AF471284

The Ladies of Hanover Square

'Lay out my peacock satin, Garfield,' Dulcima continued. 'And I will wear the emerald earrings, but not the necklace – one doesn't want to be over-dressed for a quiet dinner at home. And some wine, Dillon, right away, please. I seem to have been travelling all day, and Miss Yorke must need refreshment too after the harrowing time she has been through. My poor cousin's revered father was buried only yesterday. Such a loss to the Church – a man in his exalted position.'

With her arm round her niece's shoulders, Dulcima drifted away, while Garfield walked upstairs in stony silence, carrying the Asprey vanity case and the velvet cloak and the enormous hat, plus the long black suede gloves which Dulcima had dropped negligently on the floor – immediately retrieved by Dillon, who handed them loftily to her maid. It had taken all Garfield's self-control not to snatch them, and even more self-control not to look back as the drawing-room door closed behind her mistress and this unwelcome guest.

The Ladies of Hanover Square

Rona Randall

Hamlyn Paperbacks

A Hamlyn Book

Published by Arrow Books Limited
17-21 Conway Street, London W1P 6JD

A division of the Hutchinson Publishing Group

London Melbourne Sydney Auckland
Johannesburg and agencies
throughout the world

First published in Great Britain 1981
by Hamish Hamilton Ltd
Hamlyn Paperbacks edition 1983
Copyright © 1981 by Rona Randall

Set in Baskerville by PRG Graphics Ltd, Redhill

Printed and bound in Great Britain by
Anchor Brendon Ltd, Tiptree, Essex

ISBN 0 600 20788 9

ONE
Dulcima

1

Deborah's scandalous Aunt Dulcima walked into her life on the afternoon of February 4, 1901, and promptly changed the course of it. Had all the angels in heaven tried to work such a miracle, they could not have succeeded more dramatically, though her father would have declared it to be the devil's work, since he always regarded him as Dulcima's most intimate companion.

Although she had never set eyes on her, Deborah recognised her aunt at once. So did the Reverend Samuel Brown and his wife, who had arrived this very day to take over the vicarage and were kindly suggesting she should remain.

'After all, my dear, you are accustomed to the work of this house, and to undertake the running of it with only that old woman as a servant would be too much for such a frail constitution as mine. Nor would we think of turning you out of your home – an orphaned young woman without any prospects. Twenty, are you not? In your circumstances, such an age offers little hope of marriage, but you look healthy and strong – and I would even let you occupy your present room.' Mrs Brown held up a far-from-frail hand, quelling an answer. 'I know what you are about to say, Miss Yorke – that free bed and board is munificence itself and the last thing you expected, but . . .'

It was at that precise moment that Dulcima Howard descended from her carriage and sailed towards the front door, Titian hair aflame against the upswept brim of an enormous black hat crowned with flowing black ostrich feathers, skin magnolia cream against her elegant black cloak. She was in mourning, although on her, luscious black velvet looked far from sorrowful. The whole nation was in mourning, Deborah doubly so since her father's funeral had taken place only yesterday, the same day as Queen Victoria's. An irreverent streak in her regarded that as characteristic timing. Everyone had revered her father, including himself, and to escort the country's equally revered her father, including himself, and to escort the country's equally revered queen to the gates of heaven would have been considered, by him, as nothing less than his due.

Mrs Brown's words died. So did the wild answer on Deborah's lips, the instinctive refusal to remain in this house any longer as an unpaid servant, even though she hadn't the faintest idea where else she could go. Now she saw startled recognition in the woman's glance as it took in the incredible vision mounting the front steps in full view of the parlour windows. She saw it also in the Reverend Samuel Brown's, but underlying his astonishment was male appreciation, indicating that he was going to be a very different vicar from the one this parish had known throughout Deborah's lifetime.

Recognition of Dulcima Howard was inevitable, for her face (sometimes a great deal more) was freely displayed on postcards and chocolate boxes and calendars and hoardings up and down the country; in newspapers, too, though smudgy newsprint could never do justice to her spectacular beauty. This was more than made up for by their reports of her spectacular success – mainly, it was hinted, as a courtesan.

'A wanton, that sister of yours, a veritable wanton!' Deborah had heard her father declare to her mother many times, and seen her wince because of it.

'Oh, no, Horace, no! I am sure the newspapers exaggerate. Dear Dulcima was always flirtatious, but never wanton.'

'All actresses are wanton. Your sister especially.'

Ever loyal, Sarah Yorke had pleaded, 'But many Gaiety Girls have married very respectably – even into the nobility, dear Horace. One named Denise Orme, though I believe her real name was Jessie Smithers, became the Baroness Churston, and another named Sylvia Storey became the Countess Poulett, and the musical-comedy soubrette Olive May married Lord Victor Paget, heir presumptive to the Marquess of Anglesey, even though her real name was only Meatyard. So you see, dear husband, not all are wanton.'

'And has your sister married so well?'

'N-no . . . but she owns a fine house in Hanover Square, I believe.'

'Without the blessing of holy matrimony, which speaks for itself. No actress could afford such an establishment without male support, especially one whose only histrionic talent is to bare her bosom beyond the bounds of decency and to lift her skirts to reveal a great deal of calf. Those shocking pictures testify to that. And how do you know where she lives, pray? I forbade you long ago to hold any communication with her.'

'I . . . I think I read it somewhere, Horace.'

'Then you will read about her no more. Turn your eyes away from any paragraphs featuring her name. Since they appear only in the scandal columns, you should not be reading them in any event, for you know how greatly I disapprove. And now we will discuss her no more. Her name is forbidden in this house, as is she herself.'

Inevitably his wife subsided. She had always been timorous, but Deborah loved her nonetheless because of it. Standing up to a man like Horace Yorke was tantamount to defying God. His daughter had only to glance along the pews on a Sunday to see awe on the faces of his parishioners, and when he thundered from the pulpit, even the strongest would quail under the threat of hell and damnation, so how could anyone so gentle as her mother be anything but submissive?

Even so, Sarah Yorke had her moments of secret defiance, inevitably discovered. Deborah had been dusting the hall when her father came storming downstairs one unforgettable morning, a cardboard shoebox in his hand. Totally unaware of her, he headed for the kitchen, where old Martha was washing up after his substantial breakfast and his wife was preparing his even more substantial luncheon prior to preparing his gargantuan evening meal. If nourishment for the body was nourishment for the soul, the Reverend Mr Yorke's soul was amply fortified.

'*Sarah!*'

His anger echoed amidst the chill stone walls, and in the ensuing silence Deborah heard Martha's heavy footsteps beating a hasty retreat across the flagged kitchen, followed by a hurried closing of the scullery door. Not even so faithful a servant had the courage to give moral support to the mistress of the house when its master was on the rampage.

Deborah did not hear her mother's reply, but could imagine the whispered 'Yes, Horace?' and the familiar apprehension in her eyes.

'*You have disobeyed me!*'

This was more than average wrath. In a flash, Deborah was at the kitchen door, reaching her mother's side at the precise moment that he snatched the lid off the box, revealing its private hoard of Dulcima's pictures. Some had been cut from newspapers, but there were postcards as well, secretly bought and stored away.

Sarah Yorke's slight figure tensed within the curve of her daughter's arm.

'Explain,' commanded her husband, '*if* you can. How long have you been collecting these things and hiding them in that trunk in the attic?'

He tipped the hoard on to the kitchen table. From the changing hairstyles and fashions flaunted by the delectable Dulcima, it was obvious that his wife's secret extended over a long period of time.

'And from where did you get the money to buy them?' The tone was now one of sorrow and reproach. 'Since you have none of your own, it can only be from the weekly housekeeping allowance provided by me. That is theft, my dear wife. Theft.'

'*I* bought them, Papa. That collection is mine.'

'No, no! Deborah is trying to protect me.'

Horace Yorke paid no heed. His florid face turned slowly towards his daughter, deepening in colour as wrath increased.

'I might have known. I might have guessed. I did you an injustice, dear wife, but our daughter's confession merely confirms my opinion that you have been a weak and indulgent mother. I have always said as much, have I not, though magnanimously consenting to this modern extravagance of pocket money for an unmarried young woman? Half a crown a week for doing tasks in the home which are no more than her duty, half a crown a week spared from your housekeeping allowance – and what does she do with it? Squanders it so guiltily that she stoops to deceit. Had I not searched that trunk for discarded footwear for workhouse inmates, I would never have stumbled on this dreadful betrayal.'

He was at the kitchen stove by then, flinging the pathetic hoard of a devoted sister's mementos into the flames and ignoring her cry of pain. Then the iron lid was slammed back in a final demonstration of righteous anger.

'From now on our daughter shall not have a penny of her own. She will be fed, housed, and clothed as necessary, but no more. And guard your purse, wife, lest she succumb to temptation.' He had cast a victorious glance at the solid iron stove, as if seeing Dulcima's laughing face writhing into blackened ash. 'As punishment for your deceit, daughter, you will partake of neither luncheon nor dinner with your parents today. Instead, you will study passages from the Bible extolling the virtues of chastity and obedience. I will select them myself, and you will repeat them to me in my study this evening after I have worked on my sermons for the weekend.'

'But you fall asleep following your evening meal, Papa. Would it not be better if I repeated the passages to you before you imbibe?'

Never had red turned to puce so rapidly, but Deborah was indifferent. He had hurt her mother, and it was satisfying to retaliate, to let him know that his pretence of working behind the closed door of his study fooled no one, least of all herself. Thoroughly wined and dined (he had a great partiality for the sacramental wine), he would lower his girth into his huge fireside chair and snore until the ashes were cold in the grate.

She said blandly, 'I am being considerate, Papa, because I have no desire to disturb your evening slumber, and I am aware of this customary relaxation, whilst your curate writes your sermons, only because not even the doors of this old house are thick enough to muffle the sound of your snores.'

'Insolence! *Insolence!* Are your suggesting that I overindulge? If I occasionally nod beside my fire, it is due to fatigue. Labouring in the Lord's service takes its toll of a devoted servant's strength. Seven days a week do I toil in his name, visiting the sick, saving people's souls, preaching the gospel, working night and day and never begrudging a moment because great is one's reward in heaven . . .'

Then I wish you'd go and collect it! The words leapt un-

bidden into her mind and remained unuttered, shaming
her nevertheless. Perhaps Papa was right when remarking, as he so often did, that there was a deplorably irreverent streak in her nature which must surely have been
inherited from her mother's side of the family, by which
she knew he meant the shameless aunt who had rebelled
against convention at an early age. Dulcima had run away
to London and become a Gaiety Girl at sixteen, and the
primrose path she had trodden from then on must have
been a great deal more enjoyable than the straight and
narrow her sister had known.

Deborah was aware then of her mother's tremulous
figure, of the nervous clasping and unclasping of her
hands, of the tension which always seized her when the
wills of father and daughter clashed, and at once she
turned away, but not before her arm had tightened re-
assuringly.

'I apologise, Papa. I will go to my room, as you
command.'

'And go down on your knees to the Lord, begging his
forgiveness.'

She did nothing of the sort. She went straight to the
drawer containing her underwear and withdrew a hidden
purse. Periodically her father inspected her room, as he
did all rooms in the house, searching for imperfections or
signs of sloth, but to inspect a drawer containing ladies'
underwear was a profanity he would never indulge, so her
own secret was safe. She had little on which to spend her
weekly half-crowns, apart from the silver threepenny
pieces for the collection plate at Holy Communion,
matins, and evensong (at the Sunday-school classes with
which she helped, she was permitted to put in only one
penny), so there was now enough to buy several postcards
featuring Dulcima.

And this she did before the week was out, saving further
pence by walking all the way to Brighton from their

outlying home. At a penny a card, tuppence tinted, her savings went a long way and she returned with a store concealed beneath the household shopping that had served as an excuse for the expedition, choosing Kemp Town's market day to satisfy her father's perpetual cry for economy. Nothing could have testified so well that, at last, she was becoming a dutiful daughter.

She had exactly threepence left when reaching Roedean Village again, where, to her astonishment, she saw the last of her purchases in Mr Mulligan's window. Mulligan's store was the hub of the place, selling groceries and vegetables and sweets and newspapers – and picture postcards of Brighton's promenade and the Prince Regent's preposterous Royal Pavilion, but none of these caught her eye; only one of Anvil Dulcima, printed in a new and experimental colour process which emphasised her flaming auburn hair so that it appeared to be a blazing red, her skin waxen, her eyes a startling blue, all highly unnatural but quite unable to diminish her beauty. However tawdry the picture, her delicate features could never be anything but classically beautiful.

Deborah tried to ignore Mulligan's quizzical glance when she bought it, negligently handing over the three pennies this masterpiece cost, but she was conscious of his scrutiny. For the vicar's daughter to buy a picture of a professional beauty astonished him. It was men who collected these popular postcards, some of which were extremely décolleté and highly suggestive, but the sale of professional beauty postcards to the female sex was confined mainly to working girls who dreamed of joining their ranks. No wonder Mr Mulligan was surprised.

She braved it out by remarking casually that he appeared to be stocking a new line, to which he replied, in that tone which was characteristic of him and always unlikeable – half servile, half insolent – 'Came in by mistake, miss. Half a dozen of these ogling ladies wot I never ordered. Fast women, all of 'em. Must be, to bare 'emselves like that. "Let 'em be a warning to you," I sez to me girl Millie, but I don't have to warn that daughter o' mine about such things. *She* knows how to behave. Still, if the likes o' you want to buy 'em, Miss Yorke, maybe I'd best be ordering more.'

Deborah ignored him and walked to the door.

His voice followed. 'Couldn't be any relation, could she, miss? Struck me as soon as I saw it, it did. Younger than your sainted ma, o' course, but there's a kinda look. "Tart the vicar's wife up a bit and wipe the lines off her face, and she could be the famous Dulcima Howard to a T," I sez to my missus. Laughed, she did. "Dulcima Howard's the toast o' Lunnon," she sez. "Anyone wot looked like *that* wouldn't be buried alive down here!" And, o' course, she's right. Me missus always is.'

He dropped the pennies into the till automatically, his eyes on the vicar's daughter as she went out, feeling as he always felt when he saw her – provoked and resentful and grudgingly admiring. Provoked by her aloof profile; resentful of her coolness, which male instinct told him was only for the likes of him; grudgingly admiring of her dignity despite the shabbiness of her clothes. Mean old bastard, that father of hers. His wife always looked like a drab, and so did his daughter. No wonder she was still unwed! What chance had she of getting a husband, other than that pimply-faced curate? And what a waste that would be! Beneath her drab frock was a fine body, and would anyone so meek and mild as a curate really know how to enjoy it?

Mulligan had inspected Miss Yorke's figure with a connoisseur's eye on many an occasion, seeing a great deal more than its serge or alpaca covering. He watched the movement of her waist now as she turned to close the door behind her. It curved in supple and wholly unconscious invitation, making a man want to slip an arm in the right place in the right way, but, as always, she hadn't a glance for him, even though he flattered himself he was in the prime of life (confirmed by the innkeeper's widow over at Patcham regularly twice a week).

His resentment stirred again. What did it matter that the hoity-toity Miss Yorke was only two years older than his own daughter, and what right had she to look down her nose at him? The creature was as poor as a church mouse, and his village shop had a ready flow of cash through the till—more than she ever saw in her lifetime, he had no doubt.

So he scowled as she turned away, showing her cool profile fleetingly and startlingly — a profile so like the notorious Dulcima Howard's that he wondered why he had failed to notice it before. From beneath the counter he took out a further batch of postcards and riffled through them until he found the one he wanted — that of a red-haired woman with naked shoulders and head uplifted, a side-view portrait showing those beautiful features etched against an artificially painted backdrop of sea and sky. Mulligan neither knew nor cared that the background was artificial; all he was interested in was the similarity between the profile he was now looking at and the one which had just left his shop.

'Hey, Nellie!' he called to his missus in the back-room-cum-parlour. 'Come'n look at this! 'Tweren't the vicar's *wife* we were thinking of this morning . . .'

Deborah kept that secret store of Dulcima's pictures for the rest of her mother's short life. During the six months that remained of it, they retreated to her room whenever her father was absent from the house, and she would watch while her mother gazed at them and occasionally wept over them.

'She was so warm and affectionate and lovely – more like a baby to me than a younger sister. She was twelve years my junior, and I was married to your father just two years before she ran away. You were a year old then. I remember her coming to see me to say good-bye. 'If I stay,' she said, 'my fate will be the same as yours – an old maid at twenty-six, and forced to take any man who offers. There must be a better way of living, even for a woman.' She didn't mean it unkindly. I am sure she realised what a virtuous man Horace was, and admired him for it. She swore me to secrecy, and since she was going to stay with an old school friend who had moved to Hampstead, I felt sure she would be all right. Unfortunately, she didn't go to the school friend. I have often wondered where she did go and how she managed to become a Gaiety Girl, though her looks, of course, were outstanding and would ensure acceptance. But she never told me. In her letters she only talked about her success, and then eventually stopped writing – why, I don't know. I am sure your father would not have interfered. You don't think he did, do you, my love? I know it is a wife's duty to obey her husband, but when he read one of her letters and forbade me to answer, I was very wicked – I did write, but even so, I never heard from her again. Dear Dulcima. Never will I believe the stories about her. Always I remember her as the warm, affectionate creature I knew . . .'

And here she was now, walking into Deborah's life. A drift of perfume preceded her into the room, delicate but exotic, matching the bird of paradise who entered. Martha was mouthing incoherently as she ushered her in, and Dulcima herself was pausing on the threshold to smile down at the woman, patting her cheek with an elegantly gloved hand.

'Struck dumb, are you, Martha? I know you are Martha, because not only did my poor sister refer to you many times in the days when we corresponded, but I recall seeing you as a young woman the day I came to this house to say good-bye to her. And you recognised me as soon as you opened the door, did you not – as everyone does, wherever I go, and may the time never come when they cease to, or, by God, I'll know my days are numbered. Bless you, Martha, for staying with my poor sister for so long. How badly she must have needed your help, running this barracks of a place! As for you, darling Deborah, you alone must have saved her sanity. You are Deborah, of course. Who else could you be? Thank heaven you have grown up to resemble your mother instead of your father, because I doubt if I could live with any reminder of *him* around!'

Deborah heard Mrs Brown's disapproving gasp, but had no eyes for anyone but the lovely vision who now regarded them one by one – the vicar's wife tight-lipped above her rigidly upholstered bosom, the Reverend Samuel bemused, herself entranced. Then, very slowly, Dulcima smiled, and never before had Deborah seen a woman smile like that. A whole world of feminine voluptuousness was harnessed and then released in the divine curving of her lips. Spontaneous or practised? No matter. The effect was achieved.

'Shall I announce myself, though surely there's no need?'

Graceful arms were held out, the smile changing from sexuality to maternal warmth, and the girl went to her without another thought. 'Aunt Dulcima! I can't believe it! Never have I dreamed that we should meet.'

'Then you should have done, my dear, for I have often dreamed of meeting *you* – but in happier circumstances, I admit.'

Mrs Brown's frosty voice cut in. 'I am glad you are aware of the solemnity of the occasion, madam. The death of this poor young woman's father is indeed to be mourned.'

'Not in my opinion. I only mourn the fact that my sister

departed before he did, thus denying me the opportunity to bring some happiness into her life. So long as she was his prisoner, I was allowed no contact with her. I am quite sure my letters to her were intercepted. Mourn Holy Horace, indeed! Why should anyone? I have no doubt he is enjoying himself immensely at this precise moment, preaching to God. You gentlemen of the cloth do have direct access to the Deity, do you not, sir?'

The black velvet cloak was flung aside, falling into an elegant heap on the floor and revealing a magnificent body sheathed in more black velvet. Somehow the action suggested the unveiling of the Goddess of Love, and the new vicar's wife reacted predictably. So did her husband. He was struck dumb.

'Madam,' demanded the outraged woman, 'were you invited here? If not, I must ask you to leave. We are accepting responsibility for your unfortunate niece, and from your conversation alone it is obvious that your influence would be totally undesirable. Martha, show this. . . visitor to the door.'

But Martha was reverently picking up the black velvet cloak and Dulcima was seating herself and patting the adjoining seat, urging the Reverend Samuel not to remain standing (which he didn't), and no one paid the slightest heed to the ramrod, whaleboned Mrs Brown — or so it seemed until Dulcima tossed over her shoulder, '*I* am my niece's next of kin, and when I leave this house I will be taking her with me. Assuming responsibility for her may be a kindly thought on your part — I will at least give you the benefit of the doubt on that point — but what sort of future do you plan for her? The same dreary course her life must have taken in this mausoleum from the day she was born, or perhaps as a servant housed through charity? I will save her from that, at least.'

She cast an eloquent glance about the room. Even with the blinds now raised, it was gloomy. With a grimace she continued, 'How well I remember this place! It was in this very room that I said good-bye to poor Sarah, more years ago than I care to add up. It was as depressing then as it is now. If it has ever been redecorated, it has obviously been to the same dreary scheme. The "Sunday parlour", is it not? My dear Deborah, you will find my home very different. For one thing, I possess no "Sunday parlour". I have a salon. It is used every day of the week, and people flock to it. And they will flock even more when I am Lady Ashleigh. Your wife looks surprised, Reverend, but why? Most people are surprised only because I have not married earlier. That, believe it or not, was partially my own choice and partially because Ashleigh was not free to wed. Now he is, so he is making an honest woman of me at last.'

Her laughter pealed. The sound was like music in the sombre room, and the flame of her vitality lit up the place. Never before had Deborah realised how gloomy it was and how desperately she wanted to turn her back upon it. She saw the Reverend Brown studying the room for the first time, seeing it through her aunt's eyes instead of his wife's, who now remarked acidly, 'I am quite sure, madam, that your "salon" is as frivolous as yourself. Personally, I approve of dark paintwork. It does not show the dirt.'

'So that is the object of it – to conceal what only a slovenly housewife would tolerate?'

The dulcet tones left the other woman bereft of words, after which Dulcima turned her attention to the seat she and the vicar were occupying, a Victorian piece for two commonly known as a sociable because of the curve in the middle which enabled its occupants to face each other.

Eyes dancing, she continued, 'Do you know what the S in "sociable" stands for, sir? Sex – or so says his majesty, and he should know! How odd it will be to refer to him as "his majesty" instead of "his royal highness", though heaven knows he has waited long enough for the honour, poor man. Have you heard that at the time of his mother's

Jubilee he remarked to a noted bishop that he didn't mind bending the knee to an Eternal Father, but had any man ever bent the knee for so long to an eternal mother?'

Her laughter pealed again as the vicar's wife gasped, 'Sacrilege! Madam, I will not allow such profanity to be uttered in this house.'

Deborah burst out eagerly, 'Have you met him, Aunt Dulcima? Have you actually *met* the king?'

Wicked Dulcima brushed her black velvet lap with a negligent hand. Her legs were crossed, and somehow she had seated herself so that one soft knee projected beyond the sociable's provocative barrier and was almost touching the vicar's. Brushing away an invisible fleck of dust caused it to sway in his direction, and her niece saw him withdraw imperceptibly, though, she sensed, unwillingly. His grenadier of a wife rapped, '*Samuel!*' and only then did Deborah realise that he was covering his mouth to hide secret laughter, and suddenly she was thinking of girls like Sophie Blake, the butcher's daughter, and Mulligan's girl Millie, who always sat in a front pew so they could ogle the choristers. They were going to be in even fiercer competition when this man climbed into the pulpit for the first time.

'Of course I have met the king,' Dulcima replied, to which Mrs Brown rapped, '*In what circumstances, pray?*'

Dulcima Howard rose. Her slow, almost fluid movements epitomised a great deal more than grace, and her voice conveyed a wealth of suggestion as she answered, 'In social circumstances, madam. Purely social – though I am sure you are mentally substituting the word "impure". Come, Deborah, my love. If you have anything worth packing, I have no doubt Martha will help you, though if the rest of your clothes are anything like that depressing alpaca you are wearing, leave them behind. Bring only mementos of your mother, of which I pray you will spare me a few. I have been starved of my poor sister all these years.'

Not until they were outside did Deborah realise that the carriage was a hired one and recognise it as one of a chain which awaited the London trains at Brighton station. She had looked with envy on these luxurious vehicles when travelling by rail to places like Worthing along the coast, or inland to villages such as Balcombe and Wivelsfield, such outings occurring only annually when the Sunday school embarked on its yearly picnic. Exhausted at the end of it, fretful children and patient adults would then queue for a plodding horse-drawn bus to take them back to Roedean.

Never for her, she had thought, would there be the thrill of a hired carriage, yet here she was stepping into one which had even been instructed to wait for the return journey to Brighton. Such wealth, such wanton extravagance, filled her with so much awe that she perched on the edge of the seat clutching her straw valise until Dulcima said, 'Lean back, my dear, or you will be jolted out of your skin once this monstrosity jerks on its way.'

'Monstrosity! This carriage, Aunt Dulcima? Why, it's . . . it's *grand!*'

Dulcima laughed. 'You will ride in better conveyances than this, Deborah, that I promise. But no more of the "Aunt", if you please. It brackets me with a generation for which I scarcely qualify. I was born twelve years after your dear mother, which makes me only fifteen years your senior. I have every intention of passing for no more than ten at the most. I also have every intention of passing you off as my young cousin, so bear that in mind. Call me Cousin, if you wish, but *never* Aunt. My God, but the springs in this seat will leave me bruised, and that won't please Ashleigh next time he sees me naked. He claims I have the whitest and smoothest body of any woman he ever bedded, which is tribute indeed, considering the number there must have been.'

Her blue eyes danced with mirth. 'Have I shocked you, Deborah dear? If so, forgive me. I will try to remember that you come from a straitlaced household and do my best to help you overcome it. You cannot be saddled with a handicap like that in society. And now what are you thinking behind those lovely grey eyes? Not grey, really — hazel, like dear Sarah's. She used to look at me in the same startled way, with the same sort of bewildered questioning. You are wondering if it is true, are you not — true that I am a fast woman moving in a fast set? That is what they say of me, I know. I am quite sure it was what Holy Horace said more than once — Hateful Horace, I always thought him, driving an irrevocable wedge between my sister and me. But there, I am talking too much and you are listening wide-eyed and bewildered, and I haven't answered your unspoken question. Yes, it is true, every word of it, and if you want to step down from this carriage and walk back to that depressing vicarage, I won't let you, because your life there would be far more miserable than it could ever be with me, despite the Reverend Brown's roving eye — or perhaps because of it. At least, in my world, you won't be seduced by a man wearing a dog collar, which I am quite sure he wouldn't bother to remove during the act. With such a man as he, there wouldn't be time. The whole thing would be done furtively and hurriedly, *you* emerging distressed and *he* entirely sanguine because his clerical collar would still be in place. Oh, I could read him like a book — you too, my poor darling. You are shocked to discover the truth about me. Have you always refused to believe it? Did your mother, also?'

At last her niece managed to get in a word. One only. 'Always,' she gasped.

'Then for dear Sarah's sake, I am glad, but for yours. . . no. Evasion is not for you, Deborah. You are too clear-eyed for that. You will face the truth always, face life always, as I have done. And you will get a great deal more out of it, in consequence.'

They were bowling along the high east promenade with a strong wind blowing in from the sea. The enormous brim of Dulcima's magnificent hat swayed and dipped but never became dislodged, anchored as it was with giant stiletto pins crowned with large black-sequined knobs. She even lifted her head and took deep breaths, as if revelling in a new experience. For ever after, Deborah was to remember her like that, lolling indolently in a corner of the carriage with her beautiful face uplifted to the wind, ostrich feathers flying, her black velvet cloak wrapped around her, her skin glowing; and though she was startled by her aunt's frankness, she found herself exhilarated too.

As they turned by the Royal Albion, leaving the roar of the sea and wind behind, Deborah asked hesitantly when her marriage to Lord Ashleigh was to take place.

'As soon as I can land him.' The professional beauty laughed. 'These things take time and skill.'

'But I thought you said –'

'That he was to make an honest woman of me at last? My dear, that vicar's wife goaded me into rash statements. The truth is that for longer than I have known the present Lord Ashleigh, which is precious little time at all, I have been looking for a man to make an honest woman of me, but who would be prepared to do that for the Madame of 20 Hanover Square? Not the kind of "madam" who is generally known as such, but still a "madam" of a particular type of salon. His father, now – that was different, and in any case the poor darling died ten years ago. His heir contrived an introduction to my house recently. I had heard of him, of course. I had also seen him at the Empire and the Alhambra, and in Rule's and Gatti's, but we never met. Perhaps that is hardly surprising in view of past events . . .' She patted Deborah's hand encouragingly. 'There are few people in London, the London of money, with whom I am unacquainted, which means that before long there will be few with whom *you* will be unacquainted.'

Her blue eyes met the girl's hazel ones with candour. 'I intend to make good use of you, Deborah, my love. You are going to provide that touch of respectability I so badly need if my matrimonial campaign is to succeed. Ashleigh himself, not to mention his dragon of a mother and his gaggle of snobbish relatives, would fight tooth and nail to prevent me from sharing the illustrious family name if my own totally lacked some form of conventional respectability. A title, or even a remote link with one, can be overcome these days, otherwise no ex-Gaiety Girl would be wearing a ducal wedding ring right now, but my own needs are greater than theirs, because . . . well, I ceased to be a Gaiety Girl long ago, graduating to something far more deplorable but a great deal more profitable, and, to make matters worse, I haven't a relative in the world to prove what kind of a background I originally came from.'

'But surely, all those others – those who married so successfully – were no lovelier or better born than you?'

'But cleverer, my dear, and wiser. They took good care never to be involved in scandals, and even employed impoverished society matrons to chaperon them to and from the theatre. It was quite a common practice, I assure you. Of course, the experienced members of the stage-door brigade, the roués and the rakes seeking nothing more than a bed companion for the night, would take one look at the severe matrons accompanying certain dewy-eyed girls and know at once that the price they had to pay for *their* company would have to be substantial and permanent, but an aura of glamour combined with apparent innocence could prove an irresistible combination to inexperienced young mashers just down from university, or newly commissioned to their exclusive brigades, and before they knew where they were, they would be standing in front of the altar while their mothers wept and their fathers scowled – and the impoverished society matron who so profitably manipulated the match rubbed her hands over her bank balance and looked around for another beauty to elevate from the chorus. I, alas, never had the means to employ their services, even had I the patience to tolerate their company or to be initiated into the hypocrisy of it all – the false modesty, the calculating campaign – though I must admit I am planning my own now. My dear, isn't that fantastic Oriental palace the Prince Regent's Royal Pavilion? What a sense of humour the man must have had, to commission such a place! I am sure I would have enjoyed his company . . . Where was I? Oh, yes, my family background, such as it was. As you very well know, because it was your poor mother's background too, it was so respectable as to be positively stifling – a schoolmaster's household, and only the one I have just rescued you from could be duller than that. But there is no reason why we shouldn't hint – only hint, mind you – at a learned professor buried in his book-lined study in some remote country mansion. Learning seems to be universally respected, and so, of course, are high dignitaries of the Church. So you, my love, are heaven-sent. Quite apart from the fact that I am truly delighted to be united with you, what could be more fortunate than the production of a cousin who is the unhappily bereaved daughter of a man once ecclesiastically renowned? It lends credibility to the hints I have often dropped – but which, I know, have never been truly believed – about my kinship with a learned don.'

Deborah interrupted this spate, to gasp yet again, 'But my own father was never more than a country parson!'

Dulcima brushed that aside as casually as she had flicked away that invisible speck of dust from her black-velvet lap. 'And how is anyone to find out? Not from you or me.'

'But I cannot pretend he was anything more, Aunt –'

'*Not* "Aunt". We are Deborah and Dulcima to each other; cousins, remember? And you don't have to pretend anything. The whole art of concealment is silence. Say nothing, and nothing can be disputed. To imply is not to lie – it can be construed as reticence. And oh, how much can reticence suggest! Leave everything to me, my love, and just smile agreement when I introduce you – well, at least smile. And here we are at the station. How gloomy it looks with its funereal draperies! The whole of London looks the same, but never mind, it will be transformed when the coronation comes along, and before that there will be the splendour of the opening of Parliament, for already it is rumoured that the king is to undertake a duty his mother neglected for years. The crowds will turn out for *that* event. They haven't had a royal pageant since the Jubilee.'

As the horses trotted into the station forecourt, Dulcima continued without a break, 'Thank heaven we can now quit this abominable vehicle! And there is Garfield, waiting.'

The carriage halted, with Dulcima leaning out and calling, 'Garfield! Garfield, over *here*, my dear! Oh, my goodness, she is sniffling again. That maid of mine is one of the worst snifflers I have ever encountered. One breath of fresh air sets her off. She won't even allow me to have my bedroom window open at night in case the breeze from the Square gardens gives me pneumonia, though I fancy she is more fearful about the draught on herself when she brings my morning tea. *So* tiresome, but she is a good maid and very loyal, and quite expert with the hair, though you would never imagine so from her own. No Spanish comb, hair slide, or net can ever trap those untidy wisps.'

The driver, who had opened the door and helped down the black-velvet vision, was now bowing and touching his shabby topper ingratiatingly, so well pleased with her lavish tip that he even helped Deborah to descend too.

'Garfield, have you got a porter? Good. See he takes charge of Miss Yorke's valise. And the tickets – you have the returns safely? And the single I told you to get? Miss Yorke will travel with me, and I am sure you will be quite comfortable in Third. I do hope we won't have long to wait before the train leaves.'

Garfield's mouth had fallen open, but now she collected herself and said abruptly, 'Less than five minutes, ma'am.'

'Gracious heaven, it will take more than that to settle me in my seat! You have my dust coat ready? I must put it on the moment I step aboard. Come, Deborah, we must hurry . . .'

She was already swinging ahead, black velvet cloak swirling behind her, long skirts sweeping, ostrich feathers flying, followed by the attentive Garfield carrying a large and elaborately tooled vanity case, which only later, when London had laid its sophistication upon her, would Deborah have instantly recognised as the work of Asprey. She herself now formed a rear guard with the porter, thinking how absurd it was to employ a man to carry a straw valise so small that only one strap was needed to fasten it. She could have carried it with ease.

Inevitably, with Dulcima in the lead, the small procession was eye-catching. People stopped and stared, heads turned, fingers pointed, and through it all Dulcima sailed on serenely. After a few steps she turned her lovely head, smiling over her shoulder and stretching out her suede-gloved hand to her niece.

'Don't walk behind, Deborah darling. Garfield is my maid, not you. Porter, run ahead to the ticket barrier, and don't *dare* let them close it. And tell the guard to hold that train or I will report him to the chairman of the Southern Railway, whom I know intimately.'

The man went hurrying to obey, and as Deborah moved forward, she caught her first close view of the sniffling Garfield, nose bright red in a pinched face (how long had the poor thing been waiting in the cold?), flat tweed cap set straight upon her head, wispy hair straggling over the collar of a holland dust coat which covered her from neck to feet; a shapeless bundle of a woman whose eyes darted towards the girl and away again, baleful and malicious.

With a shock, Deborah realised the woman resented her, and for such an intensity of feeling she was totally unprepared.

She followed her incredible aunt into the train with an extraordinary sense of chill, as if an icy breath had been shed on the warmth and excitement of the day.

2

Garfield settled unhappily into a third-class seat, blinking back her tears. It would never do to allow insensitive onlookers to detect her grief – the gaping, gawping lower classes amongst whom she had been relegated so cruelly for the return journey. People of this type never hid their curiosity. 'What's the matter, love? Someone in the family died, eh?' They would question her without embarrassment, morbidly fascinated by the thought of death, an attitude typical of such people. Never would she acknowledge that she had graduated from their ranks. She, a lady's maid in Hanover Square, was far above them, and to put her to the indignity of travelling with them was one of those unexpected shafts of cruelty which Dulcima Howard could unwittingly inflict.

If she *had* to banish me in favour of that chit of a girl, thought Winnie Garfield wretchedly, she might at least have let me travel Second, amongst respectable tradespeople and suchlike instead of the lower classes.

Anger replaced Garfield's grief. On arriving at Brighton she had been told to purchase a single third-class ticket back to Victoria, but not for a moment had she suspected it was for herself – not even when she saw the young lady descending from the carriage and recognised that she was at least a lady despite the dowdiness of her dress and the cheapness of its quality. Who was she, and why was she accompanying Miss Howard back to London, and why, above all, had she replaced herself as the mistress's travelling companion? This fact alone had sent apprehension leaping into Garfield's throat, for she was always afraid of losing this situation in Hanover Square, where she basked in the reflected glory of her famous mistress.

Dulcima Howard's rise in the social world had been no surprise to the dresser who had seen more professional beauties come and go from the ranks of Gaiety Girls than she could count. Some she had liked, some she had loathed, but the instant that blazing young redhead had walked in, head high, smiling at everyone as if she had known them all her life, the wispy-haired dresser had experienced her first real impulse of maternal love. She had wanted to protect her, and did so, subtly defending her from the poisoned darts of jealousy to which such a girl was inevitably exposed.

She had also expected the girl to be snapped up by some wealthy young masher and lead him to the altar. 'Think of the future,' she had advised. 'Play your cards well.'

Little had she expected the naive girl from the country

to fulfil her words so literally, or that she would become hostess of the most fashionable card salon in London, where even the Prince of Wales had come to indulge his love of baccarat – and never had there been a scandal like the Tranby Croft affair, at 20 Hanover Square, nor ever would be. Dulcima Howard, progressing from ingénue appeal to mature beauty, proved to have a head on her shoulders. It was a pity her emotions were not equally sound, but her heart was her enemy, causing her to fall in love not only unwisely and too well, but too frequently. It's a good thing she's had *me* to take care of her, Garfield reflected now. Many's the time she's cried on my shoulder when a man has broken her heart.

Fortunately, it was a resilient heart.

Garfield had her own emotions well under control now, sitting stiffly in her uncomfortable seat, cotton-gloved hands clasped in her lap, the only female traveller wearing a holland dust coat, which was evidence enough that she was above the hoi polloi. Resentful as she was, Garfield appreciated this gift from her mistress and had to admit that she was generous in many ways – but not today. It was customary, when travelling, for her to share her mistress's compartment, anticipating just when to unfasten the silver clasps of the lavish vanity case from Asprey and take out the silver-backed mirror and hairbrush, the silver-topped bottles of rose water, witch hazel, and perfume; to dab the beautiful forehead and brush and recoil the magnificent hair to chase away fatigue. Now this unknown creature had ousted her. Even worse, the overheard exchange of first names suggested the intimacy of friendship, which could mean the termination of the companionable relationship she herself enjoyed with her mistress.

Winnie Garfield prided herself on being something more than lady's maid to Dulcima Howard. She regarded this famous beauty as her personal charge, herself as confidante. Hadn't she earned these privileges for accompanying her from the Gaiety Theatre to the house in Hanover Square when old Lord Ashleigh set her up there?

I gave up a good job for her, Garfield fretted. She can't replace me with anyone else now. She wouldn't. She *couldn't!*

But now she recalled how quiet her mistress had been on the way down, and that seemed significant, as if she had been thinking about something, planning something. And what of her bubbling good humour on returning to the station where she had left her maid shivering in the cold? And what of the future, if it held the possibility of being replaced by this chit of a young woman from somewhere in Brighton? A scandalous place, Brighton, so perhaps she was a new girl for those *poses plastiques* which dear Dulcima had unwisely exploited to supplement her income?

But no – she had mercifully abandoned all that recently, and one had to admit that this Miss Yorke looked too respectable to pose in the nude.

Garfield didn't like anything or anyone at this moment, and she was hurt to the quick by her mistress's rejection. This, in time, would be forgiven, torn as she perpetually was between disapproval of Dulcima's frivolity and rapturous admiration of her femininity.

She was also loyal. 'The world is divided between "them" and "us", ' she would insist to Cook when the woman expressed disapproval of some society scandal. In 'their' world, scandals had to be ignored. That was one of the privileges of the upper classes, and everything they did had to be excused by the lower ones. Therefore Garfield could forgive her mistress anything – except being shut out of her confidence.

That had happened not only today, but last night also, when Garfield first heard about this unexplained trip to Brighton. 'A day trip only, Garfield, but don't forget my vanity case.'

She never travelled without that gift from Lord Ashleigh, presented to her when he first set her up at 20 Hanover Square – the old Lord Ashleigh, who had died ten years ago. And a fine mess she had been in financially when he departed this life, no longer there to pay her bills and leaving her nothing but that house.

Characteristically, she had refused to sell it and invest the money. Wisdom had never been part of Dulcima Howard's makeup, so along came the alluring postcards, the chocolate-box pictures, the seductive posings for calendars and hoardings. The new business of public advertisements for soap and skin creams and pills and stays, and goodness knew what else, was growing rapidly and proving highly profitable for all concerned, though displaying a tightly laced and whaleboned waist beneath a pushed-up and almost naked bosom was to be regretted. 'You don't have to go that far, surely, Miss Dulcima? For all the world to see, too! So undignified.' But her mistress had merely shrugged and said it paid well and that was all that mattered.

'Besides, it is advantageous in other ways, making me more famous than I was even as a Gaiety Girl. It brings men to my door – rich men who can afford to lose vast sums at baccarat. So now the real card parties, the serious ones, can begin.'

That was when Dulcima Howard's shrewd streak first revealed itself. Old Lord Ashleigh had had a passion for baccarat and had taught his young mistress well.

And now Lord Ashleigh's heir had come into her life, which surprised and vaguely troubled her maid. Everyone knew the present Lord Ashleigh was a great traveller, frequently abroad, appearing only intermittently on the London scene. And there had always been vague whispers about him, though nothing for which he could be condemned in this day and age. He was a lady-killer, a woman chaser despite being married. Bella, the gossipy parlourmaid, claimed that until recently he had been visiting that middle-aged actress Chrystal Delmont, formerly at the Boswell Theatre and now leading lady at the Comet, who had an apartment in nearby Maddox Street.

'Disgusting, I call it,' said Bella virtuously, though the entire staff knew she had lost her own virtue long ago. 'Still, actresses are actresses,' she had sniffed, implying that they were inevitably fast, to which Cook had retorted that that was no way to talk about Miss Delmont, a lady if ever there was one, and besides, she had supported her invalid husband until the day he died, so who could blame her for seeking consolation when she was free?

But even if it were true, the affair had not lasted long – not after young Lady Ashleigh was seen around, pale and thin and taut, as if strained to breaking point. Had the Comet Theatre's leading lady broken it off then, moved by compassion for his wife? Whatever the reason, poor little Lady Ashleigh was gone now, God rest her soul. She had always been weakly, people said, and much given to the vapours; a drab little mouse of a wife. So who could blame her husband for looking elsewhere?

Even so, Garfield considered that stepping into his father's shoes at 20 Hanover Square was not quite right somehow. Not so soon after his wife's death, anyway. There had been a good lapse of time since his father's, and most likely he didn't even suspect who had set Dulcima Howard up in that house. One had to be fair, but it wasn't easy, because there was something worrying about him. He was handsome and charming, always courteous, speaking to servants in the way a gentleman should, but still there was that 'something' which made a body uneasy, something impossible to put a finger on, and in trying to do so now, Garfield entirely forgot about her personal anxiety and resentment, and even about that interloper Deborah Yorke. Her only concern was her mistress, whose ability to fall in love with the wrong men had become increasingly alarming since the death of her first benefactor. The only thing wrong with *him* had been the encumbrance of a wife, but his son was another kettle of fish.

Garfield had only instinct to go on, but backed it all the way, and instinct warned her that nothing good could come out of this association with the younger Lord Ashleigh, whose advent into her mistress's life was not only as unwelcome as Deborah Yorke's, but somehow a great deal more threatening.

Garfield resented intruders into the safe, comfortable world she shared with the famous Dulcima. The people who came to play baccarat represented no threat at all; they were necessary to oil the economic wheels. Even the lovers Dulcima had taken had been no more than could be expected of so popular and desirable a woman, but where the present Lord Ashleigh was concerned, all Garfield's protective instincts were alerted. What was her mistress thinking of, taking up with the man when his poor wife was scarcely cold in her grave? True, he had gone abroad for a while to recover from his grief, but he had wasted no time before consoling himself with another woman on his return.

The worrying thing was that Miss Howard was serious about him; that was all too obvious to someone who knew her as intimately as her maid did. The dear creature was up to something, planning something. She wouldn't have got rid of those girls who charmed the gentlemen with their posings if her aim had not been to give an impression of respectability, and while Garfield was thankful that such a shocking side of the business had come to an end, the termination of anything so lucrative could mean only one thing: she was hoping to land him.

More than ever Garfield wished her mistress had hooked a nice, well-heeled husband when a girl. She would have been safe then, and even if it had meant staying on as a dresser at the Gaiety, she would have been happy in the knowledge that Dulcima Howard's future was assured. As it was, the years were speeding by, and time was the enemy of the professional beauty. A few more years, and the lines would begin to show, the waistline to thicken, the chin perhaps to grow heavy. Her devoted maid would see no change in her, but others would.

So was there a hint of desperation behind this easy surrender to Ashleigh, the elaborate attention to her toilet when he was due to arrive, the fussing and the anxiety not only to look her best, but also to offer the best? Everything had to be perfect – the food, the wine, the company, the genteel atmosphere. The gay abandon toned down altogether.

And all for a man who was going to hurt her. And this time it would not be cured by a good cry on her maid's motherly shoulder. This time it would go deep. Garfield was convinced of that.

Dulcima's preparations for a train journey fascinated Deborah to the exclusion of all else. Even the awe she experienced on stepping into the first-class compartment was eclipsed by it, for her beautiful aunt's ritual commanded all her attention. Garfield had removed the velvet cloak, folded it carefully, placed it within a linen bag, then held out a fine, hand-stitched dust coat for her mistress to slip on, buttoning it from head to foot whilst Dulcima unpinned her enormous hat and threw it casually upon a seat. At that point the guard blew his whistle, and Dulcima had sent the woman scurrying from the compartment to find a place in Third.

The last glimpse Deborah had of her maid was of her signalling frantically to the guard as she ran along the platform with even more tight-lipped resentment on her face. Plainly the woman disliked being dismissed in such a way. So at least it isn't me she has a grudge against, Deborah decided in relief, and turned her attention back to Dulcima, who was now opening the vanity case and saying, 'Darling girl, do make sure the windows are well fastened, otherwise we will be covered in smuts, not to mention the filthiest smoke when going through tunnels. Now, where *is* that chiffon motoring veil – ah, I have it! Now, my love, tie it carefully in the nape of my neck.'

So saying, she placed the veil over her head and face, drawing it beneath her chin and turning so that Deborah could tie the whole thing into a loose drapery, totally covering her features and hair. Then she settled into the middle seat with her back to the engine, advising Deborah to keep well away from the window, through which smoke might seep even when closed. 'And sit with your back to the engine too,' she added, though such a thing was impossible, since the seats on either side of her were occupied with vanity case and cloak bag, and Deborah lacked the courage to remove either.

Scarcely was the chiffon veiling tied than the train jerked into action, flinging Deborah into a seat opposite her aunt, where she was well content to stay, even though it did face the wrong direction, for the comfort was superb. It seemed irreverent to bring her cheap valise into such a place as this, and against the thick carpet her sensible black walking shoes looked decidedly inelegant. As for her heavy serge coat and alpaca dress, never had they seemed more dowdy By comparison, Dulcima's voluminous dust coat and draped headgear looked positively modish. What a country bumpkin she must appear to her fashionable aunt, whose lovely face was smiling at her through the transparent chiffon.

'My dear, you are wide-eyed! Have you never travelled in a train before?'

'Of course, Aunt . . . I mean, Dulcima, but only by local train, and third-class. Never in such luxury as this.'

'You dear child, one day this mode of travel will be as boring to you as it is to me. I abominate trains, but for long distances they have to be endured, so one must do that in the greatest possible comfort. I have to confess I have no idea what third or even second class is like, and have no intention of finding out.'

'Compared with this, quite dreadful. Poor Garfield —'

'So *that* explains her bad mood! I could sense it. I thought it was due entirely to waiting on that cold station, though I did offer her money to buy a cup of tea. But Garfield signed the pledge long ago, and because station buffets also cater for the evils of drink, never will she enter them!' Dulcima's laughter bubbled. 'But a second-class ticket would have been more thoughtful, I suppose. I'm afraid I was only concerned with getting her out of the way for the return journey, so we could be alone and talk freely.'

'You mean she travelled like this on the way down?'

'Of course. I have to have someone to look after my needs. Silly woman — she has gone into one of her sulks. She does that periodically, and the best thing is to take no notice.'

'You don't think . . . surely she couldn't have imagined I was taking her place?'

'As my maid? Ridiculous. Garfield has held that position ever since I left the Gaiety, but she is a mite too possessive, and firmly believes she is indispensable to me — which, though never will I admit it, she is. And now, my love, I am going to rest.'

The lovely eyes closed, and Deborah turned her attention to the countryside flying past the windows. How many miles an hour were they travelling? She had heard that fifty was about average and eighty the maximum. The thought was staggering, so she abandoned it and dwelt instead on the events of this memorable day, scarcely believing they were true. But here she was, journeying with her scandalous aunt to London, of all places. She had never visited London in her life, nor ever expected to.

The chiffon veil lent a filmy enchantment to Dulcima's face. In repose, it looked astonishingly guileless for a woman who admitted to being a man's mistress and to moving in a fast set, and who talked so casually about her lover appreciating her in the nude. There was even a suggestion of naiveté, as if part of her character remained untouchable and even credulous. Deborah felt that such a woman could easily be taken advantage of, despite her sophistication and air of authority. And the almost imperious way in which she now withdrew, rejecting further conversation despite her statement that they were travelling alone in order to talk freely, presented a further contradiction.

In a way, Deborah was glad of the silence, for during the drive to Brighton her aunt had given her much to think about — startling revelations which a young lady from a country village had never expected to hear from anyone; and yet, illogically, they had failed to shock, because coming so frankly and honestly, they seemed in no way indecent, but merely the confessions of a woman accustomed to being loved by men and somehow implying that such love was the right of one who reigned supreme in a different world from Deborah's.

But how she herself could ever enter into it, or adapt to it, was another matter. Deborah had grave doubts about her aunt's ability to wean her away from her staid upbringing. Fragments would remain with her, standards inbued into her from childhood, and though she had rebelled against her bigoted father's tyranny, she clung loyally to her mother's edicts — as loyally as Sarah herself had clung to her belief in her younger sister's purity.

At that point, sadness replaced Deborah's excitement. She was glad her mother had died in ignorance of the truth about her sister's way of life.

Despite her pretence of sleep, Dulcima's mind was awake. Had she been wise, or foolish, in taking this step regarding her niece? There was a quality of innocence about her which might be difficult to handle. It was all very well to assume that she could be transplanted from a drab world into one which could appear, to someone so unsophisticated, as exotic in the extreme, but how would she adjust? The teachings of a lifetime, hidebound in prejudice, might prove to be shackles impossible to shake off. I may have saddled myself with an unexpected burden, Dulcima reflected, and what can I do with her in that case? I can't send her back to that awful vicarage, even if the sanctimonious Mrs Brown would re-admit her – which I doubt, since she now knows of our relationship. Besides, the girl is too nice to be thrown back as prey to that man's secret licentiousness. No, I must look after her. She is dear Sarah's child. But she must serve my purpose, as I intended, and in return for that she may well catch a very desirable husband.

The thought restored Dulcima's natural optimism, making her feel she was acting as the girl's guardian angel, just as dear Charles Ashleigh had once acted as hers. Despite his being forty-six years old to her eighteen, she had learned to love him very sincerely, and until his death she had remained faithful. Charles had been an expert lover, and the liaison had been totally satisfying until she wanted a child.

'You could give it your name, to spare the poor mite the stigma of illegitimacy. You would not be the first man to do that. Even kings have legitimised their mistresses' sons.'

His refusal had been prompt and unyielding. He had a son and daughter already, he had pointed out. That was enough.

'But not for me! You are denying me something I long for – a child of my own. Some women don't want to be mothers, but I do. Even my poor sister achieved that much.'

She could still see his aristocratic profile, turning away from her. 'No, Dulcima. You are asking too much. I will give you anything in the world but a child of Ashleigh blood.'

It had led to tears and tantrums, accusations of being slighted, that he was ashamed of her, that she was good enough to be visited in se ret, but not acknowledged openly, all of which he had tolerated patiently but with unyielding implacability.

'The whole world knows you belong to me and that I love you, Dulcima.'

'Not the *whole* world! Not your wife, living serenely down at Kingsmere. Or does she turn a blind eye? Isn't that expected of society wives, and husbands too? The eleventh commandment is the most binding of all, I understand.'

He had placed a gentle hand over her mouth, silencing her, and then replaced it with his lips until her senses yielded and she talked of his wife no more.

But sometimes she dared to ask about his children – twenty-one-year-old Justin and fifteen-year-old Caroline, wondering how they would feel if they knew their father had a mistress of their own generation, though she never put that particular question to him.

He discussed them guardedly. 'Caroline is all right. In fact, she is closer to me than to her mother, and though somewhat plain at the moment, I suspect she may grow into a striking young woman who will no doubt marry well. Justin is . . . well, Justin.'

But she knew more that that already; that Justin was in the Guards, and very handsome he looked riding out from Knightsbridge Barracks on his way to Buckingham

Palace, one of an escort of Household Cavalry on their gleaming black horses. She had seen him more than once, scarlet tunic ablaze above the white pipe clay of his skin-tight breeches, gleaming sword shoulder-high, his profile very like his father's beneath the low peak of his shining helmet. On these occasions she had been walking in Hyde Park, inevitably accompanied by Garfield, because dear Charles would never permit her to promenade alone by Rotten Row. Only the ladies of the town paraded singly. Her aging lover's diligence was sometimes irksome, but at least it was proof of how dearly he treasured her.

Even so, she was irked by Garfield's gimlet eye as the Cavalry Escort rode by, because she wanted to gaze her fill on this son of the fatherly lover who was stubbornly refusing to let her have a child. Out of the corner of her eye she would watch the Ashleigh heir go by, thinking wildly: How would you react, sir, if you knew that I go to bed with your dear papa, and that not only does he enjoy it, but I enjoy it too?

These were the only times she had seen Justin Ashleigh, apart from subsequent wedding photographs in the press. His had been one of the most fashionable weddings of the season, and it had deprived Dulcima of his father's company for a whole month because he had been forced to go down to Kingsmere at his wife's behest. Anyone would have thought he was the father of the bride instead of the bridegroom, judging by the fuss Elizabeth Ashleigh made, filling that noble country house with visiting titles and even former crowned heads from obscure European states who, though now dethroned, still commanded respect. The wedding had even been held in Kingsmere's private chapel, according to Ashleigh tradition, instead of in the bride's parish.

The catch of the season was Justin Ashleigh, and lucky was the bride to get him – or so society declared. Daughter of a wealthy industrialist who spent most of his time taking the waters at Marienbad or Homburg, she possessed a fortune, but this only made her seem more of an upstart than her self-made father. It was not Justin who was doing well for himself, but she, Norah Barnsley, whose father had managed to get himself a baronetcy for services to industry, which made him one of the worst kind of *noveau riche*. A title didn't count for much if it was not inherited.

That had been an agonising month for Dulcima; a tortured, delicious, wildly exciting month in which that damned society wedding had prevented her from making her delirious announcement to the bridegroom's father. For during that month her pregnancy was confirmed, and she was confident that all his objections would be swept aside. He had always been a kind and understanding man.

To her astonishment, this time he <u>was</u> not. He had simply stared, unable to hide his dismay, and then he had done the unbelievable thing. He had called in the most expensive gynaecologist in London to terminate things secretly before it was too late. All her grief, her tears, her pleadings, her wild protests, availed her nothing.

'I told you long ago, my love, that I would never give you a child of Ashleigh blood.'

She had never forgotten and, in her heart, never quite forgiven, but she had surrendered to his will, bowed to the inevitable, submitted to his concern and his tenderness, let him cradle and comfort her, gone on living and, in time, enjoyed his lovemaking again. But she had always enjoyed lovemaking, and she was enjoying it these days with his son. The unbelievable had happened. Justin Ashleigh had taken his father's place.

3

Deborah did not mind administering to her aunt's needs as they approached London, unwinding the protective chiffon veil, unscrewing silver tops from bottles, handing her the sumptuous velvet cloak and finally the enormous ostrich-feathered hat. She watched fascinated as her aunt smoothed her brilliant hair and then perched the creation on top of it, skewering the enormous sequined knobs into place and turning her head from side to side to judge the result.

'Not so expert as Garfield would have done it, but well enough.'

With that, Dulcima reseated herself, barred from leaning back by the vast brim of her hat; then she took a sachet of *papier poudre* from her reticule and dusted her face with it.

'You too, child,' she insisted. 'A woman should never appear in public with her face shiny – that is lesson number one.'

Deborah, who had been brought up to believe that only fast women used powder, dabbed ineffectively at her nose until Dulcima laughed and, leaning across, dusted her face all over.

'There, Cousin – you look much refreshed. And a face so lovely as yours should be made the most of. That is lesson number two.'

Being called 'Cousin' immediately broke down any

lingering barriers and established Deborah on an equal footing, so she was able to ask a question she had been burning to ask for some time. 'How did you know of my father's death? What made you come immediately after his funeral, as if knowing precisely when it had taken place?'

'My dear, I did know, thanks to his curate, who had the good sense to write to me.'

The reticule was opened again and a letter extracted. Deborah read it in surprise.

Dear Miss Howard,

I believe you are related to the Reverend Yorke's daughter. For this reason I venture to inform you that the Vicar of Roedean, whom I served, has passed away and is to be buried beside his wife in the parish church-yard at ten o'clock on the morning of February 3. Holding Miss Yorke in esteem, and feeling concern for her future, I feel it my duty to notify her relatives that she is now alone in the world, and must needs be cared for. I can trace none, other than yourself, and even the relationship between you is one I can only claim to have suspected for some time. I have no proof, apart from overhearing the Reverend Yorke discussing you one day. I hasten to assure you that I did not listen deliberately, but the vicarage kitchen is large and echo-ing, and the late vicar had a powerful voice. Being a person frequently referred to in the press, it is known that you reside in Hanover Square. Nor was it difficult to trace the number . . .

Deborah leaned back in astonishment. That subdued, mild-mannered curate — who would have expected it of him? Never revealing he had overheard that memorable scene in the kitchen was only natural, since his living depended upon her father's goodwill, but to concern himself with her future and to actually do something about it touched her deeply.

'The letter came by last night's post. The young man timed it well, and naturally I came at once. I have to confess that I would *not* have come to Holy Horace's funeral, for I could never have pretended to mourn him. The day after was more than suitable. And here we are at Victoria, thank heavens. No, my dear, don't burden yourself with that vanity case. Garfield will deal with it . . . and no, do *not* carry your own baggage. No lady does. That, Deborah my love, is lesson number three.'

No wonder her aunt had despised that hired vehicle in Brighton, Deborah reflected as Dulcima's waiting landau bowled on its way to Hanover Square. Gleaming with polished brass and shining bodywork, it rocked gently on well-oiled springs, and its upholstery of dull gold velvet seemed too good to sit on. There was even a tigerskin rug for the knees.

This time Garfield travelled with them, facing her mistress but resolutely refusing to look at this upstart from Brighton who could not disguise the fact that she had never glimpsed London before. There she sat, eyes agog, taking in the splendour of Buckingham Palace as they wheeled past it and exclaiming aloud at the sentries with their tall bearskins, scarlet tunics, and bayonets, until Dulcima gently pressed her arm.

Lesson number four: one should not stare round-eyed at every new and exciting thing, nor at the fashionably dressed ladies and gentlemen driving by in other elegant carriages.

By the time they had turned from the Mall and up St James's Street to Piccadilly, Deborah was sitting as sedately as her aunt. Dulcima Howard driving in London was a very different Dulcima from the one exulting in Brighton's sea breezes. In London she was on display, recognised by passers-by and inclining her head in response to the raised hats of admiring gentlemen on the pavements. Apart from this gracious recognition, she exchanged intimate greetings with acquaintances in other smart vehicles, waving her suede-gloved hand to fashionable women and blowing an airy kiss now and then to immaculate gentlemen who either smirked with pleasure or squirmed beneath the disapproval of their accompanying spouses. It seemed to Deborah that her aunt blew these seductive kisses only to gentlemen who *were* so accompanied, dimpling with pleasure at their discomfort and laughing at Garfield's disapproving frown.

'Stop scowling, Garfield! You have had the sulks ever since we left Brighton. I hope you do not intend to keep it up when we reach home, or Miss Yorke's arrival will be spoiled. I want my cousin to be happy in my house, and to have you trailing around with a sour face will spoil everything.'

Garfield gave a start. A *cousin?* That these two could be related had not even occurred to her. She had never heard her mistress refer to any relatives – except once, very casually, when guests were present; a vague reference to a learned father, a distinguished scholar supervising her lonely upbringing in a remote country mansion. 'That was why I ran away, and who could blame me?' But of course Garfield had not believed a word of it, and she doubted whether any of the guests did either. Dulcima Howard was always romancing, and had she been the daughter of an intellectual father, some touch of learning would have left its mark. But never a book found its way through the doors of number 20. Not even a novel from Mudie's. 'I don't want to *read* about life, I want to *live* it!' she had declared.

Garfield's suspicious glance darted now to the younger woman, seeing for the first time a resemblance to the famous profile. She had failed to notice it because the unfashionable hat did nothing to draw attention to the girl's features, any more than the dowdy clothes to her figure, which was slim and trim and could look quite good if made the most of. But why couldn't Miss Dulcima have *told* me she planned to bring a poor relation into the household? And where will she sleep – in one of the attics, near my own? Where else? Poor relations were admitted to the homes of better-off kinfolk only in some subservient capacity. They had to earn their keep, and quite right, too. So in what way was this Miss Yorke going to earn hers? As sewing maid or some sort of private secretary?

Many women in society employed female secretaries these days. There was a certain *cachet* about it. The only qualifications needed were neat handwriting and good manners and the ability to know their place. Some, like Mrs Cornwallis-West, called them social secretaries, delegating to them the task of answering begging letters, accepting or declining or issuing invitations, going on shopping errands, and keeping social diaries up-to-date – but never personal ones, of course. (What wouldn't the world give for a glimpse of Lady Warwick's, or Lillie Langtry's, or Mrs Keppel's, or any other of King Edward's close women friends, were they so unwise as to keep such things!) But despite the superficial duties of these social secretaries, everyone knew that their chief function was to chaperon daughters of the house to affairs their mammas were not prepared to endure – also to keep the girls well out of the way when an unobtrusive brougham, drawn by a single horse, came to a halt outside the front door.

That well-known brougham had now temporarily halted on its rounds, though no doubt it would be active again when the whirl of the coronation was over, if not before. Shocking as she considered its owner to be, Garfield had to acknowledge that, if all she heard was true, he did at least treat his favourites well. Even after discarding them, he remained a loyal friend to each and every one.

Garfield came back to earth as the carriage passed St George's Church and entered Hanover Square. Once halted, Briggs, the coachman, climbed down to open the door, and very annoying it was when he automatically turned to Miss Yorke after helping his mistress to alight. Why couldn't he leave the girl to fend for herself, as he did the mistress's maid? Surely he didn't imagine there was any social distinction between a poor relation taken into the household through charity, and a personal lady's maid?

Still ruffled, Garfield followed the two women indoors.

When Dulcima entered her house, it came alive immediately, the quietness dispelled by her gay voice and imperative demands.

'Send Cook to me, Dillon. I want a full report on the preparations for tonight's dinner party. It is very important. And Mrs Crowther – has she prepared the blue room for Miss Yorke, as I instructed?'

The blue room! One of the best guest rooms, and situated immediately above Miss Dulcima's own! There had been enough shocks for one day, thought Garfield, without this. Accommodating Miss Yorke in such comfort was more disturbing than anything else so far, elevating her to the level of an equal instead of a poor relation expected to earn her keep.

The idea was so unbearable that Garfield switched her attention to Dillon, the butler, who, as always, was hovering solicitously, taking his mistress's black velvet cloak with a reverence which, to Garfield, never concealed his desire to let his hands accidentally come in contact with her body. You can't fool *me*, Dillon, she thought for the hundredth time. You're a lecher, and if you ever touch her with so much as a finger, I'll kill you. Keep those hands for Bella, when you think no one is looking.

Very hoity-toity had Bella become since Dillon started creeping up the back stairs at night, and highly undignified behaviour *that* was for a butler. In his position he was ruler of the household, king of the domestic domain – but if the king of a country was a lecher, no doubt Dillon thought he had the right to emulate him. But what kings could do, butlers and servants could not, and Garfield had made that plain long ago. Not that it seemed to have the slightest effect. All her sniffs of disapproval and her pointed innuendos fell on deaf ears as far as Dillon was concerned, which somehow confirmed her suspicion that until he came to this house when Dulcima launched her card salon, he had known some other occupation.

In time she ignored him, as he ignored her. They went about their duties without speaking to each other unless compelled to.

'Lay out my peacock satin, Garfield,' Dulcima continued. 'And I will wear the emerald earrings, but not the necklace – one doesn't want to be overdressed for a quiet dinner at home. And some wine, Dillon, right away, please. I seem to have been travelling all day, and Miss Yorke must need refreshment too after the harrowing time she has been through. My poor cousin's revered father was buried only yesterday. Such a loss to the Church – a man in his exalted position.'

With her arm round her niece's shoulders, Dulcima drifted away, while Garfield walked upstairs in stony silence, carrying the Asprey vanity case and the velvet cloak and the enormous hat, plus the long black suede gloves which Dulcima had dropped negligently on the floor – immediately retrieved by Dillon, who handed them loftily to her maid. It had taken all Garfield's self-control not to snatch them, and even more self-control not to look back as the drawing-room door closed behind her mistress and this unwelcome guest.

As she climbed the stairs, Garfield knew full well that

Dillon was watching her with a smirk on his face, pleased because her nose was put out of joint. He had even helped the interloper to remove her outdoor clothes, adopting a fatherly air which he would never have displayed had he not known who she was. That meant Dulcima had confided in Mrs Crowther when giving instructions for the blue room to be prepared, and the housekeeper had passed on the news belowstairs.

So everyone in this household, except herself, had already been aware of the coming of their mistress's cousin, who, from the sound of things, was the offspring of a high-ranking Church dignitary. So perhaps the story of the professor had not been fiction after all. . . .

Smarting acutely, Garfield went on her way, pausing en route to glance into the blue room. She was startled by what she saw: flowers between the tall windows and on the bedside table, a welcoming fire in the grate, toiletries ready and waiting, and one of Dulcima's loveliest nightgowns laid out; even a pair of satin mules and matching négligé. Nothing was too good for this visitor – if visitor she was to be. Dulcima had said nothing about the length of the girl's stay, but there had been no need. Garfield sensed that Deborah Yorke had come to take up permanent residence here and that nothing was ever going to be the same again.

Dulcima had ordered a meal to be served in Deborah's room.

'You must be fatigued, my dear, and scarcely in the mood to meet guests. Besides, we must attend to your wardrobe first. I will send for my dressmaker first thing tomorrow. Thank heaven, we are not bound by the rules of court mourning – black is never a kind colour for the young. My dressmaker is a genius: she can copy any style from *Les Modes* or *Petit Courrier des Dames* or *Journal des*

Demoiselles, and by the time she and I have put our heads together, you won't recognise yourself. And your hair – we must do something with that, also. I suppose your tyrant of a father insisted on that plastered-down style, despite its natural tendency to curl. Dear Sarah had the same chestnut hair when she was a girl. She used to romp in the fields with me, letting it fly loose over her shoulders, and very lovely it was, but when she married Holy Horace, he insisted on a centre parting and a bun at the back, just the way you wear yours. But you will do so no longer.'

The lovely hands reached out, removed the restricting hairpins, and down tumbled Deborah's hair.

'It is beautiful, Cousin! We must create a style to do justice to it. And now I must dress. I have an important guest tonight – no doubt you can guess who. Not entirely alone, alas, but let's hope the others leave early . . .' Dulcima planted a fond kiss on the girl's cheek and led her upstairs. 'Your room is on the second floor, in the front above my own. The ceilings are high in this house, so you shouldn't be disturbed by sounds from beneath.' She gave Deborah a slant-eyed, roguish glance, which brought a rush of colour to the girl's cheeks. Inexperienced though she was, she guessed what her aunt meant, and was embarrassed. On entering this magnificent house, she had doubted her ability to adapt to such a background; now she had an even greater doubt. The magnificence she might grow accustomed to – she had heard that one could quickly become used to luxury – but adapting to her aunt's mode of living was indeed another matter.

'I hope you won't find me too naive,' she said uneasily.

'Don't worry, my dear, I will soon cure you of that!' her aunt assured her with a beaming smile.

That had been more than an hour ago, and while she had been in the drawing room with Dulcima, someone had unpacked Deborah's valise and hung her meagre supply of clothes in the wardrobe. They looked like a pathetic group of orphans, and she closed the door on them quickly.

What was she expected to do now? Nothing, apparently, but wait for her evening meal to arrive, which would surely not be attended to until after Dulcima's dinner party had been served. So she sat for a while, gazing around at the new and awe-inspiring room, then at the darkening square outside, watching the lamplighter walking by with his long-handled pole and the gas lamps flaring at a touch, and hansom cabs depositing passengers or halting to pick up others. Immediately he had a fare, the cabby dropped a shield over the oil lamp flickering on top of his cab, and uncovered it when free, and in the streetlights she saw top-hatted and becloaked gentlemen lifting silver-topped ebony sticks to hail them.

Such figures had never been seen in her native village – satin-lined cloaks flung casually over one shoulder, opera hats or silk toppers at a rakish angle, patent-leather evening pumps and white silk scarves and immaculate doeskin gloves! Only sombre suits at church socials and plain, respectable gowns for the ladies were worn in Roedean Village, though in nearby Brighton, she had heard, evening fashions were startling. As she was never allowed to visit Brighton after dusk, she had only hearsay to go by, but here she had the evidence of her eyes. Flickering gas lamps illumined front steps down which fashionable ladies descended on the arms of their escorts, ablaze with jewels as if in defiance of the edict about national mourning, their glittering adornments offsetting the required sombre colours of their gowns.

No miserable faces here; only gaiety as they set out to enjoy themselves – perhaps in anticipation of a rumoured early coronation, for already the new king was asserting himself, travelling from Osborne to London by train the very morning after Queen Victoria's death, to attend a meeting of the Privy Council at St James's Palace and startling everyone, when taking the oath as the new sovereign, by rejecting his mother's specified wish that he should be known as King Albert Edward the First. (It would be *impossible*, she had once written to her son in her italicised fashion, for him to *drop* his father's name. 'It would be *monstrous* and *Albert alone* would *not do* . . . as there can be only *one Albert*.') But the double-name form, established and accepted in Germany, was disliked by the new king, who announced that he had resolved to be known by the name of Edward, which had been borne by six of his ancestors. 'In doing so, I do not undervalue the name of Albert, which I inherit from my ever-lamented great and wise father, who by universal consent is, I think deservedly, known by the name of Albert the Good, and I desire that his name should stand alone.' Thus he revealed a decisiveness and diplomacy unexpected in the prince of playboys, except amongst the few who knew him well, to whom his resolution came as no surprise at all.

So would there be an early coronation, after the customary year's mourning? The thought was exciting to a village clergyman's daughter who had never expected to find herself in London at the time of such an event.

A tap on the door, and a maid entered to draw the curtains.

'Good gracious,' said Deborah, 'I can do that for myself!' and did so, at which the maid raised expressive eyebrows and departed. Instantly Deborah felt she had betrayed herself. I suppose that should be lesson number five, she thought impatiently. Never draw your own curtains, never unpack your own valise, never reveal your humble background (though surely the contents of that valise had already done so). Such *faux pas* would let Dulcima down in her attempt to pass off her 'cousin' as wellborn.

Suddenly impatient with pretence, Deborah left her

magnificent prison and descended the stairs again, hardly aware of where she was going, or why, but surely it wasn't Dulcima's intention that she should remain out of sight, and surely there was somewhere in this house where she could find a book to occupy her mind? A library, perhaps – though she suspected that intellectual pursuits would hold no interest for her aunt. But at least a comfortable morning room in which she would feel more at home? Not the drawing room again – Dulcima's guests would be shown into that, and it had been made plain that she should not appear there until groomed for presentation.

Again that irritation, that impatience with pretence, followed by a feeling of guilt for such ingratitude.

In this mood she began to descend the stairs, and looked down at a man who, she knew instinctively, had not arrived in his own carriage or even by hansom, but on foot, and surely he was not a dinner guest in that suit of rough tweed and caped coat of ill-matching material, casually flung on as if it had been the nearest thing to hand. Such rugged individualism seemed unfitted to this splendid house, and the expression on Dillon's face confirmed it – also that the visitor had walked in uninvited.

Deborah paused, unseen.

'Are you expected, sir?'

'Of course not. I don't even know Miss Howard, though I am aware she owns this establishment. And it isn't she I have come to see, but Ashleigh.'

'Lord Ashleigh, sir, has not yet arrived.' Dillon held the front door open wide to encourage the man's departure. 'If you have come to deliver a message, I will make sure he receives it.'

'No, thanks. I'll wait.'

'I don't think –'

'You don't have to think. That isn't the function of butlers, is it, except in private, when they can think what they like?' The man seated himself, crossing his legs and folding his arms, his whole attitude pugnacious and matched by the expression on his face.

'Sir, I must insist –'

'And *I* insist that you shut that damned door, go about your business, and leave me to deal with mine.'

She should slip away, of course – back to her room, unobserved. Instead, Deborah remained where she was, halfway down the stairs, highly interested. She instinctively disliked Dillon and enjoyed this man's handling of him, particularly since he seemed as out-of-place as herself, though he was in no way ill-at-ease and certainly not awed by his surroundings. Even so, a less sophisticated background seemed more natural for such a man; a down-to-earth background, though somehow she felt he was not wholly an outdoor man despite the ill-fitting tweeds.

He remained seated, his long legs out-thrust and his arms folded, unyielding in his determination and indifferent to the butler's disdain.

When the front door remained open, the visitor rose and shut it very pointedly. It was then that Deborah noticed a pronounced limp.

'If the doorbell rings again, I will answer it,' the man said, reseating himself and ignoring Dillon's indignation. 'Then Ashleigh won't be able to escape me, though no doubt he has his own key?'

At once the butler demanded, 'What are you? A debt collector? If so, I have my mistress's instructions never to admit your kind.'

The visitor's laughter filled the hall. Deborah saw an almost ugly face lightened by amusement, a wide mouth revealing white and very even teeth.

'No, I am not a dunner, though the idea of being mistaken for one is vastly entertaining. And I imagine a debt collector would pursue his lordship to his own front door, not his mistress's – unless of course, he too was at pains to keep them out, which wouldn't surprise me, knowing my brother-in-law as I do.'

'Your *brother-in-law*, sir?'

'I appreciate your surprise – I am hardly the society type – but now you can go about your business with an easier mind.'

At that moment the doorbell pealed again, and this time the guest was far more suited to Dulcima's fine house – top-hatted, tailed, white-tied, becloaked, and every inch the gentleman. He sauntered across the threshold, handing his hat to Dillon with an easy and amiable greeting which earned from the butler a deferential inclination of the head. Next came the newcomer's opera cloak, lined with scarlet satin, and then his white doeskin gloves, delicately removed finger by finger and dropped into his extended hat. Finally, as the man adjusted his bow tie before a gilt-framed mirror, the butler said, 'Sir . . . a gentleman to see you.'

Throughout this time the intruder had remained where he was, arms still folded and legs out-thrust, his eyes on the newcomer. Now he said easily, 'Yes – to see you, Justin.'

Ashleigh, for Ashleigh it obviously was, jerked round. 'Good God, Simon, what brings you here?' A nod dismissed Dillon, and when he had gone, Ashleigh continued, 'And how did you discover this address?'

'I have known it for a long time. So has Caroline, as I am sure you know. It was she who first told me about it. Since you are consistently unavailable at those rooms of yours in Albany, I came here.'

'Then I hope you will explain your purpose and leave as soon as possible.'

'I intend to. I came to tell you that your sister has gone off on one of her jaunts again and I am resolved to remove Delia from Kingsmere.'

'You must be out of your mind. As for Caroline's escapades – if indeed she indulges in any – do what other husbands do. Turn a blind eye.'

'I have been forced to do that for too long. I have no intention of becoming permanently blind.'

'More fool you. Freedom to do what you will without a troublesome wife round your neck seems an ideal marital arrangement to me. But no divorce, Simon. No scandal. Handle your affairs as discreetly as I handle mine, and as my father did before me.'

'Bloody hypocrisy!'

'Bloody common sense. The trouble with you is that you are bourgeois, too much middle-class morality. I warned Caroline, but her heart was set on you. You know the penchant she has for celebrities, and an archaeologist hitting the headlines was a distinct novelty to her, though she couldn't understand, any more than I could, why you then decided to do your bit in the South African war. Luckily for her, you distinguished yourself further in the cause of it. Perhaps you derived a masochistic enjoyment out of your long spell in hospital with other maimed heroes? But after so much separation, you can hardly expect her to reorganise her life yet again, though I understand heroics appeal to women, especially when advertised by facial wounds like yours. Why do scars across a man's cheek fascinate the female sex? As symbols of masculine daring, I suppose. Personally, I prefer to rely on my inherent charm. I also have the good sense to avoid skirmishes. The Boers interest me not at all.'

'Nor the horrors they inflicted on our troops?'

'Precisely. I confine my interest to the home front, as does my sister, so you can't blame her if the novelty of a husband like you has worn off — further aggravated by your stupidity in abandoning fame for obscurity. What a letdown for my scalp-hunting sister! Caroline collects celebrities the way other people collect bric-a-brac, the odder the better. You were the oddest of the lot. Still are, to me and my dear mother. Which brings me to Delia. The old lady will never permit a granddaughter of hers to be taken away from Kingsmere, particularly to be brought up against such a background as the one you would provide. You would turn the child into a middle-class blue stocking, and we have never had such a thing in the family, nor want one.'

'I am aware of that. Frightfully bourgeois, as you put it, to be interested in anything but doing the London season, then grouse shooting in Scotland in August, bagging pheasants in Norfolk in October – or have I mixed the game and the months? – then back to London for the same social round. A life as predictable as the liaisons and postmarital affairs which are entirely permissible so long as they are conducted in secret. 'Thou Shalt Not Be Found Out' – the eleventh commandment you expect me to acknowledge; no doubt my daughter too, eventually, which is why I intend to take her away from Kingsmere and bring her up as an ordinary Davidson, like her father, never as an Ashleigh. Nor can your mother, enthroned in her dower house, stop me. So tell me where your sister is. If anyone knows, you do.'

'On the contrary, I know nothing of her whereabouts or her affairs – nor care. And think twice before you try to make a scandal. You could live to regret it. Certainly Delia would. Unless I produce a male heir, she is in line for Kingsmere eventually. You must know well enough that I am the last of the Ashleigh men. I have no male cousin to inherit. My father's line could die out altogether, certainly the name would, unless I marry again and perpetuate it with a son. I had hopes that Norah . . .' A shrug, then a sigh. 'But you know what a weakling my late wife was. And the only cousins I have are female, daughters of my father's brother, one married to a Canadian lumberjack –'

'Rubbish. She married a very wealthy forester.'

'What's the difference? No matter how many lumberjacks he employs, he is still one of them, since timber is his trade. As for the other daughter, she did even worse for herself – an American schoolteacher.'

'A college professor.'

'Same thing, only slightly more elevated. Since their father died almost penniless, they did quite well for themselves, I suppose, but they certainly don't stand in line for the Ashleigh estates. Your wife, therefore, does, if I don't produce a son. And after Caroline, your daughter. Would you rob Delia of such a heritage as Kingsmere?'

'She is being robbed of other things, more important things.'

'It's all a question of values, I suppose. You are boring me, Simon. Take your woes or your threats, or whatever else prompted you to come here, with you. And I haven't the faintest idea where Caroline is. We have never been that close, nor wish to be. Anyway, why do you want to see her, if your aim is divorce? – which I hope, for the sake of our family name, it is not. To give her one last chance?'

'No. To tell her fairly and squarely what I plan to do about our daughter. And don't sweat under your expensive collar about the scandal of divorce. The illustrious name of Ashleigh will remain unscathed, because all your family forces will be enlisted to protect your sister, and any lawyer *I* could afford would be powerless against them. Nothing can erect an invincible barrier so effectively as money, of which you now have plenty and I little. In any case, I am indifferent – except about my daughter.' Simon Davidson limped to the door. 'I am wasting my time. Good night to you.'

As he opened the door, he looked back briefly, and saw Deborah. Despite the distance between them, she was aware of his comprehensive glance – he would remember her, should they ever meet again. Eyes so penetrating missed no detail. Then the door closed behind him, and, hot with embarrassment and thankful that the other man's back was towards her, and he, at least, unaware of her presence, she began to retreat quietly upstairs.

Ashleigh's voice came after her. 'Well, little eavesdropper, I hope you enjoyed that conversation?'

He moved to the foot of the stairs, smiling up at her, thoroughly amused. He was the most handsome man she had ever seen, and his smile was kind.

'Come,' he said, holding out his hand, 'don't stand there looking embarrassed. And don't apologise. No doubt you remained there because you have no desire to draw attention to yourself, though why, I do not know. You are extremely pretty, and even my eccentric brother-in-law would have noticed that, and forgiven you. As I do. But why did you halt on your way down? Because I arrived, or were you there already?' The hand gestured encouragingly. 'Come, don't be afraid. I am not an ogre. And don't you think we should get acquainted?'

She moved downstairs slowly, aware that her hair was still tumbled about her shoulders in a way no lady wore it except in the seclusion of her boudoir. She wished she had coiled it more decorously; it would have given her more poise, more confidence.

'When did you notice me, Lord Ashleigh?'

'As soon as I walked through the front door.'

'It would have been kind to have given some indication. I could then have retired more easily.'

'But I didn't want to. And I am not kind.' But his smile continued to be. 'Since you know my identity,' he said when her hand was in his, 'shouldn't I know yours? You can't be one of Dulcima's girls – you're not the type.'

'Dulcima's girls?'

'Don't look so startled. She never ran a brothel, if that is what you are fearing – merely a group for *poses plastiques*. What they did when out of her sight was none of her business. They came to entertain the gentlemen after the evening's card playing, and this they did supremely well, I understand. Any other form of entertaining was up to them, provided they did it away from this house. She disbanded the girls when I came on the scene, though she imagines I am unaware of that. Dear Dulcima—she can be very self-deluding. I suppose she imagined that nude posing, however artistically staged, might undermine the impression of respectability she wanted me to receive.'

Deborah withdrew her hand sharply. 'You are speaking of my cousin, sir.'

'Your *cousin*?' This time it was he who was startled. 'I had no idea she had any relatives, much less any so respectable. Of course, I knew she must have had a family of some kind once upon a time, but assumed she had turned her back on them, or vice versa. Well, what else could a man think, knowing her reputation?'

His eyes glinted, not with amusement this time, but with a kind of sparking interest, and it was then that Deborah noticed the colour of them — a pale amber, almost opaque. They reminded her of a tiger's, or how a tiger's might look when scenting a prey. She stepped back instinctively.

'When did you arrive here?' Ashleigh asked. 'Don't tell me darling Dulcima has been keeping you hidden?'

'Of course not. I came today, thanks to her kindness. She is giving me a home.'

'And why should you need one?'

Deborah disliked the interrogation, even if prompted by kindly interest. The smile had returned, the strange light in his eyes had disappeared, but curiosity and speculation remained. The sooner she escaped, the better, for it would be difficult to avoid his questions and even more difficult to support Dulcima's pretence that she was the daughter of a high-ranking churchman. Nor would it be very convincing in this cheap alpaca dress, which, as yet, he did not appear to have noticed. His eyes had been continuously on her face.

Dulcima's voice, from above, answered for her. 'Naturally she needs one, left alone in the world. I am glad you have met Cousin Deborah so soon, though she is just off to a quiet meal in her room and an early bed. After the stress she has been through recently, she needs both.'

Dulcima came sweeping downstairs, magnificent in peacock satin, her shoulders bare, the deep neckline revealing as much of her beautiful breasts as decorum permitted – very different from those blatantly revealing picture postcards. This was the real Dulcima, the Dulcima whom Sarah Yorke, and now her daughter, loved. Deborah felt a rush of pride in her beauty, the Titian hair upswept and coiled on top of her head, emeralds glinting on the small ears. Her only other adornment was an emerald ring on the hand which now cupped Deborah's chin and lifted her face to kiss good night. There was warmth and affection in the kiss, but dismissal too. She was not only giving Deborah the opportunity to escape, but also making sure that she did.

4

It had been a successful dinner party, and the few other guests had left obligingly early. Even better, Ashleigh had wasted no time in taking Dulcima to bed.

But once there, he seemed in no hurry to make love. Usually he was impatient, sometimes not even waiting to arouse her, but taking her without delay, unlike his father, whose preliminaries had always been considerate and loving. The late Lord Ashleigh had never forced himself on her, the way his son sometimes did – and was doing more frequently of late. Fortunately her responsive body was quickly aroused, but Justin's sexual appetite was often satisfied before her own, and he did not consider this to be his fault, even when he thrust into her before she was ready to receive him. She could not help comparing his father's tenderness and perfect timing with Justin's indifference to her needs, but mercifully he could perform again and again, so she rarely failed to reach a climax, even if it did not coincide with one of his. He would use her until he had had his fill, and although she had known more considerate lovers, she accepted him because he was Ashleigh, and her desire to bear an Ashleigh child had been reawakened.

Tonight, she prayed, she would conceive. She also prayed it would be a son. His wife, whom he sadly admitted had been frigid, had given him no heir, and Dulcima knew how greatly he wanted one to carry on the line. He had told her so more than once, so she was positive that he would not only acknowledge any son she gave him but also legitimise the child by marrying her, and what a triumph that would be!

She lay naked beside him, dreaming about it, waiting for him to turn to her and more than ready to receive him. She did not mind him tantalising her like this, because it made her own body grow increasingly hungry, and there would be no discomfort when he took her without any advance titillation of her senses. She flung one leg across him, trying to draw him to her, and, to her surprise, found he was quite unready. It was the first time she had ever known him to be in such a state once they were in bed, and the shock was like a rebuff.

She withdrew to her own side of the bed, waiting, her aching need becoming more insistent. After a while she touched him with an exploring hand and felt him begin to respond, whereupon, to punish him, she withdrew. Lovers sometimes played these games, and she always enjoyed them. A man and woman could spend a long time like this, tantalising each other until they could bear it no longer, and the ecstasy was doubled. Perhaps, for the first time, Justin planned to do the same. The thought excited her, because such a passionate animal as he would be infinitely satisfying after such delicious dalliance, much preferable to his normal approach, which was so impatient that it almost amounted to rape at times. Especially of late. She had even sensed a threatening though indefinable undercurrent which was inconsistent with the personality he presented to the world, and which, because he was dear Charles's son, she believed to be his true one.

Sometimes they left a lamp burning so they could enjoy not only the sensation but also the sight of each other as they mated, her own face displaying the agony of mounting desire and his the triumph of conquering and reconquering, but tonight they lay cocooned in darkness and she decided that if the touch of her limbs was not sufficient to stir him, perhaps the sight of them might do so. There was an oil lamp and a box of Swan Vestas on the table beside her. She leaned over him and whispered, 'Shall I light the lamp?' He lay on his back, and her breasts brushed above him and her hand strayed again, only to discover that his first impulse was gone. He was cold once more.

'If you like,' he answered indifferently.

Angrily she reached for the matches and struck one. The flame flickered in her trembling hand and she could scarcely remove the glass funnel of the lamp and turn up the wick to receive the light, but as the flame spread into a steadying circle, she gained control of herself. She replaced the ruby-red glass and saw the rosy glow on her body, and knew it was beautiful. She lay back to enable him to see it too, only to find him staring at the ceiling, hands behind his head, thoughts miles away.

He is trying to torment me, she thought. And succeeding, the brute.

She dragged one hand from behind his head and placed it between her thighs so he would discover for himself how ready she was. His fingers moved, exploring her, but all he did was smile a little.

'All right,' he said indulgently, 'you are impatient tonight, and I am not. It won't hurt you to wait.'

'You are callous!' she cried, realising for the first time that this was actually true.

He ignored her, lost in thought again.

She cried out angrily. 'You may as well leave! Now. Right away.'

'I am not ready yet. Neither to go, nor to make love. Be patient. We have all night before us.'

She subsided, frustrated and close to tears. 'Then tell me what is on your mind,' she pleaded. 'That way you will get rid of it and perhaps have time to spare for *me*.'

'All right. If you must know, it's that girl upstairs.'

If he had struck her, he could not have shocked or hurt her more. Nor so insulted her. No man had ever lain in her bed with his mind on another woman.

She jerked upright, staring at him incredulously, at which he laughed and told her not to be silly. 'There's no need to be jealous. I am curious, that's all, and not a little surprised to find you have a cousin so respectable. And obviously poor. That appalling gown! What sort of a home did you rescue her from, and was your own background as poverty-stricken?'

She lay down again and, without looking at him, told him his judgment was wrong.

'Her father, my uncle, was a very high-ranking member of the Church – an intellectual, like my own father. Such men are always unworldly, unaware of the needs of their womenfolk; hence the drab gown, and hence my own reason for running away from home when a girl. Deborah would never have done the same. She lacks the rebel spirit, as her mother before her.'

'I wouldn't be too sure of that. In any event, it would be interesting to find out.'

'You will have no opportunity – that I swear. I brought her here because I am her only relative and intend to take care of her, which means –'

'– that you hope to find a husband for her.'

'Why not?'

'A penniless young woman!'

'She is not penniless. I have *told* you, her father held an eminent position in the Church, as my own father did in the scholarly world, which means she won't be going around in drab clothes now she has control of her own purse strings. Does that satisfy you?'

She prayed it would, because it all sounded so convincing that it satisfied herself very well.

'For the time being,' he answered lazily, and his hand crept back between her thighs. 'Sorry to have kept you waiting, my love – what a state you are in!'

And without further preliminary he was astride her. As quickly as that, he could be ready to take her, and this time she was glad, welcoming the long-delayed release. Her eyelids drooped, then jerked wide open with each rise and fall, with every deepening wave of physical response, and she knew that tonight he was going to be insatiable. He was always like that when his eyes changed from their pale amber colour to that strange but brilliant opaqueness. It seemed to herald other things too, those threatening undercurrents which had not been apparent when he first became her lover. His eyes had remained the same then, sharpening only into a more vivid colour as excitement rode him, but giving way more and more frequently to this strange transformation.

Did the eyes of a wild animal look like that when devouring its prey? she wondered remotely. Then the tide of passion carried her to a blinding climax, obliterating thought. She was unaware of her wild, ecstatic cry.

Long after her spent body lay supine beneath him, he had not finished with her, and she dared not halt him. He was an even greater stallion than his father had been, and though she longed for sleep, she exulted in her power to inflame him – for surely, tonight, she could not fail to conceive as a result of such an onslaught?

5

London at a time of national mourning was infernally dull, reflected Ashleigh, despite society's attempts to brighten it with private dinner parties and entertainments. Even after the old queen had been interred at Frogmore following ten days of lying in state at Osborne, and then in Westminster Hall, the aftermath of state sorrow lingered on. Towards the end of her sixty-four years' reign, the longest in British history and the last forty of which had been spent in virtual isolation, feeling had changed from criticism of her apparent neglect of royal duties to an attitude of affectionate reverence, now intensified by her death.

Ashleigh could not remember a time when that squat little figure had not ruled in obscurity over her ever-expanding empire, and to him she was no more than a dumpy little representative of the monarchy whose death cast an unreasonable gloom on things. He could not share the grief of the crowds on the Isle of Wight, who had wept as her body, within a coffin covered with a white pall and surmounted by the crown, the orb, and the sceptre, was conveyed on a gun carriage to East Cowes, with the king, the German emperor, and other mourners following on foot, and thence aboard the royal yacht *Alberta*, to be borne along the Solent through endless lines of battleships and cruisers, their flags flying at half mast. A last solemn salute was fired in her honour as she passed by, for she had requested a military funeral, but the story quickly spread of how the king, following his mother through the Solent on the yacht *Victoria and Albert*, had noticed the royal standard on his own vessel also flying at half mast, and demanded to know why.

'The queen is dead, sir,' the captain had replied, aghast at such a question, to which the king snapped, 'But the King of England lives,' and promptly ordered the royal standard to the full height of the mast – another indication that he had already shaken off his mother's shadow. This was demonstrated even more at the opening of Parliament on February 14, which Edward made the first public function of his reign, surprising the politicians and delighting the populace. During her long widowhood, and despite angry scenes with Gladstone, who declared it to be a dereliction of her public duty, Queen Victoria had performed this royal task barely more than half a dozen times, and then, on her own insistence, in a much modified fashion. She had also refused to wear the robes of state and to read the speech made from the throne. Now, to everyone's astonishment, Edward restored the traditional splendour of the occasion, personally supervising all details of the first full state procession for forty years.

He also made it plain that he considered this to be an honoured tradition designed to emphasise a sovereign's role in the constitution, so the gilded coach, for which

George the Third had paid seven thousand pounds, was brought from its long storage and carefully renovated, and a new throne built for the queen, which, also on the king's insistence, was to be as grand as his own and placed beside it in the House of Lords, not slightly in the background, as with previous queen consorts.

Then further news began to fly. The king was at loggerheads with his ministers over the wording of the declaration pronounced in Parliament by each new sovereign.

'What fun!' declared Dulcima. 'Everyone expected the dear man to be putty in their hands, and he is proving quite the reverse!'

But Ashleigh merely shrugged. Politics held no interest for him, and he regarded all this excitement over the state opening of Parliament as merely hysterical reaction to the mournfulness of the past days. *He* was not going to gape at the royal procession even though his title qualified him for a seat in the House of Lords, and if Dulcima wanted to find some vantage point, she could look to her friends who had convenient windows along the route.

'Very well, I will,' she declared. 'I am resolved that my dear Deborah isn't going to be cheated out of her first glimpse of a royal occasion. The dear girl will revel in it.'

And so Deborah did, though it was from no convenient window along the route but from a pavement jam-packed with cheering crowds, held back by stalwart police, for on the morning of the great day, Dulcima was unwell.

'I must have eaten something disagreeable to me,' she said, lying pallid against her pillows. Even so, she insisted that Deborah should find her way to Whitehall, where her friend, a prominent cabinet minister by day and a regular patron of her card salon by night, had invited them to view the procession from his office window with a party of other guests.

'I shall be perfectly all right,' Dulcima declared when Deborah announced her intention to stay at home. 'I have

Garfield to look after me if necessary, though feeling the way I do, I prefer to be alone.'

Sick as she obviously was, Dulcima seemed not in the least concerned about it. In between bouts, she seemed positively happy.

But it was late when Deborah set out, only to find the crowds so dense that it was impossible to reach Whitehall. She abandoned the carriage, sent Briggs to battle his way home to Hanover Square, and headed on foot for the Mall, only to be trapped there by excited crowds. Frustrated, she decided to make the best of things and let the general excitement take over. She was here, actually *here* in London for a state occasion, and with luck she might catch a glimpse of the golden coach and the Guardsmen's gleaming helmets, plumes waving in the breeze; she would hear the military bands and the cheers of the populace and the clatter of the Household Cavalry. It was all a fantastic dream which she was savouring to the full when a familiar voice said beside her, 'My dear Miss Yorke, you will be crushed to death if you linger here. Let me take you to a safer place.'

It was Ashleigh, and this was the first time she had come face to face with him since their initial meeting, for Dulcima had not yet invited her to the salon of an evening. 'You must learn to play baccarat eventually, Deborah, but there is plenty of time for that.' So for the most part Deborah spent her evenings alone after dinner, while Dulcima entertained her guests, waited upon by the obsequious Dillon, who, Deborah had noticed, was always in attendance when card sessions were under way. Occasionally she had dined with Dulcima and some of the patrons, now being in possession of some new and very presentable gowns, but never when Ashleigh was present, for then Dulcima preferred to make it a *tête-à-tête* affair.

Now she saw his strangely brilliant eyes appraising her. In the morning sun they seemed paler than she remembered, and the expression in them was frankly admiring. 'No dull alpaca gown this time,' he said teasingly, 'and a good thing, too. I wanted to tear it from your body; not with any ulterior motive, but because it was such an abominable covering for one so lovely.'

He was steering her out of the crowd towards the opening leading to St James's Palace and thence to Pall Mall. 'I shall miss everything!' she protested, pulling away. 'Please, Lord Ashleigh, let me go! I was trying to reach Whitehall to view the procession from Sir William Coward's windows, and now I shall see nothing at all. I have lost the place I managed to seize, and I might have caught a glimpse between people's heads!'

'I shall find you a better view. Here . . . mount these railings on the corner. Stand on the middle rung, and I will hold you. You will see over the heads of the crowd, and in much greater safety.'

His hand was beneath her elbow, helping her to mount, then both hands gripped her waist, supporting her. This barrier of railings had been erected to prevent people from climbing on to the walls of St James's Palace grounds, also from trampling on the verge skirting the Mall, and he was right – they made a much better vantage point.

Wreathed in smiles, she thanked him, and he studied her excited face, thinking how pretty she was and how like, and yet unlike, her features were to Dulcima's. The difference between them was a question of innocence, of course, and though this quality normally lacked appeal for him, he found a certain novelty in Deborah Yorke, whose face was now alight with enchantment. He thought her amusing as well as endearing – or did he mean challenging? People did not endear themselves to him greatly, but they could certainly challenge, especially women. So he let his eyes dwell on her face as she gazed towards the Mall, and beneath the clasp of his hands he could feel her tremor of excitement as the sound of oncoming music swelled and cheering broke out, pouring from a thousand throats as the cavalcade rode by, and mounting in a crescendo as the state coach appeared.

'I can see it, I can *see* it!' she cried. 'I can see the king himself – how magnificent he looks, and what a wonderful smile he has for everyone! Look, Lord Ashleigh, *look!*'

He was vastly entertained. Not for a moment had he intended to stir from his rooms in Albany on such a day as this; the great unwashed were anathema to him, but on an impulse, and because he was bored, he had decided to call on Caroline, enjoying the idea of taking her and her new lover by surprise. It was a way of passing the time. Besides, he needed to get in touch with her, because an idea had been stirring in his mind, a way in which to escape from the boredom imposed since the old queen's death and which would inevitably set in again once today's excitement had passed. Public holidays always subsided like deflated balloons.

En route to Caroline's current hideout, some inexplicable impulse had made him cross Pall Mall at the foot of St James's Street, instead of walking straight on to Bryant Meredith's apartment at number 54 (an essentially fashionable address for a noted actor, whether he could afford it or not), and at the far end of the turning into St James's Park, he had suddenly espied Deborah Yorke jumping up and down behind the crowds lining the royal route. He had scarcely recognised her in that fashionable costume of rust velvet, which did wonders for her copper-coloured hair. Funny, he had not even noticed how rich the colour was when they first met, though he had admired it tumbling about her shoulders. Now he saw that in contrast with Dulcima's glorious Titian, this girl's had the warmth of a newly shelled chestnut, and he remembered how, in bed with Dulcima, he had imagined that thick hair spread over bare skin and how he had resolved to see it that way sometime. And *how* his preoccupations had inflamed Dulcima!

It amused him to recall her fury when realising that his usual lust for her was temporarily abated due to thoughts of her cousin. Then, of course, everything had been forgotten in their ensuing passion – everything but his increasing urge to indulge his stronger impulses, now too long denied. The memory of that brought him right back to the matter he wanted to discuss with Caroline, the necessity to escape from London's present dullness, though he would naturally withhold from his sister his true motivation. Meanwhile, this precise moment, holding an excited girl, would pass soon enough. It was a temporary amusement, no more: a welcome moment in a tedious day. Tedium was something to be avoided or overcome, and he had already decided just how and where he was going to overcome it.

He let one hand slip from Deborah's waist to the gentle swell of hip below. No rigid boning there, thank heaven; with such a slender figure, it was unnecessary. The softness of her velvet skirt suggested the softness of her flesh beneath. She wore a neat little bolero jacket above the long flaring skirt, hugging her small waist and curving into the delicious mound of her breast above. Inching his fingers upward, he could feel the gentle weight of it, and the temptation to cup it in his hand was almost overpowering. He always found a woman's breast sexually exciting, but his hands never wanted to remain there, but to slide upward to the base of the throat, for the neck of a woman was so supple and yielding. He could see the slender neck of this girl rising from the round sable collar of her enchanting little jacket, and longed to slide his fingers round it and press very gently . . . very, *very* gently at first . . .

The world seemed to retreat. The pageantry a few yards away, the stirring military music, the brilliance of the Household Cavalry on their magnificent coal-black steeds, the yells and the cheers of the crowd, all were miles away as far as he was concerned – as far away as the days when he himself had belonged to the Household Cavalry, from which he had retired quietly, and, thanks to his father, with the minimum of fuss and absolutely no publicity. Justin Ashleigh rejected tiresome or unpleasant memories with ease, for there had always been someone with influence to make sure that occasional lapses were covered up – thus he was able to enjoy the present moment to the full. Excitement, right now, was confined to this spot. He could feel it pulsating through him and knew that this girl must be included in his plans, though he would pretend indifference when putting them to Dulcima.

A voice cut into his thoughts, shattering the moment. 'Well, Justin, you are the last person I expected to bump into on a day such as this, and in such a place. I would never have imagined pageantry of this kind attracting you. And surely you could have taken your place in the House of Lords and seen the whole thing at close quarters? I even thought it was a peer's duty.'

Unbelievably, it was his brother-in-law again, standing right beside them, his observant eyes taking in the situation – the arm about the rust velvet waist, the girl clinging to the railings, the closeness of the pair of them. Damn the man. Did he have to turn up like a bad penny everywhere?

The procession had passed. People were surging in all directions, but some were stubbornly clinging to their places in order to see it return to the palace.

Deborah gave a sigh of satisfaction and jumped down. 'Thank you, Lord Ashleigh, and good-bye. I intend to stake a place there in the Mall so I may see even more when the procession comes back . . .'

She broke off, recognising the man she had seen in the hall of Dulcima's house, whose conversation with his brother-in-law she had overheard – husband of the unknown Caroline and father of a daughter named Delia.

At close quarters his looks suffered in comparison with Ashleigh's. He wore the same tiered coat of rough tweed which he had worn on that memorable night, and no hat covered his thick thatch of hair. His height surprised her; viewed from above, he had seemed shorter. And there was a scar running from his right eye across his cheek, almost to the corner of his mouth. Perhaps it was that which drew attention to it, the shape resolute but the lips not thin. Even in repose they curved in a way which suggested that both amusement and gentleness could come easily to them.

Ashleigh was presenting him, but only because courtesy demanded it. 'Miss Yorke, allow me to present my brother-in-law, Simon Davidson.' He was plainly determined to dispose of the formality, as well as the man's company, as quickly as possible, but Davidson lingered.

'Miss Yorke and I have seen each other, but not met. Isn't that so, Miss Yorke?'

He remembered her, as she had known he would, and though his tone held amusement, she was embarrassed, remembering the moment well. The man's eyes lingered on her briefly; then, deliberately, she felt, he changed the subject. 'So the king is asserting himself at last – even over the Declaration, though he hasn't won his way with that yet. Today he will have to utter the words he so dislikes.'

Ashleigh shrugged. He was indifferent, but Deborah was not.

'What words?' she asked. She had no knowledge of the full Parliamentary Declaration which was pronounced at every state opening, though she had once heard her father, strongly anti-papist, declare to a neighbour, whom he knew to be Roman Catholic, that he thoroughly approved of every word and prayed the day would never come when a single one was changed, so obviously part of it had some religious significance. All Deborah knew was that it had been drawn up in 1689, set out in the Bill of Rights after the flight of the Roman Catholic King James the Second, its purpose being to ensure the succession of his Protestant daughter Mary the Second and her husband, William the Third.

Simon Davidson looked at her with interest. Few people had paid much heed to Edward's protests regarding certain words the sovereign was compelled to utter, and this girl's curiosity surprised him. Though tradition, for the new king, had always been sacrosanct, today's Declaration in Parliament was the one thing from which he had striven to depart.

'He maintains that certain phrases are an insult to his Roman Catholic subjects and that he finds it particularly offensive to assert that "the invocation or adoration of the Virgin Mary or any other saint and the sacrifice of the Mass as they are now used in the Church of Rome are superstitious and idolatrous", also to vow that his Declaration is made "without any evasion, equivocation, or mental reservation whatever". He demands that this passage be deleted, or at the very least altered to an attestation that he is a faithful Protestant willing to uphold and maintain the enactments to secure the Protestant succession to the throne, but on no account to condemn the beliefs and practices of the Roman Catholic Church or to offend its adherents. But a special Act of Parliament is needed to reshape the Declaration, and time prevented that lengthy business before today's opening. So the poor devil has to utter the words he disapproves of. All the same' – and here Simon Davidson's smile flashed out for the first time, startling Deborah with its vividness – 'I am willing to bet he mutters that particular passage into his beard, so no one can hear. Rake he may be, but he is proving decisive and progressive already, and that is all to the good.'

Even more to the good, thought Ashleigh, was the

moral release which the Edwardian era promised to bring, already foreshadowed by Edward and Alexandra and the Marlborough House Set, when they were Prince and Princess of Wales. But meanwhile, how to amuse oneself in the metropolis in this otherwise dull period of time? Court mourning meant the deepest black for six months, followed by another six in semi-mourning, not to mention a reduced social round, which he himself had no intention of observing.

He doffed his hat to Deborah Yorke and bade Davidson a curt good-day. The girl he would see again; for the time being, this morning's encounter would suffice. As his brother-in-law went on his way, luckily in the opposite direction, Ashleigh walked up St James's Street towards Piccadilly and his rooms in Albany, abandoning any idea of calling on his sister at Meredith's place. He would write to her instead, and send his man to deliver the letter.

As he let himself into his exclusive apartment, he reflected with relief that the circles he moved in held no false creeds, nor clung to the Victorians' morbid fascination with death, but until London was back to normal, periodic escape seemed essential, hence his resolve to renew Kingsmere's long weekend house parties, filling the place with friends of whom his mother disapproved and about whom even Caroline sometimes protested, when she dared.

Not that her own friends were much better, but at least, as she was prone to point out, they were people who achieved things, names well known in the theatre and the arts and other spheres. Stupid Caro, basking in reflected glory and discovering, all too often, that its light could quickly wane – like her husband's.

Why the devil had she married the man? 'Take him as a lover and get him out of your system,' Justin had advised, fully aware that his sister never heeded any advice he offered. Other things she accepted without protest, such as a home at Kingsmere because Davidson could offer only a modest one in Kensington, and such a middle-class life was not for her, and certainly not the life she had anticipated when she met him at the height of his fame.

His name had been emblazoned throughout the length and breadth of the British Isles when, after successes in Egypt and other parts of the Middle East, he discovered a sacred tomb in Syria, yielding treasures for museums throughout the world, though he had quixotically insisted on the Syrians having 'their just share' over and above the terms of his licence to excavate. However, he had been honoured by the queen, who appreciated any achievement which added glory to her empire.

Naturally, everyone expected the man to go from success to success, from honour to honour, instead of going off to fight the Boers and then, after being discharged from the army due to war wounds, followed by prolonged hospitalisation, retiring into obscurity to write some profound tome on archaeology – a subject few people were interested in, except the experts who hailed his mammoth work. The public was enchanted only by newspaper headlines of exciting and spectacular events, and forgot Simon Davidson once his name vanished from the front pages.

'And he doesn't even care!' Caroline had wailed. 'Fame actually means nothing to him!'

Poor silly Caro. No wonder she consoled herself with others – though, very sensibly, she did so with such discretion that she had never yet been found out. A pity she had borne Davidson a child, but luckily it was only a daughter. A daughter was unlikely to take after her father. She could be brought up as a replica of her mother and be a credit to the Ashleighs in looks at least, for already Delia was a pretty child, with a marked resemblance to Caroline, who, in her way, was quite good-looking.

But enough of his sister and her problems, though she should be wary of that husband of hers. Davidson had a mind of his own, as well as a stubbornness not easily deflected, so the sooner she was back at Kingsmere, the better. For the past days she had refused to leave London, despite her brother's warnings, and luckily her husband had failed to trace her. People in high society stuck together, shielding each other from scandal because its ripples could spread, overlapping into one's own life and causing not only embarrassment all round, but worse besides. Betray someone, and you could yourself be betrayed.

So Caroline's hideout with Bryant Meredith, the well-known actor whose scalp was the latest to dangle from her belt, was a well-kept secret, as yet shared only between brother and sister. Although they had little in common, they did at least adhere to the ethics of their social world and respect the eleventh commandment, at which Davidson had been uncouth enough to sneer. No person of taste would ever commit the sin of being found out, and at least her brother had to admit that Caroline had her wits about her in that respect. Luckily for her, Meredith was between productions at present and therefore willing to idle his time away with her in private. This was very much to Caroline's liking, because she was in the throes of early obsession when the outside world held little allure, but once this phase passed, there could be trouble, especially if Bryant Meredith grew restless and began to chafe against their isolation – which wouldn't surprise Ashleigh, since he suspected that the man enjoyed the publicity attached to a scandalous love affair and would not be above exploiting it to his advantage. But the greatest danger was Simon Davidson's white-hot determination, demonstrated when he called at Dulcima's house that night, and despite his bland manner today there was no reason to believe it had diminished.

Of course, Meredith might tire of Caroline as rapidly as others had done in the past. For some reason unknown to

Justin, his sister lacked the ability to hold a man for long. But in any case, something would have to be done about her, and he now ensured this by writing to her at Meredith's apartment.

It is time Kingsmere's house parties began again, and because I am a widower, you, as my sister, must act as hostess. We will start with a damned good one after these past dreary weeks, so bring whomsoever you wish. Don't forget, there is safety in numbers, so you can indulge your pleasure just as privately there as in London; the place is vast enough, and with a fair number of guests, everyone will be too busy with their own *affaires* to heed those of others.

The more people, the better, he reflected; then, if Simon did turn up, even he would be discouraged from making a scene. And that would add spice to the situation. The behaviour of others was always amusing; their cover-ups, their deceits, their pretences, and most of all, the desperate measures people like his sister adopted in order to avoid being found out. *'Lord, what fools these mortals be!'* He could enjoy the stupidities of others as greatly as Puck ever did.

Caroline having been dealt with, Ashleigh turned his mind to his own guests. Never had he contemplated inviting Dulcima to Kingsmere – as with his father, she was a woman to be kept tucked away out of sight – but suddenly the idea held a wicked appeal. It would be delicious to include his father's ex-mistress, now his own. There had been a piquancy about the situation from the start, because his relationship with Dulcima was the only thing he had ever had in common with his father – unfortunately too late to hurt or embarrass the old boy, but satisfactory for all that. He had sought acquaintance with her out of curiosity in the first place, but underlying this was a quixotic motive. He had never cared much for his father, and in deliberately claiming his mistress, even after so many years, Justin Ashleigh experienced a malicious satisfaction, a feeling of triumph, as if scoring over the old man at long last.

His father's association with the 'Madame' of 20 Hanover Square had not been the well-kept secret he had so fondly imagined. Even his wife had known about it, although, being a model Victorian spouse, she pretended not to. There was nothing she could do about it, anyway. A man could divorce his wife for infidelity, but not vice versa, unless accompanied by much blacker offences, none of which his esteemed father would ever have indulged in. Charles Ashleigh had loved his daughter, but not incestuously; he had never been physically cruel to his wife; quite surely he had never been guilty of rape (probably because he had never discovered how enjoyable rape could be); and as for homosexual practices, in his creed they had been taboo, quite apart from holding no appeal because he had been as heterosexual as all Ashleigh men, including his son. And even in that respect, Justin was sure, his late father had indulged in no divergencies, however lusty he may have been.

So there had never been any possibility of divorce, even had the proud Elizabeth wanted one. Such was the accommodating law of the land, and Justin was confident it would never change. A man's rights had to be protected.

So why not invite Dulcima to Kingsmere? It would taunt his mother and needle Caroline, which would enhance the piquancy. He might even have his father's bedroom opened up and hope the paternal ghost hovered around when he made love to her in the vast bed in which he and Caroline had been conceived – after which, duty done, his mother had withdrawn to a room of her own and never again shared her husband's. Even as a boy Justin had guessed that his parents' marriage had merely been one of convenience, like his own eventually.

And if dear Mamma (spying from the dower house, as he knew full well she did) saw the notorious Dulcima arrive, the old lady would be unable to do a thing about it. His mother had no authority at Kingsmere now. Only he, the owner.

The childless owner.

Damn that insipid Norah for failing to give him an heir. What use had she been to him, except financially? He deserved every penny of her fortune for marrying her and for enduring her timidity in bed. He remembered with contempt the way in which she shrank from certain things he liked to do. If she had only been more co-operative, she need not have died at all, so it really was not *his* fault that she snuffed out so easily that night.

But Dulcima – now, there was a woman! Within a week or two of bedding her he was confident that eventually there need be no holds barred. She was highly sexed and enjoyed his lovemaking. She was also strong enough to endure his demands even when they exceeded her own. Only the self-protective instinct which warned him never to go too far with a woman until he had tested her well, thereby lulling her into the belief that he enjoyed nothing more than a hearty sexual appetite, had prevented him from giving full vent to his lusts, though surely by now she had begun to sense them. She was experienced enough to know that some men wanted more than ordinary, routine sex with a woman. Dulcima had had lovers aplenty, which convinced him that when the time came for him to throw off all restraint and resort to the varieties of violence he so enjoyed, she should not be taken by surprise.

The idea of using his father's bed for the purpose was titillating. Besides, it was sufficiently isolated from the rest of the house for no one to hear a sound – which was desirable, since he was already so well acquainted with Dulcima's ecstatic cries that he expected them to echo lustily when he finally released his pent-up desires. He was confident that she would be very different from Norah, who had frequently fainted before her screams had a chance to penetrate the thick walls of her room, which was lucky – particularly on the night she died. It had been easy to leave her there and return to his own room and sleep peacefully until morning, his senses fully satiated and his conscience untroubled, because he felt nothing but contempt for such a creature.

He had still been asleep when his wife's panic-stricken maid hammered on the communicating door next morning, crying that her mistress was unconscious and blue in the face. 'Convulsions, it looks like, sir! Leastways, I think so – her face all swollen and her tongue hanging out. And her eyes – oh, God, her eyes!' Fortunately the girl had been too terrified to touch her or to pull back the bedclothes, which Justin had carefully replaced right up to the chin, for even he had not found the marks of strangulation very pretty after the event.

Thank heaven, his mother had taken control of everything, even having the presence of mind to fetch that unreliable doctor from the other side of the village – whose fondness for the bottle rendered him not only inept but also responsive to bribe – instead of Sir Joseph Freeling, the eminent court physician whose country house was nearby and who was a personal friend of the Ashleighs. For one horrible moment Justin had feared Sir Joseph would be called, for he was in residence at the time, but of course dear Mamma had more sense than that. She departed alone in that unobtrusive dogcart she used about the estate, revealing no emotion at all. He alone had seen the horror in her eyes when she first looked down at Norah – a horror swiftly concealed because that sobbing maid was lingering in the doorway.

With equal self-control she had announced, 'The poor girl has choked on something – a fish bone, no doubt. I recall her coughing so violently during dinner last night that she had to leave the room . . . I really must have a word with Cook about her filleting — so careless of late.'

Good old Mater, she thought of everything, sending the shocked maid about other duties, then hastily dressing Norah's naked body in the gown she had worn at dinner the night before, though little could be done about that betraying face other than to release her hair and tumble it wildly, as if disarrayed when writhing on her bed, which was then put partially in order to indicate that she had collapsed on to the turned-back covers. And when good old Mater returned with that seedy doctor, the man's breath reeked of brandy despite the hour (another thoughtful touch, much admired by her son).

Further, she had insisted on paying the man highly for his services, though all he had done was hang on to the bedpost and nod agreement with her emphatically stated opinion that her daughter-in-law had choked violently on that wretched fish bone and died when gasping for breath. She even apologised for bringing the man so far and in such a state of fatigue, thereby planting in his mind the conviction that he was indeed swaying on his feet through tiredness — a useful recollection, which, if and when he sobered up, would dismiss any befuddled idea that he had somehow overlooked something. Then she played her master stroke, naming a sum which made the man's eyes widen and his mouth close forever, for after accepting such a figure, he would never dare to reveal why he had done so.

Nor had she stopped at that. Once the death certificate was signed (she steadied the doctor's hand as he wrote it), the quiet funeral had been expedited so speedily that by the time his father-in-law arrived from Marienbad, Norah lay in the family vault, and not even he would have asked for the coffin to be opened to let him take one last look at the daughter he had so successfully married off to a title —

particularly when her mother-in-law had telegraphed so promptly and considerately, allaying any possible doubt or suspicion.

Good old Mater indeed – though Justin had never been able to understand why she moved to the dower house immediately after the funeral, no longer unwilling to take up residence there, nor why she seemed to find the very sight of him painful, nor why she announced, before departing, 'I have arranged for you to have treatment again, Justin, and for a longer period this time. As always, I will put it around that you have embarked on one of your trips abroad.'

He had gone willingly enough. Why not? A grieving widower could be expected to seek forgetfulness in travel, and the sanatorium in Switzerland was a familiar and comfortable place. And good old Mater had merely intimated to them that he had had one of his breakdowns again, carefully concealing the final culmination of this one. He had a lot for which to thank his mother, but it never occurred to him to do so.

6

Justin was thwarted in his desire to entertain quickly and lavishly at Kingsmere. An unexpected postcard from Paris arrived the next day.

Bryant and I have escaped to enjoy ourselves here. His idea, bless him. He really is the darlingest man! I will get in touch on returning.

Caroline

So she had not even received his letter, nor would until she came back. It would lie there in Meredith's apartment; and Justin could not contact her in Paris, since she had omitted the address. He guessed, rightly, that she would not be so unwise as to stay at the Crillon, where the Ashleighs were well known, but would insist on some hotel where she would not be recognised. Damn the creature. He was faced with the choice of relying solely on Kingsmere's domestic staff and playing host alone, or controlling his impatience until his sister returned.

The first choice was not an impossible solution, but undesirable, since the housekeeper could not be expected to allocate guest rooms with the knowledge or discretion of his sister, always well-versed in current liaisons. Many a society house party had been ruined by certain guests being inconveniently accommodated. It was not unknown for some so thwarted to depart indignantly and reject any future invitations. Such a situation had never arisen at Kingsmere, and rather than risk such embarrassment, Justin preferred to await his sister's return.

Two months later, she did so, and then alone. One glance at her face told him the *affaire* was over, that it would be wise to ask no questions, and that in the circumstances she would be more than glad to fall in with his plans.

Dulcima was overjoyed by the invitation. She had hoped for it, prayed for it, but never dreamed that it would come so soon — perhaps when Ashleigh heard her news, of which she was now certain, but not until then. Yet here he was, inviting her as if it were the most natural thing in the world to open the doors of his illustrious home to her and to present her to his friends. In what capacity did not matter. She was proud to be his mistress, and he must be equally proud of her to say so matter-of-factly, 'You will come, of course.'

It was a command, not an invitation, which emphasised his proprietorship and raised her hopes that parenthood would make it permanent. But she wouldn't tell him about that yet, though she had rushed to meet him with the news on her lips. Now she halted. To announce it at Kingsmere would be the right setting and the right timing; meanwhile, she hugged her secret to herself, anticipating his delight.

His wife had failed him in this very important respect, poor thing. Dulcima pitied the dead Norah for that, but was elated because it was now her own destiny to give him an heir. Pray God for a son, since it meant so much to him, but if she failed the first time, she might succeed the second, or even the third. She was not afraid of childbirth, even though she was in her mid-thirties and many a physician nowadays anticipated difficulties for a woman having her first child at such an age.

What nonsense! She was strong and healthy, she had never been ill in her life; she would welcome a large family, revel in having children – and yes, she would persuade Justin to call his son after his father. Dear Charles, it would be a nice way in which to remember him. She now felt nothing but tenderness for that kindly man, his refusal to let her bear a child of Ashleigh blood both forgiven and forgotten now that she was succeeding in doing so. This time there would be no secret termination.

'Bring your loveliest clothes,' Justin was saying. 'You must be a credit to me at Kingsmere.'

Dulcima tilted her beautiful nose. 'All my clothes are lovely – you have said so often enough. And do you think I don't know what sort of a wardrobe to bring to a country house party?' Her voice was teasing, not resentful. She was too happy for that. 'And Deborah will do you credit, too.'

'Deborah? That young cousin of yours? What makes you think she is invited?'

'Oh, but surely . . . Darling, I can't leave her alone in this house, without a personal friend or acquaintance in London. She would be lonely.'

His reply was offhand. 'Your concern does you credit, but parading your poor relations doesn't enter into my scheme of things.'

She wanted to ask what did enter into his scheme of things – marriage? – but refrained. Instead, she pleaded with him not to be cruel, pointing out that he had met her cousin only once. 'I promise you she is not dowdy any longer, and meeting people will help to bring her out of her shell.' But Ashleigh only expressed doubt about having a sedate churchman's daughter at a sophisticated gathering.

'She is pretty, I grant you, and I will take your word that she is now better dressed, but transforming someone's appearance does not transform either her or her background.'

'It helps. And I should have thought you would be pleased to have evidence of my good connections.'

He smiled indulgently. If she wanted to pretend, why not? There wasn't the faintest possibility of any guest at Kingsmere believing a word of it. Everyone knew that Dulcima Howard was not only an ex-Gaiety Girl, but the Madame of an expensive card salon which, until recently, had exploited a delectable sideline in entertainment in a well-concealed rear parlour. No whitewashing was ever going to cover that up.

'Very well,' Ashleigh said with a shrug, 'bring your dull little cousin if you wish.'

Dulcima was as pleased by his indifference as by his consent, for it finally allayed the secret concern which had lingered with her ever since that memorable night when his thoughts had been temporarily absorbed with 'that girl upstairs'. He had never explained why, and he had never referred to Deborah again, but Dulcima had not forgotten.

Now she could, and did, for his attitude confirmed that his interest had been no more than passing curiosity, no doubt due to surprise on discovering that she had such highly respectable connections. It would be good to arrive at Kingsmere accompanied by her 'cousin', thereby not only establishing the fact that Dulcima Howard was no solitary adventuress, bereft of background or family, but had relatives of good manners and refinement. Deborah, bless her, possessed both, and with her at her side Dulcima knew she would be able to hold up her head amongst the best of them, no longer pretending to be on an equal footing with so-called society, but actually feeling it. And when Justin married her, as he surely would since he was free to do so and, on his own admission, was desirous of an heir, life would be wonderful both for herself and for dear Sarah's girl. They would have reached the top.

Dulcima's excitement at the prospect of the weekend house party was not shared by pessimistic Garfield, who had accompanied her mistress to such affairs before, usually in homes less grand than the famous Ashleigh country seat, but humiliating for all that. As personal maid to the least socially important guest, she ranked equally low in the servants' hall, where distinctions were as marked as abovestairs, and respect delegated accordingly. It made no difference that Dulcima Howard was invariably the most beautiful of all the women guests, for everyone knew she was totally unconnected and invited only because she enlivened any party. But belowstairs her maid would receive no deference at all, and at Kingsmere it would be even worse because the staff there, Garfield had heard, was enormous.

And so it proved to be. The line of carriages waiting at the local railway station, each with driver and footman, bore testimony to the importance of the stately home which owned them; broughams, landaus, victorias, flies, growlers, and finally wagonettes for the retinue of visiting servants – for every woman had brought her personal maid and every man his valet. There was also a fleet of waggons for the mountains of luggage without which no self-respecting guests would travel even for a weekend. Winnie Garfield eyed the individual piles of trunks, hat-boxes, boot and shoe boxes, vanity cases, gun cases, carpetbags, and innumerable valises, noting with satisfaction that her mistress's array rivalled the best of them, and confident that her wardrobe was unlikely to be eclipsed.

She would be proud of Miss Howard this weekend, and that would make up for the indignity of being the least important member of the visiting staff. From Friday to Monday she would bask in the reflected glory of Dulcima Howard's beauty and not conceal her disdain for those who were plainer and less elegant. 'Your mistress may possess a title,' she would say to any snooty lady's maid who dared patronise her, 'but you must have to work endless hours to make her even presentable . . .'

As the cavalcade pulled out of the station courtyard for the four-mile journey to Kingsmere, Garfield saw Deborah Yorke seated beside her beloved mistress and grudgingly admitted that the girl did them credit, though she had not yet learned to hide her wonder over every new sight and experience, betrayed now as she surveyed the long line of carriages bearing the Ashleigh insignia on the doors. She was Alice in Wonderland, except in looks. The travelling costume she wore had been made by Dulcima's own tailor, who was second to none and charged accordingly, and the small sable toque tilted over one eye was excep-tionally becoming. She was almost, but not quite, as noticeable as her famous cousin, and it did Garfield's heart good to see the indignant glances of others as his lordship's personal carriage, prominent because it headed the queue and bore his crest more opulently, carried the pair away ahead of everyone. The triumph was all Dulcima's, but it was Garfield who preened. What a stupendous start to the weekend, and how every other visiting maid must be envying her! *That* was one in the eye for them to begin with.

Kingsmere's head groom supervised the allocation of carriages under the authority of his lordship's man of affairs, who bore a list of guests in order of priority. Consequently, this singling out of Dulcima Howard enraged everyone, particularly the old Duchess of Dorking, who, by rank, was entitled to precedence. Her grace's maid had automatically stepped forward to make sure that the footman tucked the carriage rug well over her mistress's rheumatic old knees, and at the maid's outraged gasp, Garfield turned a proud and disdainful glance upon her, eyebrows raised, mouth curling contemptuously as she murmured, 'Beauty before age . . .'

She would have liked to make it even more pointed by saying, 'His lordship's mistress first, and rightly,' but discretion checked her; apprehension, also, because Ashleigh's marked preference had already created animosity towards Dulcima Howard, particularly from the women guests, who, though later they might flatter and fawn upon her because she was their host's current favourite, would nevertheless hate her for it. Bar the old duchess, who was past it, there wasn't a woman amongst this distinguished group, married or single, who would not leap at the chance to step into Dulcima Howard's shoes, and Garfield suspected that Ashleigh was fickle enough to give any one of them such a chance at the prompting of a whim.

The thought deepened her apprehension, which had

been growing of late, along with disturbing premonitions. Just how long would the relationship last when Ashleigh learned of Dulcima's recent bouts of morning sickness? Garfield knew well enough that for the last month or more this early indisposition had increased daily, and how her mistress had managed to hide it from Ashleigh when he spent a whole night with her, the woman did not know. Possibly the fact that he was a heavy sleeper, never waking before ten, had helped. By that time the worst was usually over, and he was too selfish a man to notice when his mistress left her breakfast untouched, and because it was a fad of hers never to completely face the light of day for an hour or two after rising, the pallor of her face passed unnoticed. When Ashleigh stayed until morning, breakfast for two would be served in Dulcima's boudoir, where the windows were clouded with ruched chiffon blinds through which light filtered only gently. In any case, Ashleigh was never interested in anything but food at that hour, and, once breakfasted, would drop a light kiss on Dulcima's brow, murmur something about seeing her soon, and be off.

Garfield hated him. Apart from mistrusting him, she didn't like his eyes, and now acknowledged that she could never condone his stepping into his father's shoes. Dulcima she forgave, convinced that her treasure had accepted Justin Ashleigh as a substitute for his father because she had loved Charles Ashleigh, and, since his death, finding no one to completely replace him, sought in the son a replica of the father. Garfield only hoped the son did not resemble the father in one way at least. She could not bear the thought of a repetition of former events, with Dulcima suffering through being denied her child.

Tweeds for morning wear, unless one were taking an early-morning ride, after which one would be permitted to partake of an informal buffet breakfast clad in one's riding habit, provided the ground had not been too heavy, and to change into a morning gown after it, then a more elegant one for luncheon, an elaborate tea gown at four, followed by full regalia for evening, and never the same clothes worn twice – thus ruled social etiquette.

It was to be an endless parade of fashion and, inevitably, endless rivalry. There would be comparisons and criticism and covert inspection. The whole thing terrified Deborah, but she would be spared the early-morning canter, much as she envied those who could participate. Lack of prowess in the saddle did at least save the cost of a riding habit, for which she was thankful, since conscience weighed heavily over the enormous expense she was causing Dulcima. There was also a feeling of obligation, though her aunt considered she was under none at all.

'My dear, I delight in transforming you!' This was precisely what she had done during the past weeks, summoning dressmakers and corset makers and milliners and shoemakers and hairdressers and beauty specialists, though Deborah was too young to need the latter to the extent Dulcima did. Her aunt was accustomed to having her face creamed and massaged daily and then delicately made up. Now she vowed, 'My little Cinderella must become a princess,' not counting the cost and enjoying it as much as Deborah did, but without the guilt.

'I don't see how I can ever repay you, Dulcima.'

'You don't have to, my love. I only wish dear Sarah could see you now – *and* Holy Horace, though I can imagine his reaction on seeing his duckling turned into a swan!'

Was she really so transformed? In the Sheraton swing mirror on her dressing table at Kingsmere, Deborah studied her new coiffure, carefully unpinning the sable toque as she did so. She would never have dared to wear so sophisticated a hairstyle in Roedean, upswept at the back and piled into curls on top, on which the little fur master-piece perched precariously despite its anchorage of stiletto pins. And the sable cloak (lent by Dulcima on her insistence) slung over her immaculately tailored jacket, with very wide revers and only the slightest hint of leg-o'-mutton in the sleeves, was matched with a small sable muff.

She looked, Dulcima had said, as if she had stepped from the pages of America's leading fashion journal, *Harper's Bazaar,* and the reflection now looking back at her made Deborah think that perhaps her aunt was right. It was a wonderful feeling. And in the basket trunk, now being carried into her room by two hall boys, was a complete change of wardrobe for each day of the visit, a wild extravagance she would not believe was justified.

But Dulcima had indulged herself equally, deeming several new outfits as nothing less than essential. Despite Ashleigh's peremptory invitation, giving her less than a fortnight in which to prepare, dressmakers had been expected to complete all work in record time, and did so, stitching away from dawn to darkness, because such was their lot and they accepted it. Disraeli had been right when saying that England consisted of two nations, the rich one and the poor one, and just how rich the former was had been thrust upon Deborah as the weekend cavalcade drove down Kingsmere's endless drive and across acres of parkland before the ancient house came into sight.

House? Could such a place be classed merely as a house? It was a world within a world, one man's kingdom, and seeing Lord Ashleigh awaiting his guests at the head of an impressive flight of steps emphasised the fact. Deborah felt ill-at-ease with him, despite his welcoming smile, and even more ill-at-ease with the woman at his side – so thin she seemed almost brittle.

Ashleigh introduced her as his sister, Caroline, adding suavely, 'Caro, my dear, I don't think you have met

Dulcima Howard, thought I am sure you have heard of her . . .'

Brittle Caroline failed to conceal her surprise. It shot across her face in a spasm hastily controlled, to be replaced by an expression of apparent equanimity which did not deceive Deborah for an instant. She had seen her own mother conceal shock in such a way when the Reverend Horace had been in a threatening mood, clutching at a lifetime's training in self-control to conceal her fear of him. But Lord Ashleigh's sister was not concealing fear; she was concealing astonishment laced with disapproval, and the only possible reason was that she knew of Dulcima Howard's relationship with her brother. How could she fail to, since it was the talk of the town and beyond, with hints appearing in a press which was ever eager to link the scandalous Dulcima's name with yet another man, the more prominent the better?

In the weeks of Deborah's residence at 20 Hanover Square, she had accepted the liaison between Ashleigh and her aunt, never condemning her for it. Dulcima loved him, her code for living was her own, and such was her nature that she gave generously in emotion as in all things. There was no guile in her, and no ability to deceive. She welcomed the world and everyone in it, which was more than brittle Caroline was doing now.

Deborah's anger stirred. If this was the Caroline whose husband had called at Hanover Square demanding of Ashleigh the whereabouts of his sister, the Caroline who had been 'off on one of her jaunts again', she had no right to frown upon Dulcima Howard's relationship with her brother, or disapprove of her coming to Kingsmere.

Then Caroline smiled and politely held out her hand, and gone was the suggestion of shocked disapproval. Was I wrong? Deborah wondered. Had the woman merely been startled by Dulcima's loveliness, as so many were? Deborah had noticed quick glances when they boarded the train at Victoria, two first-class coaches being reserved exclusively for Ashleigh's guests. The instant Dulcima stepped aboard, those already in their seats stared through their compartment windows, some even craning their necks for a glimpse of her as she followed her maid along the corridor, with Deborah bringing up the rear.

In response to Dulcima's dignified inclination of the head, they had had no choice but to acknowledge her, though with scarcely perceptible nods. Rules of etiquette should not be broken with self-introduction. Such formalities would be effected in the proper way, at the right time and place, and by their host. Meanwhile, though all were bound for the same roof, they remained strangers by the dictates of convention.

Deborah had detected a tremor of amusement on Dulcima's lips, plus an imperceptible wink which said, *'Let's shock them, shall we?'* but the next moment her expression had become as composed and haughty as the other women's and, leaning serenely back in her corner, she made it plain that she had forgotten them. She had been quite undisturbed by their scrutiny, though it had disconcerted Deborah. Dulcima not only took it in her stride, but expected it.

She wore no dust coat this time, and Deborah, who was becoming familiar with her aunt's little vanities, guessed why. Her newly tailored travelling costume of grey *gros grain*, with revers of matching satin and pockets trimmed with the same material, was too handsome to be concealed on such an occasion as this, travelling with the *crème de la crème* of London's society and determined not to be outshone by them. Her careful choice of pale grey, to show critical fellow guests that she was aware of the niceties of behaviour although not bound by court mourning, looked anything but subdued on her. Against the silver gleam of *gros grain*, her flaming hair was dramatic and well set off by a cossack hat of silver fox and a long matching coat which she shed with superb negligence. Russian fashions and Russian furs were much favoured because Queen Alexandra's sister Dagmar was the czarina, but no one wore them so spectacularly as Dulcima.

Because Deborah had no maid of her own, a housemaid unpacked for her, and although she was the last guest to be attended to and was tempted to do the task while waiting, she refrained. She was determined not to commit any social solecism, and, unbeknown to her mistress, Garfield had discreetly proffered a little book on etiquette.

Discreetly? Well, let her imagine I took it to be, Deborah decided, well aware that Garfield's patronage was prompted by a jealousy which was to be pitied. So she had taken the little book with a smile and a word of thanks, in return for which the woman had darted a suspicious glance, as if guessing that Deborah had accepted it only because she had no desire to hurt her feelings.

Now, to Deborah's humiliation, the book appeared in the basket trunk, placed there without her knowledge. It was found by the maid, who put it on the dressing table, her expression so impassive that Deborah knew the girl grasped the implication — that here was a guest unaccustomed to visiting great houses and anxious not to put a foot wrong.

Hints on Etiquette and the Usages of Society — With a Glance At Bad Habits. The words leapt from the cover, and Deborah's sense of humour mercifully overcame her embarrassment. What if she were to carry this small volume around, ticking off the bad habits of others? Garfield would not expect that.

A tap on the door, and Dulcima entered.

'I came to see if you were comfortable . . .'

She broke off, recognising at once that Deborah had

been given the least important room for the least important guest. Her anger stirred, for she had been given the most sumptuous apartment, which, she knew instinctively, had been opened up especially for her, and the fact that it was situated far away in a private wing emphasised her distinction, setting her apart from others in isolated splendour as his lordship's favourite.

Now her gratification changed. She had had to walk through endless corridors to find Deborah's room, and the contrast with her own was marked. The best suite at Kingsmere for its master's mistress, the poorest for her relative. Dulcima would not allow Deborah and, through her, dear Sarah, to be slighted, and decided imperiously that as a mark of her anger she would demand to be moved from her own sumptuous apartment. Either that or a better room for her cousin.

Then Dulcima saw the book and exclaimed, 'My dear, *you* need no lessons on how to conduct yourself!' She picked up the volume, scanned it, and burst out laughing. Then she read aloud:

> 'Etiquette is the barrier which society draws around itself as a shield against the intrusion of the impertinent, the improper, and the vulgar . . . a guard against those obtuse persons who, having neither talent nor delicacy, would be continually thrusting themselves into the society of those to whom their presence might be offensive, and even insupportable.

My dear cousin, *you* could never be impertinent, improper, or vulgar! Where *did* you get hold of this?'

Deborah said vaguely that she had picked it up somewhere. Why give poor Garfield away? Life had not poured into her lap the unexpected good fortune which had come into her own on the day her aunt had taken charge of it.

' "Never use your knife to convey food to your

mouth . . . it is unnecessary, and glaringly vulgar . . . Ladies should never dine with their gloves on, unless their hands are not fit to be seen." And oh, do listen to this! "Do not pick your teeth *much* at table, as, however satisfactory a practice to yourself, to witness it is not a pleasant thing." And *this*! "Finger glasses, filled with warm water, come with the dessert. Wet a corner of your napkin and wipe your mouth, then rinse your fingers, but do not practise the filthy custom of gargling at table – because it is a foreign habit, it can only be disgusting." Oh, Deborah, how I would love to shock everyone by doing that! *And* there is more. "You cannot use your knife, or fork, or *teeth* too quietly." I am quite sure the old Duchess of Dorking's dentures clatter like castanets!'

They were sitting on the bedside, laughing, when Garfield entered without so much as a tap on the door. At the sight of her mistress with the book in her hands, she halted abruptly, then said in some embarrassment, 'I was looking for you, ma'am. It is time to change for luncheon,' but her discomfort was plain, and Dulcima's brow met in a puzzled frown.

'What is wrong, Garfield? If we failed to hear your knock, it was because my cousin and I were having such fun with this ridiculous book.' Dulcima turned the flyleaf. 'Published in 1834 – no wonder it is so droll!'

'That's as may be, but it is still used in the best circles.' Garfield's tone was defensive.

'How do you know? Have you seen it before?'

'I have indeed, ma'am. Many a leading lady I dressed at the Gaiety had cause to be grateful for that book.'

'So you thought my cousin . . .!'

'I . . . I wanted to help Miss Yorke, to put her at ease in unfamiliar society.'

'You wanted nothing of the kind!' When Dulcima became angry, a quiet note crept into her voice and a sharp light into her eye; both were there now, and Garfield retreated before them. But there was no escaping the lash of Dulcima's tongue. 'How dare you insult my cousin! Dear heaven, Garfield, I never knew you had such a cruel streak. And how did you make sure she brought it with her? No, Deborah, don't try to protect her by saying you brought it yourself, because I won't believe you. It was put into your baggage so a maid would unpack it and you would be humiliated. *Wasn't it, Garfield?'*

The woman winced, but her mouth set stubbornly. 'I put it in her trunk, yes, but only because I thought Miss Yorke would need it, not being accustomed to moving in the best circles.'

Dulcima stormed out of the room and back on the long trek to her own quarters, her maid panting anxiously at her heels.

'Please, oh, please, ma'am!'

'Be quiet, or you will goad me into saying things I may regret. Help me to change, and then go straight back to my cousin and apologise. Meanwhile, you can apologise to me. You seem to forget that Miss Yorke and I are related, and any aspersion on her background is an aspersion on mine.'

'Oh, no, ma'am – dear Miss Dulcima, I do apologise, truly I do. Forgive me! You are the last person I wish to hurt.'

'My cousin being your main target? Don't imagine I haven't noticed your attitude towards her ever since she came to live with me. Anyone would think you were jealous.'

'Well, ma'am, I don't deny that, and with good reason. Until she came, you had time to spare for your devoted Winnie, but not any more. Oh, no, it's Miss Yorke who is taken into your confidence now, not your poor old maid who's served you loyally all these years. I daresay *she* knows your news already.'

Dulcima stopped dead. 'What news?'

'About the baby, of course. You've all the signs.'

'Rubbish. No one could possibly tell yet.'

'Not by your size, they couldn't. It's too early for that. But you can't hide anything from me. I know you've been having morning sickness for several weeks now.'

'Gracious heaven, you don't miss a thing!' Dulcima walked on, head lifting with pride. 'Well, I am not denying it, but keep your mouth shut until I say you can open it. And it so happens I have *not* confided in my cousin or anyone. Lord Ashleigh must be the first to hear, so don't you dare gossip in the servants' hall.'

'Talk to that lot! *Me?* I wouldn't stoop so low, ma'am.' Garfield was appeased. To be the first to share her mistress's secret reinstated her at once. But as for eating humble pie to Miss Yorke . . .

'Good,' said Dulcima, swinging ahead with her graceful stride. 'But don't forget to apologise to my cousin as soon as you have finished dressing me. No apology, no job. Understand?'

Garfield understood only too well, for when her mistress spoke her mind, she meant every word. It would be galling to sink one's pride before that interloper, but better than banishment from the person she loved most in the world. She resolved to humble herself as briefly and curtly as possible and avoid the young woman at all costs thereafter.

Deborah emerged from her room as Garfield approached, and it irked the maid to see that her appearance could not be faulted, despite lack of assistance from someone so skilled as herself. Even more irksome was her smile, which implied that she had forgotten the incident of the book. So why bother to apologise? It would be the easiest thing in the world to walk on – except for the fact that Miss Yorke's room terminated the corridor and could therefore be her only destination.

'You were looking for me? My cousin wants me?'

'Miss Dulcima needs no one but me, ever.'

'Then why were you coming to my room? Obviously you could be bound for nowhere else.'

Garfield took a deep breath. 'I came at her insistence, not of my own free will. I am afraid she misunderstood my reason for trying to help you.'

'You mean she sent you to apologise.' Deborah's smile was compassionate, which didn't please Winnie Garfield, because it made her feel even more in the wrong. 'Don't fret,' Deborah continued. 'If questioned, you can say the matter is settled. Will that make you happy?'

And now I suppose I ought to thank her, Garfield fumed inwardly, but I won't.

She inclined her head stiffly and murmured, 'Very well, miss. I have nothing to apologise for, but so long as it makes my mistress happy —'

'— that is all that matters,' Deborah finished, and walked on, leaving the maid in a confusion of gratitude and humiliation, and it didn't help in the least to realise that it was entirely her own fault.

The rustle of Deborah's shot silk gave her a feeling of confidence. It was altogether different from the brown merino which had been her Sunday best for more years than she could remember. To have morning gowns, afternoon gowns, tea gowns, and dinner gowns was an overwhelming experience, but the addition of an elaborate evening gown seemed a wild and unnecessary extravagance. But Dulcima insisted upon it, just in case dear Justin planned something on the grand scale, something worthy of a setting like Kingsmere.

'It is just the sort of thing he would do, to surprise everyone. These past weeks have been atrociously boring for him, and the dear man cannot tolerate boredom. Nor can I. Even attendances at the card salon have declined, but only temporarily. Social life in London will be stirring again – which means you must learn to play baccarat, Cousin. You cannot remain an onlooker for much longer.'

'But I have never played cards in my life!'

'Then it is high time you did, especially since I will have to rely on you when I am unable to run things. Don't worry – it will be only for a short spell.'

Dulcima did not indicate why, and Deborah refused to think about such a daunting prospect, however brief. To act as hostess to Dulcima's gambling clientele would be beyond her powers. They were skilful, experienced, adroit, but the most terrifying thing about them was the way in which their amiable faces sharpened into alien masks once the six new decks of cards and the strange box called the shoe were produced. Then they reminded her of wolves holding down their hunger, eyes aglitter, expressions avid, glances riddled with suspicion so that they seemed to become enemies rather than friends, and when the night's play was over, they departed either smiling or scowling, according to whether they had won or lost.

Throughout it all, Dulcima would sit there, never losing her good humour, however her fortunes went – perhaps because, for the most part, they went very well indeed.

'I will say this for old Charles, he taught you well,' someone once growled when fortune had gone continuously in the bank's favour, at which Dulcima smiled and patted the man's hand consolingly, then tactfully auctioned the bank and lost six consecutive games.

'You see, dear Hardcastle, a run doesn't always continue,' she had pointed out, at which the man laughed and regarded her affectionately as he drawled, 'So it seems – I wonder why.'

'Chance, my friend. What else?' Her eyes, widening in naive question, had made the man smile even more.

'You're a witch, Dulcima. A damned clever witch. I'd give a lot to know how you manipulate the cards.'

'Nonsense, my dear man. Games of luck cannot be manipulated.'

After which Dulcima continued to lose for the rest of the evening, not a whit distressed. 'What did I tell you, Hardcastle? Fortune is fickle. When she is on my side again, I shall win it all back.'

And so she did, and more besides, but not until the man had had a good run for his money for the rest of the week and all his doubts were laid.

The prospect of stepping into Dulcima's shoes for even a brief spell was therefore doubly alarming to Deborah, since she lacked not only her aunt's experience but also her confidence.

'Don't worry, my love. We have a few months in which to train you and I guarantee that at the end of the time I will have passed all my skill on to you. You are intelligent – and I am a good teacher.'

A few months seemed little enough, but why should they be necessary? Did it mean that Dulcima intended to take a holiday, perhaps with Ashleigh who, Deborah had now learned, was a frequent traveller abroad? In her aunt's unconventional world such jauntings were not unheard of and history was full of immoral liaisons, from George Sand and Chopin to Lady Caroline Lamb and Lord Byron, not to mention the woman who wrote novels as George Eliot and lived unashamedly with a man who was not her husband. Deborah was forced to accept things which, back home at the vicarage, would have shocked her as deeply as they would have shocked her mother and which would certainly have been loudly condemned by her father.

In her room at 20 Hanover Square she was well aware when Ashleigh shared her aunt's bed in the one below, and though at first she had covered her ears with the bedclothes, she now willed herself to ignore the murmurs and impassioned voices culminating in ecstatic cries which not only disturbed her but made her feel shut out from an unknown, exciting, and strangely desirable world.

But still she doubted her ability to adapt fully to this new way of life, with its different moral values, and she doubted it now as she walked along the corridors at Kingsmere, searching for the way down to the banqueting hall where, Justin had told her, luncheon was traditionally served at individually grouped tables. 'An informality we enjoy at Kingsmere when we have company, in contrast with dinner in the long dining room at night. It helps to break the ice and gives my guests a chance to mingle. You will feel at home, I promise you, Miss Yorke.'

He had seemed anxious to put her at ease, perhaps afraid that in this vast and impressive place she would not relax as she had on that memorable day, watching the state procession go by – a man and a woman amongst the great mass of the British public. Nothing was such a social leveller as spectators amongst other spectators, especially on the pavements of London. But Kingsmere was different. Kingsmere was vast, exclusive, and intimidating, and her footsteps echoing along these endless corridors were those of a stranger in an alien world ruled over by a man who, against his own background, seemed equally alien.

She longed to return to 20 Hanover Square, where the only visitors were rich gamesters who never stood on formality for long, but this group of weekend guests who had journeyed from London, ignoring those whom they did not know, even though bound for the same destination, had struck a chill into her, and the effusive way in which those who were already acquainted greeted each other when meeting at the country railway station on arrival jarred even more.

'Leonora, darling, how too, too *deevy* to see you! And beautiful as ever! Tell me, is that handsome masseur still visiting you when Peregrine is absent at his bank in Cheapside? Surely so, for you have lost at least two inches round the middle – or is that due to the new wasp waist invented by that clever *couturière* in Brook Street? If so, I hope you don't find it *too* agonising to wear . . .'

Poison in a perfume could not have been more subtly administered than the false honey of those words – and others.

'George, dear! And how is that charming wife of yours? Not with you? But why not? I trust she is not unwell? Never mind, I am sure dear Lady Moira will console you, as always.'

In the milling crowd waiting for the allocation of carriages, Dulcima had been totally ignored, though feminine glances of hostility and envy had been impossible to conceal, made worse when Lord Ashleigh's personal landau had given her priority over all. The recollection of that moment sharpened in Deborah's mind as she struggled to find her way down to the banqueting hall. The whole weekend was going to be one continuous embarrassment – or would be, if one were foolish enough to let it.

At last she found a main corridor, thickly carpeted and lined with portraits, and ahead opened a vast stairwell, with gilded banisters curving from a broad landing. Here were more portraits, better lit, and she glanced up at them as she passed, recognising the unmistakable Ashleigh features, which seemed to go back for generations, judging by the varying centuries of dress. The portraits continued from the corridor to the landing and down each side of the sweeping stairs to the banqueting hall below, from where she could already hear the hum of voices.

From the sound of things, most of the guests were already assembled, for which she was thankful, because her own arrival would therefore pass unnoticed, but even so, her steps slowed as confidence wavered yet again.

In a desperate attempt at nonchalance, she studied the portraits more intently, and was struck by the fact that one particular feature in this family recurred again and again. The eyes. Pale amber eyes, reminding her once more of a tiger's, but now she observed that they appeared only occasionally and only in the men of the family, sometimes skipping a generation or two, sometimes not.

'Dull, aren't they? I think they are dull because they're not smiling. Perhaps they hadn't any teeth.'

Deborah spun around. A small girl was standing beside the gilt banisters at the point where they curved down the stairs. She had dark hair and alert eyes and a thin little body, and there was liveliness in her movements as she danced across to Deborah; also intelligence in the pointed little face.

'Smiles showing bare gums would be horrid, wouldn't they?' She appraised Deborah frankly. 'You look nicer than the people down there.' She jerked her head backward towards the stairs. 'I've been watching them. Don't they make a din? Everyone talking at once, and not listening to a word anyone else says. I'm going to hate it, but Mamma says I must go down with her. She wants to show me off – that's why I'm all dressed up. She is being motherly just now because she has been away and feels guilty – not about going away, but because she feels people will say she has neglected me, so she wants to prove them wrong. She doesn't admit that, of course, but I can feel it. In a day or two she will be irritable again and I'll be left alone and I'll be glad.'

Startled not only by the child but also by these confidences, Deborah asked, 'And what do you do when you are left alone?'

'Oh, the usual lessons with Pymmy.'

'Pymmy?'

'Miss Pymm. Governess. She's nice really and tries to make lessons interesting, but she won't let me read what I want to read, so that's what I do when I am really alone. There's a big library here, and I read whatever I want to. And my father sends me books – lovely stories about Arabian nights and classic fairy tales, and now Greek myths, because one day he is going to show me Greece and all its ancient places, like Knossos and Lindos and Delos and lots more, though Mamma says they are nothing but ruins and very boring. My father doesn't come to Kingsmere often. Of course, he couldn't anyway for a long time because he was in the hospital, but even when he was better, he didn't want to come to live here. I heard him tell Mamma so, and I listened. They don't like each other very much, I can tell.'

So this was Delia, the child Simon Davidson planned to remove from Kingsmere, and very pathetic she seemed to Deborah, who had never met a solitary and precocious child before. Roedean village had been full of children of large families; this was her first encounter with a child who knew no family life. And the detached way in which she announced her parents' dislike of each other, without pathos or any idea that it was to be regretted, struck Deborah as even more pitiable. However, unquenchable Delia chattered on, unaware that for a child of . . . how old – eight, nine? – her conversation was unchildlike.

'Do you like books, ma'am? If you do, you'll find all sorts of strange ones in the library, all belonging to Uncle Justin. I remember Aunt Norah saying they should be burned. I was listening again, it's the best way to find things out, but he only laughed and said it was his library now and so he could add to it as *he* wished, and it would do her good to read more of them. He had given her one, I think, and she refused to read any further. She said, "I won't! I won't! Why do you want me to read things like this?" That's how I guessed he had given it to her. And do you know what he said? "Because it will do you good and make you less damned squeamish." And she flung out of the room and came racing by me, not even seeing me, and she was crying. She used to cry an awful lot, and that made me sad, because I liked her.'

Deborah wanted to stop this flow, but how did one dam the outpourings of a neglected child who eavesdropped because she lacked company and dipped into goodness only knew what kind of books, without anyone's knowledge? Even if she understood little of them, impressions could be left and questions aroused in a young and enquiring mind.

Mistrust of Justin Ashleigh started to stir in Deborah. 'You know, Delia, *I* think you should stick to the books your father sends.'

'How do you know my name?'

'I guessed it.'

'Then what's yours?'

'Deborah Yorke.'

'I suppose I will have to call you Miss Yorke. Well, it's better than "ma'am", though I can't see why children can't call grown-ups by their first names. Grown-ups call children by theirs. But it "isn't done", says Pymmy. To her, things are either "done" or "not done", though she can never explain why.'

Deborah laughed. 'Nor can a great many people. It is simply custom, I suppose. When you come to think of it, manners have largely grown out of custom and fashion, though they should also be out of consideration of others.'

The little girl looked at her admiringly. 'That sounds sensible, Miss Yorke. Thank you for explaining. Things should always be explained, that's what *I* say. Pymmy says I shock her sometimes, like when I asked why weekend guests are paired off the way they are. Mamma spends *ages* doing the room list, and it's funny the way she doesn't always put husbands and wives together, or even next to each other. Did you notice the names on the doors as you came along? I've been watching you, wondering who you were and why you seemed so lost, and if you were really interested in these stuffy portraits or only pretending to be because you wanted to do something instead of going downstairs. I thought that if you were looking hard at everything around you, you must either be nervous or curious, so before you reached the portraits you probably concentrated on the bedroom doors and saw the little cards in slots. That's a new word I've just collected – con-cen-tra-ted. It means to think hard. You can use it to look hard, too. But I don't have to look at the labels to know whose rooms will be next door to each other's. Lady Moira Balcombe is sure to be next to George McWhirter – Sir George, I have to call him, Mamma says. And that horrible woman Sybil Clarke, who kisses me sloppily just to pretend she's fond of children, will be across the corridor from that fat stockbroker man called Bentley, who is only invited because he gives good tips to Uncle Justin. I don't mean tips like Pymmy gives to railway porters when she takes me to London to visit my father – those are the really wonderful times, the times I look forward to most – but tips about shares to buy at a place called the Stock Exchange.'

'Do you visit your father often?'

'Not as often as I would like, or as he would, either, but he only has a small furnished flat in Kensington. He sleeps on a couch in the sitting room and gives me the bedroom when I stay. He takes me to the museum he runs and shows me all sorts of things – ancient things people have dug up all over the place – and the way he talks about them makes it all fascinating. And he takes me for walks about London because he says that's the best way to get to know it, and London is full of places I ought to see because they are historical. But then Pymmy comes to bring me back home. There's certainly more room to move about here than in my father's tiny flat, but all the same . . .'

The hum of voices was louder. More people had been

descending the stairs as Deborah and the child talked.

'Perhaps I should go down now –' Deborah began.

'Not yet! Please don't go down yet. I have to wait for Mamma, and she always takes ages, and luncheon can't start until she is there, because she is hostess.'

In which case, thought Deborah, she should be down there now, mingling with her guests. She glanced over the banisters and saw Justin Ashleigh moving amongst them, one hand beneath Dulcima's elbow, propelling her with an air of proprietorship which also struck Deborah as being tinged with determination, as if forcing visitors to acknowledge her. Deborah didn't like that, but Dulcima, characteristically, seemed amused. She was enjoying herself, just as she had enjoyed herself in the parlour back at the vicarage when an unwilling matron had been forced to receive her. How long ago that seemed . . . a whole lifetime ago, in another world.

Delia peered over the banisters too. 'You see, Miss Yorke? No one will miss you if you don't go down yet. I shouldn't think anyone is even missing Mamma. All they are interested in is talking and drinking champagne before luncheon. Did you ever hear such a din? Grandmamma won't come near these weekend house parties.'

'Why not?'

The child shrugged. 'I don't know. Perhaps she doesn't like them, or else she isn't invited. I did once hear her tell Uncle Justin that she didn't care for his friends, but I don't think she cares for anyone very much, except Uncle Justin himself, and that's funny, because he often upsets her, though somehow I know she loves him better than she loves Mamma. *They* don't get on together at all. "You should have married someone in your own class," Grandmamma once said to her, and I didn't have to listen outside the door then, because she said it in front of me. Mamma said, "Intellectually, he *is* in my class," and Grandmamma laughed, and that made Mamma lose her temper. Me too, because I knew they were talking about my father, though somehow I felt Mamma was angry for a different reason. Sort of . . . well, as if she felt Grand-mamma was laughing at the idea of her even trying to be intellectual. That means "clever", doesn't it, Miss Yorke?'

Delia was pleased because she had mastered the word and could now add it to her collection. Her father had given her a notebook during one visit and encouraged her to write new words in it, even if she didn't know how to spell them. 'I can go through it with you next time we are together,' he had said. 'That way you will compile your own dictionary.'

' "Compile"? What does that mean?'

'Well . . . "collect". That's the simplest way of putting it. You can collect words this way and call it Delia Davidson's Dictionary.'

The idea had delighted her, and she had stuck to it ever since. Why couldn't Pymmy think of a clever thing like that, learning the meanings of words you took a fancy to instead of reading parrot fashion from some dreary text-book which didn't make it interesting at all? She repeated now, ' "Intellectual" does mean "clever", doesn't it, Miss Yorke?'

Deborah smiled and nodded, wishing Delia's mother would come along and stop this spate of chatter, which in many ways was too revealing. Yet she was enjoying the child's company. She liked the little girl. She liked her honest eyes, her open manner, her endearing face, her alert mind. All that mind needed was guiding in the right direction, and this, at least, her father seemed to be trying to do when he had the opportunity.

'I must say I'm beginning to wish Mamma *would* hurry – I'm getting hungry. But I think she's sulking a bit. I heard her telling Uncle Justin that someone called Bryant couldn't come because he suddenly had rehearsals, and somehow I think that's the reason for her sulking, because she added that she didn't believe him and she had actually had to write to ask him and he'd replied very curtly, so my uncle told her to cheer up and forget the man. "Find someone else," he said, "if you have to, though you'd be wise not to for the time being." I don't know what he meant by that, unless finding someone else meant finding someone to pair off with like everybody else does. It seems to me that grown-ups always need to be paired off. Who have you got, Miss Yorke?'

'No one,' Deborah admitted, helpless before this child.

'I expect Uncle Justin will find someone for you. Why don't you ask him? *He* has someone, I know. He always has, and it is always someone different. It was just the same when Aunt Norah was alive, but she pretended not to know. I could tell. So why Mamma should be angry with him for inviting someone for himself this week-end, I just don't know, but she says the woman is bad all through —'

'*Delia!* You talk too much.'

The voice was sharp, and it belonged to Caroline Davidson. Her footfall was soundless on the thick carpet, and she continued to talk as she approached.

'I apologise for my daughter, Miss Yorke. She is an incurable chatterbox.'

'You have no need to apologise on her behalf, Mrs Davidson, only on your own, for saying unkind things about my cousin Dulcima.'

'And what makes you think Delia was referring to her? Since she didn't mention her name, you must recognise the description, which means it must be a true one. Come, child, we must go down.'

If that is a sample of high-society manners, thought Deborah angrily, the sooner Simon Davidson removes his child from this place, the better. She turned to the stairs as Caroline Davidson held out a long thin hand to her daughter, who took it reluctantly.

'If my father were here,' the child piped, 'you would have a man to go down with you, Mamma, then you wouldn't need me, but I don't suppose he is likely to come this weekend. I know Father doesn't like house parties.'

' "Papa",' Caroline corrected automatically.

'He likes me to call him Father. He says Papa is a Victorian affectation and I must say it sounds silly to me too. *Ha-Ha, Pa-Pa!*' she mimicked comically. 'See how stupid it sounds? "Father" is much better. It sounds kind of stronger. Don't you think so, Miss Yorke, and is it really your cousin who is bad?'

'Be quiet, Delia,' said Caroline's voice, descending the stairs behind Deborah. 'And remember your manners when you meet people, *and* during luncheon.'

Delia grimaced, then fixed an angelic smile on her face as they reached the banqueting hall. It had the effect she expected. Gushing Sybil Clarke swooped upon her and bestowed the usual wet kiss, and Lady Moira cooed, 'The *dear* child — she grows more like you every day, Caro!' and that sharp-faced Leonora Crossley tugged her hair affectionately, but only succeeded in hurting her, and the old Duchess of Dorking's moustache pricked her mouth most horribly. Heavy male hands patted her head, and she knew quite well that everyone was competing with everyone else to display their fondness for children. Then they promptly forgot all about her, for which she was thankful.

Nearby, a man's voice boomed, 'Such a pity you haven't a family, Justin old chap. You really must marry again and produce one, if only for the sake of Kingsmere.'

Delia couldn't see the speaker, concealed by a little knot of people, but she did see her uncle's reaction, because he was in her line of vision. He smiled, but it was a smile of annoyance, as if he didn't like being told what he should or should not do.

'I am aware of my duties, thank you, Edgar. May I remind you that my dear wife has been dead a comparatively short time?'

Inexplicably, Delia wanted to cry. She often felt like this when someone mentioned Aunt Norah, though she herself could talk about her without tears. But that was different. That was what she secretly called 'unloading'; emptying her mind of troublesome or unhappy thoughts. Memories of Aunt Norah came under both categories – troublesome because she had heard one of the housemaids whispering to one of the footmen that everything seemed to have been done in a great hurry ('I mean, the funeral and everything, and bringing that drunken doctor all secret-like . . .'), and unhappy because she had been fond of her uncle's quiet little wife, who always had time to spare for her when others had not, and who seemed even to seek her company in preference to anyone else's. Delia missed her, and the thought that she would never see her again made her unutterably sad.

It had happened so suddenly, too. One day she was alive and the next she was not, which was very strange indeed, because on the day she was alive they had gone for a long walk together and picked wild flowers, which Norah had then helped Delia to press for her dried-flower collection. She had been smiling and happy during that walk, not ill at all, and not even tearful as she so often was – except when Uncle Justin was away. She always seemed to come alive then, to eat more and smile more, but when he came back, she would wilt and become a shadow about the place.

Delia turned round, searching for that nice Miss Yorke, but she was lost in the crush. Instead, the child found herself looking at the most dazzling woman she had ever seen, and the woman had a warm and genuine smile for her with no pretence about it. Oh, but I like *you*, thought Delia, and I can tell you like me. Immediately her spirits rose. There were two nice people here this weekend, so perhaps it wouldn't be so bad after all.

Then she saw her uncle's arm about the woman's waist, and disappointment touched her. This couldn't be the woman who her mother claimed was wicked! But from the way her uncle held her, Delia knew she could be no one else. To see a man's arm about a woman's waist was no new experience for the child; she had seen it in a fatherly manner, a bold manner, and what she called a belong-to-me manner, and this was wholly the last, even though it lay so lightly and loosely as he introduced the lady to everyone. And the way in which people met her was revealing. They gushed, they smiled, they flattered, but their eyes were cold. With the unerring instinct of childhood, Delia knew they were not only jealous, but felt the woman should not be here at all.

Her own response to the dazzling creature dimmed a little then, because perhaps they were right. Aunt Norah had been dead only a few months. Was this woman replacing her? Already? Delia's loyalty to the frail creature she had liked so much rebelled at the idea, though perhaps her uncle was more to blame than the woman was. Perhaps she didn't even know he had had a wife who had died so suddenly such a short time ago.

Delia had never cared much for her uncle, even though he indulged her. 'Let the child stay up late – why not?' 'Let her have a glass of wine – why not?' He seemed to enjoy countermanding orders her father had issued. 'How is he to know? He's not here. You are her mother, Caro. Exercise your authority, and to hell with your husband.' That always meant that Mamma promptly yielded, for not only was Uncle Justin head of the house, but everyone knew his will was the stronger.

'If only I had Justin's determination, I would get *my* way too,' Mamma frequently said, and though it seemed as if she did, judging by the way she came and went as she pleased and quarrelled with Grandmamma over it, it took a child's wisdom to know that it really wasn't the kind of 'way' she wanted – though precisely what her mother did want, only her mother knew.

Dulcima felt compelled to look back at the little girl. She rarely came into contact with children, but always responded to them when she did, and they to her. To see a child, to talk to a child, even to see one passing by, awakened in her the strongest maternal instincts. At such moments the whole of her adult life seemed to have been wasted.

So she looked back at Delia, hardly aware that Justin was introducing her to yet more guests, thereby compelling them to acknowledge her. Nor was she interested. She wanted to shake off his possessive arm for the time being and go over to the child, but even as she looked back, she saw the little girl pushing her way frantically through the crush, and above the noise her piping voice carried clearly.

'Father! Father, you've *come!*'

Through a gap Dulcima saw her leap into the arms of a man who looked singularly out-of-place in this house, but what surprised her more was Justin's muttered 'Damn . . . he *would* turn up! Thank heaven Bryant didn't come too . . .'

'Who is Bryant?' she asked, wondering why Justin should look so displeased at the sight of the child's father. 'And who is the little girl?'

'Caroline's daughter.'

The resemblance was there, in the dark eyes and the thin frame, which, with maturity, would no doubt be as tall and thin as her mother's, but the warmth Dulcima sensed in the child was lacking in Caroline, whose frigid reception had momentarily halted Dulcima in her tracks. There had been more than coldness in the woman's welcome, there had been hostility, but Dulcima had encountered that in women before and therefore tried to dismiss it as on a par with the rest, though she knew it was not. Caroline's animosity indicated a hatred so strong that it might have been there all her life, which was impossible, since she could never have heard of Dulcima Howard until her brother met her, except perhaps as a professional beauty. Hostility like Caroline's could not be justified because of a brother – only, perhaps, because of a father?

The thought was shaking. When dear Charles had become Dulcima's protector, his daughter had been fifteen – three years younger than herself – which meant that Caroline was twenty-two at her father's death. Between those ages a young woman could feel bitter towards a father's mistress, if she knew about her.

But Charles had been discretion itself. His family could not possibly have known. Justin would never have come near her, had it been so.

'And who is Bryant?' Dulcima repeated, turning back to Justin because she had lost sight of Delia and her father.

'Bryant Meredith, the actor — and Caroline's latest lover. Or was. I suspect the affair has gone adrift somehow, which is fortunate. Can you imagine what the situation would have been like had she persuaded him to come? Luckily, she failed. Rehearsals, he said, though she didn't believe him. My guess is that he has tired of her already, and I can't say I'm surprised. Too much of my sister would wear any man down. She's a restless, possessive creature, and she doesn't like any man to tire first.'

Justin dismissed Caroline. Let her sort out her own problems, he thought indifferently, though she never seemed to do it successfully. He had never been able to understand his sister. Only their father had come near to doing that, and Caroline had withdrawn from him when Justin learned of the relationship with Dulcima Howard and revealed all he knew.

He remembered that moment well, because he had chosen it carefully and with secret relish – at dinner one evening, when his mother was present. He had wanted to see dear Mamma's face, but he might have known it wouldn't move a muscle. Only Caroline's had cracked, crumpling up in horror and pain.

'I don't believe it! You are lying, *lying!*'

Their mother had rapped authoritatively, 'No hysteria, Caroline. One should never give way to hysteria. And, Justin, surely you are aware that a son never discusses such matters, any more than a wife does?'

'You . . .you mean . . .you *know?*' Caroline had gasped.

'Of course. I have known for years.'

'He has even set her up in Hanover Square. Number twenty,' Justin had added.

'Oh, God, no! Not Papa, of *all* people!'

Caroline's chair had fallen over with a crash as she fled from the table, and Mamma had looked on impassively as Barker stepped forward, picked it up, and replaced it. Later, Justin's mother had reprimanded him for being indiscreet in the presence of servants. That seemed to matter more to her than his father's association with an ex-Gaiety Girl. Was a scandal a scandal only if it became known? And did refusing to discuss it make it any less scandalous, like brushing dirt beneath a carpet and pretending it wasn't there? Damned funny, really – both his mother's attitude and his sister's reaction. He had enjoyed pointing out to his mother that she had been equally indiscreet in confessing that she knew of the affair, and had laughed when she claimed to have been goaded into it by his sister's hysteria. He was astute enough to guess that jealousy had played its part, for Caroline had always loved her father more than her mother, and well did the old girl know it. Toppling him from his throne had no doubt given her satisfaction.

*   *   *

'There is something I want to talk to you about,' Dulcima was saying, and he turned his attention back to her willingly enough.

She was looking very lovely, and, for that matter, so was that young cousin of hers, who still sparked his secret interest and was still mentally filed away as a possible interlude to be sampled later. He still wanted to see her hair tumbled over naked shoulders and breasts, but there was one possible snag – her virginity. She was almost sure to be a virgin, coming from a Church background, and that could be a bore. He liked a woman who knew what it was all about, one he could tumble into bed with and waste no time on preliminaries. God, what a time he had had with timid Norah! The marriage night had been disastrous, because she had not even known what to expect. Her mother had died years before, and that fool of a father considered it a husband's duty to introduce his bride to the facts of life.

Dulcima tugged at his sleeve. 'You haven't heard a word I've said.'

'Sorry, my love. What was it?'

'That I don't like Deborah being accommodated almost in the servants' wing.'

'Is she? I didn't know. I leave it to my sister to see to the rooms, so if you have any complaints, make them to her.'

'And did *she* decide to open up that grand apartment allocated to me? I can't imagine so, disliking me as she does, though I can't think why. If she has a lover herself and wanted to bring him here, she shouldn't disapprove of her brother's mistress. But she does. Oh, no, Justin, it was not *her* idea to put me in that beautiful suite well away from everyone.'

He gave a meaningful smile. 'You are too astute, sweetheart. All right, I admit it – I gave orders for those rooms to be allocated to you. Officially, that is, though of course for both of us.'

'Which she surely guessed, so why should she look so thunderstruck when you presented me?' Alarm flickered in Dulcima's mind as she added lightly, 'Unless, of course, she was expecting you to bring some other woman?'

'Now, whom else would I bring?' he answered indulgently, knowing this was the answer she wanted. 'You know you are the only woman in my life at present.'

She didn't like that 'at present', but dismissed it with equanimity, because when he heard her news, 'at present' would become 'forever'. Meanwhile, she refused to relinquish the subject of Deborah.

'Unless you make sure she is given better accommodation, I won't occupy that magnificent suite,' she said calmly.

'Is that a joke?'

'Indeed not. I dislike her being slighted.'

'She isn't *in* with the servants, I am sure.'

'No. Merely on the fringe.'

'Even guest rooms "on the fringe" are well furnished at Kingsmere,' he answered frigidly.

She had angered him. Quenching momentary apprehension, for Justin in a temper was something she never enjoyed, she gave him her most honeyed and coaxing smile, and it worked, as it always did. He melted.

'Very well, I'll have a word with Caroline and she can instruct the housekeeper. Now, are you content?'

She nodded, well pleased.

'And I promise you the most wonderful night in that beautiful room,' she murmured, but didn't add that it would be even more wonderful because of the news she would announce there. She had no intention of doing that until they were alone, because news so momentous should be announced in privacy, even perhaps in a moment of the greatest intimacy, though she doubted if she could wait that long. It would be hours yet before they would be in bed together, so she had to be content with anticipating the moment, and this added to her underlying feeling of triumph as she walked with him amongst his guests and acknowledged their greetings with a gracious inclination of her head and her most charming smile, knowing full well that the responses of the women were forced, but not those of the men. She saw open admiration and desire in male eyes, jealousy and resentment in the women's, but being accustomed to both, neither troubled her. The men hoped that what Ashleigh enjoyed now, they might be lucky enough to enjoy next, her reputation being what it was, and the women believed that when he tired of her she would never be received here again. 'So let us pretend goodwill towards her, for the time being . . .' She read their thoughts well.

Bitches. She dazzled them with her smile. Bitches, she thought yet again, and went on smiling. Bitches, all of you. But wait – just wait until I become Lady Ashleigh. I will see that none of you is ever invited to Kingsmere again.

She anticipated her moment of triumph with confidence.

7

Simon Davidson, his daughter's hand clinging to his, saw his wife moving sleekly amidst the crowd. Caroline's lissome figure had been one of the things which had first attracted him. She was like a reed. He had thought that if he spanned her waist with his hands she might snap, but when he eventually did so, she proved to be anything but brittle. Her body moved sinuously, smoothly, with a slow and fascinating grace, but sexually she had astonished him, for then she writhed with animal lust, impatiently, greedily. There seemed to be an insatiable hunger in her, which, for a long time, he could not analyse, but eventually he succeeded. It was a need to dominate, to conquer, linked in an alarming way with hatred. Hatred of men. Gradually he had sensed that the act of love was not an act of love to her at all. It was an act of revenge.

Inevitably their marriage foundered. He felt she had wanted to destroy it, just as, when she gave her body to him, her eagerness seemed to change to a destructive impulse. She made love savagely. Before marriage he had made love to other women who responded with animal passion, but never ferociously, with a desire to wound.

She was always penitent; often she would cry. Then he would comfort her and tell her to relax next time. His own instinct was to be tender with a woman: hers, inexplicably, was a desire to be hurt so she could hit back.

They had had no physical relationship with each other before marriage. He had recognised her as a young woman of conventional upbringing and respectability, and knew she would never consent to any anticipation of the wedding night. But she was impatient for the wedding, and determined upon it.

'You know I am not of your world,' he had pointed out. 'My people were what you would regard as lower-middle-class. Yours would never accept me.'

'They would have to. In any case, I wouldn't care if they didn't. You would be marrying me, not my family. And look who you are, all you have achieved! They should be proud to have you, as I am. I respect you for what you have accomplished. None of the men in my set do anything but idle their time away.'

'That's because they have too much money. Which

brings me to another thing – I have none.'

'I don't believe it. A man so successful can't possibly be poor.'

'Can't he, indeed! Success in my field doesn't bring wealth. An archaeologist who isn't rich enough to finance his own expeditions has to seek employment either with one who is or with some archaeological society or organisation who can sponsor him, as I was sponsored in Syria, in which event any financial rewards go to them, not to him, and the best finds go to museums. I work on a fee basis, which I find perfectly satisfactory for my tastes and my needs. The work itself interests me most, the satisfaction of carrying it out, the excitement of discovery – I ask no more.'

'That is truly noble,' Caroline had said reverently, and meant it. 'And it makes me even more proud of you. I shall go on being proud of you, darling.'

And so she did, until he ceased to attract public acclaim, but by that time they were married, despite parental opposition.

'Mamma is against it, as I knew she would be, but that doesn't worry me, Simon, because she has always been against me anyway, or at least indifferent. It is Justin she dotes on. Ever since he was a small boy he has been the apple of her eye, and has become increasingly so since his teens, though his behaviour is abominable. She defends him in all he does – like the time he seduced one of the servant girls and made her pregnant. It was whispered in the village that he had raped her, but I didn't believe it. Anyway, Mamma bought the girl off. Papa was upset, but Mamma only said that Justin was at the wild-oats stage, and *he*, my father, was hardly in a position to criticise. I didn't know what she meant, at the time. I do now. He keeps a whore in London.'

Her voice had hardened, though her eyes filled with tears. Simon realised then that she had been deeply hurt by her father's secret liaison.

He had tried to comfort her, telling her it probably meant nothing and that many a man had a fling in middle age.

'A fling!' she had cried. 'It has been more than a fling for years. Justin told me. He set the woman up in a house in Hanover Square – number twenty. You see, I even know the address. And she is still there. A man like my father wouldn't give a woman like that her own establishment unless it was a permanent arrangement.'

'Your brother shouldn't have told you. What made him?'

She had shrugged. 'What makes Justin do anything? I used to wonder about that when I was a little girl and saw him torturing wild creatures, pulling the wings off live birds, and horrible things like that. I used to run away, and he would laugh at me for being squeamish, and then chase me to smear the blood on me, but when I tried to tell Mamma, she would never believe me. "You are making it up," she would say, "because you have always been jealous of Justin." I have to admit that Papa felt differently. He was outraged by Justin's cruelties, and used to punish him – and comfort me. And yet he is capable of this horrible deception.'

'Don't sit in judgment on your father. There may be reasons why he turned to another woman.'

'Reasons? What possible reasons? If you mean sex, he doesn't have to *keep* the woman, or give her a house in one of the most expensive London squares! He could find satisfaction elsewhere as and when he needed it.'

'I don't think your father is that type of a man. He strikes me as being exceptionally nice – kind and honest.'

'I thought so too, once upon a time.'

It was a long time before the logical association between Caroline's act of love and act of revenge occurred to him. She had idealised her father, and he had disillusioned her.

Justin had forever humiliated, disgusted, and hurt her, and been favoured above her. And now, in his own way, he himself had let her down. She had expected him to become more and more famous so that she could compare him with other men to their detriment. 'Look what *I* have won for myself!' She wanted him to be the most successful of men and she the most envied of women. In both he had failed her.

Poor Caroline, restlessly seeking an ideal to replace the first she had lost, and blindly hitting back with the only means in her power. Spoilt materially throughout her life, she expected its rich rewards to continue, chief of which had to be someone to place on the pedestal from which her father had toppled. It was useless to tell her she was seeking a perfection which did not exist, but as it still continued to elude her in marriage, so had her act of love become an act of hatred, driving her husband away, striving for freedom in order to seek again, and again, and again . . .

She was at his side.

'Well, Simon, so you're here. I wasn't expecting you, or I would have had a room prepared.'

Because his daughter was with him, he checked the observation that, as her husband, he might be expected to share hers. For one thing, he had no desire to, and for another, Delia, not yet eleven, knew a great deal too much already. On her periodic and all too brief visits to him, he became more and more concerned about the things she knew and commented upon. Already she thought it perfectly natural that guests at Kingsmere should be judiciously placed next door to people to whom they were not married, giving them access through communicating doors or, at the very least, with the space of only a corridor between them. 'Pairing off', she called it, obviously assuming that this was the natural order of things with adults.

It was after a revealing visit to him that he had stormed along to the house in Hanover Square, frustrated because Miss Pymm had confirmed, in answer to his discreet questioning, that Delia's mother was not at Kingsmere and that she had no idea where she was, except that she might be off on holiday.

These 'holidays' in Caroline's life had become more frequent and more unpredictable. She simply went off without telling anyone.

At the dower house, when he had travelled to Kingsmere to visit the old lady, determined to glean some information from that ramrod figure and, as he might have expected, extracting absolutely nothing, he had met with a total lack of interest.

'My daughter is your responsibility, not mine. If a wife does as she pleases, it is the husband's fault. You refused to live with her at Kingsmere —'

'She refused to live with *me* in London, though my work is there.'

'How could you expect her to, since you can house her only meagrely? A poky flat, she told me, already furnished, and badly, too, without room even for a servant, and only a daily woman to clean the place – and the baby in a cot in a corner of the bedroom! Squalor, from the sound of it. And then to go off to that tiresome Boer War, for which the whole of Europe, if not the world, is condemning Britain! At least one good thing came out of that – Delia was brought here with her mother, where she has every advantage and the right background. But when you were invalided out of the army, you could hardly expect Caroline to bring her child back to you.'

'I could and I did. I am Delia's father, and Caroline knew – and still knows – that my ultimate intention is to find larger accommodation, provided it is within my means.'

'Whatever you could afford would be totally inadequate. How can you imagine that a girl brought up as Caroline has been, accustomed to a home like Kingsmere and servants at her beck and call, could adjust to poverty?'

'Poverty be damned!' He had sounded boorish, and knew it, and did not care. 'I could show you real poverty in the East End, but not in Kensington. In any case, she knew what to expect. I made it clear before we married.'

'Which, alas, she would insist on doing, despite my warnings. And I recall *you* were eager enough to marry *her*. For money and position, I thought, though her father contradicted me.'

'He was right. I loved her.'

'Past tense, I notice. You could have saved your marriage had you realised your obligations to Caroline.'

'I realised all my obligations, and fulfilled them.'

'Indeed you did *not*. Your greatest obligation was not to uproot her from the standards to which she was reared. Marrying into the Ashleighs, you could easily have fulfilled that one. You could have lived here at Kingsmere without any need to work at all.'

'You mean I should have been content to be supported by my in-laws?'

'Why not? Many a man has married a rich bride and done precisely that.'

'Not a man like me.'

'Then put your house in order without my help, Simon Davidson.'

There was no hope of doing that, but at least he would put his daughter's life in order. That was why he was here, to tell Caroline frankly that he was resolved to remove Delia from this vast place which seemed doomed to become nothing but an anachronism. How long could places like this survive in a country already bled by the expense of continuous wars, and possibly more costly ones to come, not only in money but in life? Meanwhile, Kingsmere slept in a placid dream of continuity amidst its endless acres, with its farms, its workers' cottages, its stables – the best-stocked in the county, some said; its workshops for carpenter and glazier and blacksmith; its slaughter-houses, where the chief gamekeeper and his staff hung up deer killed in the chase within its own parklands, killed not only for the exhilaration of the hunt but also to feed the large number of inhabitants within the estate. Then there were the grounds, tended by no fewer than fifteen gardeners, and its hothouses and kitchen gardens and orchards, and the encircling Kingsmere woods demanding the attention of a permanent forestry staff.

And the house itself, with its turrets and towers, its spreading wings, its countless bedrooms, its banqueting hall and endless reception rooms; its sprawling kitchens and sculleries and servants' quarters; its still room, laundry, dairy, brewery, stone-floored larders perpetually chill and innumerable pantries perpetually full; its strong room to which only the butler and milord himself held a key, and its wine cellars and storerooms, which held enough supplies for a siege. There were servants to be fed too; nearly forty of them in the house alone, many of whom were never seen by the owners or members of the family. It was the task of butler, housekeeper, cook, and stewards to hire their own staff were it impossible to fill vacancies in the traditional way, from the estate families.

Then there were outdoor employees – gamekeepers and wardens, park-keepers and foresters, gardeners and handymen, coachmen and grooms, stable boys and black-smiths. Everyone indoors and outdoors at Kingsmere was dependent upon milord for housing, food, and security in old age.

The size of the house could be measured by the span of its crenellated roofs, which amounted to just over five acres in all. Five acres of roof sheltering a family once proud of its heritage, and rightly so, thought Davidson, though, through association, he had come to dislike the place. Nevertheless, he had a strong feeling for history, and because the best of this system, which had risen voluntarily from ancient feudalism, was its sense of duty towards its dependants and its responsibility towards its employees, he held it in respect.

But did Justin? Did he keep as watchful an eye as his own father had kept on the state of cottages and farms? Charles Ashleigh may have sought escape in London with a woman he loved, but his sense of duty towards his heritage never wavered. Simon had met him only a few times, but he had sensed the man's devotion to the place, and admired him for it. It would be sad to see Kingsmere crumble, and the traditions it held most dear vanish forever.

Simon's most memorable meeting with Charles Ashleigh had been when he had had the temerity to ask for his daughter's hand in marriage. There had been mutual liking between the two men, though Charles had not minced his words when saying that in his opinion he and Caroline were ill-suited.

'I love my daughter, and at one time we were close to each other, but in her late teens she seemed to withdraw. If you are the man to make her happy, then both of you have my blessing, but frankly I cannot see the union being anything but difficult.

'Because of my background, sir?'

'Because of your *differing* backgrounds. You are not undertaking an easy task, Davidson.'

Beside him, Caroline was speaking and, mercifully, Delia had danced away to join a young woman standing with her back to them.

'Why didn't you let me know you were coming, Simon?'

'There wasn't time. I came on impulse. If I have chosen

a bad moment, I'm sorry.' His glance took in the crowded guests and his ears, distastefully, their conversation, which consisted of prattle and gush and very little else. Was there a serious thought in the head of any one of them?

'I see you don't approve of the company,' Caroline said. 'They are Justin's guests for the most part, so you don't have to.'

'Some friends of yours too, I imagine.'

'A few.'

'No one special?'

'Of course not. Why should there be?'

'Because I understand you have been off on one of your jaunts again. Alone?'

'Naturally, alone, apart from my maid.'

'Whom you could not possibly do without, having again become accustomed to being waited on. How could you now go back to dressing yourself?'

'If you are going to be sarcastic . . .' she began, and turned away.

Simon caught her arm.

'We must have a talk, Caroline.'

'About what?'

'Not about *what* – about whom, by which I mean our daughter. As I have already told your brother, I intend to take her away from Kingsmere.'

'I won't let you.'

'I am her father. You cannot prevent me.'

'I refuse to be parted from her.'

'You part from her easily enough when the whim takes you.'

'Do keep your voice down. People are listening.'

'I don't particularly mind if they do, but if it renders you incapable of serious conversation, I can wait until later. Tomorrow, or even Sunday before I leave.'

'So you intend to stay?'

'Of course. I don't journey from London just to see my child for a day. And perhaps it's a good thing I chose this weekend, otherwise she would spend it entirely with people such as these, so it was worth taking Friday afternoon away from my work.'

'At that stuffy museum! I never imagined you would settle to anything so dull. Why don't you go on expeditions now? You have recovered from your wounds, and even your limp isn't so pronounced. I can't see that it need stop you.'

'It doesn't. I stay because I won't travel any more. I was separated from Delia long enough when in South Africa and in hospitals later. Now I can at least see her from time to time, though not as often as I wish.'

'Your own fault. You refused to live with us here.'

'We won't go into all that again. Even your mother has expressed her opinion on that point, and so have I to her. I am not cut out to be a parasite, and I'm damned if I'll be obligated to your family for my support, though no doubt you would like that. It would emphasise my inferiority and your own superiority. That is the basis of all your restlessness, Caroline – your desire to dominate a man. Unhappily for you, you cannot dominate me. Have you succeeded with others?'

She shrugged and made no answer. The truth she kept strictly to herself – that some had been willing to accept her patronage and her bounty, and how she had enjoyed seeing them crawl for it! But others had turned away; even Bryant Meredith, surprisingly, for most actors were born parasites. But the last time they had made love he had surprised her by saying wearily, 'Go home, Caroline. Go back to England without me, for God's sake. You're a tiger cat, and while it was stimulating at first, I can take no more of it. Get out of my life, and stay out. From my point of view, this whole affair has been a bloody waste of time.'

He had packed, left the hotel, and she knew she was

never going to see him again.

At least her husband had never ordered her out of his life. She had left that poky flat in Kensington of her own free will, and gladly; his departure for the South African war made an admirable excuse. Returning to Kingsmere had been an incredible relief, for she was able to hand the baby over to a nanny and not have the responsibility of it any more. Of course, she had promised to rejoin her husband when he returned, and of course she had not. And because Kingsmere offered the child so much more than he could, handicapped as he was on his return, he had been forced to acquiesce, though she had sensed his unwillingness, also his belief that it was to be a compromise only, and a temporary one.

When he had been discharged from the army and sent to a hospital for nearly a year, followed by a spell in what was known as a convalescent home for the wounded, she had had a long and additional respite during which both knew that the intimate side of their marriage would not be revived. When finally discharged into civilian life, he had devoted himself to writing that mammoth work on archaeology which led to an invitation to become curator of that stuffy museum. What a decline for a man who had once made headlines!

The young woman, to whom Delia was now chattering sixteen to the dozen, turned sideways, her profile to Simon. He was startled, and although he recognised her at once, he asked, 'Who is she – the girl Delia is with?'

'Oh, her. Nice enough, I think, though I find her scarcely acceptable. Needless to say, she is not here as a guest of mine.'

He guessed why. The girl came from 20 Hanover Square, the house belonging to Dulcima Howard, who had once been the mistress of his wife's father and was now his brother-in-law's. He remembered seeing this young woman on the stairs as he left the house that night, also the direct glance they had exchanged. He had been instantly aware of her in a manner he chose not to recall. He had forced himself to stop responding to women in that particular way for a long time now, by the simple expedient of avoiding them, but now interest reasserted itself.

'Who is she?' he repeated, though Ashleigh had introduced them as the king drove by to open Parliament, and he remembered her name well enough. He had thought her intelligent and attractive, with a dash of something more potent thrown in, and perhaps for the latter reason had taken his departure quickly. He intended to get no woman on his mind.

'Her name is Deborah Yorke.'

'Yes, but *who* is she?'

'You mean her family? She hasn't one, as far as I know. She claims to be the daughter of a high-ranking member of the Church, but I don't believe it. She is cousin to that Howard woman, who claims to be related to a learned professor, which I also don't believe. They are here at Justin's invitation, and how he can have the effrontery to bring Dulcima Howard to this house is beyond me – unless, of course, it is to taunt me with the memory of Papa. I would put nothing past Justin.'

She realised that Simon was scarcely listening. He seemed to be interested solely in Miss Yorke, which surprised Caroline and aroused in her an illogical jealousy. Despite the rift in their marriage, she knew full well that no other woman had caused it, and complacently believed that her husband was no longer interested in women. She attributed that to his war experiences, his disabilities, and his slow rehabilitation, never to herself.

Across the wide hall she saw her reflection in a large Venetian mirror, and knew she was as good-looking as ever. Her father had been gratified by her development from a somewhat plain-looking child into a young woman of striking looks. 'I knew my duckling would turn into a swan,' he had said fondly when seeing her in her presentation gown. In the traditional white, with the snowy ostrich feathers in her hair that court etiquette demanded, the simile had not been inapt.

'You are lithe and sinuous as a cat—a beautiful she-cat,' Bryant Meredith had said when he first made love to her. 'I noticed you the first time I ever saw you walk into a room, and wanted you at once.' Only later did he call her a tiger cat, and want no more of her.

Incensed by Simon's interest in Deborah Yorke, she said impulsively, 'Share my room tonight, Simon. Why not?'

He looked at her in astonishment. 'You know we don't love each other any more. We are not really married any more.'

'But we are not divorced.'

'Bound by a piece of paper? Do you call that marriage?'

'We have a child. We could have another. And even if it were a son, it wouldn't be one of the pale-eyed Ashleighs, because they are only sired by the male line.' Simon looked as if he didn't understand. 'Oh, come, Simon, you know what I am talking about. Take a look at the family portraits and read the family history. Periodically, pale-eyed Ashleighs like my brother have come down through the family, but only ever through the male side, thank heaven.'

'And what is so significant about them?'

'I can't name it exactly, but I know it is bad. Every man born with those eyes has been different from the rest. Only hints are contained in the family archives, but they seem to indicate . . . not exactly an abnormality, but an ability to become associated with violence. There is even a legend about a male ancestor named Alric, who finally disappeared. Perhaps he was put away. The myth concerns an ancestral bride who was terrified by a cheetah kept by her husband as a pet, caught on a hunting trip and brought back by him and tamed in captivity. The story goes that the bridegroom made so much of it that his wife actively resented it, and the creature hated her as much as she hated him; also that her husband laughed when it tormented her. The story also goes that the day her child was born, a son, she fled through the park with the animal at her heels; she tripped and fell and gave birth prematurely, and because she had been terrified by the animal and he was the last thing she looked upon before her birth pains began, the child was born with the same-coloured eyes, so the mother would never look at it, nor have it near her. She refused to have another child unless her husband got rid of the cheetah, but he refused, so she retired to one of the towers here and lived out her life in solitude, but the son became the apple of his father's eye and could do no wrong. He called him Alric, and the servants feared him so much as he grew up that if his glance turned on them in anger, misfortune befell them — and worse.'

'What utter rubbish!'

'Perhaps, but people were superstitious in those days, and the belief was widely held that birthmarks were caused by a mother being frightened shortly before labour, or that looking upon something abnormal and terrifying could cause freak characteristics to occur to a child. And perhaps there is something in it. Who knows?'

'I hope to heaven you have never told this nonsense to Delia.'

'Of course not, though she may well stumble upon the legend herself, since she spends so much time in the library. The family archives are all there, some in diary form, some in letters, some, such as the legend, by hearsay, and some by authenticated documents. And even hearsay can be founded on fact.'

'I'm willing to wager that ridiculous legend hasn't a word of truth in it.'

'But Delia is fond of legends, thanks to your sending her all those Greek myths, so if she delves deeper, don't blame me.'

'It is up to you to keep an eye on what she reads.'

'*I* am not her governess.'

'Miss Pymm then, though she can't be expected to fulfil a mother's duties. Does she supervise the child's reading?'

'Away from lessons, you mean? Why should she? Even a governess has free time. And you have always encouraged Delia to read, so you should be pleased that she has developed a penchant for it.'

'What about that expensive nanny you hired?'

'Which one? There have been so many. None lasted long. They unanimously declared she was too precocious to handle.' Caroline laughed. 'She even drove the last one away by regaling her with things she had read and pictures she had seen in the library. Some of my brother's books, no doubt. Justin has what one might call a catholic taste in literature. Of course, I told the child she was not to look at them, but I am quite sure she took no notice. And since the library belongs to Justin, I can hardly protest about the volumes he adds to it, nor ask him to keep them elsewhere.'

'All the more reason for my removing Delia as soon as possible.'

'You are unwise to forewarn me, Simon. What if *I* take her away?'

'I have already anticipated that. Wherever you went, I would make it my business to find you, and by that time you would be so tired of playing mother you would gladly hand her over. And I won't allow her to be used as a pawn between us, or to be tossed from one home to another. Circumstances made it necessary for her to come here, and I had to make the best of the situation, but the picture has changed. She now needs a father. She needs stability and an ordinary home life, which means living it as an ordinary person, not closeted in this great house with only a governess and servants for company, in between spasmodic contacts with her mother, occasional visits to her grandmother at the dower house – once a week, for afternoon tea, I understand – then bursts of weekend house parties, such as this one, when she is fussed over by insincere "friends" of her uncle and yourself, all anxious to curry favour by displaying a fondness for children whilst their own are left in the care of nannies or packed off to expensive schools – anything, so long as they are off their hands. I understand Delia isn't even allowed to play with the estate children! I won't have a child of mine growing up to be a snob, so it is time our positions were reversed. I would rather we arranged it quietly and amicably, but I am quite prepared to do battle, if necessary, though not in front of our daughter. I will take on the united front of yourself, your mother, and your brother if I have to, but no ugly scenes in the child's presence.'

Caroline shrugged. '*I* won't make a scene. I dislike them. And your idea could be tried, as an experiment.'

'Not as an experiment. Permanently. I will be wholly responsible for her, look after her well, and keep an eye on her teaching in conjunction with sending her to a good day school.'

'She will hate that. She will soon be wanting to come back to Kingsmere. Justin has always said you would turn her into a horrible little blue stocking if you had the chance, though I doubt whether Delia has the capacity for it. Miss Pymm says she woefully lacks concentration.'

'That depends on the way she is taught. Any child's attention will wander if a subject is not made interesting.'

Caroline shrugged again, anxious not to reveal that on the whole his suggestion had much to commend it, not the least of which was her own relief from any form of responsibility. Even part-time motherhood was irksome; she now resented ties of any kind. Without them she could have been another Hester Stanhope, Aphra Behn, Elizabeth Chudleigh – any of those dramatic women of history who seemed to be surrounded by an aura of glory, to Caroline's way of thinking. Surely none could have achieved so much fame if shackled by family ties and responsibilities – or, if they had possessed any, surely they had shed them?

It suddenly occurred to Caroline that this was what life had intended for herself – notoriety as a woman of achievement; not the notoriety of that dreadful Dulcima Howard, or even the fanatical Emmeline Pankhurst, masochistically drawing attention to herself with frenzied demonstrations, finishing up in prison, but notoriety of a more glamorous kind; the fearless traveller across deserts, the intrepid female penetrating into remote parts of the East where no Western woman had ever set foot before. Why had she never thought of it?

Caroline had never been self-perceptive, but now she had a brief flash of what she fancied to be the truth – that she was never intended to be merely the woman behind the man, basking in his reflected glory, but famed in her own right, if only she knew in which direction it lay. That, she alone could decide.

Excitement caught her. There need be no more brief sojourns away from Kingsmere solely in release from boredom, no more love affairs curtailed cruelly by men or terminated by herself because boredom reclaimed her. No more furtive interludes, desperately covered up because *she* wasn't going to be the woman taken in adultery. Her name had remained unbesmirched through her own skill and determination, and she would not have had to work at that if her husband had fulfilled all her expectations. Her disappointments and frustrations could therefore be laid at his door, and it was wholly unfair that one betrayal, one slip, would have enabled him to divorce her, for it needed only one infidelity on a wife's part for a husband to take such a step.

But she was becoming tired of playing with fire. The challenge was petering out, and life held greater challenges if a woman had the courage to go out and find them. In the process, she could achieve for herself the fame her husband valued so little. She might even go down in history, like those memorable women before her. Her mind took wings in the face of such a dream, so that her husband's voice seemed to penetrate only from a distance. He was saying something about a legend. Who knew, perhaps she would be a legend herself one day.

'Yes, Simon? You were saying?'

'That someone must have made up that ridiculous legend to account for those strange eyes recurring every now and then in the men of your family. It is probably no more than a biological quirk. Even so, I won't have Delia frightened by such a tale.'

'I doubt if she would be. She is a most unimaginative child.'

'Despite her fondness for reading?'

'That probably makes up for her lack of imagination. She is disconcertingly practical in some of her remarks – I doubt if an imaginative child would be.' Caroline shrugged, implying that their daughter was to be his responsibility from now on anyway. 'As for the Ashleigh eyes, as they are called, women find them fascinating – including Deborah Yorke, from the look of things. She has been absorbed in Justin for the last ten minutes.'

Only then did Simon notice that his brother-in-law had joined Delia and her companion, together with a spectacular woman who could be none other than Dulcima Howard.

Turning back to his wife, Simon said gently, 'I'm sorry, but as regards your suggestion that we should come together again, you know there is no hope. Nor do you really want it in your heart, which is eternally set on hitting back at men. You idealised your father too much, and neither I nor any other man could ever fill the niche he occupied.'

'Are you suggesting there was something abnormal, wrong, in my love for Papa?' she asked indignantly.

'Nothing incestuous, if that is what you mean, but because he proved to have the normal frailties of man, you let yourself be disillusioned and embittered, filled with a desire to hit back. That, my poor Caroline, is why you make love the way you do.'

He moved away from her. Pitying her was one thing, loving her another, and all he felt now was the former. He could not help her because she would not be helped, but he could help his daughter – and would.

He moved across to the little girl, and so met Dulcima Howard for the first time, and understood why his father-in-law had loved her – not merely because she was beautiful, but because she must have given him the greatest warmth and affection he had ever known in his life. She was that kind of woman.

He also met Deborah Yorke and knew, the moment their eyes met, that she remembered the glance they had exchanged across the hall of 20 Hanover Square – the potency of it, the depth of it, the disturbing awareness; and the fact that he too had been unable to forget it held an almost alarming significance.

He took his child's hand and moved away.

Moodily Caroline watched him. Though antagonised by his frank home truths, she recognised that he was still an arresting figure, despite his limp and his scarred face. She saw recognition in people's eyes as he passed and, in those of the women, attraction mingled with eager curiosity. Soon they would be whispering behind their hands, speculating on his presence here, wondering if it were possible that he and Caroline were picking up the threads of their marriage again. ('Such an *extraordinary* man for her to have fallen in love with!' . . . 'My dear, haven't I always said so?') Oh, she knew perfectly well what they were thinking and saying – Papa had said much the same before she married. 'Are you sure he is the man for you? I like him and respect him, but my daughter's happiness means more to me than anything else.'

Lies, all of it. His own happiness with that dreadful woman had meant a great deal more; otherwise he would never have continued with the association to the day he died, leaving her so lavishly housed. And now Justin had taken up with her – and what malice had prompted him to do that? Even worse, he had dared to bring her to Kingsmere and have his father's suite opened up for her – which, of course, meant for both of them. They would make love in *his* bed.

Not for a moment had Caroline dreamed that the woman her brother was to bring this weekend would prove to be their father's former mistress, though she had heard that Justin was visiting 20 Hanover Square, and not merely for the gambling. But never had she suspected that the creature meant anything more to him than an occasional diversion. There had always been passing women in her brother's life, even when Norah was alive, and he had never hesitated to invite one or other of them to Kingsmere's weekend parties, but always they had been accommodated in a room beyond his own, which, in its turn, was next to his wife's. Perhaps insipid Norah had not minded when he chose to visit next door but one. She had always struck Caroline as being a sexless sort of creature, which could certainly not be said for Dulcima Howard.

But to occupy the master suite was unusual, for Justin had always disliked it. 'It is too reminiscent of its last occupant, and I don't particularly want to be reminded of him. I never felt as you did about our revered father. Mamma always understood me better. In any case, the room is too far away from the rest of the house – by the time my shaving water arrived in the morning it would be cold in the jug!'

Now he had changed his mind – for this weekend, at least. That magnificent bedroom had had to be aired and made ready, every detail attended to according to his advance instructions, curtains and carpets and bed hangings cleaned personally by the housekeeper and specially chosen staff.

'She must use only the best workers,' he had written, 'and you, Caro, must choose the finest hothouse blooms when the weekend arrives.'

The flowers, obviously, were for a lady, for whom he was setting a splendid stage, but when Caroline discovered her identity, she had recoiled.

Now she guessed why Dulcima Howard's name had not appeared on his guest list. Justin had withheld it in order to surprise and shock her, and possibly Mamma too, should she find out. Everyone else, with the exception of someone named Miss Deborah Yorke, for whom he intimated that a modest room on the fringe of the servants' quarters would suffice, was known to his sister. Miss Yorke, she had therefore presumed, was a companion to one of the older women, perhaps that eccentric old Duchess of Dorking, who was notoriously incapable of keeping either a nurse or companion or lady's maid for long, but whom Justin always invited because she amused him.

Later, when Justin indicated that Miss Yorke was the daughter of a high-ranking member of the Church, Caroline had sensed his disbelief, and shared it. The girl looked nice enough, but because she had arrived with the notorious Howard woman, she was tarred with the same brush in Caroline's eyes.

'Actually, she is the beauteous Dulcima's cousin. If you look closely enough, you will see a resemblance, especially in profile. And though you may not believe it, sister, dear Dulcima herself claims to be the offspring of a learned don. Now, doesn't *that* impress you?'

'Nothing about her impresses me. How can you expect it to? And how can you do anything so outrageous as to bring her here? Even worse, to share Papa's bed with her!'

'As to that,' Justin had said in the soft tone which he always used when quelling an answer, 'I have my reasons.'

She did not ask what they were, because she had no desire to know. She remembered moments throughout her lifetime when her brother's acts of sadism had been preceded by the softest and gentlest of tones. 'Let's play hide-and-seek, Caro,' he had suggested once when they were children. 'I will choose the place for you to hide, and to make sure you can't escape, I will lock the door.'

'But that's against the rules! You are not supposed to know where I am hiding.'

'Ah, but this is a different kind of hide-and-seek. I hide you and then rescue you, like knights of old rescuing damsels in distress.'

And before she had known what was happening, he had pushed her to the floor, crammed a handkerchief into her mouth to stop her screaming, then tied her hands and feet and rolled her into the schoolroom cupboard, locking her in the dark. She had always been terrified of the dark, and he knew it, and he had laughed outside the door, enjoying her inarticulate and terrified sounds. She had been almost fainting when at last he released her, his opaque eyes shining in a way which terrified her even more, his breath excited, his lips parted. She knew then that he was actually enjoying her terror, the way he enjoyed hurting wild creatures caught in the park.

Mercifully their governess had walked in at that moment and promptly rushed off to find their mother, fortunately meeting Papa first, for Caroline knew that

Mamma would have defended Justin somehow. Not so their father, swift with his punishment, followed by an inexplicable alarm. Caroline remembered how he had looked at his son, long and hard and anxiously, and shortly afterward Justin had gone for a few days' holiday to London with his father, or so Mamma said – and while they were away she dismissed the governess and found another, and when Papa returned, Justin was not with him.

'A place in Switzerland,' she had heard him say. 'A very good place, highly recommended.' Then he had added compassionately, 'You have nothing to worry about, Elizabeth. With time and treatment, they hope for good results.'

'Treatment for *what*, pray? There is nothing wrong with my son, and how dare you imply that there is?'

Trust Mamma to defend Justin. She always had, and she always would.

That had been the first of her brother's trips abroad, and though Caroline guessed that they were always to Switzerland for treatment of some sort, she never enquired about them or talked about them, or even thought about them, because the excitement in his opaque eyes on that long-ago day was not something she cared to recall. It reminded her too forcibly of the Ashleigh legend, though she had never heard of her brother being involved in anything worse than seducing that servant girl, whose charge of rape had been quickly dropped when Mamma waved her financial wand. Even that had not been as bad as the case in Kingsmere's woods some months later, when a girl's body had been found, sexually assaulted and strangled. Never for a moment had her brother's name been linked with that, and the crime had passed into the limbo of those unsolved, some passing tramp being blamed by local gossip and every village girl being warned by her parents, 'Look what happens to those as are no better'n they should be!'

8

Deborah escaped from the stifling atmosphere that afternoon. While others retired to their rooms to sleep off the effects of an over-hearty luncheon, or to the card room to play bridge, or to the long room spanning the south side of the house, which was known as the garden room, there to lounge idly and gossip until it was time to change for tea, she set out for a brisk walk, and met Delia and her father doing the same thing.

Simon Davidson's limp proved no handicap. He had accepted the hindrance long ago, and therefore ignored it. Nothing jarred so much as solicitude from others, or the assumption that they should slow their pace out of consideration for his own, and he was thankful when Deborah Yorke made no attempt to. From the sweeping lawns surrounding the house they headed towards the open spaces of the park, and it was a long time before they retraced their steps. As they did so, they saw Dulcima coming towards them. She was alone and hatless, stepping out as if she had not had an opportunity to enjoy such freedom for many a year – which was true.

'I tried to entice Justin outdoors,' she announced, 'but the bridge table attracted him more. Hardly complimentary to me!'

She laughed, not minding in the least, because the whole weekend was before them and, not so far distant, the whole night. Still relishing her secret news, she had

149

good reason to look forward to tonight; meanwhile, getting away from the rest of the company was very much to her liking, for though she had always aspired to the highest society, she was finding this sample of it incredibly dull, their false charms and high voices tedious, their veiled patronage galling – but not galling enough to worry her, knowing how effectively she would be turning the tables upon them, and soon.

'I haven't taken a country walk since I was a young girl,' she said, falling into step beside them and lifting her head to the sky as she did so, breathing deeply and appreciatively and reminding Deborah of that ride to Brighton from Roedean, and her aunt's enormous black hat, ostrich plumes flying in the breeze as she relished the sea air. 'I shall do this more often – come to the country, I mean. Hyde Park is an inadequate substitute, lovely as it is. Did you know I was born in the country, Mr Davidson? Oh, yes, I am a country girl at heart!'

He laughed, as she had meant him to, and little Delia laughed as well, dancing along beside her.

'*I* don't believe you are wicked at all, Miss Howard.'

Startled, Dulcima demanded, 'And who said I was?' and the child's father immediately changed the subject, insisting that they should walk in shorter grass than this.

'Over there, by the driveway, the verge is kept mown. It will be easier for you ladies in those sweeping skirts.'

'Oh, no!' cried Delia. 'There is Grandmamma! She is sure to stop and ask all sorts of tiresome questions, like how am I behaving and have I stopped being difficult about eating rice pudding. Please – let's go the other way!'

It was too late. The ancient dogcart in which his mother-in-law drove about the estate was almost upon them and Simon could not deliberately march his child away. Nor did he want to. In many ways he felt sorry for Elizabeth Ashleigh, despite her attitude towards him, which at best was veiled hostility. Then a faint gasp at his side reminded him that Dulcima Howard was there, which could make matters a great deal worse. Since Caroline had known about this woman's relationship with her father, he had no doubt at all that her mother had also known, and, in keeping with all Victorian wives, had kept silent because she had no choice. A meeting between them would mean embarrassment on both sides, though possibly Dulcima herself had no suspicion that Justin's mother might be aware of her long-ago relationship with Charles.

Simon was caught between the choice of doing an about-turn on the spot, a discourtesy which would set a bad example to his child, or risking an unpleasant encounter between the two women. The first choice was out of the question, so the women would just have to come face to face and make the best of it.

By this time they were walking on the verge and the dogcart was slowing down a few yards away. When it halted, he saw his mother-in-law's erect back stiffen even more and knew that at close quarters her fading eyesight had not prevented her from recognising the notorious Dulcima.

Delia bobbed an automatic curtsey, wondering why her grandmother suddenly seemed sterner than ever, with not so much as a glance for herself. She wasn't afraid of Grandmamma, she even liked her when she ordered those special macaroons for tea at the dower house because she knew Delia liked them, but she was one of the few people of whom the child stood in awe. Pymmy had drummed into her that when in her grandmother's presence she must never speak unless spoken to, and what could be more difficult than that? So she stood waiting for the usual keen inspection, followed by the usual reprimand: 'Stand up straight, child! I cannot abide slouchers.' She could almost recite the old lady's comments before they were uttered, but to her astonishment, none came. Then she realised that Grandmamma's face had gone quite pale and her lips tighter than ever, and that her eyes were staring at the spectacular Miss Howard in undisguised shock.

Her father was speaking. Delia heard him mention Miss Yorke's name and saw that young woman incline her head and perform the slight bend of the knee which was obligatory from younger women to older ones in polite society, but his remaining introduction was silenced by a glare from the old lady. It was the first time Delia had ever seen her father look uncomfortable, though he skated over the moment by asking after Grandmamma's health and expressing the hope that her rheumatism was not troubling her so much, and a lot more to which her grandmother paid no attention. But the most surprising thing was that Miss Howard was standing still as a statue, her head lifted proudly but her eyes full of sadness. Then Grandmamma's voice rapped out, 'An introduction is superfluous, son-in-law. I recognised Miss Howard immediately. How could I fail to, with her picture forever flaunted before the public?' Then, turning frigidly to Miss Howard, she added, 'You cannot expect me to welcome you to Kingsmere, madam, and if you have any sense of the fitness of things, you will remove yourself forthwith.'

Dulcima's hand flew to her throat. Dear God, she does know! She has always known – all these years, when I have thought she was in complete ignorance about Charles and me! Ten long years since he died, and still she remembers and therefore hates me . . . and who can blame her?

Mixed with Dulcima's shock was compassion for the proud figure now looking down upon her so disdainfully, for she sensed behind that vigilant mask a sternly repressed pain which could only be attributable to grief over her husband's long infidelity. Cushioned as she was by luxury and wealth, what else could be responsible for it?

Elizabeth Ashleigh was saying, 'I presume you are here at my son's invitation. My daughter would never have invited you, that I know.'

Dulcima answered quietly, 'Since Kingsmere belongs to Justin, you are right in assuming the invitation came from him.'

The words were an effort, but she too had her pride and had no intention of revealing that the woman's slight had gone home. At the same time, she made it plain that no one but Justin was really in a position to invite her to Kingsmere or to ask her to leave, and with an inclination of her head in farewell, she turned her back upon the aging figure and walked on.

'Say good-bye to your grandmother, Delia.'

The dogcart jerked to action and clattered away, the child's obedient curtsey ignored.

Dulcima walked back to the house, her mind awhirl. If Justin's mother knew the truth, and apparently Caroline too, then what about Justin himself?

Impossible! He would never have sought her company had he suspected that his own father had once been her lover, so she dismissed that question with confidence. And perhaps the statement that Caroline would never have invited her to Kingsmere merely implied that a woman of good birth would never seek the company of one whose pictures appeared on chocolate boxes and calendars and hoardings and postcards, not to mention advertisements for the newest stays and corsets featured prominently in ladies' journals.

Dulcima's natural optimism rallied at the thought. She even persuaded herself that Elizabeth Ashleigh's disapproval could be based on similar grounds, until reason argued that so strong a dismissal must be due to something much worse than the cheap exhibition of feminine beauty. Beneath the pain in the woman's eyes had lurked the same animosity Dulcima had encountered the moment she met Caroline, and the memory of that stirred her anxiety anew.

Quickening her footsteps, she reached the house well ahead of her companions. Solitude was essential. She needed to regain her composure before rejoining Justin and the bevy of weekend guests for tea, but Delia's flying feet caught up with her. The child tugged at her sleeve, begging her not to hurry away. Her piquant little face looked up in pleading, and Dulcima immediately stooped and kissed the young cheek. Her hand lingered there, the soft skin of childhood reminding her that soon she would have a child of her own to touch and caress.

Immediately all the pain she had experienced out there in the park was wiped away in the joy of such anticipation. When Deborah joined them, she was even capable of summoning a smile.

Accompanying her aunt upstairs, Deborah said anxiously, 'Don't be upset, Dulcima. I was angered, too, but some mothers can be jealous of the women in their sons' lives, I understand.'

With forced lightness Dulcima answered, 'My dear, I have already forgotten the incident. I am only sorry that you and Simon Davidson were caused embarrassment.'

She had to say *something* to erase that anxious expression from Deborah's face, for naturally the girl knew nothing about Charles Ashleigh. Dulcima never discussed the past. Life was too full to waste in looking back over her shoulder, and her present cup so filled to overflowing that she wanted only to dwell upon the promise of more to come. Wife, mother, mistress of Kingsmere – all this bounty was within her grasp, so she could afford to dismiss any alarms and fears.

The fashion parade continued, with the women vying

against each other in elaborate tea gowns for the afternoon ritual, and the men lavishing compliments upon them, which echoed falsely in Deborah's ears. Apart from the walk in the park with Simon Davidson and little Delia, she was finding the company extremely boring; already she was seeing through the artificiality of society manners, a fact which both surprised and pleased Dulcima. The girl promised to be less naive than she had feared, and therefore less likely to be duped or hurt. She displayed unexpected common sense, a commodity much needed by women. Thank heaven I have plenty myself, reflected Dulcima, and looked forward to the day when she would be able to devote herself to being Justin's wife without further anxiety about her own future or Deborah's.

She would be a good wife, too; loyal and loving and a credit to him socially, for her beauty could pass muster in the most fashionable drawing rooms, and once such a marriage had put the seal of approval on her, no one would dare to regard her askance. Caroline and her mother would have to accept her, and in time, she prayed, they would even learn to like her. Incapable of bearing animosity herself, she found it difficult to believe that others could nurse it forever. For a long time now she had looked back on the blow Charles had dealt her, with complete forgiveness, remembering only his love and devotion.

As for Deborah, surely her future would be equally rosy, for with a little more self-assurance she should have no difficulty in annexing a husband; then they would both be secure forever. No more baccarat, no more trickery, no more straining one's resources to the utmost and paying Dillon, her model butler, for his co-operation and silence.

Her contentment was increased by the fact that Justin was obviously taken with Deborah, going out of his way to make the girl feel welcome at Kingsmere. Had he spoken to Caroline about changing her room? Dulcima was confident that he had. Everything she had asked of him since he became her lover had immediately been granted. Even when his lovemaking had threatened to become too rough, he had controlled it at her first plea. He was a passionate man whose desires had been repressed through a marriage which had proved disappointing, and passion too long pent up could be hard to control. She understood this, and knew her ardour would continue to be more than sufficient for his needs. Because she loved him she visualised their relationship stretching ahead in a harmonious pattern of warmth and understanding, both physically and mentally.

Never had a day passed so slowly; never had a night been so long in coming. If he comes to my room while I am changing for dinner, I will dismiss Garfield and tell him then – I cannot wait until we go to bed! The thought of coming downstairs together, united in their wonderful secret, made Dulcima's heart glow. Across the room, her eyes met Justin's, and he promptly came to her, lured by her loveliness.

'My dear, country air must agree with you. You look radiant.'

She smiled up at him, the curve of her lips full of unconscious invitation. 'Country air has nothing to do with it,' she murmured.

'Then what?'

'Happiness.'

'Just because you are at Kingsmere?'

'No. Much more than that.'

'Tell me.'

'Later. Tonight. When we are alone.'

'Later, tonight, when we are alone, there will be no time for talk.'

His light eyes smiled back into hers, then subtly changed. She had seen that happen many times before. It meant he wanted her – right now, this very moment.

Fortunately he had his back to the rest of the room, or surely others would have noticed his ill-concealed desire. Not that she would have been displeased had they done so, thereby establishing her ascendancy over every other woman present – but there was a time and place for everything, and her answering glance said as much.

The glow in his eyes faded at once. He even looked angry, knowing she was not responding with the immediacy he desired and expected. He enjoyed arousing her with meaningful glances and, highly sexed and in love as she was, he rarely failed. Now he realised there was something else on her mind, something she was relishing in secret, and he didn't like that. He took it as a rebuff for which she should be punished, and he would do that tonight, in that very private room well away from the others. It was time she learned precisely what he expected of her and precisely how he intended to enjoy her, and, by God, she would submit to all of it.

He turned his back deliberately and walked across the room to Deborah Yorke, whom he had also arranged to be accommodated in convenient seclusion. It amused him to go from one woman to another when his house was full of guests; Dulcima tonight, Deborah tomorrow? Perhaps. If Dulcima complied with his wishes tonight, then the little virgin could wait for some future occasion. Meanwhile, the recollection of Dulcima asking for her cousin to be moved to another room entertained him as much as the knowledge that she actually believed he would arrange it. Really, in some ways dear Dulcima was incredibly gullible.

Dulcima was aware that her gown of saffron slipper satin, wasp-waisted, hip-padded, and extremely décolleté, was the loveliest at the dinner table that night and that she need make no attempt to draw attention to herself by joining in the conversation of the ladies when they withdrew, leaving the gentlemen to their port. She knew well enough that the women eyed her secretly and enviously, and with good cause. She both felt and looked magnificent, lit with an inner happiness she had not experienced since that long-ago day when she had flung herself upon Charles Ashleigh, crying out her wonderful news. But there the resemblance to her present situation ceased, for Justin would not react as his father had done, because Justin wanted an heir. He had admitted that more than once, mourning the fact that poor Norah had been unable to give him one. That had been the biggest disappointment in his marriage, he had told her, but in an hour or two he would learn that she, Dulcima, would soon make it up to him.

The wonder of it, the blessed miracle of it! Did all women feel as she did when discovering they were to have a child? Did they too feel that no other woman had ever experienced such joy or such triumph?

Poor Justin, he had been hurt by her reaction, or lack of it, this afternoon. In some ways he was like a spoilt boy with a tendency to sulk if people did not respond to him the way he wished, either with admiration or eagerness to please, but he would understand when he heard the reason for it. Two months had gone, and there could be no possible doubt.

Impatiently she glanced at an ornate gilt clock on the mantelshelf, an elaborate piece which, with the rest of the furnishings, was no doubt worth a fortune. Kingsmere was famed for its treasures. It was said that the Ashleigh collection constituted a museum in itself. Dulcima appreciated the beauty of it all, but at this moment had no interest in material things, nor in the conversation about her. She awaited the return of the gentlemen with impatience, eager to see again Justin's approval of her appearance, which had been unstinting when she descended the long staircase, the train of her gown held up with a ribboned loop over her wrist that exactly matched the sash encircling her hourglass waist. God bless the new corset, which flattened the abdomen, left the breasts free, and had two vertical strips of whalebone in front which tilted the body back at the hips, producing the S-silhouette so typical of the time. (S-for-sex, as the king would say!) To carry this figure well, a woman required a good carriage and ample bosom and hips; the corset did the rest, and with such breasts as hers, she needed no pads to uplift them.

Unlike the rest of the female guests, she had abstained from wearing jewellery, guessing correctly that they would be rivalling each other with an excess of it. Her only additional adornment was a single flower in her hair and a small upstanding aigrette of feathers tinted saffron to match her gown. In this mood of confidence and contentment, conversation floated over her, only registering when she saw Deborah's expression and realised that one of these chattering magpies had uttered something the girl had never expected to hear from women regarded as well-bred.

'My dear, he is an absolute *ram* – it is common knowledge! King Edward is lusty enough, but Prendergast! No wonder his wife looks perpetually worn out. "Enough is enough," I always say when Arthur becomes too greedy. "You have had your ration for tonight, my love."'

The old Duchess of Dorking gave a coarse cackle, and someone else cried, 'Oh, Leonora, you *don't*! I absolutely refuse to believe you. But abso*lute*ly!'

'Well, you must admit that too much of it can be very exhausting.'

'Really, dahling, you are too, too terrib*lino!*'

Oh, the affectation of those Italian terminations added to English words, regardless of whether they were verbs or adjectives! Although she had indulged in this current form of slang herself, merely because it was fashionable, along with 'deevy' and 'ghastly', which could be applied indiscriminately to almost everything, Dulcima suddenly found the whole thing irritating and stupid. What bores they all were with their empty prattle and their belief that it was clever to be outspoken about sex just because the subject was taboo! Didn't they realise that anything so lovely and natural and, above all, private, could be debased by their kind of discussion, and that to talk this way in the presence of an inexperienced girl was not only in bad taste but also inconsiderate? Dulcima had admitted to her niece, right at the outset, that Ashleigh was her lover and therefore accustomed to seeing her in the nude, but never would she dream of referring to the more intimate details of their relationship. Besides, it was disloyal to Justin.

Suddenly the old duchess, famed for her outspokenness and the fact that she could swear like a trooper, declared, 'Well, it is better for a woman to be married to a ram like Prendergast than to the other kind. Far too many women have to shut their eyes to *that*.'

'I wouldn't, and no woman has to. It is one of the few things we unfortunate women *can* use as grounds for divorce.'

'Try proving it, Moira dear, try proving it!' That was sharp-faced Leonora again. 'When a man goes out on the town leaving his wife at home, how does she know what he gets up to? Where sex is concerned, men can get away with anything.'

A plump, coquettish, dimpled blonde piped, 'Well, *I* don't believe many men are like that, and I ought to know, because so many pursue me.'

Titters echoed Leonora's derisive laughter and the old duchess's renewed cackle.

'My poor Kate, I had no idea you were such a blessed innocent!'

'Leonora, you cat, I am *not*, as many a man can vouch for!'

There was triumph in silly Kate's voice, which everyone knew to be unjustified. All her hints of amorous conquests were never more than imaginary, and the vicious Leonora made that plain when she retorted, 'If you were really the *femme fatale* you pretend to be, dahling, you would know that lots of men like it both ways. Of course, it isn't done, to talk about such things, but since we are all alone and the men can't hear, we can at least be frank amongst ourselves.'

Dulcima's voice cut in briskly. 'I would be obliged if you would curb your conversation in front of my cousin. Her upbringing has been more refined. Deborah, my love, shall we take a breath of good clean air in the garden before the gentlemen return?'

Deborah went gladly. She was not so innocent as to be unaware of the meaning behind the talk of these women. What she found distasteful was the unsavoury relish of it, typical of the insincerity behind the glitter and the gold of Edwardian society.

Dulcima's moment had come. She was waiting for Justin. Garfield had unlaced her and helped her prepare for bed, saying before departure that she had only to pull the bell rope beside the fireplace should she need anything more. 'It rings straight through to my room, ma'am. All the personal maids have communicating bells direct to their mistresses, so if you don't feel too well in the morning . . .'

'I shall feel splendid, Garfield. Those wretched symptoms have already passed.'

She hummed contentedly as she began to brush her hair, scarcely heeding the woman's departure. When uncoiled, her hair reached to her waist. Justin loved to see it cascading down her bare back, vivid against the white of her skin. Sometimes he entwined his fingers in it or buried his face in it. Once he had taken a long thick strand and wound it about her throat, saying teasingly, 'Shall I choke you with it, my lovely? At the gorgeous moment of climax, shall I pull it tight so you die at the peak of delight? It would be a lovely way to depart this life, wouldn't it, soaring into oblivion at that blinding moment? And no man would ever sample the enjoyment of you again. I would like that. You would drift into eternity through *my* love, *my* strength, bearing *my* mark.'

Then he had released the coil of hair abruptly. 'Darling, don't look so startled. Surely you didn't think I meant it?'

'If I thought that, I would never let you make love to me again.'

Why recall that moment now? Why remember the strange way he had looked at her in answer, saying nothing – just looking hard at her with those pale amber eyes.

'Do you know that your eyes change when you are passionate?' she had asked, and he had jerked, 'Change? In what way?'

'In colour. They gleam like a tiger's.'

'So do yours,' he had teased, 'though I suppose I should say "tigress".'

'I don't make love like a tigress.'

'No – you make love like a warm and wonderful woman, but I could make you behave like a tigress, if I tried.'

'Never. I can only love in a way that comes naturally to me, as you can.'

'All sorts of things come naturally,' he had whispered, stooping to put his lips to her throat, then opening his mouth so that she felt the sharp edges of his teeth.

She shivered. What was the matter with her, recalling moments of apprehension which he quickly dispelled with his ardour? Why remember now the occasional feeling that beneath his passion something was held in check, only waiting to be unleashed?

Fancies. She had heard that pregnancy could bring all sorts of fancies.

But she had experienced that feeling before she conceived, so pregnancy as a cause could be dismissed.

She rose and paced the room – such a beautiful room, with tall windows draped with rich brocade and the bed turned back ready to receive herself and her lover. The thickly piled carpet beneath her bare feet was warm and luxuriant. She curled her toes in it, wondering how many women before her had done the same thing and if this was the room to which Charles had brought the young Elizabeth on their wedding night; this the bed in which she had become his wife, conceived, borne his children. The master bedroom *must* have belonged to Charles.

To Dulcima, it still belonged to him, and for this reason she could never occupy this bed with another man. Especially his son.

She was kneeling before the fire when Justin walked in, magnificent in a quilted robe of royal blue satin emblazoned with gold dragons, but she didn't even notice how handsome he looked. She just went on kneeling there, staring into the flames. He saw that she had drawn her wrap tightly about her, her arms folded across her breasts, almost as if she were cold.

He was immediately irritated. If she was going to be moody and uncooperative, he would have to show who was master, but the lovely curves of her body beneath the transparent robe drew him inevitably, and he went to her and pulled the robe apart, cupping her bare breasts in his hands.

She lifted her face then, and to his astonishment, her cheeks were wet.

'What the devil's the matter now? Downstairs this afternoon you looked radiant. You said you were happy, and very secretive you were about the reason for it, to my annoyance. If you hadn't behaved like that, deliberately ignoring what must have been very obvious to you, I would have taken you to bed for an hour immediately after tea.'

She forced a smile. 'So that was why you went back to the bridge table – to punish me.'

'You deserved it. Anyway, you look far from radiant now. What has come over you?'

She asked bleakly. 'Was this your father's bedroom?'

'Of course.'

'Then take me to the one you usually occupy. *Please*,' she added helplessly.

'Why, in heaven's name? What's wrong with this one? You were delighted with it when you first saw it; flattered because you had been given the finest in the place. And that's the way you should feel.'

'I have changed my mind. I would rather sleep with you in your own bed.'

'Don't be childish. Or are you squeamish about making love in *his* bed? Is that it? Do you actually think it disloyal, or something ridiculous like that? Good grief, Dulcima, you owe no fidelity to a man who is dead!'

She jerked to her feet, clutching her robe about her again. He could see he had shocked her, but why, he could not imagine.

She gasped, 'You *know*?'

'About you and my dear papa? Of course.'

'For how long? How long have you known?'

'For years. Well before he died I found out he was keeping the most beautiful whore in London. Damned amusing, I thought.'

She backed away. She looked stricken, shaking her head from side to side in a bewildered sort of way. He went over to her and tried to take her in his arms, but she backed away again, whereupon he seized her and shook her hard.

'Stop behaving like a fool. You're a grown woman and an experienced one. I wouldn't have come near you otherwise. Surely you're not insulted because I called you what you are?'

'I have never been a whore.'

'But you have had lovers. You've been kept by men. So what else would you call yourself?'

'I have never sold my body. I have given it only in love. And only one man has ever kept me. That was because he loved me and wanted to look after me. He *cared* about me. I was barely eighteen and I needed protection, and in return, I loved him. In the seven years we were together, I looked at no other man.'

'My dear father? He left you well housed, I'll say that for him, so I suppose he must have cared. But surely we don't have to talk about all that now? It is in the past. We are alive and he isn't, so come to bed. You know damn well I've been wanting you for hours.'

She made no answer. She stood there hugging herself as if in pain. She had a strange, stunned look both on her face and in her eyes, a look which told him that something else was troubling her. Whatever it was, he was not interested. He seized her impatiently and pulled her towards the bed, saying he had had enough of this nonsense.

She wrenched free.

'Don't touch me!'

'By God, I will. I didn't invite you to Kingsmere for *your* pleasure. I can't make love the way I really enjoy in that house of yours, with your cousin in the room above and servants who could overhear as well. No doubt Deborah has heard sounds from time to time already, but compared with . . .' His patience snapped. *'Why do you think I chose this room?* Because my own is too close to others. Here I can do things I want to do. I can whip you if I choose. Many women enjoy being whipped. And there are other ways . . . Do you imagine I am content with what is regarded as normal lovemaking or conventional passion, however ardent? My dear Dulcima, you have greater potential. That body of yours could take a hell of a lot from a man, and, as I say, there are all sorts of ways . . . You would get used to them . . . even enjoy them.'

'*No!*'

He struck her. Once across the face, and then again. She cried out in pain and then began to sob; hard, dry, racking sobs accompanied by words torn from her throat. 'Don't you dare hurt our child! Don't dare do anything to me which could damage him! *I warn you, Justin, I warn you* . . .'

His hand dropped. His pale eyes stared. 'What did you say?'

'I am having a child. Yours. Justin, I beg of you – whatever goaded you into this terrible mood, don't make me lose my baby by brutalising me.'

He walked away from her. Turned. Looked back. 'You expect me to believe this?'

'Yes.'

'Well, I don't.'

'It is true.'

'How long?'

'You mean before it is born?'

'Of course not.'

'Oh. Two months.'

He laughed. 'That's too early to be sure.'

'It isn't.'

'Well, it is early enough to get rid of it. And don't they say that three months is the most likely time for a mis-carriage?'

'Oh, no! Not you, too!'

'What do you mean – me, too? Have you tried fobbing this tale off on some other man, who said the same thing?'

'How could I? You know there has been no one else since I fell in love with you.' She took a deep breath. 'It was . . . your father.'

This time he laughed louder and longer. 'The old devil! Got you with child, eh, and made you get rid of it? Bloody dark horse, my father. He evidently had more sense than I thought. Well, darling Dulcima, since you've been through it once, you can't mind going through it again.'

'I do mind. And I won't.'

'If my father was able to persuade you, why not I?'

'I am older now. My will is stronger. I wanted his child as passionately as I want this one, and this time I won't be cheated out of it. Besides, you have told me many a time that you wanted an heir.'

'You surely can't expect me to marry you!'

'Why not? The child is yours.'

'So you say – but don't try slapping a paternity suit on to *me*.'

Stunned into silence, she looked at him for a long, hard moment, then said contemptuously, 'I wouldn't even want to.'

'Good. I have no intention of being trapped by a card-sharping strumpet.'

Her knees gave way. She sank into the rug in front of the fire. The flames lit up her blanched face. He felt no pity.

He walked to the door, opened it, looked back, and said, 'A carriage will be put at your disposal first thing tomorrow morning. I will leave orders for breakfast to be sent to you here at seven. The carriage will get you to the station in time for the nine-o'clock train.'

9

She uttered no word for three days. The house in Hanover Square became silent as the grave. Garfield walked around tight-lipped with anxiety, her eyes swollen with tears.

'I knew it,' she declared to Deborah after they had finally reached home and Garfield had put Dulcima to bed while Deborah hurried for a doctor. 'I knew he was going to hurt her. I had a premonition about it, right from the beginning.'

'Lord Ashleigh? But he loves her!'

'That kind only loves himself, the bastard. And I make no apologies for my language, miss.'

They were standing outside Dulcima's bedroom door. The doctor had left after diagnosing severe shock, administering a sedative, and ordering complete rest and quiet. His concern had been greater when Garfield told him her mistress was expecting a child.

'It's early days yet, sir, and no one knows about it in this house, except me.' Her glance had darted to Deborah's startled face, feeling triumph even at a moment like this.

'What about her husband?' the doctor had asked.

Their silence told him there was no husband, and he said nothing more until he had examined her and pronounced that all was well physically, but her condition demanded the greatest care. 'Is it her first pregnancy?'

'Yes, sir. Well . . . not exactly.'

'You mean an earlier miscarriage? How long ago?'

'Fifteen years,' Garfield admitted, knowing that for her mistress's sake the man had to be given the facts. She added reluctantly, 'She was twenty then, and it weren't exactly a miscarriage, sir.'

She looked at Deborah again, standing on the other side of the bed with Dulcima's hands in both of hers. She knows what I mean, thought Garfield, and she's shocked, but she isn't sitting in judgment . . . *and* she'd better not! To Garfield, 'that Miss Yorke' was still on probation.

'An abortion,' the doctor said impassively, making no comment on the legality of it, 'and now she is in her mid-thirties. She must take the greatest care. Coupled with that, and now severe shock of some kind, her condition demands it.'

'We will both take care of her,' Deborah said before Garfield had a chance to speak again.

Well, at least she includes me, the woman thought grudgingly, though she would have liked to impress on the doctor that she and she alone would nurse her mistress.

Now Dulcima slept, and they were alone.

'*How* did he hurt her?' Deborah demanded, feeling anger raging up.

'God alone knows, miss, but my guess is that he just didn't want to know about it. The child, I mean. Told her to get out and stay out, I'll wager. And there she was, the poor love, curled up on the hearth rug when I went along with her breakfast tray, and the fire dead and the bed not even slept in. She'd dragged off the quilt and wrapped it around her, and there she lay, waiting for daylight. I wasn't half shaken, I can tell you. And that wasn't the first surprise, either. "You have to serve your mistress's breakfast at seven sharp," that uppish housekeeper told me when the servants all came down at six. "That's an order from above," she said, and I didn't like her tone either.

Yours was sent along at seven too, wasn't it, miss?'

Deborah nodded. The early arrival of breakfast had not struck her as odd. People rose early in the country, as she knew from her own upbringing. The surprise had therefore not been on her part, but the maid's. Finding the door locked, she had to knock for admittance.

Precisely why she had locked her door, Deborah had no idea. Perhaps the isolation of her room had given her a feeling of vulnerability. At some time during the night she had even imagined that the knob turned slowly and that pressure was being exerted against the solid wood. In the cold light of day she had dismissed the idea as fanciful, until she saw the note pushed beneath the door and concealed it in her hand as she admitted the maid.

Why lock me out, Miss Yorke? You deny me the opportunity to say good-bye. Your cousin leaves in the morning, and to spare you the embarrassment of being questioned by inquisitive fellow guests, you, alas, must go with her. But we will meet again someday. I am resolved upon that.

Ashleigh

Never, she vowed now. Never will our paths cross again if *I* can help it.

One pleasant thing had happened before they left. She had been standing beside the carriage, waiting for Dulcima, when Simon Davidson came riding by, heading for the stables.

At sight of her, he had reined, his glance taking in the waiting carriage and her basket trunk being hoisted on to the back.

'You are not leaving, Miss Yorke?'

'I am afraid so, Mr Davidson. A sudden call back to London.'

'Delia will be disappointed. She has taken a great fancy to you.'

'Say good-bye to her for me.'

'Not good-bye. I hope we may both see you again in London.'

'So you intend to take your daughter away from here?'

'More than ever. And soon. She will return with me tomorrow.' Then he had added, 'I am glad you are leaving, too. There is no place here for either you or me, Miss Yorke.'

That was the last she saw of him, and the last she would ever see of him, no doubt.

She could not understand why a man so unprepossessing in appearance should stamp himself on her mind so vividly, but she knew she would remember his every feature, the scar on his cheek, the almost ugly face. Nature had not endowed this man with looks, but it would be a long time before she could forget him. The thought of never seeing him again left her feeling strangely bereft.

It was Garfield who forced Dulcima to take an interest in life once more.

'What are you trying to do?' she demanded when, yet again, her mistress pushed food away. 'Get rid of that child? And there was I believing you wanted it!'

Slowly, then, the broth was sipped. Slowly, colour returned. On the fourth day, Dulcima sat up of her own free will. 'I want to see Deborah.'

They were the first words she had spoken, and though they were not the words Garfield wanted to hear, she fetched Deborah promptly and closed the bedroom door on the pair of them.

'We must talk,' Dulcima said.

'Not yet. The doctor says you must rest.'

'I have rested enough. I have thought about myself enough. In fact, I have thought of nothing else, lying here in self-martyrdom. Now I must think about the future. I cannot escape it, nor intend to.'

'There is plenty of time —'

'How can one be sure? In any case, before long I will be unable to run the card salon for a while, so you will have to take over.'

'*I?* But I couldn't.'

'Dillon will help. He is part of the enterprise. That door is properly shut, I hope? I know Garfield has always had her suspicions, but I don't want to confirm them.'

'She is devoted to you and would never listen at keyholes.'

'You champion her more than she champions you. Poor Garfield, she has been jealous of you all along, but she will thaw in time. Dillon she will never like, nor trust. Many a time she has hinted at her disapproval of the man, and I know she can't understand why I employed him in the first place, never having had a butler. It was necessary, I said, to impress the card-playing patrons, and to supervise refreshments. That is still his official role.'

'Don't talk now. Remember the doctor's advice.'

Dulcima's old spirit came flashing back. 'To hell with the doctor's advice! I have had enough of that, lying here brooding, grieving, wanting to die, railing against fate when I have no one but myself to blame for every twist and turn of it. And I actually believed I had plenty of common sense! I prided myself on it, and now I realise I have never possessed a grain. Today,' she finished resolutely, 'all that is at an end. I shall get up. And you, Deborah, my love, must learn to play baccarat.'

For weeks Deborah was tutored. She grasped the rudiments of the game, but had no great liking for it.

'I haven't your flair for cards, Dulcima.'

'You will master it, my dear. You will have to.'

'Have to? You mean it is essential to run this card

salon?'

'Absolutely. It is my only means of livelihood. I can't become a Gaiety Girl again – not at my age, darling!' The trilling laughter was back, but forced. 'Now, let's go through it once more. All you have to remember is that baccarat is really very simple, not unlike chemin de fer except that the bank is held by us – either you or me, whichever of us is presiding for the evening – or else it is auctioned to the highest bidder, in which case he pays a percentage of winnings as commission. I demand ten per cent, to undercut other gaming rooms, which demand more, but for us to hold the bank is much more profitable, for reasons I will tell you. Now, deal again, my love. Three hands only, remember. One to the players on the left, one to the players on the right, and one to yourself as banker. That's right – one card only first, face down, and remember that the players to your left and to your right are playing on behalf of all those on their side of the table. They pool their stakes to equal the amount put up by the bank, but don't forget that a player may call *"banco"* and bet against the bank single-handed. Only the clever and confident ones do that, so they are the ones to beware of. But you will be safe so long as you keep an eye open for the cards Dillon has had treated, and when holding the bank, you are in a position to spot them quickly.'

'Treated?'

'Marked, my love.'

'You mean . . . cheating?'

'Don't call it that, darling. Such an ugly word! One has to be astute in this business, as in any other.'

'Being astute isn't the same as swindling!'

'Oh, yes, it is. As much sharp practice goes on in the world of commerce as in my own line of work. I don't run a card salon for either charity or pleasure. The expenses are too great, and I have to safeguard against losses in whatever way I can. There *is* no other way in the gaming world.'

Deborah was too shocked to answer. To her, fraud was fraud, no matter what name you called it by.

Dulcima sighed. 'I see you disapprove. That is tiresome of you, and not a little unfair. If I had not used my head and found an able man like Dillon to help me, I could never have afforded to rescue you from a lifetime of drudgery in that dreary vicarage, and more besides, if my judgment of your father's successor was right, which I am convinced it was. I have never demanded gratitude from you, but I am surely entitled to your loyalty?'

The reproach went home. It was family loyalty that had brought Dulcima hurrying to Brighton to befriend her niece.

'I do want to help you, Dulcima, but I was always taught —'

'I know what you were taught, darling, but does that give you the right to sit in judgment on me?'

'I'm not, I'm not!'

'Nevertheless, you are shocked.' Dulcima held out a pleading hand. 'Help me, Deborah, I beg of you. It will be for only a short time, and I am not asking you to participate in marking the cards. Dillon takes care of all that. Please, don't turn your back when I need you most.'

In the face of such pleading, Deborah was helpless. 'You are asking me to go against all my principles,' she said unhappily.

'We all have to go against our principles at some time in our lives, and often to a far greater degree than pitting our wits against people who wouldn't hesitate to defraud *us* if they could. Do you imagine the players who come here don't pull a trick or two if they can get away with it? I even allow them to, once in a while.' Dulcima moved impatiently. 'Darling, you must learn to bend your conscience a little, and remember that if we didn't beat tricksters at their own game, we would be out of business in no time. It is all a question of self-defence, don't you see?'

She made it sound so convincing that Deborah was lost for an answer, and Dulcima continued in a tone which was understanding but sad, 'You are hating the whole business, aren't you, my love? But for my sake, for both our sakes, for the sake of my child, I beg you to go along with me. After all, it will be for a very short time, and after that you need never enter the card room again, I promise.'

Deborah was cornered, though every instinct urged her to refuse. At the same time, instincts equally strong reminded her that she owed a profound debt to her aunt and there was no other way in which she could repay it.

'I will try,' she said wretchedly, 'though I doubt if I shall be any good at it. I am more likely to make a mess of things. And if players spot the cards . . .'

With a sigh of relief, Dulcima assured her that no one had ever done so, nor was ever likely to. 'Detection is impossible. Dillon sees to that. He was once a master printer, and though he can no longer ply his trade, for reasons I don't investigate, he has useful connections. He has his own code printed at source – a minute variation in the design on the back of certain cards, a mere speck or a fleck in the centre of a twirl or a whirl, which only someone looking for it could detect. Many is the time I have auctioned the bank and watched the player deal from one of Dillon's decks without the slightest suspicion. Delicious! I enjoy those moments immensely, particularly when the important cards appear, face down, at the mouth of the *sabot*, and only I, and Dillon standing by, can detect them because we know what to look for. Marked cards are usually done by hand and therefore risky, but a minute variation in the actual printing is never detected, nor would anyone imagine it could be done. I swear it is infallible. And of course all packs arrive freshly sealed and wrapped to comply with the rule that only new and unopened decks must be used for every game as a guarantee that they have not been tampered with, and opened only in the presence of all the players. If anyone did suspect that anything was . . . unorthodox, shall we say? – they would have a hard time proving it.'

For a fleeting moment Deborah thought she detected a shadow across her aunt's face, like a reflection of remembered pain, but if so, it was hastily dismissed. Nor could she know that it was caused by the echo of Justin Ashleigh's voice calling Dulcima a card-sharping strumpet.

For weeks the initiation dominated Deborah's life. In her sleep the terms *la grande* and *la petite* haunted her – as did Dillon's face when he stood behind Dulcima's chair during occasional lessons, his eyes studying Deborah and summing her up with obvious doubt. He viewed her as a risk, and not without justification, for she floundered helplessly for the most part, her aunt's determination alone pulling her through.

'You will have to hold the fort only while I have my baby, and Dillon will support you. He will even hold the bank for you when necessary, as he does for me sometimes. Visitors accept him as my deputy, so they will accept him as yours. You will help my cousin in every way, won't you, Dillon?'

'Indeed I will, madam.'

He spoke deferentially, but Deborah knew his support was for his employer, not for her country cousin. For Dulcima, the man would do anything, but if things went wrong, would he be so loyal to anyone else?

During these weeks Dulcima drove herself with feverish energy, avoiding idleness because she was afraid of it and dismissing Garfield's insistence upon rest.

'I rest enough when asleep,' she declared, not revealing

that she slept very little and dreaded the long hours of wakefulness, when memory took over. At such moments her whole life seemed to parade before her: her childhood with her elder sister, who had indulged and petted her because the arrival of a new baby in the family was a wonder and a delight to an only child who had comforted herself with dolls; her indulgent mother and father, to whom she had been born at an age when they no longer had the patience of younger parents and let her have her own way because it was easier than trying to exercise parental control; the loneliness of the house when Sarah had left it to marry that sanctimonious clergyman because her parents considered it a good, safe match for a young woman who, at twenty-six, was obviously going to remain an old maid otherwise; the restlessness of adolescence, the longing to escape from stifling respectability, the fear of following in Sarah's footsteps and marrying some dull man who would bore her for the rest of her life.

Inevitability had stretched ahead like a long and dreary road, enlivened only by the attentions of local boys, on most of whom her parents frowned. 'You will marry some nice respectable man one day, as Sarah has done. Meanwhile, you must not demean yourself by heeding the attentions of boys who dare to ogle you in the street.'

Little did they know that she not only heeded such attentions, but encouraged them, because she enjoyed flirting and could see no harm in it, but quite soon the distinction of being the prettiest and most pursued girl in the neighbourhood began to pall, and being a dutiful daughter palled too. She wanted wider horizons and a more exciting life. The prospect of remaining within the narrow confines of her present existence, waiting only for the arrival of a suitor of whom her parents would approve and she would undoubtedly dislike, became unbearable. So she ran away.

Only now, when she was about to become a mother

herself, did she realise the grief she must have caused to the quiet woman who had borne her when close to middle age. Undoubtedly her mother had found her too boisterous to control, and her father too recalcitrant to understand, but they had loved her. They had done their duty by her always, as her father's letter of reproach, when she let them know her whereabouts, stressed heavily.

We are appalled to hear what you have become – a daughter of ours, on the stage! You have been an anxiety to us always, Dulcima, but, as our son-in-law pointed out when you dealt us that mortal blow by running away from home, we all have our crosses to bear, and you, alas, are ours . . .

It did nothing to make her want to return, despite pangs of guilt. She was a Gaiety Girl by then, earning her own living and enjoying it, and although neither Sarah nor anyone else had ever asked how she became one, they would have been surprised to learn that it was by no dubious or immoral route.

The story about staying with an old school friend, which she had told Sarah when saying good-bye, had been a necessary cover-up to allay anxiety. 'No, I won't tell you her name, so you can truthfully say you don't know it when Mamma and Papa, and that husband of yours, press you. I don't want anyone chasing after me. I promise to write when I am settled, and in the meantime you are not to worry. But I cannot go without saying good-bye to you, of all people, dear Sarah.'

She could remember, even now, the distress in her sister's gentle eyes. 'Take care of yourself, Dulcima, I beg you, take care of yourself!'

She had taken care of herself very well, going straight to London and thence by cab to the stage door of the Gaiety Theatre, sitting agog on the edge of the seat as the vehicle bowled along the Strand, and catching her breath when the theatre came into sight on its prominent corner. Never for a moment had she felt either doubt or apprehension, for she had always met life head-on and unafraid. Presenting herself at the stage door had been an exciting adventure, holding no terrors or doubts of success.

All she had to do, she believed, was to ask for the stage manager and say she had come to be a Gaiety Girl. She had heard of stage managers and presumed they must be very important and influential: only later did she learn that they were only one step above the assistant stage manager, and by no means so important as stage director or producer.

'They're not casting at the moment,' grunted the stage doorman, returning to his study of *The Racing Times*.

'Casting?'

'Booking arteests, miss. Show's full an' runnin' well.'

'But surely they could add one extra young lady? I wouldn't mind coming on last of all, at the tail end of the line, really I wouldn't. For a start, that is. You see, I have made up my mind to be a Gaiety Girl, and a Gaiety Girl I shall be.'

'Come back another day, ducks, but not for a long time yet.'

It was not in her nature to acknowledge defeat, so she ignored the man and pushed her way through some swing doors into a long stone passage, deaf to his ineffective shouts. The passage led directly to the stage, where she tripped over something in the gloom of the wings. Ahead of her the backs of scenery rose like a great wall, beyond which lights shone and music swelled and voices sang. It was like entering another world, and after steadying herself, she stood still, half-blinded, half-dazzled, and a man walking by, clad in top hat and tails and carrying an ebony stick with a silver knob, paused and said, 'Not hurt, are you, dear? Angle props can be the very devil, but without them the flats would fall down.'

Her eyes were becoming accustomed to the half-light backstage; she could even see that he wore make-up, and never having seen a man wearing make-up before, she found it both grotesque and fascinating.

'Are you an *actor?*' she breathed.

He answered with a smile, 'I try to be, dear, but mostly I sing and dance.'

'So do I! In fact, that's why I am here. I have come to be a Gaiety Girl.'

'Have you, now?' He sounded amused, but not unkind and certainly not dismissive like the stage doorman. 'What experience have you had?'

'None, so far, but I shall get it here. My sister says I have never stopped singing and dancing from the time I heard my first tune.'

The gentle amusement increased. 'I can imagine it.'

'So if you would please direct me to the stage manager?'

'He's over there, sitting in the prompt corner with the cue copy, but he'll be no use to you. *I* will, so don't go away —'

'Mr Loomis, sir, you're on!'

Billy Loomis, singing and tap-dancing and wise-cracking his way into the hearts of Gaiety audiences, had taken her under his wing from that moment. Star of the show, and, at that time, indispensable to it, he was powerful enough to insist on her being put on the payroll whilst being coached for the chorus. Only years later did she find out that until she was ready to join on the end of the line, the two pounds a week she received had come out of his own pocket.

He had even taken her back to his lodgings that night, and given her the couch in his sitting room.

'No need to fear molestation from me, dear. I'm no ladies' man — if you know what I mean. No — I can see you don't. You *are* a blessed innocent, aren't you? Never mind, dear, it only means that your honour won't be threatened by the likes of me.'

Dear, kind Billy Loomis, who sank into obscurity as rapidly as he had risen, when scandal of the Oscar Wilde kind banished him from public grace. It had been her turn to lend a helping hand then, and they had remained friends until he died. Long before that, Charles Ashleigh had come into her life, and taken charge of it, and loved her with the generosity of his kind heart.

But not enough to let her bear a child of Ashleigh blood.

Why, Charles? Were you afraid it would turn out to be like Justin — cruel and callous? But no child you and I produced could ever have been like that, and I shall take good care that his child won't be. I shall love it, and bring it up properly, and try to imagine it is yours. And if it is a son, I shall call him Charles.

In that way she might eventually cease thinking about Justin Ashleigh's sadistic treatment and the humiliation of her dismissal from his home.

The child was born prematurely, a seven-month baby who came into the world with difficulty and drained its mother of life. When the battle was done, Garfield, weeping, watched the midwife lay it beside the beautiful exhausted face, and Deborah, stooping over her, said softly, 'You have a son, Dulcima — a wonderful handsome son.'

The tired eyes tried to open, and failed, but the lips which had curved so exquisitely in happiness scarcely moved as she murmured the child's name.

Much later, Deborah managed to say to Garfield, 'I heard what she was trying to say. Charles. That must be the name she wanted for the child, so that is the name he will be given.'

Garfield nodded mutely.

After a while, Deborah spoke again. 'He — the baby — is my only living relative. I will look after him and bring him up.'

The woman stared. 'You can't do that on your own, miss.'

'Why not? Dulcima would have done so.'

'With me to help her.'

'And I? Would you help me? I know how you feel towards me, but perhaps, in time, you will feel differently. Meanwhile, for her sake, would you try?'

Garfield was silent. She had not anticipated this. Through a haze of grief she had clung to one thought — that she and she alone would take Dulcima Howard's child and look after it. She would work for it and care for it, for her sake — her adoredMiss Dulcima, her treasure. But now Deborah Yorke was claiming the child, and what she said was true — it *was* related to her, so she had every right. Garfield straightened her shoulders. 'Very well. But only for her sake.'

'Thank you. I am grateful.'

'No need for that. I won't be doing it for you, remember.'

'So long as you do it, that doesn't matter. Only the child matters, but there must be no antagonism between us or he will sense it as he grows up, and that would be bad.'

'One thing I'd like to ask, miss. Are you going to let the father know of his birth?'

'Never,' Deborah answered vehemently. In the weeks prior to Dulcima's death she had grown very close to her aunt and had glimpsed the depth of pain the man had inflicted. Bit by bit, in moments when Dulcima found it possible to talk about that night, Deborah had collected fragments to piece together into one distressing whole, and as a result she hated Justin Ashleigh and knew that if it ever came within her power to strike back at the man, she would do so.

And never would his son come within his influence or learn the truth about his parentage. If he asked questions, as he undoubtedly would when he was old enough to become curious, she would invent a convincing story to satisfy him; there was time enough to think about that.

Meanwhile, she had to be a mother to this child and give him all the love and protection that warmhearted Dulcima would have given him. And he would learn how courageous and lovely his mother had been, of her generosity and gaiety, her love of living, her beauty and wit. He must know the true Dulcima as she had known her, and be proud of her, as she was.

Deborah did not delude herself that the task would be easy. Bringing up another woman's son was a heavy responsibility, but fate had placed it upon her and, like Dulcima, she would shirk nothing.

She realised then that Garfield had spoken.

'I'm sorry.' She jerked herself back to the present. 'You were saying . . .?'

'That I'm glad you're not going to tell Lord Ashleigh. Like as not he'd have a change of mind if he saw the child. Couldn't deny it was his then, could he? Not with those eyes.'

TWO
Deborah

10

The letter was concealed in Dulcima's jewel case, and addressed to her niece.

> I beg you, Deborah, if anything should happen to me, take care of my child. All I have will of course be his (I know in my heart it will be a son), but I want you to take whatever clothes or jewels or anything else you may fancy, in remembrance of me . . .

There the writing tailed off, as if the hand were too tired to continue, or her mind too distressed, and since it was penned on Kingsmere's embossed notepaper, Deborah guessed the exact time and place in which her aunt had been driven to write it. Where else but the bedroom she had later described in moments of painful recollection? ' . . . a most beautiful room; his father's, of course. He was a great collector, a lover of antiques. Of all the pieces, I think the Queen Anne escritoire was the most lovely . . .'

Deborah knew instinctively that Dulcima had dragged herself to that escritoire to pour out her pathetic plea before curling up on the floor to await the cold light of dawn; writing when her spirits were at their lowest ebb, her stunned mind driven by fear, then thrusting the letter out of sight — shocked that she could even imagine her life ending.

Deborah found it when going through her aunt's personal things sometime later. The day was also memorable for another reason. Simon Davidson called.

'I have been wondering how you were and what you intend to do.'

She hid her pleasure at seeing him after all these months.

'Do? Carry on as usual, running this house and the card salon, and looking after the child with Garfield's help. You have heard of his birth, of course?'

Simon nodded. The whole of London had heard of his birth, and the whole country of Dulcima Howard's death, for the passing of so famous a beauty could not be overlooked by the national press.

'Isn't that a big undertaking for a young woman of your age?'

'Why? Many young women of my age are mothers.'

'Usually with husbands to care for them.'

'I have not only Garfield to help me, but also staff — though I doubt if I shall be able to keep all of them, nor if I really want to. I know how to manage a large house, but am not accustomed to handling servants other than a daily woman. In fact, I think I would rather clean and cook than try to run a professional card salon. But as to that, I really have no choice. I have no income of my own, and, as yet, no knowledge of any other financial source Dulcima may have had that could be used to support her child.'

She closed the lid of her aunt's bureau, hiding papers she had found thrust haphazardly into pigeonholes. Alarmingly, all appeared to be unpaid bills. Others had been discovered in various drawers, and even in discarded reticules, and though Dulcima's current account at the bank was not overdrawn, the balance was quite in-adequate to meet them, nor was there a deposit account or any other form of investment. It also appeared that at no time had she employed a solicitor or made a will, which indicated that apart from material possessions she had nothing else to bequeath, and since she had admitted that gaming was her sole source of income, Deborah's summing up of the situation appeared to be right. But none of this was she prepared to reveal to anyone yet, not even to this sympathetic man who now enquired whether he could help in any way.

'Yes, Mr Davidson. Bring your daughter to see me.'

'I will be glad to.'

His wife had surrendered the child with the minimum of fuss, apart from making a great display of maternal affection when saying good-bye. Very shortly afterwards she had startled everyone by departing for the Middle East. 'I have always wanted to see immortal Petra, "the rose-red city half as old as time". ' To the press she had trotted out the cliché as if she had just coined it herself. 'Other women before me have proved that my sex can penetrate regions hitherto regarded as too dangerous for them. I follow in their footsteps, unafraid!' She spoke as if she were answering a clarion call.

Poor Caroline – what was she out to prove now, and did she really imagine that hiring Arab servants and professional guides would prove to be an open sesame to a region into which only groups of armed explorers could still penetrate, and where the local inhabitants, for many years after Burckhardt discovered Petra, were so unfriendly that they murdered the first members of the Arab Legion stationed at the police post, in the village of Elji, to protect travellers? Even now the Bedu on the outskirts of Petra, and the Eljyites from Elji, considered this region their exclusive territory and were so suspicious of foreigners that they tried to discourage their visits by intimidation and force. Simon had shared the experience with members of an archaeological expedition before the start of the Boer War, and it had made little difference that the Anglo-French members of the group had been accompanied by Palestinian officials.

Somehow Caroline had to be deflected from her course, but he knew well enough that any verbal argument would only set her heart more firmly on this latest whim. It was wiser to let her depart and, without her knowledge, contact an influential member of the Turkish government at Al Salt, who controlled Palestinian excavations, ensuring that guides be provided to take her only to places like Jerash and Madaba, but that no aid be granted for more remote and as yet more uncertain regions. This he had done, knowing she would dislike being thwarted, but that against adamant Arab courtesy all her tempestuous protests and pleadings would avail her nothing. He owed protection to the mother of his child, but Caroline would never suspect who had organised it.

He became aware that Deborah was offering tea, which he accepted only because he wanted to remain. Somehow he had never been able to forget this quiet young woman whose face oddly belied its impression of passivity. Beneath her self-control he sensed an impassioned will, and, by God, he thought, she was going to need it now, plunged into a life she had obviously not been brought up to. There was still a basic lack of sophistication about her, of which only someone so perceptive as he would be aware. To his discerning eye it was not concealed by her modish clothes, all of which bore the hallmark of Dulcima Howard's taste.

Against his will, he was intrigued by Deborah Yorke, and anxious about her future under the pressure of responsibilities from which many another young woman would have fled. But he had to go carefully, afraid that she might regard any offer of help as an intrusion, but also because he had no desire to become too closely involved with her. It was for Delia's sake that he was here, or so his mind insisted, and in Delia's life that he wanted this young woman to be included, because the child had taken a great fancy to her. Anything beyond that, he would not acknowledge.

So he accepted the tea, fully prepared not to remain for long, once a further meeting with his daughter had been arranged.

'She is attending a girls' school in Kensington and settling in well,' he said, 'though I fear her taste in literature is a little more advanced than those in her class, and her aptitude for arithmetic and kindred subjects sadly behind. I am helping her to pull up in that respect, but she is no orthodox schoolgirl.'

'Do you want her to be? Delia struck me as highly individual, and since you are highly individual yourself, Mr Davidson, that should please you.'

He was surprised by such direct speech from one whom he had judged to be reticent, but all along he had suspected that much of this young woman's docility was a façade, an outer veneer imposed by a lifetime of strict and conventional upbringing. So he smiled and said, 'It does please me, of course. I want Delia to think for herself, to be a person in her own right.'

'No one will ever be able to prevent that. It is part of her nature.'

'You sum up my daughter well, and yet you have seen little of her.'

'Enough to make me want to see more, so shall we say four o'clock on Sunday, Mr Davidson, again for tea? That is the only day of the week I am likely to have to myself, for I must reopen the card salon as soon as possible, which means six nights a week and busy hours in between. And thank you for calling. It was kind of you to remember me. Thank you also for the letter of sympathy you sent.'

'You must have received a great many.'

'I did indeed, from Dulcima's admirers up and down the country.'

'Then I am surprised you noticed mine.'

'Naturally, I read them all, but I am glad to have this

opportunity to thank you personally instead of by the routine acknowledgement.'

Stilted, polite conversation which seemed to form a barrier between them, rather than a bond. But it was a beginning. And of course it was important only for Delia's sake, because she had taken a liking to the young woman.

Garfield's sharp eyes spotted the emeralds at once. Her dear Dulcima's necklace round the throat of a young woman who did not belong, and never would belong, in 20 Hanover Square! She was outraged. How dare the chit help herself to her darling's jewels, presents from the late Lord Ashleigh himself? But everything was awry in this household now. It wasn't the same place, nor ever would be. The staff, once devoted to the mistress of the house, were also watching the new one with a wary eye, a fact which gave Garfield satisfaction and, for the first time, even a feeling of comradeship with them — except with Dillon, whose patronage was rapidly becoming arrogance, as if at any moment he intended to take over the reins and heaven help anyone who got in his way.

Meanwhile, Garfield had more to worry her head about than an unlikeable butler; there was the mite upstairs, bless his angelic little heart, on whom she was already lavishing possessive devotion and bitterly resenting any intrusion from Deborah Yorke.

It wouldn't be so bad, the woman fretted, if the young woman kept away from the nursery, but she didn't. She visited there as often as possible, and even insisted on alternating the three-hourly feeds — for as a seven-month child he was not yet strong enough to advance to four-hourly. 'I will give him the very early-morning one, so you won't have to rise so soon,' she had said, for all the world as if she were being considerate, when she must know well enough that Garfield thought nothing of rising shortly after dawn. Every morning now she lay awake listening to

Miss Yorke coming upstairs, picking up the baby in the next room, crooning over him, comforting his cries until they were silenced with his avid sucking at his bottle. He was a healthy, hungry child, a happy one too, already smiling, though he was barely a few weeks old.

Garfield remembered his first smile very well indeed, because it had been for that Miss Yorke, who had exclaimed in delight, 'He is smiling, Garfield! Just look at that!' And Garfield had looked, and seen those bright, pale eyes sparkling up into Deborah Yorke's, the baby lips parted in toothless happiness, and she had thought jealously that the wonder of such a moment should have been for her, his mother's devoted slave, not for this upstart from the country who should have the good sense to go back there.

And that wasn't all. Miss Yorke seemed to have taken over the task of bathing him every morning and top-and-tailing him at night. She even left the card salon to change his nappy, give him his final bottle, put him across her shoulder to bring up wind, and hover over his cot until he dropped off to sleep again. 'Dillon is in charge down there, he can manage very well without me,' she would say when Garfield acidly pointed out that she knew well enough how to handle the child.

If you ask me, Garfield thought wryly to herself, she's glad of an excuse to get away from that room. She doesn't belong there, any more than she belongs in this house. And all she wants *me* for is to wheel the darling out in his perambulator and cope with nursery chores – me, a lady's maid! Not that I wouldn't do anything for my dear Dulcima's baby, short of accepting this young woman as his mother, which for two pins I'd like to remind her she is *not*.

And now look at her, wearing the famous emeralds as if they were her own!

Grudgingly Garfield admitted that it was the first time

she had seen Miss Yorke wearing her cousin's jewels, or any jewels at all for that matter. She also grudgingly admitted that the girl looked very lovely in that off-the-shoulder gown of moiré taffeta, so pale a grey that it looked almost silver, against which the emeralds shone brilliantly – a colour combination which Miss Dulcima would have admired. The girl had learned a lot from her beautiful cousin: how to hold herself, how to groom herself, how to make the most of her fine wardrobe.

She also had to admit that Miss Yorke had become very skilful with her hair, ringing changes in style according to what she was wearing; simple coiffures to go with ankle-length dresses by day, more elaborate for sweeping gowns by night. The silver-grey moiré, worn with the obligatory long gloves demanded by a décolleté neckline and Empire puffed sleeves, had a wealth of frills round the base and even more in the train, and although elaborately ornamented with lace, the line and cut simplified the gown into dignity and elegance. This evening she had coiled her hair and bound it, Grecian style, with silver-grey ribbon – simple and unfussy and highly becoming. In fact, so effective was this style that Garfield regarded it with not a little displeasure. Had the girl even sought her advice or opinion, she would have been faintly mollified. Instead, she was annoyed to discover that her services in the matter of hairdressing were totally unneeded.

What was more, the coiffure displayed the emerald necklace and earrings to the fullest advantage. Oh, yes, mused Garfield sullenly, she looks very presentable indeed, I will say that for her, but I wonder what she has done with the rest of my darling's jewels?

The woman would have been shocked to learn that Deborah had been forced to sell them to clear outstanding bills, and that the emeralds would have gone too but for the fact that they were the most valuable of all and something compelled her to hold on to them for the child's sake. They represented capital which he might need one day, and although Dulcima had told her to take whatever she fancied, Deborah had been unable to bring herself to do so, apart from a cameo brooch which somehow seemed to epitomise Dulcima's purity of feature. With that she was more than content. But tonight she had decided to wear the emeralds, not only because the silver moiré was the ideal gown to display them, but for another and more subtle reason.

She wanted to impress Dillon. Not from vanity, but as a means of defence. Increasingly she had sensed the man's watchfulness, his assessment of her appearance and social graces, his criticism of every game of baccarat she presided over. It was as if he were waiting for her to fail, even hoping for it, so that he could step in and take control of the sinking ship. She was afraid of the man, and afraid that he knew it, for she was not yet completely expert at hiding her feelings. She also knew she had angered him by refusing admittance to Justin Ashleigh, a man who played for high stakes that invariably proved profitable to the bank.

Two weeks before the card salon reopened, she had searched Dulcima's cluttered bureau for a list of patrons. All needed to be formally invited by the new hostess, despite the fact that news of the reopening would pass by word of mouth. Instinct warned Deborah to keep out the undesirables, and surely Dulcima had kept records of some kind? But there appeared to be no such list, and her overcrowded address book did not distinguish between gamblers and non-gamblers, or between friends and baccarat acquaintances.

Dillon had found her at the task and politely enquired if there were anything he could do. 'You appear to be look-ing for something, Miss Yorke.'

Not 'madam'. He never called her that, because he did

not regard her as on a par with Dulcima Howard. Nor did the servants, with the exception of Cook, who, to Garfield's surprise, viewed her with something bordering on respect. The remainder addressed her almost sullenly with 'Yes'm' or 'No'm', clearly indicating their inability to accept her in place of their former mistress.

She had created further enmity by reducing the staff by half, including Mrs Crowther, taking over the housekeeper's responsibilities herself, and surprising everyone with her ability not only to supervise a household but also to run it. Household accounts were vetted and found wanting, the departing housekeeper's protests silenced by the production of this evidence, and even Cook's ordering was now carefully examined, the week's bills studied item by item, costs discussed, tradesmen listed and compared. She spent time going round various shops and listing their various prices, then advised Cook to deal with suppliers in the area of the Marylebone High Street instead of ordering from fashionable establishments such as Harrods and Fortnum & Mason. 'Splendid stores, Cook, but too expensive for us. There is an excellent greengrocer in Blandford Street, a good general emporium in Marylebone High Street, and a French butcher in Thayer Street who certainly knows his business. I propose to give all a month's trial.'

No 'I hope you agree, Cook?' A decision was a decision, and because Cook recognised in this young woman someone who knew how to buy, how to order, how to choose the best meat, the best groceries, the best vegetables, the best fruits, and when and when not certain foodstuffs were in season, the woman's immediate reaction changed from rebellion to respect. It was either that or follow others through the door at the foot of the area steps.

Where did she come from, this quiet young woman with a head on her shoulders for the day-to-day business of household management? From a servants' hall in some superior household? Doubtful, thought Cook, but certainly from a home that had taught her wot-was-wot. And of course, Cook now recollected, there had been some talk that she was the daughter of a bishop or suchlike. A bishop's household would surely be well supervised and well run, and a bishop's wife and daughters very knowledgeable about such things, so what was a body to do, but knuckle under? Jobs weren't two a penny these days, and being a cook in Hanover Square wasn't to be sneezed at.

All the same, even Cook knew that things were never going to be the same again. No more lavish entertaining, no more grand dinner parties for rich patrons. Catering had been cut down to cold collations presided over by Dillon, assisted by Bella, the parlourmaid (who had become even more uppish since being chosen to wait upon the gentry). Even so, it all seemed to be working satisfactorily, though no doubt the gentlemen recalled Miss Dulcima's splendid fare to the detriment of Miss Yorke's – apart from the wines, which the new hostess seemed to know little about and therefore relied on Dillon to order as before. That didn't prevent her from keeping a record of the number of bottles consumed, to the butler's chagrin. Dillon was accustomed to helping himself freely from the cellar, and his extravagant former mistress had never even noticed.

There was certainly a new regime in this household, and a stringent one, but perhaps, thought Cook optimisti cally, when things got back to normal and Miss Yorke became as well known and as popular as Dulcima Howard, lavish entertaining would begin again . . .

But pretty as she was, would such a young woman ever become so famous or so pursued? Her face had not been seen on a thousand hoardings, adorned men's clubs from January to December with a more seductive pose each month, been collected as picture postcards by infatuated males, or shocked the matrons of Britain by smiling winsomely above a pair of voluptuous breasts upheld by wasp-waist stays.

Still, give the young lady a chance. She had to feel her way, and perhaps there wasn't so much money as everybody had thought. Things like the elegant carriage and pair had been the first to go, and that seemed significant, since people of quality, and many who were not, maintained such an equipage as a symbol of their social standing.

It was of vital importance to any lady to drive in an elegant turnout, her coachman immaculately uniformed and preferably with a footman mounted behind. Miss Howard, lacking the distinction of a crest or armorial bearings on her carriage door, had had the good taste to do without a footman – a mark of vulgar ambition in untitled folk – but she had never failed to catch the eye on her daily drive along the Ladies' Mile, mainly because of her beauty but also because Briggs, the coachman, kept her landau in immaculate condition, coachwork and brasswork gleaming, and the groom, who slept above the stables, took an equal pride in the high-stepping greys. Alongside Rotten Row she would drive in all her splendour, sweeping round the curve of the Serpentine, then wheeling smartly round and back along the same route, to commence all over again at the start of the Ladies' Mile just within the entrance at Hyde Park Corner.

This fashionable daily parade was a routine with members of the smart set, and it seemed very sad to Cook that young Miss Yorke was not to be part of it. What a to-do there had been in the kitchen when Briggs announced what had happened – the new mistress of 20 Hanover Square selling the carriage and pair, dispensing with himself and the groom, and actually renting out the stables to a jobmaster! Briggs had departed in high dudgeon, only too willing to seek employment with some establishment that was not going down in the world.

Cook, like the rest of the household, kept a wary eye on the new mistress, and none so closely as Dillon when he found her sitting at his late mistress's bureau studying her address book page by page.

He had repeated his question. 'You are looking for something, Miss Yorke?'

'Yes, Dillon. A list of regular patrons. I am sure Miss Howard would have kept one.'

'She did indeed, miss, and placed it in my care. But I am willing to let you take a look at it.'

The note of condescension jarred. Deborah decided to ignore it, just as she was schooling herself to ignore the man's underlying insolence and increasing self-confidence.

'I will do so at once,' she told him.

'For what purpose, may I ask?'

How did one tell a man so impervious to snub that it was none of his business, especially when anything to do with the card salon *was* his business, for without him the place would not survive? All she could do was answer coolly, 'To consider which guests are acceptable and which are not.'

'All guests are acceptable so long as they have money. You can rely on me to know whether they have it or not. They become unacceptable only when they can't meet their losses.'

'Even so, I will see the list immediately, if you please.'

He drew a folded sheet of paper from an inner pocket, holding it out almost casually. 'As you wish, Miss Yorke.'

She had to stretch out a hand to take it, for plainly he had no intention of placing it politely in front of her. She hid her annoyance by remarking, 'Do you actually carry it around with you?'

'Of course, miss. That is a private document, and

private documents are best kept safely on one's person.'

'I commend your diligence,' she replied, goaded by the hint of disdain in his voice and not attempting to restrain a touch of sarcasm in her own. She had little defence against this man, but patronised by him she would not be.

Many names on the list were familiar to her, some as public figures, some as friends of Dulcima, some as regular gamblers whom she had already met, but some were totally unfamiliar to her, and these, she judged, must be spasmodic visitors. There was no way of knowing which were the richest, the most respected, or the most acceptable, but at least one name should be deleted. She dipped a pen into Dulcima's silver inkwell and scored it through heavily.

Over her shoulder, Dillon protested, 'You can't do that, Miss Yorke! You can't cross Lord Ashleigh off!'

'I have already done so, and I am unaccustomed to anyone looking over my shoulder.'

She folded the paper, tucked it in her waistband, and rose with an air of dismissal. 'From now on I will take charge of the list, but thank you for keeping it so carefully, Dillon.'

'But that's *my* property, miss! I wrote the whole thing out, names and addresses and all.'

'For Miss Howard. I am sure she appreciated it as much as I do. I will now be able to refer to it, and to add or remove names whenever I wish, without troubling you.'

The man scowled. He was a handsome fellow, somewhere in his early forties, Deborah judged, and plainly unaccustomed to being thwarted by women. Nevertheless, she recalled how he had been willing to take any amount of scolding from Dulcima because the next moment she would be laughing, treating him almost as an equal – but not quite. In this way she had kept the man on a rein which he very much enjoyed, tantalised and provoked by her, but admiring too, because not only was she beautiful, but she knew how to play baccarat like a real professional. Deborah guessed that working alongside such a woman, in the guise of her butler, had meant a lot to him, and that in his eyes she herself had no such assets to commend her, least of all a skill with cards.

Dillon's attitude worried her increasingly, but she was determined not to be unnerved by it. Winning the battle with him over the elimination of Ashleigh's name from the visitors' list had been the final spark to his animosity, worsened by the fact that she had despatched a polite note to Ashleigh informing him that he would no longer be received at 20 Hanover Square. Dillon had been horrified, telling her bluntly that she must be insane to banish one of their wealthiest clients.

He spoke as if theirs were an equal partnership, and his manner ever since had suggested that it would become a very one-sided partnership eventually, and in his own favour. He seemed to have forgotten the promise he had made to Dulcima, to uphold her cousin. No doubt he felt that promises given during someone's lifetime counted for nothing after they were dead.

Garfield had not been far wrong in concluding that Deborah was glad to escape from the card room during the evening's play. To visit baby Charles was like returning to a safe, happy world from a decidedly threatening one.

Wisely, she had kept a personal check on the financial side, knowing that Dillon did the same. Dulcima had been content to leave all that to him, but because she was incapable of winning the same loyalty from the man, Deborah kept her own records. He was therefore in no position to make the picture appear blacker than it was in order to compel her to surrender the reins. She knew well enough that profits, since Dulcima's day, had taken a downward plunge, but at least she knew by how much and was not prepared to yield to premature defeat, much as she disliked her involvement with the business.

'You auction the bank too often,' Dillon now grumbled as she gave a final inspection to the gaming room prior to the evening's play.

'Perhaps, but at least we earn ten per cent that way.'

'Ten per cent!' He spat the words contemptuously. 'You could make that at least fifty if you spotted the right cards, not only when you have the chance to pick them up, but when others do. That way, you know what they have in their hands.'

'Such tiny marks are hard to detect.'

'Not if your eyes and your wits are sharp. And how would you prefer them to be marked, may I ask? With signs that everyone else can see? We would be out of business overnight that way. From now on, you'd better let me take the bank more often.'

The awful thing was that she knew she would have to. He was not only the better player and the more experienced one, but his brain was quick and cunning. For what reasons had he ceased to be a master printer? she wondered. Dulcima had declared that she preferred not to enquire, which meant she had a shrewd idea, and *that* meant they did not stand investigation. But to know just one thing about Dillon, one thing to his detriment, would be a weapon with which to arm herself against him. Meanwhile, she stuck to her ruling that if Ashleigh ever presented himself at the door of 20 Hanover Square, he would be refused admission.

Dillon remarked sagely, 'If you had any sense, you would aim at being as successful with him as Miss Dulcima was.'

A comment like that indicated Dillon's increasing arrogance, and though she was angered, Deborah's only defence was self-composure, a cool front hiding a deepening unease, and the exercise of authority because she was mistress of the house. She therefore forced a firm note into her voice as she replied, 'Please confine your remarks solely to your duties, Dillon. And Lord Ashleigh's name will never be mentioned again. Do I make myself clear?'

'Very clear.' His voice was sullen, but his glance was bold. 'Miss Dulcima never mentioned it either, after you all came back so quickly from his place in the country. There must have been a reason for that, I thought to myself, and it could only be that child upstairs. It's his, isn't it?'

The man was detestable. Deborah's only retaliation was to check her anger, because she knew he was deliberately trying to provoke it. She turned her back on him and walked from the room, but that only amused him. She heard his quiet laughter following her, and shut the door more sharply than she intended.

Oh, dear God, if only I could get rid of him! If I could put an end to running a business I dislike, earn money some other way . . .

She was halfway across the hall when Dillon followed. 'Miss Yorke . . .'

She walked on, heading for the drawing room, where she always received her guests, but Dillon caught up with her, saying with quiet ferocity, 'You know you haven't a hope in heaven of making a success of things the way your cousin did. Not as a baccarat player. But you have other assets, and if you are wise you'll make use of them, as she did. You look very lovely tonight. That gown and those emeralds become you. You are very handsome and could feather your nest very well indeed if you would melt towards the gentlemen. Charm them, Miss Yorke. Use your feminine wiles. I never knew a woman yet who lacked them. Even the plainest of women has a body, and yours is a fine one. Now, don't slam the drawing-room door in my face!' His foot shot forward, preventing it. She whirled away, cheeks flaming, and he marched into the room after her, seizing one wrist and pulling her round to face him. She raised her free hand to strike him across the face. He caught it, held it, and laughed. 'My word, Miss Yorke, if Ashleigh could see you now, he wouldn't be able to resist you. He liked a spirited woman, I could tell.'

Damn the man's insolence. Damn his familiarity. Damn his arrogant face and scheming brain.

'Get out,' she said, deadly quiet. 'Get back to your duties.'

'And just what are my duties, Miss Yorke? Rescuing you from financial disaster? You're heading that way, and you know it, so you're not in a position to order me around any longer. You and I had better have a talk, which means *I* talk and *you* listen. This whole organisation now depends on me. You are no card player and no gambler. Miss Dulcima was both. Her kind isn't born twice, and though you may look like her in some ways, there the resemblance ends. So you'd better let me take the reins, and for the time being, I'll be generous. A half share of the profits. An equal partnership until things improve, then we'll talk again. If you don't agree, you may as well sell this house and get out. Only that way are you going to keep your head above water. All these economies you've been making speak for themselves. And they're not helping all that much, I can tell.'

'The house isn't mine to sell.' In her confusion, she spoke without thought, then regretted revealing even that much to the man.

He answered reflectively, 'Of course – I should have guessed. Miss Dulcima's child would inherit. But you? What did she leave you?'

She couldn't believe this was happening, or that the situation had deteriorated so much that this man, an employee, was now in a position to be so personal and contemptuous. But when failure stared a person in the face, wasn't the whole world contemptuous?

'My cousin's bequests are no concern of yours,' she said icily.

He shrugged. 'Well, if you can't sell the house – though many a guardian or relative would have no compunction about doing so *and* pocketing the proceeds – you'd best make the most of it. You could use the place to good advantage. There are plenty of rooms and plenty of ways, and the first is to welcome men as rich as Ashleigh.'

She checked a stinging reply, and only a man so thick-skinned could have missed the intimidating note in her voice as she retorted, 'I hear the front doorbell. The first visitor has arrived. They will expect to be admitted by the butler – and that is your position in this household.'

But stand up to him as she might, uncertainty possessed her. His voice, drifting back to her from the hall as he courteously greeted the arrivals, was a jarring reminder that the man had a hold on her. If he chose, he could expose her as a fraud and a cheat, and at the same time protect himself, for he would certainly deny allegations of being party to any deception.

'I am merely the butler here,' he would say. 'How could a butler have any knowledge of his mistress's affairs? My duties are to serve the wines and supervise the buffet. Deputising for Miss Yorke at the card table is a duty I perform only to oblige her. She purchases the cards herself. From what source, I have no idea. I had no suspicion that deception was being practised. How could I, a mere household servant? Any private arrangement Miss Yorke has made with a supplier is her own secret. I was puzzled when I noticed those slight discrepancies in the design on the backs of certain cards, and thought attention should be drawn to them. So I drew it.'

She would put nothing past him. The man could wriggle out of incrimination and land her into it as smoothly as he was now welcoming guests.

Standing before the fire beneath the portrait of Dulcima painted by Sargent at the height of her loveliness, Deborah placed her arms on the mantelshelf and rested her head upon them, eyes closed. A nagging headache threatened. She was tired before the evening began. Thank God, tomorrow was Sunday, the one day of the week she really looked forward to, because it meant seeing Delia. Simon would bring her after lunch and call for her at the end of the afternoon. Sometimes he stayed for tea, but recently he had made work an excuse. New exhibits had arrived and Sunday gave him the opportunity to unpack them without interruption, or a new catalogue was being prepared and the printers were waiting for the first pages, or arrears of correspondence demanded attention. Running a museum was apparently a seven-day-week occupation. But soon she began to feel that the excuses were devised in order to avoid her.

For a time, that hurt; then common sense told her it was better that way, for her own sake. It was never wise for an unmarried girl to become interested in a married man, even one who saw so little of his wife. Caroline Davidson was *there*, in the background all the time, part of his life, mother of Delia. She might be vain, selfish, even unfaithful, but the fact remained that she was Mrs Simon Davidson and could walk back into their lives at any moment she chose.

Never had this reminder come to Deborah so sharply than at one particular moment when Simon had taken hold of her hand, Delia's in the other, to guide them across Marylebone Road to the York Gate entrance of Regent's Park. The touch of palm against palm, flesh against flesh, had sent an excitement through her which he had surely felt too, for he had dropped her hand as soon as they reached the other side and taken good care not to touch her again. She had known instinctively that caution urged him to resist such betraying moments.

He had spent no further Sunday afternoon with them, but always lingered for a while when calling to take Delia back to Kensington. He seemed anxious to know how Deborah was faring, frequently stressing that if she felt the need for advice or help, she should turn to him. It was good to have a friend, even one who set up barriers against emotional involvement.

Now she wondered wildly how he would react if she went to him and said, 'I am frightened of my butler. I run a dishonest gaming table with his help and connivance, but if I were found out, *I* would be held responsible. I could not prove any accusations I made against him, because there is no evidence. He makes sure of that. I am trapped. I have to carry on because I have this house to maintain. I cannot sell it because it is not mine. I have to take care of it for little Charles. I have no other means of earning money. I am not equipped for anything except housekeeping. Had my father lived, I would be running the vicarage for him in place of my mother to this day. That is all I am any good at. I haven't a head for baccarat, nor for manipulating marked cards. I don't even detect them half the time. So I am lucky if I make enough profit to meet servants' wages and household bills, after paying Dillon his percentage. And that has to be in cash, because the arrangement began that way. Never anything in writing. So if the worst came to the worst and exposure came along, he could deny involvement. Dulcima had no cause to worry, because she was brilliant at the game and made a handsome profit, which she squandered just as lavishly. She lived for the moment, but I cannot. I am frightened, and I am trapped. And all the time, Dillon is watching and waiting. He reminds me of a bird of prey.'

Deborah let out a tired sigh and lifted her head as she heard the first guests entering the room. Above her, Dulcima's portrait smiled down, serene and untroubled.

She envied her aunt's assurance and the optimism that had deserted her only toward the end of her life. Had she lived, it would undoubtedly have returned, being part of her nature, but already Deborah felt the tight knot of apprehension which always seized her when these inveterate gamblers arrived one by one. It was even worse when they took their places at the table and Dillon presented her with the first six decks, stacked neatly on a silver salver borne in his white-gloved hands. She would take a deck at a time, unwrap the cards in front of the players, and place them face down in the *sabot*. On a side table, further decks would be waiting. If play were fast, they would get through the lot in the course of the evening, but after the first six were disposed of and others were brought across, she would hand them round for the seals to be broken and the wrappers removed, so everyone could see that the cards were mint-new and untouched.

She was challenging fate, terrified all the time. As the new Madame of the card salon at 20 Hanover Square, she was totally unfitted to the role, and knew it.

Now she braced herself, turned with a forced smile to welcome the arrivals, and looked across the room at a young man totally unknown to her, a blond young man surely not yet out of his teens. He had a sensitive face and a smile so engaging it was irresistible. Whoever this handsome boy was, she liked him. She felt the tautness go out of her, and catching sight of her reflection in a mirror, was instantly bolstered by the knowledge that she had never looked so lovely as she did tonight.

11

That was the way Peter Maynard first saw her and the way he was always to remember her. Foolhardiness alone had brought him here, urged by his old friend Bruce, who had been his senior at Bedford. Bruce had always had a great deal more money than he himself ever had, but then, Bruce was a Whitney, and an only son, his father's Liverpool shipyards reputed to be richer than the famous Camel Lairds' across the Mersey in Birkenhead, whereas he himself was one of four, his father a Kentish country doctor who recognised that further expensive education would be wasted on this particular member of his brood, because the only ambition the boy possessed was to become an artist, and that was no way to become financially prosperous.

'When do you hope for recognition?' he had barked. 'After you are dead? That's the only time artists ever get it, and you're no Turner or Gauguin or that chap who went mad and cut off his ear – what's-his-name – Van Gogh? And Gauguin finished up a leper in the South Seas or somewhere. As for Turner, well, I confess I know nothing about Turner except that he painted damn fine sunsets. Can't say I know much about any of those impecunious chaps, for that matter. Unless you are prepared to go in for something practical, young sir, I'm not wasting another damn penny on you, and that's the truth.'

Peter didn't blame him. His father was forthright, impatient, hardworking, and ambitious for his children but not for himself. Half his patients never paid their bills, but by rigid self-denial he managed to give his four sons a good schooling. But no university for Peter, which was fair enough. He didn't hanker after one, anyway. But an art training – even twelve months at the Slade? Couldn't he have just that? Learning the basic techniques, how to mix pigments and so forth? After that it would be up to him. An artist didn't become an artist by using a blueprint, only by working at the job. All right, said his father, he would advance the small legacy due to him at twenty-one under his mother's will, but not a penny more, and if he failed to make a living, he would have to come home to Tenterden and find steady employment. He could have a word on his behalf with the local bank manager.

It was a deal, and Peter had agreed, but his mother's legacy had supported him for barely a year, by which time he could afford no more tuition. He was now living from hand to mouth.

Where his foolhardiness came in tonight was in listening to Bruce Whitney's persuasion. 'I promise you, old chap, you can win substantially in an evening's play. I wouldn't say that if Dulcima Howard were still the Madame of 20 Hanover Square – my God, what a head for cards that woman had! – but her young cousin can't hold a candle to her. It's obvious she isn't making a success of the place. I can see disgust in her butler's face whenever she holds the bank. Sharp fellow, that butler; held Dulcima in tremendous esteem, but doesn't feel the same way for dear Deborah, I can tell. You should have visited number twenty in Dulcima's day, by Jove! The food, the wines, the standard of play – you can't imagine it, old boy, you really can't. Gaiety and elegance combined with challenge and excitement. Deborah Yorke is charming, but she ought to unbend a little, the way her cousin did. Of course, that sharp-eyed butler gives the place a certain tone with his presence, but there's little gaiety now, and even less excitement. Still, the quality of the wines hasn't gone off — only the quantity, alas, which speaks for itself. So it's an easy wicket, I promise you, Peter ol' boy. Come along with me tonight and you can win more than that tenner I lent you last week. More than that and the previous tenners, in fact. How much is it already, Pete? At least fifty, I'm afraid. Lucky I'm a friend, isn't it, and don't charge interest? And because I'm a pal, I tell you what I'll do — I'll stake you for a hundred tonight and I'll guarantee that with all the blunders dear Deborah makes, you'll more than treble it and be able to pay me back every penny. How's that for an offer?'

Instinct had warned Peter to resist, so he seized on the first excuse that came to mind. 'I haven't any evening togs.'

'That's no problem. We're the same height and more or less the same size, except that you are thinner than I — what are you doing, starving yourself? — so I can fit you out.' Bruce had dismissed further protests with a wave of his well-manicured hand. 'No, no — I'll take no refusal. Everything's settled. Expect you at my place at seven sharp. We'll dine and then go on.'

There were moments when Peter regretted bumping into Bruce in Piccadilly Circus. He had been walking all the way home from Bloomsbury to save fares, and by the time he had trudged down Tottenham Court Road and into Leicester Square, he had begun to feel very tired indeed. He had had little food for several days, but now he felt rich with five pounds in his pocket from the sale of a painting to a dealer near the British Museum. If he had had the courage to bargain, he might have got more, because it was a good painting. Peter could view his work objectively. He knew when it was good and when it was bad, and even the pangs of hunger didn't drive him to peddling his worst stuff around. But five pounds was all the dealer had offered, and because he was afraid the man might change his mind if he tried to push him higher, he had accepted gladly. He owed three weeks' rent for his basement room in Pimlico; at ten shillings a week that left three-pounds-ten in his pocket, and he wasn't going to waste a penny of it on fares.

But by the time he reached Piccadilly Circus he felt light-headed and was forced to sit on the steps leading up to the statue of Eros, well aware that the sight of anyone sitting there attracted disapproving attention. No well-behaved person would do such a thing. It was the exclusive territory of flower girls by day, and the occasional down-and-out by night, who would immediately be removed by a keen-eyed bobby and carted off to Marl-borough Street police station, there to be given a good strong cup of tea and despatched to the nearest doss house for a bed.

The steps of Eros were becoming sacred to Londoners, although the aluminium statue of the God of Love was barely nine years old and despised by many as too modern to be revered, and by the artistically snobbish as far from a masterpiece, but gradually he had become the much-loved hub of the capital. There he stood, poised above his tumbling fountain, empty bow and outstretched arm pro-claiming that an arrow had just winged its way across the world. By day he seemed to rise from a bed of flowers and perfume, for the flower girls of London who grouped about his base, their baskets ablaze with colour, sold anything from a buttonhole to a 'bookay' and dipped their wares into the Eros fountain every now and then to refresh them.

Most of the 'girls' were matronly and russet-cheeked, competing not only with their wares but also with their variety of bonnets and vivid shawls. Those who scraped enough pennies together to buy the traditional flower seller's shiny black straw boater would tuck a nosegay in

the ribbon, ready to be taken out and placed in a gentleman's buttonhole.

They were one of the sights of London, and proud of it.
Many top-hatted and frock-coated gentlemen were their
regular customers, buying their daily buttonhole from the
same woman and remembering her with a pound at
Christmas, and sometimes as much as two – enough to
buy a Christmas dinner for her family. These flower
sellers of Eros were the *élite* of women street vendors. The
fact that their billowing skirts were shabby and covered
even shabbier boots was of no account, smartness being
confined to bonnet and shawl because they were the most
eye-catching and therefore good for trade, but if any of
their number arrived looking dirty or dishevelled, she
would be despatched by the others in no mean terms and
told to come back when she had cleaned herself up. 'Not fit
to sit beneath the God o' Love, that you ain't!' And Eros,
shining in the sun, looked as if he agreed, poised gracefully
above the vivid display of blooms and sparkling water and
beaming cockney women.

But a young man sitting there after the flower sellers
had packed up and gone, a respectable young man too,
from the look of him, inevitably attracted attention. Only
tourists committed such a *faux pas*, knowing no better.
Peter knew he should get up and go, but his head was so
light that if he did so that stalwart bobby stationed on the
corner of Regent Street would think he was drunk and
perhaps arrest him. The man was beginning to come
across, ready at least to move him on as a loiterer, but
fortunately the way was blocked by surging cabs and
horse-drawn buses, and by privately owned carriages
which were cursed by the cabbies, for this was the hour of
pre-theatre dining. Peter took a deep breath to steady
himself. In a minute or two the light-headedness would
surely pass, and when he reached Pimlico he would go
into a tearoom near his lodgings and have a poached egg

on toast and a whole pot of tea. Maybe even two eggs, though he had to make three pounds ten shillings last until he sold another painting or, with luck, actually got a commission of some sort. And tonight, instead of struggling to work despite the dim basement light, he would go to bed early and sleep.

'Good grief, it's Maynard! What the devil are you doing there, sitting bang in the middle of Piccadilly Circus? What would our revered masters at Bedford think, eh? Letting the old school down, by Jove. Couldn't believe my eyes when I saw a respectable-looking bloke sitting on the steps of Eros! Not done at all, old chap. *Lèse majesté*, and all that. I say, you look white as a sheet. Better come across the Circus to Monico's Bar and have a brandy. You look as if you could do with a double.'

The brandy was the worst thing he could have had. It was large, and he drank it at one gulp and passed out. Later, he had only the haziest recollection of being bundled into a hansom and trundling across London with Bruce Whitney beside him, laughing.

'Good Lord, Pete, you've no head, have you? I wouldn't have ordered a triple if I'd realised that, but you looked so under the weather, I thought you needed a really stiff one. Never mind, here we are at my place. Cabby, help me get my friend up the steps, will you, and don't let him collapse on to them while I fish for my latchkey. Very partial to sitting on steps, is my dear old friend. Oops, Pete, here we go! Thanks, cabby, and here's a sovereign for your trouble.'

Even through his foggy senses Peter was staggered by such a lavish tip, presented so casually. The gold disc had a treble halo around it as it passed from Whitney's immaculate hand to the cabby's grubby one.

Peter had wakened next morning in his friend's Belgravia apartment, ashamed but ravenously hungry, and from that moment was indebted to him. Bruce had been appalled by the state of his clothes, and later, by his basement room in Pimlico. He had glanced around it as if he were slumming, and urged Peter to pack up and go. He could not comprehend how anyone could be reduced to living in such a place.

'It isn't necessary, you know. I have a couple of guest rooms, and you can take your pick. Pay me later. I'll chalk it up on the slate.' But Peter had taken a firm stand against that. What he had not been able to take a firm stand against was his friend's hospitality when hunger gnawed at him, for he had sold no more work. He gave himself another month, and then it would have to be Tenterden and a job in which he would mentally stifle.

Bruce told him not to be a fool. 'I don't know much about art, old chap, but I suspect you really can paint. Remember the theatrical scenery you produced for school plays? Maybe you could earn a living that way – and introduce me to some actresses on the side, eh?' A sly dig in the ribs at that. 'Tell you what I'll do, Pete – when you've attracted enough attention, I'll buy a picture or two, but I only go in for names that are being recognised – early enough to make sure of a good investment, but not when they've made their mark and the prices have zoomed. First, I want proof of a good investment.'

Now Bruce urged, 'Have a fling. Just this once. You were a dab hand with cards when we were at school. Remember those secret games of poker? You can clear all your debts in one evening at 20 Hanover Square.' So here he was, rigged out in some of Bruce's Savile Row evening wear, and hoping the looseness didn't really show. Fortified by a good meal at his friend's place beforehand, plus some excellent wine, he felt more confident as they stood on the steps of number twenty.

'She's really becoming a pushover,' Bruce was saying. 'I've watched her since she stepped into Dulcima Howard's shoes, and instead of improving, she seems more and more unsure of herself, auctioning the bank frequently for a measly ten percent. Dulcima Howard did that only rarely – as a sop to her guests, I suspect. Now the only time we have to be really careful is when that damned butler takes over.'

'A butler? Why should a butler take part?'

'He used to stand in for Dulcima occasionally – mostly after Ashleigh came into her life and the pair of them would slip away from the gaming room for a while. Dear Deborah takes a break only when she goes to attend to that baby upstairs, and a mighty long time she takes over that lately.'

'She's married, then?'

'Lord, no. And the child isn't hers. It's Dulcima's.'

'And the father?'

Bruce shrugged. 'Dulcima being Dulcima, the identity of the father is open to speculation, though most people believe it to be Ashleigh. In her way, Dulcima was capable of fidelity, particularly when she loved a man. I became a visitor to her salon pretty late, but it's well known that she'd had lovers aplenty – and not surprisingly, she was such a ravisher. Ring that damned bell again, will you, old chap? Dillon must be deaf tonight.'

But the door opened before Peter could do so, and very soon he was walking into Dulcima Howard's elegant drawing room and looking at the loveliest girl he had seen in his life. Against the silver-grey of her gown and the vivid green of emeralds, her skin was a beautiful ivory, her hair a rich chestnut, her eyes dark and warm. His artist's eye noted the high cheekbones and finely moulded chin, the full lower lip which hinted at an inviting sensuality, and the nose which was remarkably like that in the portrait above. Lovely as she was, she was overshadowed by that portrait, but Peter Maynard knew which of the two women appealed to him most. He was suddenly wildly glad that he had come.

'I would like to paint you,' he said without any preliminary, scarcely heeding his friend's formal introduction and quite unaware that the butler was trying to catch his mistress's eye. But Deborah was not. She saw Dillon's glance as he proffered champagne and knew he was trying to convey something to her, and that it must be important or he would have left it until later. It gave her satisfaction to ignore the man. Let him wait. She was hostess, and on that part of her duties no one could fault her.

She liked the newcomer, even though he came with Bruce Whitney, who, she understood, had become a regular patron about a year before Dulcima's death. Deborah summed Whitney up as a thoroughly spoilt young man with a streak of hardheadedness. At the moment he was playing at being a man-about-town, but beneath that pose she sensed an inborn shrewdness. He was swift to calculate his winnings and his losses, and Dillon would never have been able to cheat him in that respect. Whitney knew to the last farthing exactly how much he owed the bank, or vice versa. She felt it would go hardly for anyone unwise enough to get into this young man's debt.

'Produce a portrait of Miss Yorke to equal that one,' he said now, gesturing towards the immortal Dulcima, 'and I'll buy it from you, Pete.'

'It wouldn't be for sale.'

'I thought you aimed at being a professional artist.'

'I do. I am. At least, I suppose a chap may call himself a professional once he starts selling.'

Bruce tilted a cynical eyebrow. One picture only? it said. Do you call that being a professional? But only Peter understood and hoped the hurt he felt didn't show. Deborah was puzzled by Whitney's gesture and sensed disparagement behind it. So this amiable boy with the lean look and the engaging smile was an aspiring artist, but why should that be scorned?

She knew Dillon was listening and that in his assessment, also, aspiring artists did not rank high. Was he trying to convey to her that here was a visitor scarcely rich enough to be welcomed? But how could he be sure of that? And what did it matter, except that if it were true she would do all in her power to discourage Peter Maynard from playing? To her, it went against the grain to take money from those who could ill afford to lose it, but usually Dillon had a sixth sense where such people were concerned.

There were signs, he said. Poor tailoring, or dress suits hired from that new renting agency near Covent Garden. One could always tell. There was a stamp about such players, a certain look, and they would start gambling with very low stakes, increasing them only when on a winning streak, then backing down when luck threatened to turn. At that point they would leave while the going was good.

She had a strong desire to urge this young man not to play. Accustomed as she now was to the gambling fraternity, she could never become hardened to their ruthlessness or to Dillon's casualness when pressing a loser to continue. 'I am sure your luck will change, sir. Try another round, sir. Just one more . . . '

When other guests arrived and Dillon was busy pouring more champagne and Bruce Whitney was chatting with one of the salon's long-standing visitors, Deborah found Peter Maynard beside her.

'I meant it,' he said, 'about painting your portrait.' Actually, he would have preferred to do a nude study, but dared not suggest it. The ivory of her skin would be a joy to any artist. Neck, shoulders, and the hint of a valley between her breasts, which was all her low neckline revealed, were sufficient to reveal both texture and tone.

She was surprised. 'No one has ever seen me as suitable

portrait material,' she said. 'I am flattered.'

'And *I* am not flattering. Perhaps no artist has come your way before?'

She admitted this was true, and was forced to turn aside when Dillon indicated his wish to consult her about something. 'May I have a word, madam?' His tone was deferential, but beneath it was determination. She made her excuses to Peter Maynard and stepped aside reluctantly.

Dillon pretended to consult her about the champagne, though she knew there was another dozen bottles in cellarettes on the other side of the serving table. They stood with their backs to the room, and Dillon said beneath his breath, 'That boy is a fraud. Hasn't a penny. He may have come with that wealthy shipbuilder's son, but the suit he is wearing isn't his. Nor is it even hired. A renting agency would have produced something nearer his size, if only as an advertisement for themselves. It is almost falling off him – look at the shoulders, and the droop of the sleeves, not to mention the loose trousers. He has to keep the coat fastened to hide the slackness round the waist. Get rid of him, Miss Yorke. If he loses, he won't be able to pay his debts, and players like that are a liability.'

'How can I get rid of him? He has been introduced by an established patron. We can't restrict the number of players at baccarat, so I can't make that an excuse. The most I can do is to discourage him from playing. And if you felt that way about him,' she added, 'why did you admit him? You have made short shrift of would-be players before, not even allowing them across the doorstep. Where was that instinct, on which you pride yourself, tonight?'

Stung, he retorted, 'And what of your own instinct, Miss Yorke? Just because he speaks like a gentleman and has the manners of one, you believe him to *be* one, but many a so-called gentleman's pockets are to let. Mark my words, this young man's are. As a client he will be useless once he has lost what little he has.'

Dillon was right. Long before the end of the evening the bank had relieved Peter Maynard of Whitney's hundred pounds, and the exhilaration of champagne and the heady experience of falling in love were numbed. And he disliked the look of satisfaction in the butler's eye.

'Another game, sir? Just one more?'

Then Bruce clapped him on the shoulder and boomed heartily, 'That's right, old chap. Win it all back. Never quit when you're down.' And, *sotto voce*, 'You know I'll stake you.'

Deborah returned to the gaming room reluctantly after attending to baby Charles. She was worried because he had a slight cold, and Garfield had been defensive about it.

'You are not blaming *me*, I hope, miss? No one could take better care of the baby than I do. It's picking him up from the warm cot to give him his late feed that's done it, and that's your responsibility, not mine, since you always insist on giving it to him yourself. Lay there screaming for it, he did, while you had to change out of your finery, so of course he kicked all the clothes off.'

Deborah had not even bothered to answer, knowing that if she did, she would snap at the woman. She had to tolerate Garfield, because she couldn't afford to replace her. Already her wages were overdue. She was the only member of the staff who would put up with that. 'Short again, are we?' she had commented this morning, taking one look at Deborah's face when it was time to pay the wages. 'Well, my needs are few. I have all I want. Food and a roof over my head and Miss Dulcima's child to care for. I can wait for what's owing to me.'

Being under an obligation like that did not help Deborah's peace of mind, but she was grateful nonetheless. She also knew that even if financially solvent she would not dispose of Garfield's services, the woman's devotion to Dulcima demanding loyalty in return. But as she changed back into her moiré taffeta gown after giving little Charles his bottle and dealing with his other needs, Deborah's creeping despair had intensified. She knew that things must come to a head, and soon. The end was an ever-approaching shadow, one she would welcome as far as her personal escape from a shady gaming business was concerned, but an impending financial disaster when so much responsibility rested on her shoulders. The problem was how to stave off the moment and what to do when it came. Perhaps tomorrow, when Simon brought his daughter for her weekly visit, she would seek his advice.

Emerging from her room on her way downstairs, Deborah met Garfield once more. To her surprise, the woman said unexpectedly, 'Don't worry, miss. Baby colds are baby colds. They throw them off in no time, and that one's a healthy lad – look how he's thrived in spite of being premature. He'll get better, the way babies do.'

Deborah touched her sleeve in thanks, surprised by this unexpected kindness, whereupon Garfield tensed up again and hurried away. But Deborah was comforted. Little Charles *was* a healthy lad. An alert one, too. His pale eyes had been mesmerised by the gleaming emeralds at her throat, partially revealed by the wrap she wore when attending to him. She was sorry he had inherited his father's eyes. Dulcima's deep blue would have been preferable, reflecting the warmth of her personality. There had never been any coldness in her aunt's eyes; nor, she insisted, was there anything amiss with those of her son. It was absurd to regret their colour. Lots of people had pale eyes. And Charles had the sweetest smile in the world, so she could forget the reminder of his father and hope that in time his eyes would darken. Perhaps even change colour. She felt sure such things were not unheard-of, though she knew of no specific case.

Then she opened the door of the card room and saw Peter Maynard sitting very still and very white, stricken by disaster. A stab of fear halted her. It was as if the shadow of defeat had suddenly extended, engulfing herself. She had to thrust the idea aside. A player's loss was the bank's gain. Dillon would be pleased, but she was not. Instead, she was frightened, sensing that in some unpredictable way this young man's loss was to bring about her downfall.

'You played like a bloody moron,' Bruce said beneath his breath. 'An absolute bloody fool. Why I was so idiotic as to stake you, God only knows. A couple of hundred, too! You'll pay me back by the end of the month, or after that I'll charge interest. And don't forget those earlier tenners, either. Sorry, but I'm no philanthropist.'

It was the supper break. They sat apart from the rest, balancing plates on their knees and glasses in their hands. 'I hate these damned buffet affairs,' grumbled Bruce, who had not done too well himself tonight and was aware that Dillon was already totting up accounts for the first half of the night's play. 'You've certainly lost your touch with cards, Maynard. Can't believe you were ever a dab hand at poker.'

Peter couldn't answer. His mind was numb. Where he was going to lay his hands on a couple of hundred, let alone the previous tenners, which added up to another fifty, heaven only knew. He couldn't, wouldn't, appeal to his father.

He took a gulp of wine, but that didn't help, and the food tasted like sawdust in his dry mouth. Even so, he forced himself to eat. A man who knew that food was going to be short in the near future instinctively fortified himself when the opportunity arose, and though he had dined earlier, further nourishment would sustain him tomorrow and the day after, and perhaps even the day after that. Oh, God, what a mess, and all his own doing! No one else to blame. He shouldn't have heeded Whitney's persuasion, but the remainder of those accumulated tenners and the assurance that he would be on an easy wicket at 20 Hanover Square had tipped the scales. And it was true that once upon a time he had been a good poker player – at any rate, good enough for a schoolboy. But he had not been playing with schoolboys tonight.

A trim parlourmaid stood before them with a tray of glasses. 'Thanks, Bella, my beauty,' said Bruce, replacing his empty glass with a full one and letting his hand slide over her hip as she passed on, glancing at him archly over her shoulder as she did so. 'Damn,' he said, 'missed her bottom. Better luck next time.'

Peter took a sudden dislike to his old schoolfellow, set aside his food and his wine, and moved away. He had to get out of here. He couldn't think in all this noise. He needed air. Walking home might steady him, clear his brain, relieve his tension, but he knew perfectly well that it would produce no solution to his problem. He had one painting which he knew was worth a decent price, and a few lesser ones, which, with luck, might fetch a few pounds. The most he could do was tout them round the dealers, unless Bruce himself . . .

The thought halted him. He turned back. His friend was standing with his arm round Bella's waist, and she was obviously enjoying the familiarity, and across the room that lynx-eyed butler was watching them. But none of this mattered to Peter. He took hold of his friend's arm, trying to draw him aside, and the maid muttered, 'Sorry, Mr Whitney, sir, but Dillon's got his eye on me . . .'

Bruce slapped her bottom as she moved on, and she uttered a stifled giggle.

'What is it now, Pete? Not asking for leniency, I hope,

because I learned at my father's knee never to be lenient with people who owe one money.' The tone was hostile. Bruce was beginning to regret rescuing his old school pal from the steps of Eros. 'I've staked you, and that man Dillon knows it. He will demand the money from you before you leave, and I wouldn't recommend trying to slip away without being seen, because he has the eyes of a hawk. Credit is extended here only to men like Hardcastle over there and other old-timers, though I suspect naive Deborah might prove an easy touch. All the same, I shouldn't count on it if I were you. As I say, Dillon will insist on immediate payment, and when you can't meet it, he will demand it from me. He's no fool. He heard me offer to stake you for the second hundred and no doubt guessed that I'd staked you for the first. He'll take my cheque, and it won't bounce, luckily for you. Professional card players don't have hearts like mine, you know, and bad debts aren't allowed to slip through their nets. But *I* can't let you off, either.'

Peter answered furiously, 'I'm not asking you to, but at the moment there is only one way I can repay you. I'll give you the best painting I've ever done, and several others that aren't quite so good but are worth something. For the time being, that's the best I can do.'

Bruce's smile was cynical. 'And what, may I ask, is the "best" painting worth?'

'I don't know. I only know it *is* my finest work to date. Better than the one I sold the day we met.'

'For a fiver!' Bruce burst out laughing. He had a hearty laugh, and across the room Deborah heard it. She didn't like the sound of it, full of scorn and derision. She looked across and saw Peter Maynard standing with his friend, his face taut and unsmiling, and the contempt in Whitney's laughter was reflected in his expression. She had never cared for him very much; now she actively disliked him. She moved to Peter's side.

The boy was saying tensely, 'I tell you, it is by far my best work. I *know* it is good. I am offering you a stake in my future, and I wouldn't do that unless I were confident it was worth having.' He continued wildly, driven by anger and despair and smarting beneath his friend's ridicule, 'One day this painting of mine may be worth a fortune! No — *will* be. You'll see.'

'Sorry, old chap, I bet only on certainties.'

'Not always, Mr Whitney,' Deborah interrupted. 'If you did, you wouldn't play baccarat.'

She drew Peter aside. She could not bear to see anxiety in one so young. In a low voice she said, 'Come and see me tomorrow, and bring your painting with you. I would like to see it.'

Later, she wondered why she had issued the impulsive invitation. No one with any sense would stretch out a helping hand to so misguided a youth, yet she knew she was going to do precisely that, despite Dillon's warnings and even those of her own common sense. Wisdom told her to let the boy battle with his own problems, and that sensible people never let the heart influence the head, but she felt towards this boy as a mother would towards a rash young son.

He was waiting when she returned from the park with Delia the following afternoon. He was glad that Bella, not Dillon, opened the door to him, but the maid's raised eyebrows had spoken volumes. '*You?*' they said, and he knew at once that she had not missed a thing last night as she handed round refreshments and flirted beneath her eyelashes. She was sharp-faced, pert, and calculating, capable of summing up a man's worth with a shrewdness that had been acquired not merely as a parlourmaid. He had no doubt that as players emerged from the card room for supper she could tell at a glance who had won and who had lost, also those who could stand such losses and those who couldn't. Perhaps the butler had tutored her well. The man's concealed but observant glance had followed her about the room, and Peter had no doubt at all that he was as untrustworthy as she.

He had been well aware of Dillon's assessing glance and the secret appraisal of his borrowed evening wear, followed by instant rejection. Embarrassment had made him want to turn tail the moment he and Bruce had been admitted, but he would have felt a fool in front of his old school friend had he done so, and, at eighteen, making a fool of oneself was unthinkable, so he had pretended to be as self-confident as Bruce, though the façade had crumbled entirely before the evening was over. The only good thing, the miraculous thing, was meeting Deborah Yorke and falling in love with all the passionate ardour of his years.

Despite anxiety about financial disaster, the hours of waiting to see her again had dragged, his mood fluctuating between hope and despair; also between excitement at the thought of their coming meeting and fear that it might be their last, for without the means to court her, how could he hope to see her again? He had never realised that love could be like this, transcending even anxiety and guilt.

Now he sat on the edge of a chair praying for her to come. Bella's announcement that her mistress was out had stunned him momentarily. Had she actually forgotten her invitation to him? Then the maid had asked if he were expected, her tone implying disbelief, and he had enjoyed discomfiting her by saying that he certainly was.

'In that case, sir, you'd best come in and wait.'

He had been doing that for half an hour, sitting in the hall in a state of tension, well aware that this brash parlourmaid did not consider him good enough to be shown into the drawing room. So long as Deborah came, and soon, he cared little about that.

And here she was, at last. He heard her voice from the steps outside, accompanied by a little girl's piping, 'I raced you, I raced you! – *I* won!' Then Deborah's again: 'You won't next time, Delia – watch out for next time!' He loved the sound of her laughter, so full of enjoyment.

Then the door opened and her figure was silhouetted in the aperture as she halted on sight of him. She removed her latchkey slowly and her small companion darted round her skirts into the hall, halting in front of him with her hands behind her back, feet astride, frank curiosity on her face. He paid the child no attention, interested only in Deborah. It seemed characteristic that she should let herself in instead of summoning a servant to admit the mistress of the house.

But he was puzzled by her reaction, unaware that she was reminded of another man sitting in that selfsame chair and that her heart had wrenched at the recollection.

He jumped to his feet, almost dropping the canvas he had carried with such care. She had looked beautiful last night; now, in his eyes, she looked equally lovely in a coat of dark blue velvet hugging her small waist and flaring about the ankles to give the freedom that walking clothes demanded. With it she wore a blue velvet pillbox hat perched dead straight upon her head and tilted slightly forward over her brow, her chestnut hair coiled in the nape of her neck in a style not wholly unfashionable, since it lacked the addition of a frizz of false curls, but which, on her, was vastly becoming. It was also slightly tumbled, as if she had been running, and, judging by the breathlessness of the pair of them, she had. That she could be so unrestrained as to run along the street with a child enchanted him.

'Mr Maynard, I am sorry to see you waiting in the hall. Bella should have shown you into the drawing room. Dillon is off duty, but all the same she should have known.'

She came towards him, hand extended, and he found himself stuttering as shyness overcame him, nor was his self-consciousness lessened by the frank appraisal of the small girl who still inspected him with a disconcerting glance which, had he but known it, was to become increasingly familiar to him with the years.

He disliked precocious children and was glad when Miss Yorke removed the enchanting pillbox and handed it to the little girl, saying, 'Would you take that upstairs for me, Delia, and my coat too, if you can carry it?' He judged this to be an excuse to get rid of the child, who promptly perched the pillbox on top of her own sailor hat, pirouetting with a wicked grin. Then he saw the warmth in Deborah's smile and knew it was no pretext to be alone with him, but an indulgence she knew the child enjoyed.

Still with the pillbox crowning her headgear, Delia accepted the coat and flung it across her shoulders so that it trailed like a cloak. 'Bow to my majesty!' she commanded. 'Bow to my majesty!' and off she went upstairs, the long blue velvet coat serving as a train and her voice floating back, 'Bow, my subjects, or off with your heads!'

Deborah laughed and called after her, 'You may go and see Charles while you are up there, darling. Mr Maynard and I have business to discuss.'

'You are getting as bad as my father. *He* seems to have business to attend to on Sundays now. I can't think why. He never used to.'

Why that remark should bring a faint flush to Deborah's cheek, Peter could not understand, but the next moment it was gone and she was opening the drawing-room door. 'Now, let me see that painting,' she said. 'Bring it over to the light.'

She stood framed within the tall window, and as she studied the canvas, half turned, he saw the lovely outline of her profile and longed to touch it, to run a finger over the delicate chiselling of her features, to lightly feel the contours of her lips. It would be the next best thing to kissing her, and the thought quickened his blood. He was glad her attention was occupied, so she did not see his betraying colour.

He blurted, 'I want you to have it. As a gift from me. It's the best painting I have ever done, and I want to give it to you. Please don't refuse, Miss Yorke. It's all I have to offer.'

'Why should you offer me anything?'

She continued to study the canvas, her delight in it increasing. It was a scene of the Thames at dawn, the sweeping lines of the Royal Albert Bridge shadowed by mist, a hint of sunrise warming the cold grey light. She could almost feel a slow stirring of life and the promise of a day's awakening. She had not expected talent like this, but she knew that to possess this painting would give her unending pleasure.

'I am not knowledgeable about art, Mr Maynard, but it seems to me that you could sell this with ease.'

He nodded. He was sure of that himself, but *her* hands had touched it, and the thought of any others doing so was now unbearable. He was besotted, and knew it, and wanted nothing so much as to remain so.

'Last night,' she said, 'you offered it to Bruce Whitney.'

'And he refused, thank God, or now I would be unable to make a present of it to you. You will accept it, won't you? I want no one else to have it.'

'That confirms my fears that you are a very foolish young man. You are heavily in debt, Mr Maynard. How do you propose to discharge it? Mr Whitney doesn't strike me as being a generous person at heart.'

He could not answer that. The burden of his debt to Bruce didn't bear contemplating. A month, he had said, and after that, accumulating interest. Peter suppressed a shudder and wished Miss Yorke had not brought up the matter, spoiling the enjoyment of this meeting.

'How old are you?' she asked gently.

'Eighteen,' he admitted, feeling like some callow youth.

Not long out of school, she thought with compassion. Though he was only two years younger than herself, her feeling towards him was wholly maternal. She hadn't the slightest suspicion that the boy had fallen madly in love with her.

She walked across to the mantelpiece, cleared a space, propped up the canvas, and stood back to study it anew. Undoubtedly this boy had a future as an artist, but the promise of ultimate value was not her reason for wanting this painting. It was a thing of beauty with which she would never want to part. Bruce Whitney was a fool to turn his back on Peter Maynard's work. One day he would realise that, and regret it.

She took out a cash box in which the previous night's takings were locked until the bank opened on Monday, then withdrew Whitney's cheque and handed it across. 'Take this, and return it. If you give it back to him personally, he will never be able to pretend you are still in his debt. I think you have been a little too trusting where Mr Whitney is concerned.'

'He helped me when I needed it,' Peter stammered, wholly embarrassed. 'Look . . . I don't want you to do this. Nothing was further from my mind.'

'I know. But you want me to have the painting, and I won't accept it as a gift. In discharge of your debt, yes.'

'But . . . *two hundred pounds!*'

'I am sure it will be worth more than that, one day.' She folded the cheque and tucked it in the breast pocket of his jacket. 'There. That is settled.'

He was spared the embarrassment of answering by the drawing-room door bursting open and the front doorbell ringing simultaneously. Delia danced into the room, piping, 'That will be my father. Make him stay to tea, won't you? I know he always wants to, though he often makes excuses. I can't think what is the matter with him lately, really I can't.'

But her father knew. The moment Simon looked across the room at Deborah, the now familiar feeling of pleasure seized him, in the face of which resistance threatened to crumble. A man could hold out just so long and no longer.

Then he saw the bemused look on Peter Maynard's face and recognised it as an adolescent version of his own feelings. Whoever this blond boy was, he was in the throes of calf love, a state more easily recovered from than his own. A man in his late thirties, already married, could only suffer as he was suffering, knowing his emotions went deeper and were more permanent than those of a boy scarcely breeched.

Then he saw the painting, and almost with a feeling of reprieve he let it claim his attention. These moments when he came face to face with Deborah were always dangerous, forcing him to don a mask which was perilously insecure. He had given up trying to convince himself that it was only for his daughter's sake that he allowed the acquaintanceship to continue. He knew that his own desire for Deborah was the dominant motive.

He had also been tempted to visit the card salon occasionally, though he was not a gambling man. With a crowd of others, it would have been easier to hide his feelings, even to avoid more than conventional greetings with her, but because he had a shrewd suspicion of the methods practised there, he feared she might feel he was keeping a watching brief – which, even at a distance, he was, though not in condemnation. Every time he brought his daughter to this house, he saw signs of anxiety in Deborah's eyes, and knew there could be only one cause. It was not only the responsibility of this household that was troubling her, but being involved in a reckless game, using methods totally alien to her, methods established before the reins were passed on.

Very soon he would have to do something about it, but at the moment she was keeping him at arm's length, and to step in without encouragement might make her retreat further. So he was biding his time, waiting for one moment's weakening on her part, and when it came, he knew he would be unable to keep his distance any longer.

Apart from his concern for her, he was fighting a losing battle with himself, and since Caroline's departure and subsequent silence, it was almost as if she had walked out of his life. His world had become self-contained, bound by his work, his daughter, and his love for Deborah Yorke.

Staring at the canvas, caught by its quality and atmosphere, he heard her introducing Peter Maynard as the artist. 'And he has given the painting to me. It is actually mine. My first real possession.'

'That isn't strictly true, sir. About giving it to her, I mean. I wanted to, but she would only accept it in discharge of a debt.'

Simon did not ask, as he wanted to, why a boy of his age was fool enough to gamble at all. There was something likeable about the youth, and it was not for him to censure him like a father. His concern for Deborah was greater, for he already knew that Dillon had played a part in Dulcima Howard's profitable business. Justin had hinted as much, with some amusement, remarking that Dillon was a useful chap 'and as cunning as they come, which is no doubt very advantageous to dear Dulcima, though she fondly imagines I don't suspect a thing. But I have a shrewd idea that they have some kind of working arrangement. One turns a blind eye, of course, with one's mistress.'

To Simon, more alarming than the fact that the card salon was not proving so profitable in Deborah's inexperienced hands was the awareness that gestures like this, accepting payment in kind instead of monetary settlement, could only antagonise a man like Dillon, who was likely to prove a very ugly customer if provoked, for undoubtedly any working arrangement he had come to with Dulcima Howard had been inherited by her successor.

'Are you still in debt?' he asked the boy unexpectedly.

'Very little, sir, compared with last night's disaster.'

Deborah exclaimed, 'Surely you don't owe Mr Whitney any more!'

Having to admit that hunger had compelled him to accept loans during the past weeks was humiliating but unavoidable. 'But I know I can sell more work,' Peter hastened to add. 'Not so good as this, but for fivers and perhaps even tenners.'

Pride, coupled with youthful optimism, encouraged him to lie. He was by no means sure that his lesser paintings would fetch such sums, and another glance at Simon Davidson told him that the man saw through his bravado.

'What you need are firm commissions. I can give you one. You can start tomorrow at nine – the Archaeological Museum in Princes Gate. We are producing a new catalogue and I need an illustrator. It won't be a permanent job, but will tide you over for some weeks.' He cut short the boy's stammered thanks. 'Sketches of our most important exhibits, precise in detail, good in draftsmanship, perfect for reproduction – that is what I want. You may not regard it as art, but at this stage of your career you must make a choice – art for art's sake, or money for God's sake. Which is it to be?' He flashed the smile which Deborah had come to know so well – warm, understanding, good-humoured. 'You can pursue your talent for painting in your spare time. In fact, both of us will be disappointed if you don't. And one thing more – I suggest that once you are clear of debt, you take good care to keep out of it.'

The only thing marring Peter's happiness as he

departed was the uneasy feeling that Davidson was doing this not so much for him as for Miss Yorke, as a sign that he endorsed her action, or even to demonstrate his devotion. Hadn't he been linking himself with her when he uttered those significant words 'both of us'?

Perhaps his own enslavement made Peter perceive a great deal more beneath the man's façade than anyone else might. So he departed with mixed feelings. Gratitude, a reluctance to be indebted to Davidson, jealousy because he seemed to be important in Deborah's life, and a curiosity which amounted to torment. Were they in love? Was the man a widower, free to marry, or a married man without conscience pursuing a young unmarried woman?

Relief because a financial burden had been miraculously lifted accompanied the boy all the way to Bruce Whitney's place, linked with happiness because he had seen and talked with Deborah Yorke again and even touched her hand in greeting, but almost as strong was the despair of unrequited love.

When he had gone, and Delia had begged to go out with Garfield, who was taking baby Charles for an airing and even promised she could wheel the perambulator for a while ('But only under *my* supervision, young miss!'), Simon knew he had Deborah to himself for at least fifteen precious minutes.

He said without any preliminary, 'You are worried. You can't hide your feelings from me, Deborah.'

He could not recall the actual moment when they had slipped into the intimacy of first names, despite his endeavour to remain scrupulously formal.

'I want to know the cause,' he persisted. 'Could it be Dillon? I know he functions in a more important capacity than butler here. He won't be pleased about your waiving a gambling debt, unless you plan to sell the painting more profitably and put the proceeds into the kitty.'

'I would never sell! Surely you know me better than that? It is the first possession I have ever had, entirely of my own, and besides, it is too lovely to part with.'

She had pulled a lace-edged handkerchief from her waistband and now sat twisting it between long fingers, quite unaware of the action. They were sitting opposite each other, and he reached across, took the handkerchief away, and covered her hands with his. It was the first time they had made any physical contact since that betraying moment on their way to Regent's Park, and this time they did not draw apart.

She slid to her knees on the floor beside him and leaned her head against the arm of his chair, longing to draw nearer but aware that closer proximity was not for them. Even so, she yearned for it, and the awareness of her own sensuality both startled and delighted her. It was demanding and urgent. *Take me, take me now . . . don't let us fight it any longer* . . . The words cried out for utterance, but a lifetime of restricted upbringing held them in check. The frustration of virginity was a burden she suddenly longed to shed, but only with this man – a married man, to whom she could never belong legally.

He said again, 'Tell me what is worrying you – even frightening you, I think.'

She murmured, 'Not *you*, at least,' and dared not lift her face for fear of betrayal.

'It is the card salon, isn't it? You are out of your element there, and worried too. Give it up, Deborah. Finish with it once and for all.'

'I can't. It is the only way I can make money, and I have to do that in order to maintain this house and bring up the child.'

'There must be another way. One less risky.'

So he knew, or had guessed, and the realisation was humiliating. Card sharper – an ugly term and a dangerous one. Was that how he thought of her? Why not, since that was what she had become. Shame made her speechless, and perhaps because he sensed this, he stroked her hair with a compassionate hand.

For some minutes they remained as they were, held in an emotional isolation from which they were aroused by voices descending the area steps outside, Garfield's loud and clear.

'Hold on to that end, young miss. We don't want his lordship falling on his head down these steps, now do we?'

'Bother the rain!' piped Delia. 'Rain, rain, go to Spain, and never dare come back again!'

By the time the child came racing up from the basement, where the perambulator was kept warm and dry in a nook close to the kitchen range, Deborah and Simon were seated as she had left them. Now she came dancing into the room, announcing all in one breath, 'We had to turn back because Garfield says it's raining cats and dogs and that's stupid because *I* didn't see any cats and dogs coming down and why does she call the baby his lordship?'

She was unaware of the emotional tension between her father and Deborah, and too young to guess that self-imposed barriers had almost been broken down, but Deborah now knew that she was faced with the choice of going irrevocably forward or retreating forever, and the last thing she wanted to do was to retreat from this man, married or no. There was more of Dulcima in her than she realised.

'Is it because Charles has eyes like Uncle Justin?' Delia chattered. 'Pale, just like his. *And* like those horrid portraits at Kingsmere. An awful lot of Ashleigh men seem to have had eyes like that. And another thing puzzles me. I read once that babies are always born with blue eyes and that after a few weeks they change colour. But this baby's were never blue and they haven't changed at all. I wonder why.'

Simon knew that the sudden chill he felt was absurd, but in memory he was back in Kingsmere with Caroline's voice saying, 'Periodically, pale-eyed Ashleighs like my brother have come down through the family, but only on the male side . . . every man born with them has been associated with violence . . .' The words were not only an unwelcome reminder of his wife's existence, but of that unpleasant story. Thank God, for Deborah's sake, that such tales were nonsense, since she had been left with the responsibility of bringing up this child.

12

Dillon's face twisted with fury. 'You *what*? You accepted that daub in place of a debt for *two hundred pounds*? What did you do with the cheque?'

'Tore it up.'

The lie came more easily than facing up to him, though now the confession was out, Deborah felt all the better for it.

She picked up her reticule and headed for the door. She was on her way to the bank to deposit Saturday night's takings. This week they amounted to a reasonable sum even without Bruce Whitney's cheque, though still not comparable with Dulcima's profits.

'You have no cause for complaint, Dillon.' Her voice was cool. 'You have received what is due to you.'

'That I haven't! I am entitled to a percentage of that two hundred, and have it I will, or by God, you'll regret it.'

'I regret nothing.'

She walked the length of the hall. The man followed, but made no attempt to open the door for her.

'What are you up to, Miss Yorke?' His eyes narrowed suspiciously. 'Could it be that the picture is worth more than two hundred and so you plan to sell it and pocket the proceeds, swindling me out of my share? Is that the idea? By God, you're not such a fool as I thought! But I'm wise to you now.' He looked at her aloof profile, so reminiscent of Dulcima Howard's that his heart lurched. A man could worship a woman like his late mistress, take any temperamental outburst from her, endure her snubs when the mood was on her, knowing all the time that she wasn't cunning like this one, whom he had apparently underestimated.

He slipped in front of Deborah, barring her exit.

'You can't swindle *me*, Miss Yorke, so don't try.'

'If I had wanted to swindle you, I would merely have told you that I had cancelled the debt, not that I had accepted something in lieu of it.'

'You can't cancel debts without consulting me.'

'I can, and I have. The card salon is mine.'

'Oh, no, it isn't, any more than this house is. When the place belonged to Miss Dulcima, the situation was very different. Now the house and everything in it belong to that squawking brat upstairs. I suspect that running a profitable sideline on premises not belonging to you could prove quite a tricky legal problem if the worst came to the worst, but that would be your worry, not mine. Meanwhile, I do have a say in things.'

If he hoped to frighten her, he was disappointed, for she answered coolly, 'No – you have a hand in things, but no authority. Miss Howard told me the details of her arrangement with you, and you cannot say I haven't kept to them. You receive your share exactly as before. If she had decided to waive a debt and accept something in place of it, or even nothing at all, she had the right – as I have. If she decided to close the card room altogether, she had that right too, and so have I.'

His temper rose. 'I warn you, Miss Yorke – try any tricks with me, and you'll regret it. I've had enough of your whims and your fancies, your likes and dislikes, refusing admission to profitable clients and leading us slowly into ruin. Close the card salon!' He laughed. 'Before you know where you are, it will close of its own accord, grinding to a halt, and all *you'll* have left will be worthless gifts from debtors. For a minute I thought you were more cunning than I realised, but now I know I've been right about you all along. You're a fool, but *I* am not going to be a loser because of you. What if I were to blow the whole thing sky-high, as I very well could? Who would be the real loser then? Not I. I would get away scot-free, because you couldn't prove my involvement, no matter how hard you tried. But if I tipped the wink to someone about certain cards . . .'

'Would you also reveal where they come from, the printers who produce them, and the fact that you were once a printer yourself and therefore have "connections"? Just why did you cease to be a printer, I wonder, and where and how did you make these "connections"? In jail, or when you came out of it?' It was a wild shot in the dark, a desperate bluff, but she saw his eyelids flicker and his mouth tighten. 'Don't look so surprised, Dillon. My cousin knew a lot about you, and I guessed the rest.'

Caught off guard, he yielded as she brushed him aside, opened the door, and walked out into the street. He watched her descend the steps, head high, unperturbed; then he slammed the door behind her. The bitch. The damnable bitch. The time had come to deal with her once and for all.

* * *

Bella was in the drawing room. She paused, feather duster in hand, and looked at Dillon enquiringly as he marched in. She rather fancied herself with a feather duster, wielding it negligently, as if she were mistress of the house. Miss Yorke had already dusted the precious porcelain and glass in which Miss Dulcima had taken such a pride, but Bella liked to give herself airs. Since being elevated to the position of parlourmaid, she had acquired certain privileges, one of which was relief from menial tasks. What with that, and waiting on rich gentlemen who came to play baccarat, plus being admitted into Dillon's bed, she had developed a sense of importance as well as additional opportunities – though she was wise enough to conceal those opportunities from the butler. Dillon had a nasty temper, so she took care to please him not only in bed but also out of it, which meant keeping him in ignorance of the fact that she was doing very well for herself in other ways.

It was amazing how many men with a keen eye for cards also had a keen eye for a woman and were ready to pay generously for her favours. She had always understood that most gamblers were obsessed only with gambling, but since being brought into the card room to serve the gentlemen during the refreshment interval, she had learned otherwise. With luck, one of them might even set her up in a nice little place in St John's Wood – the ambition of many a woman who had learned the tricks of the trade – and by that time Dillon would have served her purpose.

Not that she would part from him without a pang, for he was a very good lover, though not so unrestrained as a certain gentleman from Albany who needed keeping in hand but was worth putting up with because he paid so well. Dillon was very satisfying and certainly less exhausting but fivers didn't come her way after a session in the butler's bed. And the last time the gentleman from Albany had booked her for an hour in that accommodation room behind a cigar shop in Conduit Street, he had promised to double the fiver if she was a good girl and pleased him even more.

'Don't I please you well enough now?' she had demanded pertly. 'Many a girl on the Dilly wouldn't be so obliging as I am.'

'Piccadilly prostitutes are not to my taste.'

Very hoity-toity he could be, his lordship from Albany, but it pleased her to be classed above those on the Dilly. Made her feel quite the lady — as indeed she was, in her opinion, since she had actually stepped into her late mistress's shoes. Well — in a sort of way she had. Meeting a titled gent in a tobacconist's back room wasn't quite the same thing as being his acknowledged mistress and living in style, but she believed it to be a step in the right direction. What puzzled her was what he meant by pleasing him 'even more'. Surely to goodness she worked hard enough at the job already, so what more did he want? She even permitted certain liberties at which many a dolly-mop and smart lorette would draw a line. What an appetite the man had, to be sure! But what a distinction for a parlourmaid to be so singled out! It only goes to show, she thought as she flicked her feather duster, that I wasn't imagining those sidelong glances in the days when Miss Dulcima was alive and he walked into this house as if he owned it.

And now Dillon was walking into the drawing room in much the same way.

'Time for you to go on an errand, Bella, m'girl.'

'Same place, same person?' she demanded airily. It did no harm to remind him that because she was a party to it, she was aware of how frequently he had kept in touch with Lord Ashleigh since the man had been forbidden the door. It reversed their positions slightly, stressing that because she carried the messages, she wielded power too: a sort of tit-for-tat for rubbing in, as Dillon so often did, that but for him she would not have been promoted to parlourmaid at all. 'It's thanks to me that you're not underhousemaid still, and don't you forget it!' He said that just a bit too frequently, claiming his reward at night.

Her own rewards, unbeknown to him, were claimed from Lord Ashleigh himself, though she had never dared actually to demand them. An arch glance, a meaningful smile, a lift of the eyebrows, a tilt of the head, an out-thrust of her bosom, and a swagger of the hips as she strolled up to him to deliver Dillon's messages were expressive enough. 'And don't you go mentioning my name when you pass the word on, Bella, m'girl, or you'll be sorry. Just tell him quietly as you walk past him, and keep right on your way, understand? Real gentlemen don't like to be seen talking to your kind in the streets.'

What an insult! One of these days Dillon would be sorry for saying things like that. Meanwhile, his command was easy to obey, since the messages were so brief they could be uttered casually out of the corner of her mouth. 'Not yet, sir,' or 'It won't be long now, sir,' or 'Things are progressing, sir,' none of which Bella could make head nor tail of, but which plainly meant something, because his lordship, from looking annoyed in the early days, had begun to look more pleased of late. So she had pressed her advantage by tempting him with her wares, collecting her rewards, and becoming very self-confident in the process.

Now she said derisively, 'You never put anything in writing, do you, Dillon?'

'Only a fool does that, Miss Impertinent.' He caught her wrist, pulled her to him, and kissed her long and hard. 'That's to keep your mouth shut.'

'You don't keep *yours* shut when you kiss me, and you make sure mine's open, too.' She giggled.

'And you know what that means. Half an hour when you come back?'

'If I can spare the time,' she answered saucily.

'You'll spare it if I say so.' The threatening note surprised her, because she could see no reason for it. He was certainly in a bad mood for some reason or other, but why take it out on her?

She tossed her head defiantly. 'So what's the message this time – *sir*?'

'Just this. "Tonight." '

' "Tonight"?' she echoed. 'I've to walk all that way, just to say "Tonight"?'

Dillon nodded. 'And it isn't that much of a walk from here to Burlington Gardens, you lazy slut.'

She bridled. 'Slut I am *not*! I take a pride in the way I look, and I've learned to speak proper, *and* I keep myself clean. You've seen me in the old hip bath often enough to know that. And there's another thing. I'm not going to hang around that Albany back entrance on a day like this unless you make it worth my while. Have you put your nose outside the door today? Damn cold, it is. Real November weather, and wet into the bargain.'

He said angrily, 'How many times have I told you *not* to wait at that entrance? Those are gentlemen's chambers, and not for the likes of you.'

She snapped back, 'I know that – you've said it often enough. "Stroll near the Burlington Arcade until he comes out of the rear gate and walks along that way to his club." You've said it more'n a dozen times, but the beadles at the gates of the arcade move a girl on if she lingers. One of these days I'll go right up to his chambers and knock on the door. Don't think I don't know the number. K1, that's wot it is. *And* I know how to nip through that back gate, private though it may be.'

'You wouldn't get far if you tried, my girl. Chambers for rich gentlemen are well portered, and if you tried to get in, you'd be out on your ear in no time.'

'Think so?' She tilted her nose. 'Wanter bet?'

'Be off with you. You know what time he goes to lunch

at his club each day. Sharp at noon. You'll do it comfortably.'

And so she did. Lord Ashleigh was emerging from Albany's unobtrusive rear entrance as she neared the end of Savile Row, directly opposite, but due to his lengthy stride, she failed to catch up with him until he reached the arcade and turned into it. Putting down her umbrella, she followed at a discreet distance until she was out of sight of the beadle at the entrance and not yet within view of the one at the Piccadilly end. She wasn't going to risk being treated as she had been on one occasion when she was late and had hurried after his lordship all the way to his club in St James's, catching up with him at the entrance, where he had dismissed her curtly in full view of gentlemen sitting in the windows.

'Be off with you,' he had ordered with a threatening gesture of his silver-topped malacca, for all the world as if she had been a pestering prostitute – and she looking so fine and ladylike in her scarlet feather boa! The next minute a uniformed commissionaire had come hurrying down the steps to chase her away, so she had spat at the man just to show how superior she was. Landed right on his gold-braided lapel, too, which made her depart in triumph.

All the same, she wasn't going to risk another massive wave of the silver-topped cane, nor a summons to one of the arcade beadles to get rid of her. You never knew with the gentry. Approach them by daylight and they cut you dead. After dark, it was different. They weren't above taking a girl down a dark alley then, but speak to them in public before dusk and you didn't get a hearing. But she had to speak to his lordship now, whether he liked it or not. She bridled a little at the thought. If she was good enough for a lay in the accommodation room of a cigar shop (though she had her orders to be there before him and to leave well after he had gone), she ought to be good enough to acknowledge in the street, especially when looking as smart as she did today, in a new bright green outfit with long skirts sweeping negligently behind her the way society ladies let them (no ankle-length walking skirts for *her*, thank you very much!), and a huge cartwheel hat covered in yellow satin and adorned with enormous green ostrich feathers, and pointed green shoes with shining buckles and high yellow heels. Every inch the lady.

And here, in the enclosed Burlington Arcade, she didn't have to shelter any more beneath the old black umbrella used by all the servants at number twenty, so now he could see the glory of her thick mane of hair, swathed about her head beneath the cartwheel, which she wore tilted almost on one side. Bella was proud of her hair, and not without justification. His lordship had quite a fancy for it, too. In the early days, when he started booking that room in Conduit Street, he had insisted on her loosening it, and a terrible nuisance that had been, because it took ages to pile up again, pin by pin, but there you are, for a fiver a girl had to please a gentleman.

When loose, her hair was so long it reached below her knees, and when she sat down, it cascaded over her thighs. His lordship liked that. He liked taking hold of her hair and twisting it into strands, but the time he coiled a long thick piece about her throat and pulled on it as he made love to her, tighter and tighter as he really got going – cripes, that was going a bit too far! If she hadn't managed to cry out, the Lord only knew what might have happened. Nearly choked her, it did. He hadn't been pleased by the noise she made, either, but he stopped at once, clamping a hand over her mouth in case the cigar vendor overheard. Owners of accommodation rooms wouldn't re-admit customers who caused trouble, and one more scream would have had the man banging on the door to know what was going on, or even bursting in.

It hadn't happened again, because she now pinned up

her hair so firmly that his lordship grew impatient with her fumbling attempts to loosen it – wasting good time he was paying for, he said, and wasting time was something he did *not* like. He was one of those men who took a woman without any shilly-shallying once he was ready for her.

Well, she thought now as she sidled up to him in the middle of the Burlington Arcade, for all the ways I've obliged him, he shouldn't have the nerve to cut me, looking as handsome as I'm looking today. So she fell into step beside him, saying brightly, 'Good day to your Lordship. And how are we today, eh? Fine'n dandy? You're not going to cut me dead this time, I hope, seeing as how you've paid for these smart clothes I'm wearing. Oh, so it's deaf we are, is it? That's a pity, because I've got a message for you. "Tonight." That's all it is. Just "tonight". "Tonight wot," I sez to you-know-who, but there wasn't any more. Just "tonight", he sez.'

He walked right on, as if he hadn't heard a word, but she had seen his pale eyes light up, and the tightening of satisfaction about his mouth. Oh, yes, he had heard all right, blast him, and the least he could have done was give her a smile of thanks, especially when she looked so elegant and spoke so proper, not dropping a single aitch or saying 'ain't' even once. And she would very much like to know when he wanted her back at the cigar shop. She was always ready for another fiver. She would have to call in at Conduit Street, as usual, to ask when the next booking was to be, and hope that this time the promised increase in pay would come along, no matter what she had to do to earn it.

Tonight. At last. He had waited impatiently for this one word from Dillon. Over a leisurely lunch Justin had turned it over in his mind with relish. *Tonight*, Miss Deborah Yorke. Tonight I will answer your insolent note of dismissal.

He walked back to his chambers along Piccadilly and through the front entrance in Albany Courtyard. No longer would he take the lengthier route through the rear gate opening into Burlington Gardens at the junction with Vigo Street, on the off chance of meeting that brash maid from 20 Hanover Square, never knowing which day she was likely to turn up with a message from Dillon saying the time was ripe. He had arranged that casual rendezvous in preference to an apparently chance encounter in Piccadilly, because the creature would have had no compunction about turning into that very private courtyard in full view of the uniformed staff and, even more embarrassing, other Albany residents going in and out.

So day after day he had taken the slightly longer route to his club to avoid actually coming face to face with her. In a crowded public street it was easier to walk straight ahead without apparently seeing a lady of the town when she sidled up, than it would be if confronted by her in a quiet courtyard reserved exclusively for the use of Albany tenants. Regular appearances there would have advertised the fact that she came expressly to meet him, and, as Ashleigh had once pointed out to his brother-in-law, appearances must always be preserved. Discretion above all things. Never any scandal. Preserve the niceties of social behaviour. Keep one's private life strictly private, so that one's public face remained eminently respectable, and always observe the eleventh commandment. That was the essence of gentlemanly conduct, even though the Edwardian era had begun and the mask of Victorian manners was beginning to slip. To him, such manners were a useful protection behind which a man could comfortably hide.

Of course, the parlourmaid had had her uses in other ways besides acting as an intermediary between himself and Dillon. She had solicited him blatantly, and naturally he had availed himself of what she offered, as any

Edwardian gentleman would – except perhaps that brother-in-law of his, who seemed to tolerate his wife's absence abroad with equanimity and, as far as Ashleigh knew, consoled himself with no other woman.

Occasional reports had filtered through about Caroline's Middle Eastern journeys. She had been seen with an entourage of Arab servants in the black basalt desert on the outskirts of Amman, and, later, heading for the Wadi Rum and Aqaba. The press were already calling her the second Lady Stanhope, though they had picked up only snippets of news from overseas reports. The eccentric English lady dressed in bedouin robes and mounted on a fine Arab horse, with a retinue of servants with camels and packs, had attracted the attention of travellers, who described the spectacle when reaching such places as Jerusalem, Ramallah, or Nablus, but no message from her had come either his way or his mother's.

Whether Simon had received any communication from his wife, Ashleigh had no idea. It was not his custom to pay social calls on his brother-in-law, but he had once, at his mother's request, visited that cramped Kensington place to see how Delia was. Mamma was concerned about the child growing up there, and no wonder, but she could not order her back to Kingsmere, and as far as he himself was concerned, his sister's child was not his responsibility. Frankly, he didn't care for her very much. She was too precocious by far, and disconcerting with her questions. After Norah's death Delia had been a positive nuisance, weeping unashamedly and asking repeatedly how a person could be alive and well one day and gone the next, and not caring if the servants heard and started asking the same questions amongst themselves, which they would otherwise not have thought of but for that pest of a child.

So the duty visit to Kensington had been a reluctant one, executed only because he deemed it wiser to humour dear Mamma occasionally. Fortunately, Simon had been at that stuffy museum and Delia on her way to have tea with a school friend in the flat below. She had seemed as unenthusiastic about receiving her uncle's visit as he had been in making it. They had met at the entrance to the building, where, characteristically hoydenish, she had crashed into him, racing her companion up the steps.

She had greeted him with surprise but no joy. 'Uncle Justin! What are *you* doing here?'

'I come at your grandmother's behest,' he had answered tartly. 'She is naturally concerned about you.'

'Why? My father takes good care of me and I like living with him and I write a duty letter to Grandmamma every week and I'm sorry I can't stop because Pru says there are muffins for tea.'

The other child was waiting beside a solid door. A matching one faced it on the other side of a black-and-white-tiled hall, typical of those depressing red-brick affairs erected half a century earlier, when Victorian architecture was at its worst, contrasting hideously with Kensington's Regency terraces and squares. No wonder poor Caro had fled from the place and, if she had any sense, would never return to it.

'I thought your father intended to find better accommodation?' he remarked to Delia, who was shifting from foot to foot in that irritating way of schoolgirls.

'He did, and he's been looking when he's had time to, but I don't see why. I like living here. It's cosy. Pru's flat is exactly the same as ours – isn't it, Pru? – 'cept that it's furnished differently, of course. I'd invite you up to ours, Uncle Justin, but Pru's mother is waiting for us and Father won't be back from the museum until half-past five, so we have this arrangement. Pru and I come back from school together and I stay at her home until Father collects me and he recip . . . recipro . . . Pru, *what's* that word I said I would write down in my dictionary?'

The other child, owl-like with spectacles and round eyes and face, shook her head dumbly.

'Bother,' said Delia. 'I do hate forgetting new words.'

Both little girls wore sailor hats held beneath the chin by elastic and trimmed with navy ribbons falling into streamers at the back, and dark blue reefer jackets with pleated skirts reaching to the tops of their laced-up boots, and both carried brown leather hand satchels in neatly gloved hands. They were as like as two peas in a pod, except that Delia's expression was more lively, thank heaven. Otherwise one couldn't tell the difference between them at first glance. What a comedown, to look like any middle-class miss after being tutored by a private governess and brought up like a little lady at Kingsmere!

'Is there anything else, Uncle Justin?' Delia was now bouncing about more impatiently than ever, and though he wanted to be rid of her, he resented her desire to get away.

'Yes, niece. Your grandmother wonders if you have heard from your mamma.'

'Gracious, no. Father says it can take weeks and even months for letters to come from the Middle East. And where would she get notepaper in the desert? No shops or anything, so she wouldn't even be able to buy a stamp, let alone post a letter, because I don't suppose there are pillar boxes either. Anyway, she hates writing letters. She did promise to bring me something back, though. I hope it's a camel. Coming, Pru!'

The door of Pru's flat had opened, a woman's beaming face looking round it. Pretty, but homely. If his brother-in-law reciprocated her hospitality to his child, Justin doubted whether it would be in any amorous way, because he imagined Simon's taste running to something more intelligent. Worthy soul as she appeared to be, this young mother's face was as owlish as her child's. He doffed his hat silently, and departed.

Well, he had made his duty call and reported it to his mother when down at Kingsmere that weekend. The old lady had merely shrugged, not surprised to hear that Caroline had not communicated with her daughter. 'Your sister is a law unto herself, and always has been. She is also a born survivor. She will simply return one day, unannounced, unless her trail-blazing has really made headlines, when she will expect red carpet and military bands, no doubt.' The rigid mouth had tilted in a wry smile. His mother even permitted herself a small joke. 'Perhaps she will find herself a wealthy sheikh, as, I believe, Hester Stanhope was rumoured to have done for a while.'

'And finished her life in lonely and forgotten old age in an isolated fortress in the Lebanon.'

'Since she built it herself, she must have wanted it that way. She could have come back to England, and so can Caroline when she feels like it. Of course, she wouldn't attract so much interest or attention on her native soil after the first flash of curiosity about her adventures died down – *if* she is experiencing anything more than dust and flies. It was solely to dramatise herself that she embarked on this ridiculous journeying. She wants everyone to notice her, to be impressed. She always hated being eclipsed by you, dear boy.'

His mother's cloying fondness had expressed itself in the touch of her beringed hand on his cheek. Sometimes her doting affection was irksome, and even worse was her everlasting anxiety about him, but both had had their uses throughout his life, so he tolerated them, made the most of them when necessary, and escaped at all other times.

Now he had no room in his mind for thoughts of his mother, his sister, or his pert niece, only for the evening ahead. He lounged in his chambers, well content, waiting for the evening to arrive. He enjoyed his London residence, in a place linked with past and present renown, with names like Byron and Macaulay and Bulwer Lytton and even Gladstone, who had lived here until his marriage, but more than all he enjoyed occupying this particular set of chambers, number K1, famed because the notorious Mat Lewis had once been the tenant. In these rooms the man had held a kind of literary court at which young authors paid homage to him, amongst them Walter Scott, who bowed low until there came a revulsion against Lewis's books, accused of being indecent and blasphemous.

What a pity no trace of them remained, for that was the only kind of literature Ashleigh enjoyed, and it would have been amusing to add them to his extension of the Kingsmere library. But alas, the only remaining souvenirs of Mat Lewis were the mirrored doors of his bookcases, from which he, and now the present tenant, could survey himself whichever way he turned.

Dulcima had sometimes visited him here, and he had often made love to her surrounded by these mirrors. She had laughed in that indulgent way of hers, and submitted. 'Why not? This couch is just as comfortable as your bed, my love.' But watching the mirrored reflections of their bodies had not meant so much to her as to him. It was the act itself that she enjoyed, giving herself up to it with eyes closed and her body gloriously relaxed. Dear Dulcima. He had rarely enjoyed a woman so much as he enjoyed her, and, so far, he had found no one to replace her. A tart in a cheap accommodation room was no substitute. A creature like that was to be used and then discarded. A man couldn't even recall her face after he had left her; it was the same with all her kind. But Dulcima's divine features remained in the mind forever, making a permanent replacement difficult. A pity she had spoiled everything by conceiving and then fondly imagining he would legitimise the child. Having a famous beauty as a mistress was one thing, but marrying her quite another. To be the wife of the lord of Kingsmere required at least one of two assets

– high birth or a substantial fortune – and Dulcima, alas, had neither.

He was vexed with himself for thinking of her now. It made him quite depressed, so he turned his mind to the evening ahead, and promptly felt better. Tonight, Dillon had said. *Tonight*.

13

Walking up Regent Street on her way home from the bank, Deborah considered Simon's counsel. Give up the gaming room; finish with it once and for all. She recognised it as sound advice and knew that the sooner she acted on it, the better. This evening, perhaps? Why not? A quick break and a clean one. Announce it when everyone had arrived. 'My friends,' she would say, 'I have reached a decision which I hope you will understand and forgive. This is the last time we shall meet, our last evening together.'

It would come as a surprise to some, but not to others, such as Hardcastle, that inveterate gambler who had come to 20 Hanover Square from the time Dulcima set up her first table, and who had been watching benignly ever since Deborah tried to step into her shoes. Hardcastle would certainly not be surprised. He might even be sorry for her in her moment of defeat, for he had dropped hints of late. 'Sure you are not overdoing things, my dear? Wearing yourself out unnecessarily? Trying to achieve the impossible?' And he was right, though not for the reasons he imagined. He thought she merely had no head for the game, whereas the truth was that she had no taste for anything involving trickery and deception and, therefore, could never succeed in it. So it was better to give up than fight a losing battle, and the relief would be indescribable.

Dillon wouldn't like it, of course, but she no longer cared about Dillon. He could be as angry as he pleased, and she would be glad to see the last of him. She would also enjoy seeing his face when she made her announcement, for after his accusations of this morning, she hadn't the slightest intention of warning him beforehand. But she wished Simon could be present to bolster her confidence. She could then look across the room and see his quiet, scarred face and know that however foolish she had been in trying to follow in Dulcima's footsteps, he understood that she had had no other choice.

Turning into Maddox Street, she felt the sting of rain and wind in her face. It was a long time since she had walked in the rain like this. Once upon a time she had thought nothing of walking along the high sea front all the way from Roedean to Brighton and back, the wind buffeting her, but in cities it whistled round corners and whipped up one's skirts to bite the ankles. It nipped the ears and the nose and the cheeks, so that one walked head down, hiding from it. There was no hard, clean buffeting, pitting one's strength against the elements and revelling in the fight. One simply bowed before it and hurried along, trying to escape, but suddenly it seemed very stupid to bow before anything, even fate, so she lifted her face and braced her shoulders, challenging the wind and the rain and feeling invigorated at once.

By the time she neared the end of the street at the side of St George's Church, both her colour and her spirits were aglow. She had reached a decision and wasn't afraid, even though she had no notion of how she was going to earn a living from now on.

Simon had said, 'There must be another way. One less risky.' But there had been no chance for further discussion, with Delia bursting into the room, pelting them with questions, followed by excited chatter about her forthcoming birthday treat.

'We are all going to Egyptian Hall, the three of us and Pru, though I hope she won't cry when the monkey loses his tail. She's a bit of a crybaby. I've warned her it's only a trick – I know, because I've read all about it. It's magic. Maskelyne's Magic! The tail jumps all over the stage and flies in the air, while Will, the Witch, and the Watchman try to catch it – and Mr Maskelyne is all of them, the monkey as well! One day *I* shall write a play, and I'll act all the parts the way Mr Maskelyne does, and you and my father, and Mamma too if she is back, can come and watch. If she does bring me a camel, I'll use it instead of a monkey, then Mr Maskelyne won't be able to say I copied.'

Mention of her mother had been the only painful thing in that afternoon, which, for Deborah, was memorable, for at last she had admitted to herself that she loved Simon Davidson, and in acknowledging the truth, she felt released, as if she had been chafing against a restriction now miraculously broken. She found herself facing the future with less apprehension simply because she was ready to accept circumstances. In standing up to Dillon, she had conquered fear. Let him rant and rave, let him threaten, let him even try to hit back, the end would be the same – he would be forced to go, and she would be forced to make ends meet some other way.

Passing the door of number 9 Maddox Street reminded her that she had already made a start of sorts, for at this address lived the leading lady from the Comet Theatre, Chrystal Delmont, who was coming to visit her at twelve-fifteen. A discreet advertisement under a box number in the personal column of *The Times*, offering for sale 'The

Exclusive Wardrobe of a Society Hostess' (copied from similar advertisements in select ladies' journals), had followed Deborah's sale of Dulcima's jewellery to a buyer in Regent Street. One could take jewellery to a dealer discreetly, but furs and clothes were another matter. Since Dulcima's death they had remained untouched in her room, carefully protected by holland covers, but finding Garfield weeping over them one day had made Deborah decide to dispose of them at once, or the poor woman would come to regard them almost as effigies of her late mistress. She had a sneaking suspicion that certain items, such as the magnificent black hat and velvet cloak, had in any case been hidden away by Garfield, but Dulcima's wardrobe had been plentiful, leaving many more items to dispose of.

The advertisement had brought a number of replies, mostly from wardrobe dealers in Soho, but some came from genuine purchasers, one of whom lived nearby in Maddox Street, an actress wanting to replenish her stage wardrobe. Garfield's awe when hearing the name had almost overcome her reaction to the news that her dear Dulcima's beautiful clothes were to go.

But now Garfield met her in the hall, wide-eyed.

'She's here already, miss, and I must say she's a very nice lady. If anyone's good enough to wear Miss Dulcima's clothes, it just *could* be her. And it would be nice to think of them being seen onstage for everyone to admire.'

Although unwilling to go beyond that, it was almost as if she were caught again by the lure of the theatre and ready to give back to it the spirit of the loveliest of all Gaiety Girls. From Garfield, this was a big concession. Deborah hid her smile as she went to meet Chrystal Delmont, and Garfield went on her way upstairs to attend to the young master.

He lay in his crib watching the dancing leaves of London's

plane trees beyond the window. The light seemed to be caught and held in his pale amber eyes, and, not for the first time, Winnie Garfield turned her glance away from them to his chubby face, which, to her mind, bore a strong resemblance to his mother's. In particular, he had her gentle mouth, and when he smiled, which was often, she could see dear Dulcima's lips curving in that spontaneous way of hers. Oh, yes, he was Dulcima Howard's child, and no mistake. There was little resemblance to the man who had fathered him, except those eyes, which could be ignored, because all his other features outclassed them. Perhaps they would change with time, but she would thank that chirpy Delia Davidson to stop asking why he had not been born with blue ones. '*All* babies are born with blue eyes,' the little girl had declared. 'I know, because I read it in a book. They are blue at birth even if they change colour later.'

'Not always, Miss Know-All.'

'Well, I don't *yet* know all, but I mean to try, and I do think it a pity that baby Charles hasn't inherited his mother's gorgeous blue. I met her once, at Kingsmere, and thought her very beautiful.'

'So she was, young miss. So she certainly was. What's more, she was as good as she was beautiful.'

'Mamma didn't think so, and I could tell my grandmother didn't, either, the day they met. She even suggested that Miss Howard should leave Kingsmere at once.'

That had startled Garfield, who had heard nothing of any meeting between the dowager and her dear mistress, and was angered to think of Miss Dulcima being snubbed. Garfield's one dread during the whole of that memorable visit had been that the two should meet, for, unlike trusting Dulcima, she had fully expected Charles Ashleigh's wife to know all about their long-standing relationship. Such things could never be hushed up, and everything about the famous Dulcima had made news, both publicly and privately. What didn't appear in the press was passed on by word of mouth, society consisting of idle gossips.

As for that Caroline, one glance at her had been enough for Garfield, who didn't like long, thin women. She was thin herself, but she wasn't long, and with such as she it didn't matter anyway, because she had never aspired to be anything more than what she was in life, but those born to better things shouldn't be on a par with the likes of herself, even physically. Women in society ought to know better than to be skinny.

To Garfield's mind, a woman was only a true woman if she had Dulcima Howard's lovely curves, and she knew every man would agree with her. That was one reason, but only one, why men had fallen in love with Dulcima. The others were her gaiety and wit, her warm abandon, her good nature, her generosity. In Garfield's eyes her late mistress had possessed every virtue and absolutely no faults, and she would dearly like to say as much to this young miss's mother, who had apparently let even her daughter know that she didn't class Dulcima Howard as a good woman. But what chance would come the way of a former lady's maid to tear a strip off Caroline Davidson, especially since she had gone gallivanting off alone to far-flung places where no respectable Englishwoman would ever set foot? Garfield wondered yet again why that nice Mr Davidson permitted it. Very likely he hadn't much choice, his wife having money of her own to do what she liked with, and somehow Garfield suspected that he didn't mind anyway, especially since meeting Deborah Yorke. Garfield prided herself on being no fool. She could tell when a man was interested in a woman, and vice versa, and guessed that these two were fighting a losing battle between their consciences and their desires, not surrendering yet, but being strongly tempted.

She was convinced that the man wouldn't be able to

keep his distance much longer, with his small daughter visiting the house regularly and he as little as possible – which spoke for itself. And there was something about Miss Yorke these days which reminded her more and more of Miss Dulcima when she had been on the brink of taking her first lover. Dulcima had been younger, but as ripe for it as Deborah Yorke was now.

Oh, yes, Garfield knew the signs, and in a way welcomed them, because being cared for by a man would be better than this card business, which wasn't up Miss Yorke's street at all.

It seemed to be common knowledge that people could win at 20 Hanover Square more regularly and more profitably than they could in Dulcima Howard's day. This meant that the new hostess was handling affairs badly, and Garfield couldn't think why Dillon let so many players in, unless it was because increased numbers meant increased stakes – or else he enjoyed flouting Miss Yorke's stipulation about limiting them.

Oh, for the good old days! It had been Dulcima Howard's beauty and personality which drew people then. Men didn't mind losing money to such a woman, but poor Miss Yorke was on a losing wicket, well advertised by Dillon's black looks around the house, plus his attitude toward her. Garfield had actually begun to feel sorry for Deborah Yorke and, if necessary, was ready to line up with her against Dillon.

Goodness only knew where it was going to end, with all these undercurrents going on, Dillon hating the new mistress for making a mess of things, and in particular for banning Lord Ashleigh, and Bella going around more cock-a-hoop every day for reasons well known belowstairs, and many more that could be guessed at, and Mr Davidson keeping his distance against his will, and Miss Deborah wanting nothing so much as to welcome him here more often, and now this row over that picture she had accepted from someone who couldn't pay up. The whole staff knew about that, for Dillon hadn't troubled to lower his voice, and Miss Deborah's clear tones had also carried, though not so loudly. And Garfield had to admit that what Dillon said made sense – fancy accepting a picture (and not even in a nice frame) for a debt of two hundred pounds! Garfield knew instinctively that such a mistake was likely to be the young lady's undoing. Dillon had a very nasty, spiteful streak in him when he cared to use it, though exactly how he could hit back, she had no idea.

She turned her attention to the child, picking him up with the familiar surge of love. The dear lamb smiled, crooning a little, and one tiny shell-like hand curled round her forefinger, clutching with the amazing tenacity of small babies.

'Now, now, my little dear, you'll have to let go, because I have to give you your bottle, and how am I going to do that with you clinging to my hand?'

But she didn't want to dislodge those delicate little fingers, the nails like tiny pink shells, the skin so soft. She brushed his forehead with her dry lips, longing to kiss his little bud of a mouth but knowing it was unhealthy for the child to be kissed in such a way. One might pass on germs, such as colds. Miss Yorke was very progressive in her outlook, and on the whole Garfield saw the sense of it, though she sneaked a tiny kiss every now and then to satisfy her frustrated mother love.

The toothless smile widened, the little legs kicked joyfully.

'There's a strong little boy, then! There's my clever little master!'

This was Garfield's happiest hour of the day, when she was entirely alone up here with baby Charles. 'My little lordship,' she murmured, 'my little lordship. That's what you are, if you did but know it. Or should be, one day, and maybe will, if *I* have anything to do with it.'

How could Miss Yorke possibly imagine that she could keep the child's parentage from him forever? Dislike the Ashleighs though she did, Garfield was beginning to resent the fact that this child was denied recognition by them. Had he been legitimate, he would have become his father's heir, inheriting that country seat in Sussex with all its riches. The idea of keeping the truth from the child, which had seemed desirable at the time of his birth, had become less so of late. It even seemed like cheating him.

Weren't there cases in which illegitimate children had been able to make claims of some kind later in life? Garfield couldn't think of any specific ones, but felt sure she had heard of such things or read about them in the newspapers. Wills had been overturned, hadn't they? Families torn apart? It would serve that Ashleigh lot right if this boy upset their apple cart and took the lot. And a better king of the castle he would make than his father. Even in babyhood certain characteristics manifested themselves, and in this child was a sweetness of nature never possessed by the man who fathered him.

When you looked after a baby every day, you got to know his nature, and Garfield knew this child's already. It was his mother's, all over again, so the pale eyes didn't matter. In time, they wouldn't even be noticed. He would grow more and more like her dear Dulcima, not only in looks but also in kindness and warmth of nature, and a wicked thing it would be not to fight to get for the child all that his mother would have inherited had Justin Ashleigh had the decency to make her his wife.

Chrystal Delmont had been standing with her back to the door studying the painting still propped on the mantelpiece when Deborah entered.

'I hope you like it, Miss Delmont?'

The woman turned, saying spontaneously, 'Indeed, I do. How could one fail to?' Her outstretched hand met Deborah's. 'Whoever the artist is, he – or she? – is tremendously talented.'

'A young man named Peter Maynard. Only eighteen, and still struggling.'

'So you bought this to help him?'

'Not entirely. I wanted it as soon as I saw it.'

'It would make a wonderful backdrop for a scene at dawn on the Thames Embankment. Good scenic artists are hard to find. The theatre could offer a good living to a young man so talented.'

'I will suggest it, but not until he has finished his present commission, which may not be so much to his liking but will help him to achieve self-discipline. Oh, dear, I sound like a schoolmarm, don't I? Blame my Church background, which was sternly disciplined, though I secretly rebelled.'

Falling into conversation so easily seemed natural to both. Deborah looked into the face of this handsome middle-aged woman and liked it immediately. Chrystal Delmont felt the same, and was glad she had come, after all. When receiving the note in answer to hers, her instinct had been to destroy it, for she had good reason to regard this house with a certain bitterness. The woman who had owned it had supplanted her in Ashleigh's life, though no doubt unwittingly. Justin had grown tired of an older woman very quickly, especially one who had almost lost the art of lovemaking after years of a physically frustrated marriage. But not a loveless one. Marriage to an invalid became something to tolerate through a sense of duty only if love went out of it, and love had never gone from hers. It had remained in the heart and the mind, along with loyalty and the memory of the union as it had been before ill health forced it into physical deprivation. There had been passion in the early years, and a desire for children, but none had come, and eventually it was too late.

It was not Joseph's fault that illness had made a wreck of him, putting an end to his musical career as well as his virile manhood, leaving him dependent on his wife's support. A woman didn't leave a man because of that, or cease to love and respect him. The greater tragedy had been that in becoming dependent upon her, he had ceased to respect himself. He had never been content to be supported by a woman.

What had made her fall in love with Justin Ashleigh, or imagine she had, when she met him several months after her husband's death, she had never been able to understand. Perhaps it was because she was at last released from a sexless life. She had almost forgotten what it was like to feel a man's body in union with her own. 'You should have taken a lover,' Justin had said brutally, 'then you wouldn't have lost the knack of things. Never mind, in time you will learn again how to perform well in bed.'

That had startled her, because although self-conscious and shy following years of self-denial, she had enjoyed renewed sexual experience. The knowledge that she was proving inadequate came as a shock, and with it the feeling that she should have known a younger man would not be satisfied with an older woman for long. And then, when she had seen his wife for the first time, something inside her had withdrawn from him. What had he done, to make the poor thing look so frozen and despairing? Does she know about me? Or have there been others?

Of course, there had been others. A man with Justin Ashleigh's lusts could never be content with one woman. He had already been pursuing Dulcima Howard before her own brief affair with him came to an end, and although she was already regretting it and deciding to terminate it, his abrupt rejection hurt her pride.

'I think it would be better if you found a man nearer your own age, my dear. Perhaps a widower seeking comfort as you are, his appetites also dulled with the years. You *are* a little *passée*, aren't you, darling?'

She had plunged back into work at the theatre, seeking forgetfulness of her vain folly, though surely she was not the only middle-aged woman in the world who had instinctively sought a renewal of love? But the sight of Dulcima Howard, that famous beauty, had been a constant reminder of her own lost youth and what some people might regard as her wasted years. Coupled with the realisation that the professional beauty had replaced her was the knowledge that, for her, the peak years had passed and Dulcima Howard had many more ahead. Many more years and, no doubt, many more lovers, if the stories one heard were true.

Which only showed how wrong one could be. There had been no long period of glory ahead of the popular beauty. The whole of London had been shocked to hear that she had gone. In childbirth, it was rumoured, though the press never printed the story. But certainly there was a child in this house. She had seen Miss Howard's maid, wheeling a perambulator and obviously doting on the child. Once or twice she had been tempted to peep at it in passing, but refrained. She had stopped looking at babies long ago, because they reminded her too painfully of her own unfulfilled longing for them.

And now she was following this young woman, who bore a decided resemblance to Dulcima Howard, upstairs to the bedroom the professional beauty had occupied. She was not surprised by its elegance, nor by the vast bed dominating it. Here Justin must have made love to her, and found her more satisfying than he had found herself. Such thoughts were foolish; they could border on self-pity, which was always dangerous. And why shrink from touching these clothes? If she had come here only to torment herself, the sooner she departed, the better.

Besides, as an actress she had to be sensible. Providing

a good and constantly changing stage wardrobe for modern productions, for which, unlike costume plays, actors had to supply their own clothes, was a very costly business, and the opportunity to acquire quality items such as these was too good to miss. As she examined them one by one, her admiration for them overcame her reluctance to try them on. Dulcima Howard had not only possessed superb taste, but had thought nothing of going over to Paris to be dressed by Worth. Chrystal also had to bear in mind that since the Comet Theatre employed her as permanent leading lady, following years building up her reputation as a supporting lead at the Boswell, she owed it to the management and to audiences to maintain her reputation as one of the best-dressed women on the London stage.

She bought the entire wardrobe, furs as well. On her salary at the Comet she could afford it. Miss Yorke looked positively grateful. Chrystal Delmont wondered why. From all accounts, there was a flourishing card salon here, so the only reason for the girl's gratitude must surely be that she found these clothes a painful reminder of bereavement. Wasn't it said that she was Miss Howard's cousin?

'Would you like me to pack them and bring them to your house?' Deborah asked.

Miss Delmont would not hear of her going to so much trouble; she would collect them later. 'And it isn't my house,' she added. 'We had an apartment there. The ground floor, because it was easier for my husband, in his wheelchair. Many owners of large London houses are beginning to utilise them in this way. But I am seeking something else now I am alone, partly because our rooms in Maddox Street are filled with reminders of Joseph, and partly because I would prefer to be on a higher floor, away from street noises. May I collect these things tomorrow? I have a matinee this afternoon and must get to the theatre early to run through a couple of scenes with my new leading man. He should be word perfect by now, but isn't. Bryant Meredith is a good actor, but too fond of socialising to attend to his work as he should and,' she finished with a touch of impatient indulgence, 'he has a great weakness for women, who occupy too much of his time.'

Bryant Meredith. The name was familiar to Deborah, but not because she was a theatregoer. Since she had begun running the card salon there had been no opportunity for such relaxation. She turned the name over in her mind, trying to recall when and how she had heard it, but another thought was more demanding. This woman had unwittingly suggested a way to earn an income without running a risky gaming establishment. Number 20 Hanover Square was too big for just herself, Garfield, and the child, and once the card salon was closed, staff could be cut to a minimum. Then there would be all those surplus rooms, begging to be lived in. She could let them, floor by floor.

She said impulsively, 'Miss Delmont, if you are really seeking accommodation elsewhere, I can offer it to you here.'

The nation was disappointed that the early coronation they hoped for was not to take place, the king deciding on 26th June of the following year in the hope that it could be celebrated in time of peace, for the Boer War was dragging on and no treaty was in sight. There was also French and German criticism to contend with, echoed by the Dutch on behalf of their compatriots. To hold a coronation ceremony at such a time was to risk ostracism by crowned heads from abroad, so the date was set for eighteen months after the accession, in the hope that this unpopular war would be over by then.

The news formed the main topic of conversation in Deborah's drawing room that night, and she was glad of it, for it kept at bay the decisive moment of which she was unexpectedly nervous. She knew that the evening marked a turning point in her life. She was taking a plunge from which she was unsure of surfacing successfully, and although resolved upon it, she was inwardly tense. Visitors were arriving desultorily and lingering over their champagne as they discussed the latest situation, and, to Deborah's surprise, Dillon was making no attempt to urge them into the gaming room. It was almost as if he, too, were in no hurry, a fact which made Deborah uneasy. Could he possibly suspect what she planned to do, or was he playing some waiting game of his own?

He was certainly avoiding her. He even seemed reluctant to share their preliminary inspection of the card room, which, in any case, was a mere formality tonight, since she had no intention of putting the place to further use. But it was necessary to carry on the pretence to allay suspicion on Dillon's part.

Now she waited for sufficient guests to arrive before breaking her news, and she was determined to be adamant about it. There would be no more baccarat at 20 Hanover Square from this night forth.

She had dressed carefully for the occasion, wearing the silver-grey moiré taffeta and emeralds because again they boosted her confidence. She saw Dillon's eyes flicker toward the jewels as she came downstairs, and immediately resolved to guard them personally until he left this house once and for all. She would put nothing past the man, not even an attempt to steal jewels which could be identified unless broken up by a master hand and disposed of as individual gems. Then his mouth had curved contemptuously, indicating that he guessed her thoughts. 'What sort of a fool do you take me for, Miss Yorke?' He had not spoken the words. It had not been necessary.

Nor had it been necessary to remind her of his threat, should she try any tricks with him.

Tension between them was now as taut as a spring. She

could not look at him across the drawing room and was thankful whenever he left it to answer the doorbell. Only vaguely was she aware that on one occasion he returned without announcing a new arrival, though she had been sure the front door had opened and closed. At that moment she had been listening to Hardcastle, who was holding forth about the expectation of the populace when the coronation did finally take place.

'To them, it will be the highlight of the new reign, and I hear the king intends to personally supervise all arrangements.'

'And the queen is refusing to follow the precedent of the last queen consort, declaring she knows better than all the royal milliners and antiquaries, and that for the coronation she will wear exactly what she pleases.'

'She is certainly proving to have a mind of her own. Do you remember how, on the king's birthday, he insisted on driving through London alone to receive the plaudits of the crowd, so she waved good-bye from the palace windows, then ordered a carriage for herself and followed the tail end of the procession, looking magnificent and stealing all the thunder?'

It was idle chatter, but interesting, and since several present were well connected, no doubt much of it was true, but the minutes were ticking by, and now Dillon's eyes were upon her, trying to convey that it was time to bring this social session to a close and move into the card room. She even sensed a sudden impatience about him, almost an excitement, and wondered what caused it. Perhaps she had imagined his earlier attitude and she alone had been playing a waiting game?

Refusing to meet his eye, she signalled for more champagne to be served. Very soon she would speak, and when everyone had departed, Dillon would be unable to put up any argument when instructed to tell further callers that the salon was closed once and for all.

At that moment the last visitor arrived. It was Bruce Whitney, and he immediately cornered her, demanding to know how Maynard had persuaded her to hand back his cheque.

'He didn't. I know a good painting when I see one. It would seem that you don't.'

He didn't miss the cool note in her voice, but attributed it only to his lack of judgment. He felt a touch of chagrin. Had Deborah Yorke, whom he had always considered rather naive, actually spotted a good investment and snatched it from under his nose?

'If it's that good, I'll buy it from you,' he said.

'Before its value increases, you mean? You don't really care whether it is a good painting or not. All you are interested in is grabbing at something you now feel you shouldn't have missed, something which must surely be of value, since it was worth cancelling a substantial debt for. That is the difference between us. I value the painting because it is beautiful, because I want to live with it, and I won't part with it whatever value it ultimately reaches. If you missed a good opportunity, blame yourself. And I don't admire the way you led your foolish young friend into trouble.'

She turned her back on him, bolstered by the encounter. If she could deal with a man as self-confident as Bruce Whitney, she could deal with Dillon. Meanwhile, she needed a breathing space, and while glasses were being refilled, she decided to slip across to the card room and put away the unopened decks. Tomorrow she would cancel further orders. It was all very easy if one acted resolutely, and she cared little about Dillon's covert glance as she departed. He was annoyed because she was offering her guests more champagne instead of getting down to the business of the evening. The thought amused her. He would be even more annoyed shortly.

She ignored his glance as she left the room: then she

crossed to the card room, opened the door, and looked straight across at Justin Ashleigh, lounging at ease beside the fire.

14

He was turning some cards over in his hands, inspecting them thoroughly, and from the way he did it, it was apparent that he knew exactly where to look, and at which ones.

Behind her, in a part of her consciousness not stunned by shock, she heard the front doorbell ringing again. Instinct made her close the card-room door before Dillon went to answer. She had no desire for any visitor to witness her meeting with a man who had been admitted secretly and hidden until play was expected to begin.

Ashleigh looked up, smiled, and rose in a leisurely fashion. 'My dear Deborah, you look very beautiful. You have blossomed since we last met. And you wear dear Dulcima's emeralds well. A gift to her from my father, I understand. You look surprised. Were you unaware that she was my father's mistress long before she became mine? Alas, if the emeralds had been a gift to her from me, I would ask you to accept them in her stead, but perhaps she bequeathed them to you anyway? From all I hear, I am surprised you have not sold them. And with cards such as these to defraud players, I am equally surprised you found it necessary to sell anything at all. Cutting down staff too, I gather. Hardly the signs of a prosperous gaming establishment! And yet you had the effrontery to refuse admission to me, who never quibbled however greatly I was swindled and would certainly never have embarrassed you with exposure. Surely you knew how attracted I was to you, that weekend at Kingsmere?'

'The weekend you treated Dulcima so callously? Am I likely to forget it?'

Quite unruffled, he continued, 'If you would have the sense, even now, to be as accommodating to me as dear Dulcima was in her lifetime, you would have no problems at all, and I would not dream of revealing to everyone that you play with marked cards.'

'So Dillon let you in for that purpose?'

'Useful Dillon. You shouldn't have made an enemy of him. Nor of me. I am unaccustomed to being refused admission to any lady's house. Not that this one belongs to you. I understand Dulcima's child inherits.'

Dillon had certainly been talking; taking his revenge, too. By bringing disgrace upon her, he no doubt expected to reap a harvest for himself with this man's aid, confident that disillusioned patrons would follow him to other premises financed by Ashleigh. At least that would finally remove him from her life, though exposure could bring her trouble with the law. The thought brought a lurch of fear equalled only by her anger. How long had Dillon been in touch with this man? From the beginning, it seemed, since Ashleigh knew so much about her forced economies and financial difficulties.

Initial shock was subsiding beneath a rage so strong that voices outside in the hall went unheeded. She was only vaguely aware that Dillon's was defiant and faintly aggressive, the other decisive and familiar. Fury over the deception practised on her, and Ashleigh's bland assumption that he held the whip hand, deepened her anger so that when he strolled toward her, murmuring, 'My dear Deborah, you have no need to be afraid of me,' she flung back, 'I am not in the least afraid of a man like you!'

'Splendid. I trust that means you intend to be co-operative.'

He reached out to her. She sidestepped, unable to conceal her distaste, and his bland smile was replaced by a frown as she rapped, 'There is absolutely no way in which I would co-operate with you.'

Good Lord, she actually meant it! This country miss from heaven only knew where was rejecting him with the cool impudence with which she had written her dismissive note. She didn't seem to realise that he had her cornered, that he could destroy her, that he had only to wait until Dillon ushered in the players for him to expose her before everyone as a card-sharping little harpy.

He said, carefully driving the words home syllable by syllable, 'Do you realise I can bring the patrons of your elegant little salon down on you like a pack of wolves, howling for repayment of losses you cannot meet?'

'If you hope to do that, Lord Ashleigh, you will be disappointed. You come too late. No more baccarat is being played in this house.'

'And do your visitors know? From the look of things, and the sound of things, I imagine not. The table is prepared, the cards ready, and a number of people seem to be gathered in your drawing room.'

To announce that she was about to tell them that play was at an end would only imply that he had goaded her into it, that she was afraid of him, and as if reading her mind, he said sarcastically, 'Perhaps a farewell party is going on in there? But it isn't too late. I can walk in and show these cards.'

She had had enough. Blazing, she flung open the door. '*Do your damnedest!*' she cried, and whirled out into the hall, pulling up sharply as she came face to face with Dillon, and, beside him, Simon Davidson. At that, she almost sobbed with relief, but her voice was steady as she commanded the butler to show Lord Ashleigh off the premises.

The man didn't move. His eyes shifted from one to the other. He was disconcerted by the turn of events. He had not anticipated the arrival of Ashleigh's brother-in-law, a man he remembered well from his first call at this house. Tonight Davidson cut a very different figure from the one he had presented then. Now he was clad in evening wear worthy of Savile Row. Even so, Dillon had tried to get rid of him, knowing instinctively that for these two men to come face to face could only spell trouble. Beneath his quiet composure, Davidson was that kind of man.

Now he rapped, 'You heard your mistress. Show Lord Ashleigh off the premises.'

Justin demanded angrily, 'What right have *you* to give orders in this house? Am I to assume that in your wife's absence our charming Deborah has been as accommodating to you as her cousin was to me? She seems to have inherited a lot of Dulcima's talents, including cheating at cards. I often wondered how that dear lady of mine won so consistently and so well – '

' – and now Dillon has told you, thereby revealing his own part in things. I recall your suspicion of him. Obviously, you have acted on it, and found it justified.'

Dillon showed alarm then, but Simon's glance was on the cards in Justin's hands. How they were marked, he had no idea, but it was apparent that Ashleigh had found out. It had been equally apparent, when Dillon opened the front door, that the man wanted no third party intruding at this moment, particularly a man known to be a friend of Miss Yorke's. Simon had seen the thoughts mirrored in the butler's eyes and heard them reflected in his blustering voice as he stammered, 'I am sorry, sir, but only regular players are admitted – '

'I am a regular visitor, and that is enough.'

Dillon had been forced to stand aside, though the blustering note had changed to truculence and a spate of protests. His mistress was with her guests . . . play had already begun . . . it could not be interrupted . . . He had continued to flounder with the bewilderment of someone trying to cope with an unwelcome situation, whereupon Simon's resolve had hardened. He had pushed past the man and walked into the house, saying, 'From the sound of things, Miss Yorke's guests are in the drawing room, not the card room.'

Dillon had answered defiantly that on the mistress's orders no one was admitted without an official invitation, and at that precise moment the door of the card salon had burst open on Deborah's blazing challenge.

The game was up. This man Davidson was astute, and the young woman's refusal to be intimidated, hurling her anger in Lord Ashleigh's face like that, was a shock. Dillon had imagined it would be easy to get his own back through someone whom he had always regarded as powerful, but now Ashleigh looked weak in comparison with his aggressive brother-in-law. Davidson was still talking, but Dillon paid no further heed, his mind bent only on escape. He edged toward the back stairs, fighting panic. If exposure were to come in a way other than planned, it would be worse for himself than for the girl, since he had been involved right from the beginning and had confided his knowledge to Ashleigh – apart from which, he had a record the police could dig up, whereas she had become part of the organisation only since inheriting. They might even claim that in her innocence she had also been ignorant.

Even more alarming was the fact that Ashleigh had been suspicious of him and therefore used him for his own ends. All those fine promises meant nothing. He would be ditched whenever it suited his lordship's book. He would get out while he still had the chance.

Cursing his own impatience and wishing he had waited

just a little longer, long enough to take over the helm as he planned (no chance of that now, no chance at all!), Dillon hurried down the service stairs and through the kitchen to the butler's quarters.

He was flinging clothes into a suitcase when Bella's voice said from the door, 'And where d'you think *you're* going?'

She swaggered into the room, still talking. 'There's no one up there to serve the gentlemen, and now what d'you think Miss Yorke has done? Walked in with that Mr Davison beside her and announced there's to be no play tonight or any other night. Couldn't believe my ears, I couldn't. Turned round to look for you, but you'd gone, so I went into the hall, and who d'you think was on his way out? Lord Ashleigh, looking like murder. He gave me a message for you. You're to leave the front door on the latch tonight. Wot's going on, eh?'

He pushed her aside and hurried to the butler's pantry, where he began stuffing items of silver into his pockets.

'Hey!' she cried, following him. 'You doing a bunk or something?'

'What does it look like? Now, get out of my way and back to your duties upstairs. Cover for me, and you'll have cause to be grateful.'

'Grateful for wot? Don't think I won't spill the beans if you run out on me.'

Damn her. Why did she have to choose this moment to come down?

'Listen,' he said desperately, 'there's no time to talk. Meet me tonight at the World's End, far end of Fulham Road. They don't close till after midnight, and since play has been called off upstairs, you'll be off duty long before then. I'll wait for you in the public bar.'

'I still want to know wot I'll have cause to be grateful for. A cut of wot you get for that silver, mebbe?'

Her head was tilted to one side, her eyes calculating, her

arms akimbo, feet astride, blocking his way. He had to promise her something, anything, then he could get out of here and never see her again.

'More than that. We'll pair up together, Bella. You don't think I could do without you in my life, do you?'

He kissed her before putting her aside and going back to fasten his case. Then he was heading for the servants' entrance, her voice following him across the kitchen. 'Hey! Wot about his lordship wanting the catch left up on the front door?'

'You see to it,' he flung over his shoulder. He didn't give a damn whether his famous lordship got back into the house or not, or what he did when he got there. He was up the area steps and away, leaving 20 Hanover Square forever.

Once Dillon had slipped off the scene, Simon had made short shrift of his brother-in-law, accusing him of trying to frighten Deborah, and wanting to know why.

'You have not been admitted to the card salon since it reopened, so what are you likely to gain by making accusations at this late date? And do you think it would have any effect on gamblers who would prefer it not to be known that they could be hoodwinked, or on those who want to keep quiet about their attendances at any gaming room? Men like Hardcastle, for instance, men in the public eye. They would thank you to keep quiet, and humiliating Deborah in front of them wouldn't cast you in a good light. It would be more likely to win sympathy for her. She certainly has mine. I know of your sadistic streak, Justin. Don't try to exercise it here.'

Ashleigh had changed colour at that, but said nothing. He had merely turned to the hall stand, reaching for his outdoor things and tossing crumpled cards to the floor. Simon pocketed them, in case someone idly picked them up. Despite his confident words, it was better not to tempt fate. Then he put his hand beneath Deborah's elbow and went with her into the drawing room, leaving Ashleigh to find his own way out.

Deborah said quietly, 'Fate must have brought you.'

'Not fate. My own choice. Something told me the time had come to step in.'

'So now you can hear what I thought I would be announcing alone.'

He stood beside her while she broke the news, and later, when everyone had gone after uttering expressions of regret, understanding, or reproach, he lingered. She told him then what she proposed to do with the house.

'I shall rent off rooms as apartments. That way it can be made to pay for itself. I don't know why I didn't think of it before. And already I have my first tenant – Chrystal Delmont, the actress. I offered her Dulcima's suite on the first floor – her bedroom and boudoir and private sitting room and bathroom. The boudoir can be turned into a small kitchen and the whole thing be self-contained. At first she seemed to hesitate, though somehow I knew she wanted to come, but for a while she looked around as if Dulcima was still in occupation. It was the oddest feeling. I know the rooms are stamped with her personality, but I promised to remove all personal mementos and leave only the main furnishings, so she can add her own things and the rooms will become hers entirely. Gradually she seemed to see them in a different light and said yes, she would take them. She has her present apartment on a monthly basis, so will move in soon. And she offered a very good rent, higher than I was going to ask! I'm so thankful I took your advice to close the card salon.'

'And what of the rest of the rooms? There are two whole floors above, aren't there?'

'Plus a large attic with a dormer window and skylight, which I shouldn't think anyone would want, but I am confident that I can let the rest. Miss Delmont tells me there is an increasing demand for apartments in the West End of London. I shan't in the least mind being a landlady. In fact, I rather think I'll like it.'

'Then promise me something — don't let those other rooms go yet. I have reasons for asking, and I'll discuss them when I get back from Bath in a couple of days. I'm off there tomorrow to lecture at an evening institute, returning the next day. I'll come to see you as soon as I get back.'

Meet me at the World's End before midnight, Dillon had said, so there was plenty of time. Bella shed her cap and apron, loosened her hair and her stays, and sat down to wait.

Mr Davidson was still upstairs in the drawing room. That was interesting. Would Miss Yorke see him out, or would she invite him up to her room? My word, Garfield would be shocked if that happened! The woman would excuse such behaviour in a person like Miss Dulcima, but never in someone like Miss Yorke. Ever so respectable, was Miss Yorke. Too damn respectable. What she missed in life! Bella looked back on an endless chain of experiences and regretted none of them. She was still alive, wasn't she? Still hale and hearty, ready for the next.

Ten-thirty. She should be going soon. But she mustn't forget to leave the catch up on the front door. What for? she wondered. So his lordship could walk in unannounced? Was he after Miss Yorke? Was she really his cup of tea? Not like *I* am, thought Bella proudly. She'd be tepid, compared with me.

Ten-forty. Sounds from above. Was that the closing of the front door, or a distant bedroom door? Had Mr Davidson taken his departure or not? And did his lordship really intend to come back? If so, when? It would be fun to confront him in the hall! But time was slipping by. The

World's End was 'way down in Fulham. Better get going, or Dillon might not wait.

But of course he would! For two years he'd been having her, so was he likely to break the habit now? Besides, she knew about the silver, and if he tried any tricks and flogged it without letting her know, she could tell the police and identify the stuff. She had been in the butler's pantry often enough when Dillon did the polishing. She knew every item. He had taken all the small ones, things easy to conceal. Snuffboxes and match holders and cream jugs and sugar tongs; dozens of little things she could describe in detail so the police would know what to look for.

Try to cheat me, Dillon, and I'll split on you, that I will. Even if I can't trace you, I'll see the police do. They'll go to every fence in London, knowing what to ask for and what to look for, and the trail will lead to you in the end.

So let him wait down there in Fulham while she sat here listening for his lordship's step. She knew it well enough, after all the weeks she had lingered in Burlington Gardens waiting for it. And down here, in the kitchen, feet mounting the front steps echoed clearly.

And now they came. She leapt up, stays still loose, hair still loose, and raced up the service stairs and along to the hall, reaching the main stairs just as his lordship set foot upon them.

'Oh, sir, don't go up there! She's not alone!'

He turned his head slowly and looked at her. She took a retreating step, alarmed by the expression on his face. Never had she seen him look quite like this, not even in his wildest moments in the cigar vendor's back room. That strange light in his eye, the fierce penetration of it – yes, that she knew, but not this other look, all white and fixed and rigid. Frightening, it was.

She took another retreating step, wishing she had gone on her way to the World's End, after all.

'Who is with her?' he asked, and at that her tension relaxed, for his voice sounded quite normal. So long as she didn't look at his mouth, all tight and savage, she could put up with the piercing brightness of his eyes, and there was nothing alarming about his voice.

'Is it Mr Davidson, Bella? *Is it?*'

'Well, sir, I didn't exactly see. I just heard, if you know what I mean . . .'

'Their voices, their footsteps? You recognised them?'

She nodded. She wished she hadn't started all this, but she couldn't back out now. A fine fool she would look, if she did.

'And they went upstairs to her room? Are you sure of that?'

She wasn't. She even thought it unlikely. She was certain it was the front door she had heard closing, but she nodded, and to her surprise, he began to laugh; soundless laughter which sent a shiver through her. Oh, for the public bar at the World's End! The noise, the smell, the sawdust, the ribald laughter, the sweaty men, the coarse jokes, the drunken singing, the searching male hands on her buttocks and breasts, and Dillon getting more jealous by the minute. There was safety there.

And there was safety here! What was she imagining? Taking leave of her senses, that she must be. She knew his lordship. A bit cranky in some ways, but she had coped with his habits before, and she would cope with them again, provided he paid her well. Was he going to want her now, peeved because he couldn't have the quarry he was after? He'd have a much better time with me than with that virgin upstairs, Bella thought proudly.

His eyes were on her hair. She had forgotten that she had left it cascading down her back. He put out a hand and touched it, passing his tongue over his lip as he did so. 'On your way to bed, Bella?'

'I . . . I was, sir, yes.'

The tight line of his mouth loosened. It seemed almost slack now. Moist and slack, while his eyes remained hard and bright.

'D'you want to come with me, your lordship?'

'No, Bella. I want *you* to come with *me*.'

'Then I'll just get ready, sir. Get my coat and put up my hair. Can't go out looking like this, can I?' She giggled coquettishly. 'A tenner, maybe?'

'Twenty, if you like, but come as you are, and hurry.'

Twenty! For that, it was worth going without a coat, cold as it was outside. *Twenty*! She had never seen that much in all her life.

Now he was really in a state. Trembling with impatience. She had never seen him so agitated, and said considerately, 'You can come to my room if you promise to be quiet, sir.'

He didn't bother to answer. He pulled her toward the door, and she went willingly enough. For twenty she would put up no opposition at all.

Nor was she able to, prostrate on the damp earth amongst some bushes in the Square gardens, hidden by the dark night, his hand clamped over her mouth and the other reaching for her hair.

It was Cook who discovered Bella was missing and that Dillon's bed had not been slept in. When Garfield came down to the kitchen, she announced, 'Done a bunk, the pair of them! Would you believe it, they've actually done a bunk! Come and see for yourself.'

Garfield entered Dillon's quarters in Cook's wake, staring over her shoulder at the untouched bed and the yawning cupboard and drawers.

Characteristically, she thought of essentials first. 'What about the silver? Anything missing? A butler has charge of the silver, remember.'

But it all seemed to be there, wrapped in green baize

and stored meticulously in the butler's pantry, though neither knew how many items made up the total.

'Miss Yorke will know,' said Garfield. 'I remember her making a list of it all – an "inventory" I think she called it, when she found Miss Dulcima had never bothered to insure anything!' She finished briskly, 'Now, what's all this about Bella?'

'*Her* bed hasn't been slept in, either. When she didn't come down, I went to her room and banged on the door, thinking the lazy creature was sleeping late. "If you don't get up right away, Bella," I shouts, "you'll miss your breakfast, that you will!" When she still didn't answer, I thought to meself, "They're in there together, that's wot." It wouldn't've been the first time, though usually she goes to Dillon's room, the butler's quarters being so neatly tucked away. So I rattled the doorknob to scare them, and lo and behold, it turned! Struck all of a heap, I was! There was her bed, not slept in either, though untidy as ever, with clothes thrown on top of it and strewn all over the place. What a slut! And the trash she spends her money on!'

'His money, you mean. And maybe others'. She couldn't tart herself up the way she does on a parlour-maid's wages. She's sure to come back, because she wouldn't walk out and leave all her stuff behind, but my word, *I'll* have something to say to her when she does turn up! Well, I'd best get upstairs and tell Miss Yorke. As for Dillon, it's good riddance to bad rubbish. I never did like him. Never liked either of 'em, if it comes to that.'

The man employed to sweep the Square gardens unlocked the wrought-iron gate used by residents and began his morning's work. Most of the autumn leaves had fallen, but still some fluttered down in the early dawn, to litter the paths and linger beneath the bushes and trees. He was an old man, and it took him some time to wield his besom, piling the refuse to be stowed into sacks and carted away for burning. Very fussy, were the residents of London's exclusive squares. Everything had to be spick-and-span, and there was always the additional trouble of litter left by vagrants who climbed over the railings seeking shelter for the night. And not always vagrants, but young bloods with their lasses. Many a time he would find a fragment of torn skirt or petticoat impaled on one of the spikes, and knew at once that he would find further evidence of nocturnal goings-on beneath the bushes. Sometimes a torn stocking, and once even a pair of stays. Scandalous, it was, the way folks behaved nowadays, and not always the lower classes, either, judging by the scraps of silks and satins torn off in hasty climbing.

There was a piece now, fluttering in the chill morning breeze, waving like a tiny flag from the railings. Someone had been trespassing again. That meant he would have to search the bushes thoroughly just in case, later in the day, some child toddled out to its nanny with a pair of lady's bloomers or suchlike. It had been known to happen, and once he had nearly lost his job because of it.

But this cloth belonged to no member of the gentry. It was a large slice of black material of the kind worn by a housemaid, and she must have been in a fine old hurry not to bother to remove it. A tiny scrap she might have overlooked, but not a rent this size. The old man had a sudden vision of a struggling servant girl, aghast because her housemaid's dress had been ruined, trying to snatch the piece back so she could patch it up somehow, and being forced to abandon it by some impatient man. Maybe she'd planned to pick it up on the the way back. So why didn't she?

He pushed the piece of material into his pocket. When he had finished, it would go into the sack along with the rest of his sweepings, but meanwhile he'd best search the bushes thoroughly in case anything else had been left behind.

Deep in the midst of them he saw a woman's bare legs spread-eagled in a fashion which urged him not to look any further. He backed away, stumbling through the bushes to the garden path. S'truth, but he'd never come across anything like that before! Shaking and breathless, he shuffled to the iron gate and out into the square, searching for a bobby and mercifully finding one across the road. Mouthing incoherently, he pointed behind him with a trembling finger. '*Oh, my Gawd, copper — in there . . . in there . . . in the middle o' them bushes!*'

15

Elizabeth Ashleigh was surprised to discover that her son had been at Kingsmere for the last two days, without her knowledge. Usually he called at the dower house shortly after his arrival, a kindness which always touched her. Dear Justin was so thoughtful. True, he had his problems, but always rose above them with her aid. His compliance when she took charge indicated, to her mind, his desire to conquer what she regarded as his 'misfortune', that occasional uncontrollable streak which he had inherited from her husband's family, never from her own. She chose to call it temper and firmly believed that her blood provided a merciful leavening to the Ashleigh strain.

Although she had been shocked by Norah's death and, for a long time, found it painful to meet her son, it had not been because she thought him capable of deliberate violence, but because her distress over the tragic outcome of what she chose to call his 'lapse' had gone deep.

'Why can't you bear to look at me, Mamma?' he had finally pleaded. 'It wasn't my fault, you know. Norah was too frail for marriage. Fragile women should never be allowed to wed. Her father should have warned me. Is it fair to palm off on to a healthy and normal man a bride who cannot even endure a long embrace? But that is what her father did. He kept quiet about her weak constitution and had no compunction about marrying her off, so long as she won a title. He fooled us all, Mother dear, and certainly defrauded *me*. I was never cruel to her. I treated her with infinite patience and gentleness.'

He had flung himself down at her feet then, burying his head in her lap just as he had done when a small boy after being punished by his father for what Charles regarded as acts of cruelty. None had ever been intentional, always accidental, and locking his sister in the cupboard that day, gagged and bound, had been nothing but a boyish prank. Small boys loved pretending to be brigands, and Caroline had been silly to have hysterics. As for the governess who had gone rushing to Charles – well, it had been wise to dispose of her, excellent teacher though she was, for she would surely have elaborated the story out of all proportion to everyone in the household. As it was, Charles had taken an exaggerated view of the whole thing.

Justin had always been high-spirited, but also highly strung and sensitive – hence the occasional breakdowns and the need for rest and treatment at the Swiss clinic. As for that servant-girl episode years ago, how many high-born gentlemen had seduced village girls? Hundreds, throughout the centuries, and many a country wench had considered it an honour. The girl had accepted Elizabeth's money without a murmur and made no trouble at all.

As for the one raped and strangled in Kingsmere's

woods months later, that had obviously been a crime committed by a tramp, and the police had been unable to prove otherwise. Never for a moment had the heir of Kingsmere been under suspicion, nor could he be, for he had been safe and sound beneath the family roof and nowhere near the scene of that hideous event. He had dined with the family and gone to bed when everyone did, and she would never forgive herself for recalling the incident when finding Norah dead that night.

Dear Justin. Poor Justin. All her son needed was to be protected from his sensitive and impulsive nature.

It had been tragic about Norah, of course, but really the girl had been a very dull creature and not good enough for her dear boy. Her death, and the way in which it had occurred, had been a horrible accident. It would have been better for her to have died in childbirth than in trying to resist a man's natural passion. That proved she was a weakling. Wives had to submit to their husbands' physical demands, but obviously Norah had resisted, and the outcome, though terrible, must therefore have been her own fault.

Elizabeth had long ago coaxed herself out of the horror of that night, and it would be to her eternal shame, she now thought, that even in a state of shock she could have considered her son to blame. She was sure he possessed no more than a man's average sexual appetite, as his father before him. She herself had dutifully tolerated that side of her marriage, until, having produced a son and daughter, she considered her duty discharged. She was left with her position and title, and her husband with his male freedom. Had he taken a mistress of birth and breeding, she would have accepted the situation with equanimity. She would even have been grateful to the woman for releasing her from the tedium of wifely submission, but for her husband to replace her with a London harlot was an insult she never forgave.

So as far as Justin was concerned, she considered her
husband to blame for setting his son a bad example. It was
regrettable that her dear boy had also taken up with
Dulcima Howard years later, but no doubt he considered
that what was good enough for his father was good enough
for himself, and the woman must have pursued him,
hoping to take the place of his dead wife.

But to keep quiet about his return to Kingsmere this
time was so unlike Justin that his mother could not, at
first, believe it was he who came riding across the park.
Every afternoon, after her nap, she would have the dogcart harnessed and then bowl through the countryside,
enjoying the gentle rocking of the vehicle on its two
enormous wheels. No dogs now occupied the ventilated
compartment at the back, as when Caroline and Justin
had been children and they had all set off for a day's sport,
but she still enjoyed handling the reins and returning the
respectful greetings of villagers and estate workers, stop-
ping every now and then to enquire after their health or
their families. Caroline sneered at what she called her
mother's 'Lady Bountiful act', but it was nothing of the
kind. From the day she married, Elizabeth had prided
herself on becoming mistress of Kingsmere, and she now
prided herself on carrying out her dowager duties.

It was on her way home that she saw her son galloping
across the wildest stretch of parkland, riding more reck-
lessly than usual and putting his mount to jumps too high
or too wide for easy scaling, whipping the creature to a
frenzy before taking its frantic leaps and laughing exul-
tantly when he cleared them. Justin was a magnificent
horseman, totally in control, completely lacking in fear,
and Charles had always been wrong when declaring that
he had no mercy for the animals.

Even so, there was something about Justin's behaviour
now which alarmed his mother. It was as if he were driven
by a devil, intent on self-destruction. She reined, pulled

the dogcart to one side, and watched with a mixture of pride and fear. Expert as her son was in the saddle, wasn't he going too hard for safety? She could feel the ground vibrating through the wheels of the stationary dogcart as horse and rider came thundering toward her. She sat very still, tight-reined in case any movement should startle the horse and throw him, but she should have known better. One glimpse of her brought him to a halt in a rush of air and flying mane, the horse rearing violently but not dislodging him. As dust fanned and swirled and began to settle, Justin called, 'So there you are, Mamma – I was on my way to see you.'

'In this direction, my son?'

'I was taking a roundabout route. I need exercise and fresh air after London.'

She believed it. She had not seen him so pale for a long time.

'Then you can return with me for tea,' she said, flicking the ponies to a trot and heading for home. Justin rode beside her, calming his horse with a brief pat every now and then. There was foam around the bit, and the massive chest was heaving.

'You have been riding him too hard, dear boy.'

'He'll recover. He's a strong animal.'

'All the same – '

'Mamma, don't lecture me the way my revered father used to.'

She fell silent, noting the tension about his mouth and the dark shadows beneath his eyes, but not until they were having tea did she ask if he were not sleeping well.

He shrugged. 'I have bouts of insomnia, as you know. They come and go. I've stayed in bed since my arrival a couple of days ago.'

'You have been here that long! Why didn't you send for me? A message would have brought me at once.'

'I didn't want to trouble you, Mother dear. You know

how you worry. I didn't want any fuss. I merely wanted to be left alone. Too many late nights take their toll, don't you know.'

Conversation became desultory. Sprawling at ease in an armchair beside the fire, long legs out-thrust, he was in no hurry to leave. The dower house was always a welcome refuge; he wished now that he had come before this, instead of taking to his room on arrival and remaining there, but never had he felt so exhausted. For that, he blamed Deborah Yorke. If she had been compliant, he would not have been driven to such a frenzy of hatred against the entire female sex. And Simon Davidson had aggravated things by saying, '*I know of your sadistic streak . . .* ' A devilish remark, touching him on the raw. Untrue, moreover, since they scarcely knew each other. Ashleigh was aware that he should not have allowed it to upset him, but, coming on top of Deborah's defiance, it had been the final spark to his fury.

Damn the man for turning up at the worst possible moment. A minute later, Deborah would have come to heel, for surely her challenge to him had been sheer bluff. One stride toward the drawing-room door to present his incriminating evidence would have brought her running after him, pleading with him, her defiance changing to submission, and then there would have been no wretched incident with that slut in the Square gardens. One had these moments of blind hatred, when punishment had to be meted out. Returning to 20 Hanover Square for that very purpose and being forestalled before he even reached Deborah's room had ignited the burning flame that blotted out reason.

'*Oh, sir, don't go up there! She's not alone!*' He could still feel the shock of Bella's words, and though they had prevented him from bursting into that upstairs room, and so betraying his presence in the house, all he now felt was regret that he had not caught Simon Davidson 'in the act' and so turned the tables. Outraged pride had prevented that, indignation because his sister's husband had apparently succeeded with Deborah where he had failed. She had admitted Simon Davidson into her bed and rejected himself – an insult which fanned his anger into avenging fury. Bella was handy. Bella was willing. Bella had to suffice.

After it was over, he felt as he always felt after an act of savagery – satiated, tranquil, at peace. He could scarcely recall the moments that followed, discarding the limp and useless body and climbing over the garden railings alone, the solitary walk back to Albany through quiet London streets, choosing the rear entrance because the night porter there would be nodding – unlike the one at the front, who had to keep alert for returning hansoms and carriages. Albany residents did not use that rear gate after an evening on the town. As he expected, he entered unnoticed, and only his man observed the state of his clothes, marked by damp earth. He had an excuse ready for that. Some damned cabby had splashed him liberally with mud – a habit of cabbies and, amongst some of the young blades about town, a subject for sport and betting. Odds were laid and then a course followed along the kerb to collect the greatest number of splashes, those most bespattered scooping the winnings when reaching either end of Piccadilly or the top of St James's Street – a notoriously bad thoroughfare when it came to slush and one where horses constantly slipped. Any gentleman's gentleman turned a blind eye to his master's ill treatment of his clothes, immediately cleaning and pressing them into respectability again.

As always, he had slept soundly and spent an idle day until the evening paper arrived. One glance urged him to escape from London to the solitude of Kingsmere without delay, for on the front page was a paragraph announcing that the body of a young woman had been found in the gardens of Hanover Square . . . sexual interference . . .

strangulation . . . thick hair knotted round her throat. No identification, as yet, but alarming even so, for this was the first time any reference to any of his escapades had appeared in the national press, though of course his name was not linked. That incident years ago, in Kingsmere's woods, had been confined merely to the local newspaper, some 'person or persons unknown' being blamed at the inquest (presumably a vagrant) and the case finally dismissed. But a London crime would involve the metropolitan police, which was something very different.

Defiantly he had pitched the newspaper into a wastebasket, drawing comfort from the thought that no one at 20 Hanover Square had seen him enter the house or leave it on his second visit, and not a soul had been in sight when he helped Bella over the garden railings. Even her cry when her dress was caught on a spike and badly ripped had been no more than an excited squeal. 'Wot a lark!' she had giggled, and made not the slightest fuss. 'But I'll have to repair it by tomorrow, so wait a minute –'

A sharp jerk had prevented her from retrieving the fragment of cloth. 'To hell with tomorrow, Bella. Tonight is ours.'

More excited giggles. 'Did you really mean it when you said twenty, sir?'

No time to answer . . . hurrying footsteps on the grass . . . the welcoming bushes, darkness, concealment . . . two animals mating on the damp earth . . . her sudden cry at his violence, stifled by his hand clamped over her mouth, and then the long thick hair twisted about her throat, tightening with every forceful thrust until his senses spiralled to a blinding climax and, satiated, he fell away, forgetting her.

But now the aftermath had set in. Perhaps Kingsmere hadn't been such a good idea after all. Escaping here alone gave him solitude, but that was all. And now he had to assume a façade for the benefit of his mother, or she would be fussing over him, fearing he was ill, and calling to see him every day, making a nuisance of herself.

He became aware that she was talking. She had had a letter from Caroline, at long last, written from a rest house at Madaba. A typical Caroline missive, saying little but implying that wherever she went she created a sensation.

'As if we haven't heard that already, through the press! I wish she would have the sense to come home and stop making a spectacle of herself. That husband of hers should go and bring her back.'

'That husband of hers,' said Justin with malicious enjoyment, 'is too busy elsewhere, and I don't mean at that dull museum.'

Elizabeth sat up even straighter. 'You mean . . . a *woman*?'

'Why the surprise? He is a man, after all, and he put no opposition in Caro's way when her heart was set on going. I suspect he even encouraged it. Surely that speaks for itself?'

His mother had been about to ask for the identity of this other woman when a tap on the door heralded the arrival of the evening paper. Idly Justin took it from the silver salver before his mother had a chance to.

The body of the young woman discovered beneath the bushes in the gardens of Hanover Square had been identified – a parlourmaid from number twenty, once the home of the famous Dulcima Howard and now of the young cousin she had introduced to London's society. 'When interviewed by the police, a shocked Miss Yorke revealed that her butler was also missing and that various items of silver had disappeared. Whether the two incidents are linked is, as yet, unknown.' But Cook had confided to a reporter that the butler and parlourmaid had had 'a certain relationship'. The man, Dillon, was being sought for questioning.

Quietly Justin began to laugh. Dillon could not have timed his exit more opportunely, nor be a more obvious suspect. The newspaper account went on to say that no one had called at the house after guests had departed that night, so neither the butler nor the parlourmaid would appear to have admitted any visitor. Why the young woman happened to be in the Square gardens was not known, but a likely conjecture was that she had gone there to rendezvous with the absconding butler. It was speculated that the couple planned to decamp with the stolen silver. Police investigations proved that Dillon had an earlier conviction, and was known to be a man with an ugly temper. Carried away by the story, the newspaper reporter even visualised a lovers' quarrel terminating in a fatal act of violence. It seemed a cut-and-dried case and similar to many city crimes committed after dark.

Justin heard his mother asking what amused him.

'Nothing, Mamma – just a political cartoon. A dig at the prime minister, and well deserved. Brilliant, don't you agree?'

He folded the paper carefully, displaying the satirical sketch and concealing the account of the murder in Hanover Square. Murder? Of course, it wasn't murder. Murder was premeditated; accidents were not. But if the press and the police chose to pin it on to Dillon, so much the better. Serve the man right for being such a fool as to run away.

Elizabeth looked at her son fondly, glad to see he had recovered his spirits.

'I hope you mean to stay at Kingsmere longer than usual, Justin. The place isn't the same without you. And Christmas is near. There will be the annual ball, which the county looks forward to, as well as the party for estate children in the great hall on Boxing Day – '

'And all the rest of the tedious rigmarole, Mamma.'

'Tedious it may be, but as master of Kingsmere it is

your duty to face it. And don't yawn at the thought, dear boy. Delia must be here, of course, even if her mother isn't, and that, I suppose, means inviting her father too.'

'If he can drag himself away from 20 Hanover Square,' Justin said absently, immediately regretting the words because he knew that fateful address was stamped indelibly on his mother's mind.

He saw her proud head jerk up, eyes startled.

He shrugged. 'Oh, well, Mamma, you may as well know. The object of Simon's fancy is Deborah Yorke, the beauteous Dulcima's cousin, who came with her that weekend. You thought she looked a most respectable young woman. "Quite unlike her fast relative." Your very words, Mother dear. But blood will out, I suppose. Do you mind if I borrow your evening paper to browse through after dinner? I don't get this edition.' He kissed her, forestalling an answer. 'And don't look so stricken over your son-in-law's love affair. After all, it is of no concern to us.'

He sauntered from the room, waving the folded newspaper in farewell and congratulating himself on so skilfully annexing it. No doubt the morning paper would feature the sordid details, though personally he now felt too detached even to regard them as sordid. He was in that comfortable aftermath of remembering only the exultation, the rest of it retreating and, as was customary, leaving him with no sense of guilt. Besides, it was apparently a foregone conclusion that Dillon was responsible, and of course his only reason for taking the newspaper now was to spare his mother any distressing reminder of the house in Hanover Square. Tomorrow the story would be crowded from the front page by news of war and politics, the fate of so unimportant a creature as a promiscuous housemaid being relegated to a few lines buried somewhere inside, so with luck the address would not even catch his mother's eye. He felt benign and self-righteous as he departed.

After he had gone, Elizabeth sat staring into the fire. She was very still, as always when alarmed or uneasy. When the parlourmaid came to remove the tea tray, she roused herself, forcing a casual note into her voice when asking if the housekeeper's copy of the evening paper could be brought to her. 'My son appears to have picked mine up by mistake.' The newspaper came at once, but she could see nothing to provoke his silent laughter. The political cartoon was not so very funny – and since when had he taken to studying political cartoons?

But something had definitely amused him. And there had been more than ordinary amusement in his laughter – a sort of gratification, as if something he read pleased him very much. She also remembered how he had folded the paper, carefully and precisely, so she copied the movements to see what, if anything, could be concealed that way.

A few minutes later she discovered what it was, and despite the heat from the fire, the room seemed suddenly ice cold.

16

The day following the discovery of Bella's body, and all the horror of identification and questioning which had fallen on Deborah's shoulders, Garfield said, 'Don't take on so, Miss Yorke. It's all over now, and you can take it from me, Bella was no better than she should've been. Her kind always comes to a sticky end.'

The thin hand touched Deborah's shoulder hesitantly. Demonstrativeness did not come easily to Garfield, but she was moved by the girl's white face and shadowed eyes. The whole ugly business had hit the poor young thing hard. No doubt she had never seen a dead person in such a state before, and having to identify Bella had brought her close to fainting. Garfield had gone with her, and Deborah had clung to her hand throughout. For the first time there had been no division between them; they were simply two women engulfed by horror.

The shred of material found by the gardener had matched Bella's muddied dress, and house-to-house visits by the police had finally brought them to the door of number twenty, asking if any person was missing. Deborah had decided to give the girl twenty-four hours in which to return, and to reprimand her for taking French leave. No one, neither Garfield, nor Cook, nor herself, had imagined she had gone for good. A night out with Dillon, perhaps, which spelled trouble for her, but nothing more terrible than that.

'She didn't deserve such a hideous death, Garfield. No woman does, whoever or whatever she may be.'

'Well, it happens all the time, miss. Or almost. The newspapers are full of them, and girls like Bella know what to expect, or ought to. Well do I remember Jack the Ripper! Not that I'd class Dillon with that maniac, nasty temper though he has.'

Deborah said slowly, 'Why should everyone assume it was Dillon? Just because he has disappeared with stolen silver doesn't mean he is a murderer.'

'Well, there was *that* going on between them, miss, and had been for a long time, and all of us belowstairs knew it. Maybe she found out he was doing a bunk and threatened to tell if he didn't take her with him, so he silenced her.'

'I don't believe it. Dillon would lose his temper, yes, threaten her, and even strike her – I can imagine him doing that, but he would do it in this house. Why entice her into the Square gardens? And for her to go so willingly, so hurriedly . . . '

'What makes you think she did, miss?'

'Because she didn't even bother with a coat on a raw November night.'

'That proves she knew whoever it was. She wouldn't go like that with no stranger, not if I know our Bella. She'd tart herself up in her best, feather boa and all, and take her reticule to put the money in, safe and sound. That's all she went with men for. You can bet she was hobnobbing with others as well as Dillon.'

'So it *could* have been some other man.'

'I s'pose so,' Garfield admitted grudgingly, 'but I doubt it. Dillon kept a sharp eye on her whenever she was on duty, especially when serving the guests. He'd have noticed if one of the gentry were eyeing her that night, and he would have ordered her back to her room to stay there until he sent for her. Things between the pair of them nearly always took place in his own quarters.'

'Which proves there was no need for them to seek the shelter of garden bushes.'

Garfield answered reflectively, 'But don't you think that proves things, in a way, miss? If he had made up his mind to silence her for good'n all, he wouldn't do it in the butler's room right here at number twenty. He'd do it away from this house, to avoid suspicion.'

'And then run off with a supply of silver, drawing attention to himself?' Deborah shook her head. 'I don't believe he would do anything so stupid, not even to supply a motive for running away. I believe he would have returned here and carried on as if nothing had happened.'

'He would have had to be on the boards to act *that* well.' Garfield gave her mistress's shoulder a slight shake.

'Come on, now, miss, snap out of it. It's all over, as I said. The police have gone, and they've taken Dillon's fingerprints from the furniture in his room, though I don't see how fingerprints could match up with marks on a woman's neck, do you?'

Deborah was too tired and depressed for further conversation, and when Garfield suggested a nice cuppa, she made no protest, even though Cook had kept endless supplies of tea flowing throughout the day. To Cook and Garfield, tea was the unfailing panacea for everything, but all Deborah really wanted was Simon, and he was in Bath. If she could only hear his voice, if the house only had a telephone, like wealthier establishments nowadays, the sound of his voice down the line would comfort her despite the crackling and the noise all telephone wires made.

From behind lace curtains Garfield looked into the square. A policeman was stationed outside to move on the morbid and the curious who had gathered to stare at the house. A pity some folk hadn't better things to do with their time, she thought angrily.

'Are they still there?' Deborah asked.

'They won't be much longer. Tell you what, miss, as soon as I've brought you a cuppa, put everything out of your mind and get on with preparing those rooms for Miss Delmont. To tell the truth, I'm thankful she's coming. She'll be company for you, though never did I think the day would come when 20 Hanover Square would be turned into a lodging house.'

Secretly Deborah feared all this ugly publicity might persuade Miss Delmont to change her mind, and was relieved when she arrived a few minutes later, climbing the front steps in full view of curious onlookers, indifferent to their stares. The signs of strain in Deborah moved her to instant compassion. Gathering her into a motherly embrace, she offered to come and stay each night until finally taking up residence.

*

The news paragraph about Bella also brought Peter Maynard hurrying from Kensington. Garfield opened the door and promptly sensed his agitation. My goodness, she thought, but he's got it badly, and wished he were older and richer, since he was a bachelor and free to wed, whereas it could mean nothing but trouble if Mr Davidson and Miss Deborah lost their heads. She hoped life was not going to play the same tricks that it had played on her poor dear Dulcima, who, though lucky in cards, had certainly never been lucky in love.

What a woman needed was stability in her life. Garfield could see neither this impressionable young man nor the older married one being able to provide either for Miss Deborah. Life seemed to have little talent for arranging the right partnerships.

'I must see her!' Peter burst out. 'She must be terribly upset.' He almost fell across the doorstep in his haste.

Garfield nodded toward the morning room and decided, as he strode toward it, that young Mr Maynard needed to grow up a bit before he would be ready for marriage. Still, if he brought her young mistress out of herself at this awful time he would serve a good purpose.

Garfield went out to the back garden to look at her precious charge, totally unaware that although 'that Miss Yorke' had long since become 'Miss Deborah', this was the first time she had thought of her as her mistress, and that from now on she would continue to.

Peter could not conceal his disappointment because Deborah was not alone; then recognition of the actress temporarily eclipsed it, followed by gratification when Deborah introduced him as the painter whose work the woman had admired.

'Miss Delmont feels you could do well as a scenic artist,' she added. 'How does that appeal, to follow your work at the museum?'

He stammered his thanks, overjoyed at the prospect, for

by the end of his first week he had realised that doing detailed sketches of pottery shards and flint artifacts would, in time, become monotonous to someone who wanted to paint with great sweep and grandeur. Even so, gratitude to Simon Davidson for saving him from the dull fate of a bank clerk in Tenterden had made him apply himself with a will.

He worked in a room off Simon's office at the top of the building, because it had the best light, but apart from an occasional glance at his work, the museum's curator left him to carry on without interruption. Peter wanted to dislike the man because he, instead of himself, was involved in Deborah's life, but found it impossible. Dammit, he even liked him.

And the museum was fascinating, items well displayed, separate rooms given over to certain dynasties and differing countries – Egyptian, Syrian, Palestinian; to prehistoric pottery and glass; to bronze heads, coins, ornaments, plaques, and tools, to bone utensils, roundels, pins, spinning whorls, and jewellery; to stone carvings and sculpture to items in marble and alabaster. The place was attracting an increasing number of visitors, and its success was due solely to the man who ran it.

Simon Davidson was passionately devoted to his museum. Every item in the place had been identified, labelled, and displayed by him personally, and visiting archaeologists were always shown around by him.

'You should hear him talking to students, too,' one of the museum guides said. 'Great enthusiasm, has Mr Davidson, and it's infectious. After hearing him lecture, you feel he has opened up a whole new world.'

But in Peter's workroom that world was confined to the objects he was illustrating. One at a time they would be carried up and placed carefully before him, and with equal care they were taken back to their showcases and locked up, handled all the time by experts. Yesterday, spent with rare pieces of ancient jewellery, he had realised that he was acquiring valuable knowledge of Eastern design. He had even thought how marvellous some of the stuff would look if incorporated into theatrical costume, and following the cheap snack he called lunch, for he diligently discharged his weekly payments to Bruce Whitney, he had lingered amidst Grecian pillars and arches and relics of ancient temples, visualising them as parts of stage sets and longing to try his hand at producing some.

Creating scenery for school productions had been fun, leaving him with a desire to work on a much larger scale. And now providence seemed to be opening another door to him – or, more accurately, Deborah was, yet again. He owed everything to her, and wondered how he would ever be able to express his gratitude and devotion. Excited though he was by this meeting with the Comet Theatre's leading lady, he wished she would go so that he would be able to show his concern for Deborah, his sole reason for being here.

Miss Delmont was asking when his work at the museum would be finished and suggesting that, in the meantime, she should arrange a meeting with the theatre management. 'Why don't you bring Miss Yorke tonight, and meet the stage director during one of the intervals? I'll see that tickets are at the box office for you.' It would take Deborah out of herself, thought the actress, and the prospect pleased Peter, particularly the idea of accompanying Deborah, who then deflated his hopes by asking if it could be another evening, because Garfield had insisted on calling a doctor to her, who had prescribed a sedative and an early night. 'And Garfield will insist on both,' she added. 'I hope you understand, Miss Delmont?'

'Chrystal, my dear. Theatrical folk are never formal. And I endorse the need for an early night and a sedative, so I will get tickets for another performance. And now I must go.' She kissed Deborah's cheek and held out her hand to Peter, promising not to forget to arrange that meeting with the stage director. Then at last he and Deborah were alone and he was pouring out his concern for her in a way which both touched and embarrassed her. She didn't want to discuss Bella's death, and skilfully changed the subject by asking how Delia was faring in her father's absence.

Peter wanted to discuss neither the little girl nor her father, and this reminder of the friendship between them was not too welcome. 'Oh, Delia's all right,' he answered indifferently. 'Staying with friends in the flat below. Her father is away for only a night.'

Deborah prayed that on his return Simon would come to her quickly. It was he whom she needed, and much as she liked Peter, she wished he would go. She moved to the door, thanking him for coming and asking him to give her love to Delia should he see her.

'See her! I can scarcely avoid her. She seems to spend all her spare time haunting the museum with a round-eyed friend who looks like an owl. Luckily the owl prefers the exhibition rooms to my workroom, but Delia comes bouncing in whenever she feels like it.'

'That shows she is interested in your work. You should be flattered.'

Flattered! he thought later when the obstreperous child invaded his room yet again, leaning across to inspect his work and jogging his arm so that the detail he was working on squirted in a zigzag across the page.

'Damn you!' he exploded, tearing the sheet off his drawing board and flinging it toward the wastebasket. Disappointed in his meeting with Deborah, he was now not in the best of moods. But Delia didn't mind. She pounced on the discarded drawing.

'If you don't want it, Mr Maynard, may I have it? I think it's lovely, squiggle and all. And I'm sorry I startled you, but what luck for me – I've been wanting another picture for my bedroom wall. Have you any more to spare, because my father told me before he left for Bath that I'll soon be moving into a much larger one if things go the way he plans. He has talked for ages about finding roomier accommodation and now he's been made director of the museum and taken on to the board, he says he plans an early move. He wouldn't tell me where, only that I would hear when he had had a chance to arrange everything. So it's to be a surprise, and I like surprises. If you have another picture to spare, may I have that too?'

'I'll have plenty if you come charging in the way you do. Why aren't you at school?'

'Wednesday half day, and I can come here as often as I like without anyone's permission except my father's,' she answered airily, 'and *he* doesn't mind how much time I spend poring over his exhibits.'

'Well,' he admitted, 'I am sorry. I lost my temper. But you ruined my work, and now I'll have to start again. If you tell your father I snapped at you, I won't blame you.'

'What *do* you take me for? A telltale? And my father wouldn't be angry. Anyway, not with you. He would probably say you were quite right to be annoyed and blame me for bothering you. But I don't think he would *really* be angry with me, because he is about the only person who doesn't find me a nuisance. Except Deborah. That's Miss Yorke, but I always think of her as Deborah because it's such a lovely name. Sometimes I wonder if they will pair off together the way everyone does at week-end parties down at Kingsmere, because when they are together I feel they want to. Mamma and Uncle Justin always did as they pleased, though I don't think my father ever knew – at any rate, not about Mamma.'

He was startled. The child was confirming all his fears. He desperately wanted to question her about her mother, 'who did as she pleased'. If she were still alive, Simon

Davidson was behaving like a blackguard in pursuing a young unmarried woman, even if his marriage was unhappy, and from the sound of things, it didn't seem to Peter like his own idea of marriage.

Peter had conventional ideas about right and wrong, categories which were strictly black and white, with no between shades. That was the way he had been brought up. Calf love now cast him in the role of knight-errant, destined to protect a maiden's honour. He wished Simon Davidson were staying longer in Bath, for to return now, after the shock Deborah had gone through, would be to find her at her most vulnerable. She had not responded to his own concern, but she might well respond to an older man who knew how to play on a woman's sensitivity and adopt a protective role.

Downcast, Peter turned back to his drawing board, and after watching for a while, Delia said, 'I think you are terribly clever, Mr Maynard, really I do. When my plays are produced, you can paint the scenery. I am writing one now, all about Cleopatra and her friend Helen of Troy.'

'Cleopatra and Helen of Troy were never friends.'

'They are in *my* play. Cleopatra comes riding in on a camel, the one I've asked Mamma to bring back for me—'

'So your mother . . .' He broke off, checking the words 'so your mother *is* alive' and substituting, 'Where is your mother?'

'In the desert somewhere. Grandmamma says she is trying to copy someone called Hester Stanhope.'

'And who are going to act the parts of Cleopatra and Helen?' Peter asked.

'I shall be Cleopatra, because I want to have long slanty Egyptian eyes and wear those wonderful headdresses. Pru can be Helen, provided she leaves off her spectacles.'

'But Helen was supposed to be the world's most beautiful woman. Wouldn't you like to be that?'

'I'd rather be the cleverest.'

'From the way you are going about it, you're starting young enough. How old are you?'

She evaded that, shifting from foot to foot in embarrassment. She longed to be mistaken for grown-up.

'Do you know what I think, Cleopatra? *I* think you'll make a better actress than a playwright.'

'And *I* don't see why I shouldn't be both.'

'In that case, I suggest you go home and get on with your play.'

'I'm not going home. I'm going back to Pru's. She's downstairs now, and getting bored, I expect. But when we've gone to bed tonight I shall finish the drama of Helen of Troy and Cleopatra.'

'And the camel,' Peter reminded her solemnly. 'Don't forget the camel.'

'You're laughing at me! But one day you won't. *You*'ll see!' She whirled away, bumping blindly into the doorpost and crying out in exasperation. '*Now* look what you made me do!' she flung at him, choking back tears.

He was sorry immediately, hating the idea of a little girl being hurt, but when he hurried after her, she was racing across her father's office and slamming the door behind her. Instinct told him to let her go because she would hate him to see her crying. He had thought her a silly little thing, a nuisance, but now he realised that beneath it all she was a very sensitive child indeed.

But an extraordinary one, also – and how on earth had she been brought up, talking about men and women 'pairing off' at weekend parties? Wherever this place Kingsmere was, guests apparently behaved as people never did in Tenterden, at any rate in the circle he had been born into, though there was that country place outside Rolvenden where its wealthy owner was known to hold very permissive weekends. His father had once been called to attend an injured guest who had broken a leg sliding down the banisters during some wild party in the early hours, the men challenging the women in a banister-sliding competition. Some stupid girl, unsteady on champagne, had fallen off the end on to the oak floor, half-naked. The whole lot had been half-naked, watched by two imperturbable footmen standing by with trays of glasses. His father had returned disgusted and angry at being called out at such a time to attend such people. A sudden childbirth, a sick woman in a remote cottage, a shepherd with pneumonia caused by cold night vigils during lambing time – all these he was more than willing to journey out to, whatever the hour and whether they could pay his fee or not, but decadent guests at wild house parties won no sympathy from him.

Was Kingsmere such a place? And whom did it belong to? He knew nothing about the Davidsons, but in all honesty, and despite his jealousy, Delia's father didn't strike Peter as the kind to enjoy gatherings where men and women 'paired off' in the way his small daughter seemed to take for granted. And why was her mother able to please herself, setting a bad example?

He was afraid young Delia was likely to grow up into a very unconventional young woman, and feeling sorry for her because she seemed to have missed an essential part of her childhood was perhaps a waste of time. That little girl had a will and a mind of her own.

He pinned a fresh sheet of paper to his drawing board, set to work, and promptly forgot her.

The newspaper report brought Simon travelling back to London as soon as he had finished his lecture. Instead of returning the following morning, he caught an overnight milk train which crawled through the darkness, unloading churns and taking empty ones aboard at seemingly endless stations. The train had no heating and no comfort, but every slow turn of the wheels brought him nearer to Deborah, until eventually it shunted into the London terminal next morning.

It was seven o'clock. He went straight to Hanover Square and found her at breakfast. She could not hide her relief at the sight of him and went straight into his arms, because it was the most natural thing to do.

'I couldn't get here fast enough,' he said, stroking her hair. 'You've gone through enough strain and anxiety since Dulcima's death without having to endure this ugly shock as well.'

'It's over now. All the questioning and . . . and everything else . . .'

His hold tightened, and for the first time in her life she experienced a feeling of total protection.

Then Simon told her what he planned to do. 'I want to rent the two top floors here for Delia and myself. You know our need for roomier accommodation, and with Miss Delmont occupying the floor below, the barrier of respectability will be safely maintained,' he finished with an ironic smile.

Must there be barriers? she thought, knowing full well that his marriage was the biggest one of all, and would remain so. She had no doubt at all that one day his wife would reappear and that not until then could either of them know which direction their lives would take.

She said, 'You mean that with another tenant in the house, a middle-aged woman of good reputation, the gossips will be silenced. But gossip these last two days has almost inured me against it – as Dulcima was. It seems the fate of any Madame of this house to be involved in scandal.'

'Not any more. And you are not a "Madame" in the sense it is used nowadays. And the tragedy of your house-maid could have happened to any promiscuous maid-servant in any establishment – unpleasant and distressing for the owners and, to someone as sensitive as you, doubly so, but this house will become a secure and happy place for you. I am resolved on that, though I won't pretend it will be easy for me to keep away from you. I love you, Deborah, but can offer you nothing and ask for nothing. All I want is to be near you and help you in any way I can. I have wanted that for a long time.'

Colour rushed to her face, betraying her. It would be a bittersweet situation, living beneath the same roof as this man, even with a dividing floor between them.

Simon continued, 'Living in the same house with you will make Delia happy too, and you know how important that is to me. So will you accept us as tenants on those terms?'

On any terms at all, she wanted to say. Whatever you ask, whatever you want . . .

'I am torn between my love for you and responsibility for my child. You understand that, don't you? She has been brought up to accept casual liaisons between men and women, relationships without stability or any sense of moral values –'

She put her hand over his mouth very gently. 'Hush,' she said. 'I understand. And *I* happen to care for Delia too. I too have ideas about the right way to bring up children, the right examples to set. I hope I can be as good a mother to Charles as you are a father to Delia. So we'll put them first and, for ourselves, hope for the future . . .' With an effort she drew away from him, letting her fingers touch his scarred face in a last caress. Then she forced a practical note into her voice. 'When do you want to move in?'

'I have the usual monthly tenancy on my furnished flat, and I must also make arrangements about Delia's change of school. If I can get her into a good one near this area of London pretty quickly, I will make financial settlements in lieu of notice on the flat, and move as soon as you can have the rooms ready. I'm afraid I'll be bringing a lot of books and papers and clutter with me.'

'There will be plenty of room for all of it,' she said, thinking how wonderful it would be to have Simon's 'clutter' in the house, and how happy it would make her just to think of him upstairs, working at his papers and writings. She was already planning which room to turn into his study when a tap on the door brought Garfield on to the scene without waiting for a summons.

'It's *Dillon*, miss! I told him to wait on the doorstep, but he walked right in, bold as brass, demanding to see you at once.'

Dillon was already unloading his pockets when Deborah and Simon reached the hall.

'I brought them back, Miss Yorke, the whole lot. You can check and see. I don't mind being pinched for robbery, but I'm damned if I'll have a murder charge slapped on to me, and I'm going straight to the police to tell them so. I'd be obliged if you'd testify that I've returned every item.'

'Of . . . of course, I will . . . but . . . '

'But where have I been? Staying at the World's End pub at the far end of Fulham, and the landlord and everyone else who works there can vouch for that. They'll also vouch that I got there around ten-thirty on the night poor Bella was knocked off, and didn't leave the place. Bella was going to come along around midnight, but didn't turn up. To tell the truth, I wasn't sorry, because I was afraid she'd be a nuisance. I even planned not to turn up there myself, but thought better of it, because if I didn't, she would split on me. About the silver, I mean. She knew I'd taken it. So I thought it best to stick with the arrangement, and thank God I did, because the landlord offered to put me up and everyone in the bar that night can testify that I was there until the pub closed, then a bunch of us moved into the back parlour and played cards until the early hours.' His eyes shifted from Deborah to Simon.

'I'm glad you're here, sir, because what I'm telling is the truth, and I'll put my hand on the Bible to it. If you'd be good enough to come along with me to the police station, you can hear me repeat all this. I'm not lying, sir.'

Inestimable as Simon thought him, he believed the man. Fear was forcing the truth from him.

'The papers say it all points to me.' Dillon ran his tongue over dry lips. 'By God, I'll prove them wrong! I'll even tell how I admitted Lord Ashleigh earlier in the evening and promised to leave up the catch on the front door later.'

'You *what?*'

Dillon nodded. 'So he could slip in when he chose, sir. He was after getting his own back on Miss Yorke. He'd been wanting to for a long time, and because of what happened earlier – all that fiasco and finding out how he'd suspected me and used me – I thought, to hell with him. Bella can leave the catch up, *I'm* getting out. But whether she did or not, I don't know. All the same, he was a bastard, that one, the way he treated Miss Dulcima, and the things he promised me if I'd get him into this house when the right moment came. He said he would expose Miss Yorke as a cheat and a fraud and frighten the daylights out of her, and then I'd be in control, if not here, then somewhere else where he would set me up. I shouldn't have listened, but I did, *and* believed him.' Fear trembled in the man's voice. 'Poor old Bella, she was no better than she should have been, but she didn't deserve a death like that – though maybe she asked for it, going into the Square gardens with a man after dark, even if she did know who he was.'

17

The last person Justin expected to arrive at Kingsmere was his brother-in-law. The station cab deposited him on the doorstep that afternoon.

He didn't like the look on Simon's face – that stubborn, determined look he had seen when Caroline had flouted her husband from time to time. It had been demonstrated increasingly as their marriage became more and more divided.

Well, thought Justin, if he has come for news of Caroline, he'll be disappointed.

He was glad his mother had come to luncheon and had not yet taken her departure. She would quell any unpleasantness Simon had come to stir up. So he met his brother-in-law blandly.

'I suppose you've come to find out if there's any news of Caroline. None, I'm afraid, old chap. Mamma had a letter from her, written at some place called . . . what was the name of it, Mother dear? Madaba? Somewhere in Palestine, I believe. Not a word since. But you should know your wife better than anyone and not be surprised at anything she does, or does not, do.'

'It isn't Caroline I want to talk about. It's you. And I think, for your mother's sake, we should talk alone.'

A slight quivering of the nostrils was Justin's only reaction, swiftly checked. 'Anything you want to say to me can be said in front of my mother.'

'Not this.'

Justin turned to Elizabeth languidly. 'Mamma? It is up to you, but from the look on my dear brother-in-law's face I'd say he is in an unpleasant mood, and women should be spared scenes, I always think. What sort of a scene Simon has come to create, I cannot imagine, but I can handle it alone. I will see you to your carriage.'

Elizabeth half-rose, then recalled that her son-in-law was involved with Deborah Yorke at that house in Hanover Square, the one that employed the wretched servant girl found strangled under some bushes, a crime so reminiscent of that long-ago one in Kingsmere's woods that it had disturbed her peace of mind. She promptly sat down again, suspicion and fear beginning to stir. She had said nothing to her son about that horrible news item, nor asked why he had folded the paper in order to hide it. She had persuaded herself that the action had been entirely innocent, that he might not have read the paragraph at all, and that he had indeed been laughing over the political cartoon. But a lifetime of maternal devotion to her son made her linger now, for she knew that Simon had never liked Justin. Not for the first time she wished the man had not become part of the family.

She wished it even more when he said, 'I think it really would be better if you went home, Mother-in-law. What I have to question Justin about is not pleasant.'

Her stomach lurched, but not for a moment did she reveal the fear that caused it. She remained seated, erect and proud, her rigid face as expressionless as ever. Then she saw the sudden whiteness about her son's mouth, the pallor spreading to his cheeks, and the innumerable occasions since his childhood that she had seen this reaction, following some deed which had outraged her husband, passed in procession through her memory. Her hands quivered where they rested on the arms of her chair, then were still again, drilled into obedience as all her emotions were.

In a high, artificial voice Justin said, 'If I am forced to put up with your company, old chap, at least I'll endure it with a drink. And being an hospitable host, I'll offer you one.'

'No, thanks.'

'Please yourself.' The decanter chinked against the brandy glass; the stopper rattled as it was replaced. Then Justin turned and raised his glass. 'Ask away, old chap, though I can't think what it is you want to know.'

'Did you return to Miss Yorke's house after your visit the other night?'

'Miss Yorke? Oh, you mean dear Deborah. Of course I didn't. What should I return for? She has closed the card salon, so why in heaven's name should I go back? I forgot to tell you, Mamma, that I dropped in at that address for a game of baccarat, only to depart disappointed. It seems that number 20 Hanover Square is at last to become respectable.'

'Then why did you ask Dillon to leave the catch on the front door unlocked?' Simon demanded.

Justin's pale eyes flickered. 'What the devil are you talking about?'

'Dillon, the butler at 20 Hanover Square. And your request to him to leave the catch up on the front door so that you could re-enter at will.'

'Why the hell should I do that when there was nothing to return for? No gaming, no baccarat, no reason at all. Where did you get this cock-and-bull story?'

'From Dillon himself.'

'When? How? The man has decamped – with silver, the newspaper said, but apparently for a much worse reason. From the sound of things, he took the silver to provide a motive for running away, and now the police want him for questioning . . .'

Justin stopped short, recalling that his mother knew

nothing. He had taken away her evening paper, and this morning's had revealed nothing further. His glance slid to her, and assurance returned, for her ramrod figure and rigid face were the same as always.

'The police *have* questioned him,' Simon said. 'He came back voluntarily, returning the stolen silver and able to produce evidence of his whereabouts at the time Bella was murdered. They have questioned independent witnesses, all of whom confirmed his story. So he is off the hook.' Simon turned to his mother-in-law. She looked as if she were carved in stone. 'I am sorry,' he said gently, 'but I did say this conversation wouldn't be pleasant. Please go now.'

She remained immovable, staring through the windows to the park beyond. It was a grey November day, the trees bare, the wind cold.

Justin gulped his brandy and then asked, 'Who the devil is Bella, anyway?'

'That question confirms you have read the news, so you must know. The report identified her as the parlourmaid at 20 Hanover Square.'

'Never clapped eyes on her in my life.'

'You must have done during your association with her former mistress.'

Justin shrugged, but his shoulders were stiff and the fingers clutching his glass were white at the knuckles. 'Can't remember her for the life of me. I don't notice parlourmaids. And when I dropped in hoping for a game the other night, it was the butler who admitted me. I left almost at once. You know I did. But *you* remained. For how long, I wonder. For the night?'

Simon ignored that. 'The police will question you, Justin.'

'On the strength of some lie told by a man who is known to have served a prison sentence? Oh, yes, that was in the report too. Also a reference to his ugly temper.' Justin recharged his brandy glass, his confidence returning. 'Why a butler should accuse a guest of asking for the catch of a front door to be left unlocked, I cannot imagine, but it seems that you can. Sorry to disappoint you, Simon, but you're barking up the wrong tree. I did not return to that house in Hanover Square. Had I done so, you would surely have seen me.'

'I left about half an hour later. I had to catch an early-morning train to Bath.'

'So you say.'

'It can be proved. I was due to lecture there.'

'And can it be proved that I or anyone else walked back into that house, finding the latch conveniently up, and took a servant girl into the Square gardens? Did you ever hear anything so ridiculous, Mother dear?'

'Never,' Elizabeth answered calmly. 'As for you, Simon, I wonder you have not been to Justin's chambers to question his manservant, since you seem capable of harbouring such vile suspicions.'

'The police have already been there.'

The silence was fractional before Elizabeth asked stonily, 'And?'

'The man confirmed that his master had returned very late that night.'

'That was all?'

'I gather so.'

Justin laughed. 'And what does that prove? Of course I returned late. I always do after a night out. After leaving that house, I dropped into various fashionable bars, watched a few entertainments, and then went home. My man spoke nothing but the truth. Let the police question me as much as they like. They'll have to come up with proof, and there is something else they will have to take into account. A man in my position doesn't pick up some low-class servant girl. He can afford high-class whores if he wants that sort of thing. Forgive the crudeness of this conversation, Mamma, but I dislike the trend of my brother-in-law's thoughts.'

If he had really known the trend, he would have disliked it even more, for Simon was recalling Caroline's story about the servant girl her brother had raped and whom her mother had bought off, and the other hideous incident concerning a village girl sexually assaulted and strangled in Kingsmere's woods.

Justin was right. There had to be proof, and where in the name of heaven was that to come from? Not from Kingsmere; not from Justin Ashleigh, wily as a fox; not from his ramrod mother, who would fiercely protect her son. Hadn't she always?

Had she done so when poor Norah died so unexpectedly? Choked on a fishbone, it was said, and apparently medically confirmed. But how many times had Delia, stricken by the loss of the aunt she loved, declared that *she* couldn't remember her choking at dinner? 'I was allowed to stay up that night, and I would have patted her hard on the back to help her cough up a fishbone! It's the sensible thing to do, isn't it, Father?' But a death certificate had been signed, and no one had disputed it.

Death by choking – or by sadistic sexual assault?

Prove it. Prove anything. Prove everything! How could anyone? The police would come, and the police would go.

As Simon thought, his journey had been wasted. He would get nowhere. No confession would be extracted from his brother-in-law, because however frightened he might be underneath his arrogance, he remained the wily fox, well aware that without positive proof no accusation could be levelled against him. No one at 20 Hanover Square knew anything about a return visit; no one had seen or heard him come back. No one knew whether the man had met Bella, and certainly no one believed that a man of birth and breeding would associate with such a creature. Dillon's story would not be enough to convict, and so long as his own hide was safe, that was all that Dillon would care about. Simon was left with nothing but uneasy suspicion, and Bella's case would be filed away with other unsolved crimes committed after dark in cities like London.

But at least Deborah would be spared the shock of learning about the darker side of the man who had begat Charles. She thought him callous, but no more than that. She knew nothing about the significance of the Ashleigh eyes, and it was better so, for she loved little Charles and believed him to have inherited nothing but his mother's nature. Please God, he had. Simon was glad he had not told her about his visit to Kingsmere today, but let her think he was returning to Kensington when they parted.

When Simon had gone, Elizabeth said to her son, 'You have had enough brandy. More than you usually drink. Did you find it so necessary?'

'My dear mother, who wouldn't when one is practically accused of murder?'

She was silent. He went on drinking, then burst out proudly, 'I got the better of him, didn't I?'

She hadn't moved a muscle, he noticed. She had sat in that chair, rigid as a statue, the whole time. He wanted to scream at her, to shock her, to make her tremble, but suddenly he found that it was he himself who trembled.

'Was that necessary, too?' she asked. 'To get the better of him, I mean.'

'Well, what do *you* think! For God's sake, Mamma, did you expect me not to put up a fight?'

'If you were innocent, a fight would have been unnecessary.'

He couldn't believe she had spoken the words. They were not even uttered in her normal voice. They seemed to come out of her throat in jerks, almost as if she were unaware of saying them. Words put into her mouth against her will.

He didn't bother to answer. He went on sipping his brandy. She rose stiffly and came and stood in front of him. 'Can you rely on that man of yours?'

'Of course. He is the soul of discretion. He has to be, because you see, Mother dear, I have a hold over him. That butler at 20 Hanover Square isn't the only servant with a police record, and jobs for such as they are hard to get – especially in a bachelor's luxury quarters, with good pay and the place to himself whenever his master is away. The threat of unemployment ensures any servant's loyalty, particularly a man like mine. That is why I hired him.'

For a moment he thought her proud face was going to crumble. He put down his glass and rose and placed his arms around her, saying in an almost childish voice, 'You mustn't worry, Mother dear. No one saw me. The square was absolutely deserted. Not a soul in sight. I made sure of that before I left.'

Dear God. Dear God in heaven, that he could confess without a trace of guilt! But only to her, because with her he knew he was safe. With others he would never crack, because he enjoyed getting the better of them. He was triumphant in his victory over Simon, but one day, when she was no longer alive to protect him, his defences would break. He had slid back now into his childhood trust of her, knowing she would look after him, and she was forced to acknowledge what she had always denied – that Charles had been right about their son.

Grief was like a knife in her heart.

She withdrew from him, and cupping his face in her hands, said gently, 'You must go back, my son. My poor, dear son.'

'To London? Oh, no, not yet – please, not yet. Let me stay here with you, where I am safe.'

'I didn't mean London.'

'Where, then? Not Switzerland again! I get so bored there.'

'They will take care of you. For always.'

'*Always*, Mother dear? But why for always?'

She could not tell him. She could not look into his pale, handsome face which now bore a look of incredible innocence, his light amber eyes blank, registering nothing but a total lack of comprehension. She could only act, and quickly, and for the last time. Put him away forever. Live without anxiety and dread, but always with the agony of loving him.

'We will leave at once, Justin. We have done it quickly before.'

He began to cry. 'I won't go, I won't go! You can't make me. No one can make me! That place is like a prison, they watch you all the time!'

'But you will be safe there. Safe forever, dear boy.'

She held her arms out to him, but he spun away from her, sobbing. Beyond the windows the lake shone amidst sloping lawns. He pointed a trembling finger toward it, crying, 'I'll kill myself, that's what I'll do! I'll throw myself in the lake and drown! I swear it, *I swear it*!'

There was nothing she could do but leave him. When he broke down like that, no one could get through to him. He had to be left alone to recover; then back would come his trust. She was not alarmed by words uttered in hysteria, because it was well known that people who threatened to commit suicide never did.

THREE
Delia

18

Delia was delighted with the move to Hanover Square, where the accommodation was more than twice the size of the flat in Kensington: two whole floors, which gave them a bedroom each, a sitting and dining room, another room which Deborah had furnished as a study for Simon, and a small guest room. Delia looked forward to having Pru to stay, the way she used to go to Pru's, though she had shared her friend's room there. Still, here they would be able to tiptoe across to each other's and talk in whispers when they were supposed to be asleep.

Deborah had been very busy before their arrival, switching furniture around and rearranging rooms on the ground floor, where she and baby Charles now lived. What had been the morning room was now his nursery, and Deborah's bedroom was the one shut off by sliding doors from the room where people used to play cards, which, in turn, was now a dining room. The only room left untouched was the splendid drawing room with Dulcima Howard's portrait above the mantelpiece. Once Delia had caught sight of Deborah through the open door, holding up the baby to admire the picture. 'See how lovely she was, Charles — your beautiful mother.' Something had made Delia tiptoe by, feeling she was intruding upon a very private moment.

Then on the first floor lived a real live actress. That impressed Delia tremendously. Chrystal Delmont — such a lovely name and just the kind she would have expected an actress to have. The thing that surprised her was Miss Delmont's age. She seemed quite old, yet people flocked to see her.

Delia hoped that one day Miss Delmont would invite her to her theatre dressing room, as she had invited Deborah and Peter Maynard. Peter had told her all about it, and made her quite envious. They had gone behind the scenes in the interval and met the stage director, and when Peter's work at the museum was finished he was actually going to work at the Comet Theatre as an assistant scenic artist.

'I'll be starting from the ground up, but I don't mean to stay there, Cleopatra. I aim to become scenic director and to have my own scenic studios one day, producing sets for other shows as well.'

'Sets?'

'That's the name for the flats produced for different scenes.'

'Flats? That's another name for apartments.'

'Not in the theatre, Cleopatra. A "flat" is a piece of scenery set with others round the stage – hence the name "sets".'

It was all very fascinating and sent Delia tearing off to write another play, which, when she knew Miss Delmont better, she would offer to let her act in, on condition that alongside the name of Chrystal Delmont the name of the dramatist, Delia Davidson, should appear in equally large letters, instead of beneath the title of the play, in smaller ones. Delia had stood outside the theatre and gazed with awe on billboards announcing 'The Incomparable Chrystal Delmont in *The Second Mrs Tanqueray*, by Sir Arthur Wing Pinero' – and obviously Sir Arthur wasn't very important, since his name was printed in small letters below. That struck Delia as most unfair, since without him there would have been no play, and without a play the actors would have had nothing to act in.

She had said as much to Peter Maynard, who had laughed at her as he always did and said, 'You should have a soapbox at Hyde Park Corner, Cleo. You're always fighting for something. I can see you becoming a suffragist as soon as you are old enough.'

'Which won't be long now,' she had declared. 'You are only eighteen yourself. I know, because when I told Deborah how you always talk down to me, just because you are older than I, she said, "Not all that much older, Delia. Eighteen only seems a great age when you are eleven. When you are eighteen and he is twenty-six, you'll find the gap has narrowed considerably." '

On one thing Delia was firmly resolved: when she knew Miss Delmont better, she would ask if she could be allowed to watch her put on her stage makeup, and where she could buy grease paints so she wouldn't have to make do with her paint box, as she now did when acting all the different parts in her plays. The results often failed to look as she anticipated, because the water colours ran.

Miss Delmont's bedroom had belonged to Miss Howard herself, and off it was the most gorgeous bathroom imaginable, the porcelain bath standing on gilded lions' feet and ornamented all over with flowers in pinks and blues and golds. Not even Kingsmere had a bathroom as ornate as that. In fact, Kingsmere had very few bathrooms indeed, maids having to carry hot water in copper jugs with lids, and even hip baths, which had to be filled from a whole line of bigger and heavier jugs. At weekend parties there was an endless parade of jug-carrying maids marching along endless corridors and up endless stairs, going almost at a trot to reach their destinations before the water chilled.

There would be valets, too, carrying shaving water for their masters and hot damp towels to steam their faces. Once Delia had glimpsed her uncle in his dressing room, leaning back in a chair with his feet up whilst his valet swathed his face in steaming towels. He looked so comical that she burst out laughing and the valet had kicked the door shut with his foot. She couldn't think why. She was amused only because her father never did that sort of thing, so it was a new entertainment for her.

By comparison with Miss Delmont's bathroom at number twenty, their own on the floor above was quite ordinary. The impressive thing was that a London town house actually had more than one bathroom. There was even one which Deborah described as 'merely functional' down in the basement, and she didn't mind using it in the least until she had enough money to install another. What Delia did not realise was that only recently had society begun to consider extra bathrooms necessary, and that Dulcima Howard had been in the vanguard, even installing a 'cloakroom' on the ground floor for the convenience of guests. These were the main advantages, as far as Deborah was concerned, when changing the function of her aunt's house.

The boudoir on Miss Delmont's floor was now a small kitchen where her daily maid prepared her special meals, though she seemed to eat very little. 'Not enough to keep skin and bone together,' Cook said down in the basement. 'I hope you and your pa have heartier appetites, miss, or my cooking will be wasted.'

Father had come to an arrangement with Cook regarding food and catering, and very pleased the woman was with the extra money; so pleased that she had no objection to carrying trays all the way upstairs, keeping the dishes hot with silverplated food covers like those used on the sideboards at Kingsmere. Delia loved the smell of cooking down in the basement kitchen and would come home from school that way, leaping down the area steps and in through the door, sniffing ecstatically when she opened it. 'Is that for us, Cook dear? It smells scrumptious!'

'Of course it's for you, Miss Eager-Eyes. Or maybe I should call you Eager-nose! Whatever I cook for Miss Yorke, I cook for you and your pa as well – and I make sure there's plenty left over for Garfield and me.' Cook chuckled hugely. 'Garfield warned me you were a one, and she was right! "Doesn't miss a thing," she said, and you don't, do you, love?'

Cook was large and buxom and beaming. She liked the way the house had changed, she said, though Garfield shook a sorrowful head and repeated, so often that no one took any notice, that never had she thought the day would come when dear Miss Dulcima's house would be 'let off.' She only hoped that when his little lordship grew up and came into his own, he would change things back to the way they had been, and live here as a gentleman should.

'But that would mean turning us all out, and we don't want to go!'

'By the time he grows up, miss, you'll be married, or living in state at Kingsmere, so why shouldn't his lordship live in state here someday?'

She still called baby Charles 'his lordship', and when Delia ventured to ask why, all she got in reply was: 'Why shouldn't I, young miss? Tell me that.'

Which, of course, Delia could not. If Garfield wanted to have her own pet name for the baby, as she said – why shouldn't she?

'I wonder you don't call him "his majesty", though he'll never be as fat as the king, I'm sure.'

'That he won't, though he does love his food, bless him. Look at him now, gobbling up his milk. There's my healthy little boy! There's my happy little lordship!' And Charles *was* a happy baby. Always smiling. 'Just like his dear mamma,' Garfield would say.

Garfield's voice always changed when she talked to little Charles. It became all soft and adoring instead of brisk and dry. Sometimes she would be rocking him in her arms down in the warm basement kitchen when Delia returned from school, for winter was now here and excursions in rain and wind weren't good for him, Garfield said.

In the two weeks they had lived at 20 Hanover Square, Delia had become very much at home, and the thought of spending Christmas at Kingsmere with her grandmother didn't appeal to her at all. But she had to go, her father said. Both of them had to go, though somehow Delia sensed that he felt he would be unwelcome. When her grandmother's letter had come, he had thrust it aside. Delia had very much wanted to read it, and once upon a time, when she had lived with her mother at Kingsmere, she wouldn't have hesitated. Reading other people's letters had been the same as listening at keyholes – the best way to find things out – but now she had learned that both things were wrong.

'What will you do at Christmas?' she had asked Deborah.

'Hang up a baby sock for Charles and decorate his first Christmas tree.'

'I wish I could see it.'

'There will be a huge one at Kingsmere, I'm sure. And a party for the estate children. Isn't that the custom?'

It was, and Delia always enjoyed the children's party, because it was the only time she was allowed to play with them. ('Damned snobbishness,' she had heard her father once remark to her mother.) She had always envied these children, living with large families and running wild until they espied her grandmother's dogcart approaching, when they would retreat to the doors of their cottages and bob respectful curtseys as she passed. Sometimes Delia had been summoned to take these drives with her grandmother, so she knew very well that once they had driven by, the children ran out again to continue their noisy games. She would look back enviously, 'until Grandmamma commanded her to sit up straight and be ladylike.

It all seemed so long ago, though it was scarcely a year since she had come to live with her father in London, and made school friends, and come to see Deborah every Sunday, and loved every moment. The first night she had come to live in Hanover Square she had knelt down to say her prayers as usual, and bubbled over in her excitement to tell God all about it. 'You'd better have my change of address, God. We've moved from Kensington Church Street to 20 Hanover Square. Don't forget, will you? And I wonder if you could arrange for me to have a chariot for Christmas to use in the play I am writing about Boadicea? There's a mews at the back where I'm sure I would be allowed to keep it, along with my camel. That is, if Mamma does bring me back a camel. I'm beginning to wonder about that. Where is she, God? Have you any idea? You must have, since you can see everyone here on earth. I'm sorry, dear Lord, but I can't say I miss her. I suppose that's wrong of me. But perhaps she doesn't miss me, either? But look after her, won't you, even though Grandmamma always said she knew how to get her own way. Mamma used to say that Uncle Justin did that. Poor Uncle Justin. Take care of him, too, because he must have felt so cold and wet when he drowned in the lake . . .'

The next day she had written to her grandmother:

Dear Grandmamma,

We have moved into a new house and I like it very much because I can see Deborah more often. That's Miss Yorke and she lives on the ground floor, and so does the baby. Garfield, who looks after him, lives in what used to be Dillon the butler's room. She grumbles because she says it reminds her of him, and she doesn't want that. Then on the next floor, the one above Deborah's and below ours, there is a real live actress

called Chrystal and she is very famous. I like her too.
Father and I have the whole of the next two floors, like
a house on top of the others, with our own upstairs, and
Father has a study. He has needed one for a long time
to write his books in. He is doing one now about ancient
Greek sites.

There is also an attic with a big skylight, and I am
sure if Peter Maynard saw it he would like it for a
studio, but I want it for a theatre. I think Peter is in love
with Miss Yorke, I can tell by the way he looks at her,
but she likes my father better, just the way he likes her.
I can tell that too.

The address is at the top of this letter, and there are
gardens in the middle of the square which we can use,
though Cook told me they were closed for a few days a
while ago, but not why.

Cook has offered to post this letter for me on her way
to visit her sister. She is waiting, so I must stop now.

Your loving granddaughter,
Delia

Two days later a reply had come by the evening post,
but not addressed to herself. Her father had sent for her at
once.

'What did you say when you last wrote to your grandmother, my dear?'

'I can't remember, Father. I've been busy writing my
new play, and that makes me forget everything else. I told
her about our new home, of course, and everyone in it, and
how Peter would like the attic for a studio if he saw it.'

'That sounds a good idea. I believe he makes do with a
dim Pimlico basement, so we will see what can be done
about that.'

'Oh, Father, I hoped I could have it for my plays!'

'I think he needs it more than you do, don't you? So
we'll rescue the young man from his basement and give

him a room with a good light to paint in. I'll have a talk with Deborah about it. It will help both of them. Meanwhile, what else did you say to your grandmother?'

Delia's forehead creased in concentration. 'That Peter is in love with her, I think. Yes, I did say that. Also that *she* wasn't with *him*, only with you, the way you are with her, though I don't think I said "love" just there, only "like". That she likes you better, which I am sure she does. That wasn't wrong, was it, because it's the truth.'

He answered gently, 'My dear, when you write to your grandmother, show me the letters first, will you?'

'I would have done, but you weren't home and Cook was going to post it on her way to Bethnal Green to see her sister, and couldn't wait. Has Grandmamma complained about something?'

'Only, as always, about the way I am bringing you up.'

'But I like the way you are bringing me up! I like it better than the way things were at Kingsmere, with all those noisy people coming at weekends and behaving the way husbands and wives shouldn't behave. Only then, of course, I didn't know they shouldn't. I've learned that from Peter.'

'And how did he come to hear about weekend parties at Kingsmere?'

'I told him. He didn't say right away that he didn't think much of them – only since I've got to know him better. And of course, you and Deborah don't behave that way, either.'

'Your grandmother, I fear, thinks differently.'

'How can she? She doesn't live here, so how can she know how anyone behaves in this house? I'll tell her when I see her. I don't think I'll be so afraid of her as I used to be. I suppose we have to go there for Christmas. Is that why she has written?'

'Partly. I am commanded to bring you.' That was when he thrust the letter aside, though there was a certain pity in his voice as he said, 'Naturally, I will take you. You must be with her, even if I have to remain in the background.'

'I don't see why you should.'

'But I do.' He had changed the subject abruptly. 'So Christmas at Kingsmere it will be, and she will hold up her proud head at the Christmas ball, which I gather she intends to hold because tradition demands it, and, she says, her son would never wish to break with tradition, and she will hold it up just as proudly at the party for estate children, where you, Delia, my dear, will help her merely by being at her side and handing out presents as she takes them from the tree. I owe her that much at least, poor soul. She must be very lonely.'

It was then that Delia began to feel uneasy. 'She doesn't want me to remain there, does she, Father?'

'At Kingsmere? I am afraid she does. In fact, she virtually insists upon it. She says your place is at Kingsmere since your uncle's death.'

'But you won't agree, surely? Oh, Father, please don't! I would miss you so terribly, and Deborah too. And I love living in London. There are so many things to do, so many to see, and the coronation is coming along – I would hate to miss that.'

His scarred face had broken into that wide, warm smile which never failed to assure her of his love. He had given her a bear hug and told her not to worry, and that not for the world would they be parted from each other.

'I shall be firm, but as gentle as your grandmother will permit me to be. A difficult situation, Delia, but I shall handle it, never fear.'

'Thank goodness! For a moment I was scared. I don't see why my rightful place should be at Kingsmere because Uncle Justin has gone.'

'It is a question of preparing you for your inheritance, she says. Training you so you will know how to handle it when the time comes. Your uncle left no heir, and there is no close male relative – not even a cousin – to carry on the line.'

'But Uncle Justin wasn't my father, so how can I inherit? Mamma comes after him, not me.'

'Yes, but your mother has not come back, and if . . .'

He broke off, kissed her on the forehead, asked how her play about Boadicea was coming along, and talked about everything except Christmas until she went to bed.

Elizabeth's letter had begun without any preliminary greeting.

> I am appalled to hear that you have taken my grand-daughter to live in the house of your mistress. I insist on Delia returning to Kingsmere immediately. Have you no sense of the fitness of things?

Simon's astonishment had been exceeded by his anger, but astonishment increased when he read on.

> And to think that I should learn of it from the child herself! I received her letter this morning.

Delia – writing such a thing to her grandmother? He didn't believe it, precocious as she was. But obviously she had said something which could be wrongly interpreted.

Well, now he knew. And regrettable as it was, it had its ironic side. Loving Deborah as he did, he could think of nothing more desirable than to share her bed and delight in her body, but the very fact that he loved and respected her prevented him from seducing her. He had known the risks of gossiping tongues when he decided to live in this house. He had known how much he wanted her and that propinquity was likely to make him want her even more. He was wise enough and experienced enough not to delude himself in any way, and this strengthened his resolve not to compromise or hurt her. Yet already unfounded accusations were being made through the inadvertent and guileless remarks of his daughter. It certainly did have its ironic side.

It is also imperative that Delia should now become aware of future responsibilities. My poor son dying childless, and no one else but my daughter being in direct line, her own child will one day inherit.

But Delia was not her daughter's child exclusively. He would have to remind his mother-in-law of that, but tactfully. Infuriating as the letter was, with its wrong assumptions and arrogant note of command, he felt compassion for this grenadier of a woman who had brought suffering upon herself solely because she had not loved enough in one direction, and too much in another. Her son's death must have been the culminating grief of her life. Walking by the lake, after heavy rain, he had slipped on the wet sloping lawn and plunged into the water. The lake was deep and his waterlogged clothes did the rest. No one saw him or heard his cries for help. Only later was his body seen, floating face down, tragically discovered by his mother, who had gone in search of him and seen the muddied grass on which he had slipped. She had pointed it out to everyone after her son had been dragged from the lake and carried indoors, though by that time milling footsteps had made the ground much worse.

The inquest had returned a verdict of accidental death, and only in Simon's mind lingered an unanswered question. Had his brother-in-law, whom he had always suspected of being basically cowardly, actually had the courage to end his life?

Some people looked on the event as confirmation of what they called 'the Ashleigh inheritance', claiming that tragedy stalked this family despite their wealth and advantages. The press recalled incidents in the past touching on earlier Ashleighs, and it all made very good reading in the Sunday newspapers, which he had taken good care to keep away from his daughter. Simon alone wondered if the iron Elizabeth had been spared the greater pain of her son's public disgrace.

No one would ever know.

After her long absence, Kingsmere appeared larger than Delia remembered.

'I had forgotten it was so huge,' she remarked to her father as they drove across the park in the late afternoon. In the gathering twilight its turrets and towers loomed like giant fists against the sky, awesome and somehow threatening. 'I feel the whole place could gobble me up!'

'Nothing would ever gobble *you* up, my dear. You wouldn't let it. Like me, you are a fighter.'

She had never thought of him that way, only as a very patient man with a strong face and a kind smile. Yet he must have been a fighter to enlist for the Boer War when he didn't really have to. 'He is mad!' her mother had declared. '*And* selfish. Justin has kept out of this wretched war, and I see no reason why your father should not do the same.'

Funny, how returning to Kingsmere made Delia think of her mother. She could even see her more clearly: very tall, very striking. Like a greyhound, someone had once said. She recalled the echo of a shrill, affected voice at a party saying, 'Bryant Meredith calls you his long, lean greyhound, Caro darling. I wonder how he comes to that conclusion, since present-day fashions hardly make us look that way. I mean, greyhounds always look so *naked* . . .'

Bryant Meredith! That was the name beneath Chrystal Delmont's outside the Comet Theatre. Had her mother actually known the man? Had he been amongst the guests at weekend parties sometimes? Delia was not aware that either her uncle or her mother had known any actors or actresses, but why not, since they had known all sorts of people – so many that their names had become as confused as their faces in a child's mind. They had been ever-changing, apart from a few regulars like that dreadful old Duchess of Dorking with her prickly moustache, and that horrible Sybil Clarke, who plonked those wet kisses on her, and that stockbroker named Bentley who made a great display of patting little girls on the head.

Thank goodness, none of them would be here for Christmas, and she and her father would be able to take long walks together, ride when they felt so inclined, and, if the weather were bad, curl up by the library fire with books he selected from the shelves. Her father had an unerring instinct for a good, readable tale. She recalled that he had never gone near that secret hoard in one of the cupboards below the bookshelves. Perhaps he had not known they were there. She had discovered them by accident, and in recollection they seemed nasty, though she could not remember why. I was probably too young to understand, she reflected, feeling very adult now she had reached the age of eleven.

She wished Deborah and baby Charles could have come too, and Peter Maynard also, because he could have painted a lot of pictures here – of the park, and the deer, and the lake, and the woods, and the towers of the house, which seemed no longer like menacing giant fists, but things of dignity and grace. That was because her father was pointing out how beautiful they were, how beautiful the whole place was. 'A magnificent heritage from a former age, full of historic grandeur.'

But it didn't seem very homelike. Not like 20 Hanover Square or Pru's place, smelling always of her mother's baking, or the friendly rooms she and her father now occupied, or Cook's basement kitchen, or Chrystal Delmont's lovely rooms into which she always welcomed Delia warmly, or Deborah's ground-floor home to which she felt she belonged as much as to her own on the floors above.

And what was Peter Maynard's like? 'A shabby country house in Tenterden, badly in need of a lick of paint, but country doctors don't have money for such luxuries. Not when they have to educate four sons. It will be great to be back there for Christmas, though, and Dad will be gratified to learn that I am standing on my own feet, though not for a moment will he admit it. He'll huff and chuff and say, "Well, get on with it, boy, since it's the life you want." '

'He sounds like a growly bear.'

'He is, a little. But bear growls can be kind growls, remember.'

'All the same, I have a feeling you would like to spend Christmas at Hanover Square with Deborah. You are thrilled with the studio upstairs, aren't you? You can thank me for that. If I hadn't gone exploring and said I would like to turn it into a theatre, my father would never have said it would make a better studio, and then you wouldn't be living in the same house as your goddess. So aren't you going to thank me?'

'It seems I must thank your father. For the studio, I mean.'

'You've gone very pink. Why? Does thinking of your goddess make you do that?'

'Shut up, Delia. You're a precocious little brat.'

The old lady had returned to live at the great house in isolated splendour. Kingsmere without its milord could at least be Kingsmere with a chatelaine who loved and respected it, upheld its traditions, and reflected its glory.

'That is what my granddaughter must do,' she

announced. 'I will train her myself.'

She sat in a high-backed chair at the end of the long drawing room. It had been placed between two windows so the light fell on anyone who approached, but left her own face in shadow. She was like a queen receiving her courtiers, Delia thought, and decided it would be a very good idea to set Cleopatra's throne in just this way, so that when Helen came begging for her favour she would feel like a supplicant, and be made to appear like one too. The old lady had watched them the whole time, and uttered not a word until they stood before her, and without glancing at her father, Delia had known that mixed with his dislike of such a reception was a sort of pitying indulgence.

'So you have brought her. I knew you would.'

'I would not keep her from you at Christmas.'

'Nor at any other time, if I so decree it.'

The indulgence faded.

'I will never prevent Delia from visiting Kingsmere so long as she wants to, Mother-in-law, and so long as it coincides with her school holidays.'

'School! She will not attend any such middle-class establishment under *my* supervision. She will be privately tutored and brought up as befits her station.'

'She is already being brought up as befits her station, under *my* supervision, and will continue to be.'

Thank heaven for that, thought Delia devoutly. Father was keeping his promise to her, as she had known he would.

Grandmamma rose, leaning on her stick. 'We will continue this discussion later. Privately. You and I, Simon Davidson.'

'We will, indeed.'

Her father's amiable tone did not deceive the little girl. He spoke on exactly that note when most determined.

Now her grandmother looked down at her, surveying her through lorgnettes the way the chemistry mistress at school examined things under a microscope.

'She has grown. But thin. Too thin.'

'I expect I take after my mother,' Delia piped. 'I once heard someone say that someone *else* had said that Mamma was like a greyhound – an actor called Bryant Meredith who is acting at the Comet Theatre with Miss Delmont. She is the actress who lives below us, Grandmamma, and I do know it was he who said Mamma was like a greyhound because I remember how the woman said that greyhounds always looked naked.'

'That is enough, child!'

Delia subsided, but only momentarily, because rebellion spurred her into defence of her father. 'I was only trying to prove that it is not my father's fault if I am thin, as if he doesn't see that I get enough to eat. Cook sends up scrumptious meals, doesn't she, Father? *And* gives me tea down in the kitchen when I come home from school – freshly baked scones and muffins and as much as I want of her fruitcake.

'You will not partake of tea in the kitchens here. I think you had better go to your room. Your bag will be unpacked and you can change out of those travelling clothes. I trust she has a suitable wardrobe?' the old lady finished, turning frigidly to Simon.

'I doubt if you will be able to fault it. Miss Yorke kindly assists in that respect, fathers not being much good at choosing clothes for schoolgirls.'

Delia fancied that Miss Yorke's name had been mentioned deliberately, in a sort of challenging way. She wondered why, but was not sorry, because Deborah really did choose the prettiest clothes for her. She seemed to know just what suited a girl of eleven who was on the thin side and tall for her age, and she took endless time and trouble over it. 'I enjoy doing so,' she had told Delia. 'I enjoy it as I would if I had a daughter of my own.'

'Ah, yes . . . Miss Yorke.' That was all Grandmamma

said, but Delia disliked the tone. She also disliked the note in the old lady's voice when she turned to her and added, 'I trust you remember the way to your room, child, or have you become so accustomed to living in cramped accommodation that Kingsmere bewilders you?'

'I *had* forgotten how huge it was, Grandmamma, but of course I remember the way to my room, and things don't usually bewilder me, so I am not bewildered now.'

'You are pert, child. But then, you always were. That will be corrected, too.'

'They don't consider me pert at school. The headmistress put on my report that I was bright and intelligent, but occasionally boisterous, which was natural in a girl of my age with a zest for life. And that didn't displease Father. He chose this new school – didn't you, Father? – because it is considered advanced in its education for girls. We even have lessons usually given only to boys, like chemistry. *And* we play hockey and netball.'

'Hoydenish. It is totally unbecoming to a granddaughter of mine to attend any school, much less take part in rough outdoor games. She should be tutored privately, and only in subjects which can be beneficial to her socially.'

'My dear mother-in-law, the fight for higher education for women was won as long ago as the seventies, and I am a firm believer in it.' To Delia, Simon said gently, 'Go to your room now, and change as your grandmother suggests.'

'I shall wear my blue. It's new and I love it. Deborah says blue is my colour, because my eyes remind her of cornflowers.' Delia turned to dance away; she wanted to slide the length of the polished floor, but managed to refrain; then she mercifully remembered her manners and turned back to bob the obligatory curtsey before walking sedately to the door and closing it quietly behind her. Father was on her side, so she was on his and would do nothing to disgrace him if she could avoid it.

He was alone with Elizabeth for the first time since he had raced down here to confront Justin Ashleigh, and the memory of that interview lay between them like an immovable shadow. He was not welcome here, but would be accommodated because he was the father of the old lady's granddaughter. He also knew that Elizabeth hoped he would depart at the earliest opportunity, leaving Delia behind. In that she would be disappointed. He had no intention of relinquishing his daughter, no matter how heavily loaded the persuasion.

He was moved to pity, all the same, for the woman seemed to have aged overnight. Now that she had left her throne, the merciless light of a cold December day revealed a face on which grief was deeply etched. But there was bitterness there too, and it was levelled against himself. 'We will have our talk, and then I trust you will have the decency to leave this house.'

'I see no reason to take my leave, nor will I, without my daughter. If I go, she goes too, and you know you cannot prevent it. Now, let us have our talk and be done with it. Perhaps it will clear the air for Christmas.'

'I might have known you would be facetious and ill-mannered.'

'If I am ill-mannered, I apologise, but your own reception could hardly be called gracious.'

'And why should I receive you with any grace at all? *You* – who sent my son to his death.'

Astonishment rendered him speechless. He had not expected her to remember him with kindness – his suspicion of Justin had been all too plain – but to blame him for that accidental death . . .

Surely it *had* been an accident? The unanswered question leapt into his mind again.

'But for you,' Elizabeth accused, 'he would never have

died. The insinuations you levelled against him left him distraught and shocked, as he had every right to be. If you had not come that day, he would not have gone walking by the lake to calm himself, and so slipped on the wet bank. He would be alive and safe.'

But where? Simon wondered. Where? 'Is this what you wanted to talk about?' he asked quietly. 'I thought you had other things in mind.'

'You are callous.'

'No. I grieve for you, but I can see it is useless to defend myself against thoughts you are determined to harbour against me. So if there is nothing more . . .'

'There *is* more, and well you know it. There is Delia – and the deplorable way in which you are bringing her up, the environment, the immorality of that house. I shall take every possible step to get her away from the influence of yourself and your mistress.'

'I have no mistress.'

'Yet your own daughter writes to me about her, about the way the young woman feels about you and the way you feel about her – so blatant that even a child notices.'

'I am quite sure my daughter has never referred to my having a mistress, though from her previous upbringing here at Kingsmere I wouldn't be surprised if she knew the term, and what it means. I believe you yourself kept away when weekend house parties took place. Unfortunately, my daughter was not kept away, and consequently learned of certain behaviour which she accepted as natural.'

'I wanted her with me at the dower house on those regrettable occasions, but her mother would never agree. Caroline enjoyed flouting me. And I will never have my son blamed for things that went on. I daresay most of the guests were my daughter's friends.'

'Some, perhaps, but by no means all. But that is in the past. Delia's environment now exposes her to nothing except a healthy home life and a normal upbringing.'

'Living in the house of your mistress, and some fast actress beneath the same roof! Carrying on the tradition of the place, I can tell.'

'Miss Yorke is not my mistress, and Miss Delmont is anything but fast.' Something in his eyes silenced the old lady, who stood clutching the silver top of her ebony stick with shaking hands.

'But you *are* in love with that young woman,' she managed to say. 'So much that my granddaughter is aware of it.'

'I will give you the truth. Both Delia *and* I love Deborah Yorke, and will continue to in our different ways. But neither Deborah nor I will set anything but a good example to my child. For this reason we keep apart; for this reason even more than the fact that I am married to a woman I would dearly like to be released from – and if I ever can be, I will marry Deborah Yorke if she will have me. I hope Caroline decides never to return. I will then divorce her for desertion no matter how slowly the wheels of God and the law may grind. Until then, I will allow no one to slander Deborah. And now, if you'll excuse me . . .'

A few moments after Simon left her, Elizabeth Ashleigh banged her stick violently to the floor. 'Damn you, Caroline! *Damn you*. Why don't you have the good sense to come home?'

Despite its bad beginning, Christmas proceeded on its smooth and well-organised way, with the customary ball the day preceding Christmas Eve, to which all the best names in the country were invited and at which everyone behaved with tact and sympathy, full of admiration for the way in which the dowager Lady Ashleigh held up her proud head in the face of recent grief; then came the carol singers on Christmas Eve, grouped below the steps of the great front door, then trooping into the ancient hall to partake of mulled wine and mince pies and to accept the Ashleigh donation to local church funds; then church on Christmas morning, the old lady flanked on either side by her granddaughter and son-in-law, with everyone in the congregation secretly glancing at the Ashleigh pew in admiration and curiosity, thinking how nice it was to see the dowager united with what was left of her family and wondering when that daughter of hers was going to return, and every woman wondering how she could bear to stay away from that very striking man – not handsome, but so interesting, with his scarred face and slight limp and very determined jaw – and the little girl, Delia, who grew more like her mother every day, though the child's deep blue eyes were larger and friendlier than her mother's, her mouth softer, and her expression warmer.

Then came Christmas dinner in Kingsmere's immense dining room, to which various friends of the dowager had been invited, all stately and elderly and who obviously believed that a small girl should speak only when spoken to, and so to Boxing Day and the party for the estate children, which, to Delia, was to be the highlight of the visit, for she was allowed to join in the games after presents had been distributed from the tree. This would be a welcome relief from supervision and restraint, from which she could normally escape only when Grandmamma took her afternoon nap, whereupon she and her father would go striding across the parklands and she was free to be herself.

'I hope you think I am behaving well, Father?'

'Very well, my pet.' His fond glance was tinged with amusement. 'Very well indeed, considering the effort it must be.'

She gave her lovable, impish grin. 'How many more days do I have to keep it up?'

'I must return to the museum in two days' time. Can you hold out that long?'

'If you can, I can. Poor Father – I think you are finding it all as lonely as I am. Oh, those long meals with Grandmamma sitting at the head of the table and scarcely speaking except when there are guests! Why doesn't she like us, Father?'

Sometimes his daughter's observations startled Simon. He had been congratulating himself on carrying everything off so well that underlying tension was firmly hidden, but children had uncanny perception, and Delia's could be unerring.

'Not *us*,' he said carefully. 'Myself, perhaps, because I don't see eye to eye with her.'

'Oh, both of us, I'm sure, otherwise she wouldn't always be saying how pert I am, or how hoydenish, or how I should be controlled or brought up or disci . . . what's that word she uses such a lot?'

'Disciplined. And if you have brought your dictionary with you, you can add it and I will tell you how to spell it.'

'Bother – I left it behind.'

Recalling the bureau where she kept it made her think of the house in Hanover Square, of Cook's spicy kitchen and the warm nursery where she sometimes played with the baby on the hearth rug, and Deborah holding him up to see his mother's picture that day, smiling her lovely smile. And Peter, chasing her out of his studio because he wanted to work and threatening to stick a notice on the door saying *'Keep out, Cleopatra!'* – but of course he never did. And Miss Delmont inviting her in for tea sometimes, and letting her look at her collection of theatre programmes, which went back years and years . . . and the lovely feeling of home she and her father shared in their two-floored 'house' upstairs.

A wave of longing swept over her which was almost unbearable. She slipped her hand into Simon's and said, 'I've just remembered it is baby Charles's three-months' birthday – he was born on twenty-sixth September. Let's go home soon.'

She felt his strong grasp and knew he understood, that he felt as she did, though all he said was, 'Time passes, my dear – and don't forget there's the children's party to look forward to this afternoon. Now, I'll race you back – ready, steady, *go*!' And off they went, laughing, aware of no one but themselves, and she thought how wonderful he was to run so well despite his lame leg – so well that she hated beating him and began to slow down to let him win.

If she had not done so, she wouldn't have seen the station cab trundling up the long drive, with her mother half-leaning out of the window, watching them.

19

'So you have come back, and not before time.'

Elizabeth's voice lacked all emotion. Not that Caroline had expected any, or felt any herself. Even so, she was shocked by her mother's appearance. She had aged alarmingly, the once handsome face shrunken to little more than a mask.

I don't believe *I* did that to her, thought Caroline. She would never grieve for me. Only for my brother.

'Yes, I am back, but not because I want to be. Only through a sense of duty. I read about Justin in a back number of *The Times* in Alexandria. What made him fall into the lake? Was he drunk?'

'Your brother never drank to excess.'

'I am sure he had other vices, probably worse.'

The familiar brittle note was still there, but it made

Elizabeth wince as it had never done before. It was the first time Caroline had ever been able to score over her mother, and she relished her triumph.

'If you have returned to belittle your brother, I wonder you took the trouble to come back at all.'

If you did but know, thought Caroline, I came because I had nowhere else to go. Stuck in that hotel in Alexandria, wondering where to go next, what to do with herself next, and hating the idea of returning to England unheralded, she had ordered meals to be served in her room and stayed there for three days before descending to the public lounge and picking up that old copy of *The Times*. She had been miserable and alone and very sorry for herself, disgusted with the minimal co-operation she had received from people she had expected to bow down to her, and particularly with the ever-extended palms she had to grease to get anywhere at all.

She had decided that Hester Stanhope's story had been overdramatised and most of it fictional, also that the woman could not have travelled as extensively as she had done without the faithful Dr Meryon and others to help her on her way. No doubt they did all the organisation while the Stanhope woman merely waited to be escorted from place to place – and footed the bills. In fact, the only part of the story in which Caroline now believed *was* her footing the bills, and there was precious little glamour in that.

From Amman – the old Rabbath Ammon of Biblical days – to Madaba, from Madaba to Karak, changing servants all the way and handing out bribes, on top of which she suspected she was being grossly overcharged on basic rates; aiming for Aqaba, and never reaching it because Arabs disliked journeying so far from their native villages, and bedouins in particular disliked serving any woman. Beneath their *kaffiyehs* their black eyes had seemed either contemptuous or amused, some even scorning her proffered money, others accepting it and then deserting her when they felt the urge to return to their families. She had never realised before that Muslims could feel such strong family ties – how could they, when allowed as many as four wives and consequently breeding apparently endless tribes of children? One would have thought they would be ready to bow in homage to an affluent Western woman proffering badly needed money. Instead, their glances had conveyed nothing more than disdain at the spectacle of a woman travelling without a man. As far as her virtue was concerned, she had been entirely safe, for if any man was willing to let his wife go off alone, he obviously did not miss her in his bed, which meant she was not worth coveting.

Petra she had never reached, and hardly cared anyway. Heading back north from the road to Aqaba, somehow she had reached Ramallah and then Nablus, from where she had travelled across to Haifa on the distant coast. At least the green softness of Samaria had been more endurable than the black basalt deserts, but the sight of the eastern Mediterranean had been more welcome than any previous glimpse she had ever had of the sea. Haifa meant ships, and places like Port Said and Alexandria. It meant the end of Spartan rest houses and unpalatable food and never-ending discomfort. It even meant a bath. Those at the rest houses had been nothing more than tin tubs filled by sloe-eyed women who regarded her with greater curiosity than did their menfolk, then ran away giggling and chattering as if they had been looking at a freak.

The laughter had been the most galling thing of all. Throughout her fruitless journeying it always occurred when her back was turned. To her face, male servants had been polite even when their black eyes seemed derisive; then behind her back she would suddenly hear high falsetto laughter, but no sign or sound of it when she spun round. Gradually her nerves had begun to jangle with suspicion, until she could stand it no longer and would round on them, snapping out commands and imprecations in very bad Arabic – only to be met with proud hauteur, for no man would accept such talk from a woman.

Packs would then be dumped, mules abandoned, padding footsteps start on the trek back to their villages, deaf to her screaming abuse and orders to return at once. And so would start the dreary business of bargaining for replacements from the nearest bedouin encampment or huddle of desert hovels, with the heat and the flies and the dust and the smells making her long for the cool peace of Kingsmere and even more for its luxuries and respectful staff.

By the time she reached Haifa she was more than ready for home, but on reaching Alexandria she had begun to recover sufficiently to realise that to return without the expected fanfare would be humiliating in the extreme. In the solitude of her room, isolating herself while she tried to think up some convincing excuse for returning, she thought of her husband and child, of her mother and brother, of friends, of ex-lovers like Bryant Meredith, and knew that none of them had really been missing her. No letters had caught up with her at any of the rest houses, forwarded by the authorities at Al Salt. Mails were unreliable, of course – she had reassured herself with that thought – but had she been wise enough to accept the official guides offered to her on arrival, she knew she would have fared better in every way, but the whole object of this adventure (as she had expected it to turn out) was to cut a dramatic figure and win the world's admiration for her intrepid spirit.

It was useless to dwell on that. All was behind her. Ahead lay home. But even now her stiff-necked pride made her shrink from returning without some justifiable excuse. Her name on a ship's passenger list would be sure to attract the press. She would be met when it docked, interviewed, photographed. 'What made you abandon your explorations?' they would ask. 'What made you return so soon?' But it wasn't soon. She had been away for several months, so what more natural than to return, her mission accomplished? 'I now intend to write a book about it,' she would announce, hiding the fact that if she did, she would have to make it all up.

On that thought she was able to go downstairs, the prospect of eating in the dining room encouraging her to dress with former pride. She made her descent leisurely, aware of her lissome body encased in the tussore silk dress she had bought in Haifa, and hoping, this time, for a renewal of male admiration. Nor was she disappointed. Various samples of the Britisher Abroad both appraised and appreciated her. Her morale rose. She sank lazily into a deep armchair and picked up a discarded newspaper from the table beside her – and read of her brother's death.

So what more natural than her immediate return? She was the inheritor of Kingsmere. Her place was now there.

She descended the gangway at Tilbury clad in hastily purchased black and ready to meet the press with every display of sorrow, only to find herself completely un-noticed. Instead, reporters flocked to interview some tire-some Eastern potentate, flanked by his elaborate en-tourage and his numerous veiled wives. Outraged and insulted, she turned her back on the lot of them and headed for home.

'You do realise,' said her mother, 'that now poor Justin has gone, you are mistress here, and after you, your daughter? If only my dear son had left an heir . . .' She choked a little, then went on, 'But that was not God's will. You now have responsibilities to face, and in your absence I have been facing them for you. I have started by bringing your daughter back to Kingsmere.'

'You mean my husband brought her, don't you? I know they are here. I saw them in the park, and they saw me. Delia first, whereupon she stopped dead and then bolted, the little savage. A fine way to welcome back her mother! Then Simon saw me. Naturally I didn't expect any reaction from *him* – he is a past master in the art of hiding his feelings except when it suits him – but instead of calling the child to heel immediately, he simply turned and walked after her.'

'So that was why you arrived in such a bad temper. What did you expect? A fanfare of trumpets, red carpet rolled down the front steps, joyous cries of welcome from a child who has probably almost forgotten you, open arms from a husband who has announced his intention to divorce you. If he can?'

'He has *what*?'

'Ah, I thought that would shock you. You really cannot sail through life doing what you please just when you please, and expect people to accept it.'

'Justin did whatever he pleased, always.'

'Justin was a man. What a man may do, a woman may not. And what the mistress of Kingsmere may do is another matter entirely. In your new position you must be circumspect in the extreme and never involve the family name in so much as a breath of scandal. And that middle-class husband of yours is a man to be reckoned with. He means what he says, and while I would be wholly glad to be rid of him, I cannot permit him to drag the name of Ashleigh through the dust. The fact that you bear his name makes no difference. You were born an Ashleigh and are still thought of by society as an Ashleigh. So go carefully, Caroline. It is a good thing you came back. Had you continued trailing around the world for a couple of years, he could have divorced you for desertion. He was hoping for that precisely, in order to marry again.'

'Marry! Simon *marry* again? Who, in heaven's name?'

'The new "Madame" of Hanover Square.'

Caroline sat down abruptly. The *new* Madame? What had happened to that shocking whore her father had kept? 'What *new* "Madame"?' she asked. 'What happened to the old one? You do mean number 20 Hanover Square, I take it?'

'Naturally. I know of no other scandalous house in the neighbourhood. But of course, I was forgetting – you haven't heard. That dreadful woman died. Sometime in September, I believe. You had departed on your hare-brained pursuit of the Near or Far East, or wherever it is you have been roaming, so I don't suppose the news caught up with you.' Elizabeth finished indifferently, 'Childbirth, I believe.'

'Childbirth! You mean there was actually a child?'

'That is what the word usually means, does it not?'

'Justin's child? It must have been!'

'That is not so. He denied it emphatically, and I believed him. It could have been any man's. You know what she was.'

Caroline nodded, for once in agreement with her mother. 'All the same, what if it really was Justin's? Was it a son, do you know?'

'I have not the faintest idea nor the slightest interest.'

'Did it live?'

Her mother answered impatiently, 'I believe Delia referred to a baby in the house, but –'

'*Delia?* How does she know about it?'

'How can she fail to, since her father has taken her to live there? My dear daughter, this is the whole point of what I am saying, the very thing I am trying to lead up to, but you keep interrupting. Your husband and daughter have taken up residence there, beneath the same roof as the Howard woman's relative – niece or cousin or what-ever she was – and it is this creature whom your husband hopes to marry. Deborah something.'

'Deborah Yorke! I remember her. She came here that weekend — the weekend when something happened between Dulcima Howard and Justin and he sent her packing next morning. I often wondered why. He had insisted on Papa's suite being opened up and lavishly decorated with blooms from the hothouses, and I was absolutely livid when I discovered for whom. I told him so, but of course he only laughed. But I was outraged at the thought of his occupying Papa's bed with *her*.'

'Please . . . I don't want to hear!'

Caroline mused aloud, indifferent to her mother's feelings, 'I wonder if that was why Justin kicked her out . . .'

'If he did, I am delighted to hear it. My poor boy, ensnared by such a woman!'

'Well, he slipped the snare very easily, *and* characteristically. No one would ever be allowed to trap Justin, Mamma, so don't delude yourself. But what a joke if the child were really his!'

'*Joke!*' Elizabeth jerked to her feet, outraged, leaning on her ebony stick for support.

'It certainly is, if the child is a boy. And it *could* have been my brother's just as easily as any other man's.'

'Rubbish. Justin had better sense than to beget bastards. He was a man of the world and no doubt enjoyed the rights and privileges of a man of the world, but he would never be so indiscreet as others of the nobility, breeding indiscriminately.'

'Perhaps he couldn't. He never had any success with his wife, did he?'

'That was Norah's fault entirely. She was a weakling, and you know it. My son wanted nothing so greatly as he wanted an heir.'

'And, of course, a bastard could not be acknowledged.'

'I have had enough of this conversation. If you will not listen to me now, Caroline, you will have to later.'

'Sorry, Mamma. I am listening. What else do you want to discuss?'

'The matter of how you are going to spike your husband's guns. If there is going to be a divorce, *you* must not be the guilty party. For this reason your return is fortunate – he cannot now divorce you for desertion. But you know how the divorce laws are loaded in a man's favour and very much against a woman's. On the grounds of adultery alone you cannot divorce him, but if he refused to live with you and if proof of adultery with the Yorke girl can be obtained, you can sue on the grounds of adultery coupled with desertion, after two years. No fair-minded judge would then refuse you custody of your daughter, and we can employ excellent lawyers to convince the court that the house she is living in with her father is highly undesirable, even disreputable. I understand there is also an actress living there, and some bohemian artist up in the attic.'

To Elizabeth's astonishment, Caroline burst out laughing. 'Sorry, Mamma, but you paint such an amusing picture!'

'Amusing!'

'Actresses and bohemian artists up in attics!'

'But everyone knows what actresses and artists are like. Loose-living. Scandalous. The very people to take up residence in a house once belonging to a whore, and now to her calculating relative, who has wasted no time in enticing your husband beneath her roof. Is that a suitable background for the offspring of a titled family? You can rest assured that no right-minded court would permit a wellborn child to remain there. Delia would be back at Kingsmere, where she belongs, in no time at all, being trained to come into her inheritance, mistress in your stead eventually, married to a man of good birth and breeding and ready to produce another generation to carry on. The name of Ashleigh would have to be linked with that of her husband to ensure that it did not die out. We would make that a stipulation.'

For the first time in her life Caroline regarded her mother with something akin to awe. 'You've thought it all out, haven't you, Mamma? And you make it sound so easy. But will it be? Accusing someone of adultery is one thing; proving it another.' As I well know, she thought complacently, and congratulated herself on her own talent for deception.

'I am aware of that, and have given the matter some thought. My first determination was to get Delia back here permanently, but on that point her father is proving stubborn – as I suppose I should have anticipated. Not having any idea when you proposed to return, I felt it imperative to have the child under my supervision, to make sure she is brought up to fulfil her future obligations, but also to avoid moral contamination in that house.'

'Oh, come, Mamma, little girls of eleven know nothing of moral standards.'

'Indeed they do, if brought up properly. And I cannot say you have been very diligent in that respect yourself. People are so lax nowadays, and I strongly suspect that applies to you too. From now on you must watch your step. Remember your position here at Kingsmere, and live up to it. You will start at the party for estate children this afternoon.'

'Oh, heavens, what a bore! Must I? Couldn't you deputise for me? Say I am fatigued after travelling.'

'Certainly not. We must both be present, and Delia with us. The staff expects it. It will be a sad occasion, without Justin to hand presents from the tree, but we must do our duty and keep up appearances.'

'And after? When Christmas is over and Simon goes back to London?'

'You go with him.'

'*What*? To that house? Never! You must be out of your

mind.'

'Indeed I am not. You don't have to stay. Not for long, anyway. All you have to do is get in there and remain until you have sized up the situation yourself, but, even more important, since I am sure that neither he nor she will act indiscreetly while you are on the premises, to show society that you are reunited with your husband and child, and any break that follows then will be his fault entirely.'

'I will never, *never* set foot in the house Papa bought for that mistress of his.'

'She is dead, Caroline, and so is he. Am *I* grieving?'

'You never did, Mamma. Not for my father. Not for anyone except my brother. You will certainly never grieve for me.'

'Not if you fail me in this. Don't you realise that you badly need to win the sympathy of society? Everyone frowned on your going abroad alone, without apparently sparing a thought for your husband and child. The press was critical too, but the headlines were soon replaced by more spectacular ones. You have to recover lost ground if you hope to regain the slightest sympathy, and you can do that only by at least pretending to be a dutiful wife and mother after all.'

'And if Simon refuses to take me back with him?'

'For goodness' sake, use your wits! Follow him. Arrive on the doorstep. The door could hardly be shut in your face, and if it were, that would be the first shot in your bow. You have only to announce that you are expected, especially if the door were to be opened by Deborah Yorke. She comes of the class accustomed to opening doors to callers, and even if there were a butler, you know how to deal with them. In any case, I doubt if the one who decamped has been replaced.'

'The one who what?'

'Nothing . . . nothing . . .'

Elizabeth began her slow journey across the room, her

shoulders bowed beneath the pain of memory. She was no longer the brisk, upright woman her daughter remembered, but though her shoulders were bent, Caroline knew that her shrewd brain was as active as ever.

'Mamma, nothing in the world would induce me to go to that house, and you know it.'

'Think it over. Think it over well. You may change your mind if you do. Meanwhile, we have about an hour in which to prepare ourselves to face that bevy of children in the great hall. And from your looks, you need rather more preparation than formerly. You have returned most unbecomingly sallow.'

Furiously Caroline pulled the bell rope beside the fire, then marched out of the room without waiting for it to be answered. In her agitation she had no idea why she was summoning the housekeeper, but she had automatically given the three short tugs which set the bell jangling in the housekeeper's room. Her bags would have been taken up, and be already unpacked. Simpkins, her maid, would have seen to that. Not for a moment did she doubt that Simpkins was still here; niece of the cook, daughter of the head gardener, she was as much a part of the household as every other member of the staff. Tradition in the servants' hall was as strong as family tradition abovestairs, and now she would have to uphold it more than she had ever done before.

To find herself suddenly mistress of Kingsmere left her with mixed feelings – gratification, pride, and a sense of restriction. To be free of her brother's domination and arrogance was a relief, as was the knowledge that she would no longer be overshadowed by him, nor rank as second in the servants' regard, but only now did she suspect how strangulating the tentacles of duty could threaten to be. A curb on her freedom, without a doubt.

But how easy it was to accept once again the magnificence of the Ashleigh home, how quickly one expected, and received, subservience! Kimberley, the butler, Barker, the first footman; even the hall boy who hurried down the front steps on Kimberley's order and took her bags from the cabdriver – all had been immediately respectful after their first display of surprise, swiftly checked. Thank God she was back in a civilised country, with civilised servants, in a regime which could never change.

In return, to stand on the dais in the hall, beside the Christmas tree, and make a welcoming speech to the children, was really a very small duty to perform. She began to rehearse what she would say.

'I hope you are all having a wonderful, *wonderful* time? You certainly look as if you are! And now for the tree and the presents you are all waiting for . . .' Oh, no, that wouldn't do. She must first make some reference to the sad loss the Family had sustained. 'On behalf of my dear mother and myself . . . this, alas, is not the happy Christmas we all would wish . . .' No, that wouldn't do either – she had forgotten to mention Delia. 'On behalf of my dear mother and my darling daughter, not to mention myself and the brother for whom everyone at Kingsmere mourns, I would like to wish you all a very happy Christmas and a bright new year, and to thank all your dear parents for their loyalty and service throughout these past twelve months . . .'

But how ridiculous! She had not been here for the whole of the past twelve months, so how did she know what sort of service they had given or how loyal they had been? She had no doubt at all that their tongues had wagged incessantly at the time of Justin's death and that speculation had been rife as to how it happened. 'Had a drop too much, if you ask me. You know his lordship . . .' and 'I wonder if it really *was* an accident? I wonder if his mother wasn't covering up for him again?' Good heavens, what was she thinking? What put such thoughts into her head? Imagining servants' gossip was a stupid thing to do. Why heed the tittle-tattle of such parasitical creatures, over-indulged and overpaid and probably not in the least grateful?

But after the present giving, and a last brilliant smile coupled with a gracious wave of the hand, she could retire to the drawing-room fire, thank God, and sherry before dinner, and service she had not experienced since she left this place – this beautiful, magnificent place of which, she realised, she was immensely proud.

With the presentation of toys from the Christmas tree she would have accomplished her first duty as the new mistress of Kingsmere, but what of the other responsibilities? The weekly conferences with Cook about menus, and, even worse, the checking of household accounts, a task she had never undertaken in her life. Perhaps she could prevail upon Mamma, always so managing and efficient, to undertake that duty again. And then, of course, there was the staff, for even with senior members responsible for others below them, real supervision always emanated from the mistress of the house, and though butlers and housekeepers were prepared to relieve bachelor employers of such irksome responsibilities, they would have no respect for a mistress who was not prepared to shoulder a great deal more. And, of course, she would be expected to tutor her daughter in such responsibilities throughout the coming years.

Delia! She had forgotten the child. Where was she? Upstairs in her room, or still out in the park with her father? Finding Simon here was something she had not expected, though she had anticipated that Delia would have come to spend Christmas with her grandmother. I should have known he wouldn't let the child out of his sight, Caroline reflected as she went on her way upstairs. He made it plain before I went away that he was determined to have her with him permanently, and I must admit I thought it a good idea at the time.

But now? She had come home to a very different scene. The picture her mother presented was an alarming one, but how true was it? Perhaps Mamma was getting a bit senile; at the very least, imaginative. Simon, in love with another woman? Simon, wanting to marry someone else? Simon, hoping for a divorce? She could scarcely credit any of it, but even less could she credit the story that he had actually moved into the house in Hanover Square and the woman he had fallen in love with was the new 'Madame' there.

As for visiting the place herself, Mamma must be out of her mind. There must be other ways of avoiding scandal than grovelling to one's husband to be taken back. Their marriage wasn't a marriage any more, he had said during that memorable weekend. She wondered now whether that had been due to Deborah Yorke's presence. She had had a feeling even then that he knew the young woman by sight. Perhaps their *affaire* had begun even before his wife embarked on her travels. Had that been the reason why he put no opposition in her way? It could be, it could be . . .but how to find out? Only, as her mother said, by visiting that hateful house herself, and nothing in the world would make her do that. It would be better to tackle Simon as soon as they met; ask him if what Mamma said were true.

Which, of course, he would deny, and then where would she be?

Her thoughts were going round in circles by the time she reached the long landing at the top of the stairs and saw her daughter standing beneath a portrait, hands behind her back, head uplifted, studying the painting with unusual intensity. On the thick carpet, Delia had not heard her tread, so Caroline was able to study the child unseen. My goodness, how she had shot up in a matter of months! And there was something else about her; she was less gauche. Even from this distance, that fact was noticeable. The way she held her head, the way she stood, not kicking her heels in that infuriating way she used to, but quite still. Very still.

'Delia.'

The little girl turned but did not come toward her.

'Why did you run away in the park?'

'I was taken by surprise. We both were.'

'That was no reason for running away. Surely you wanted to see me? Surely you knew I was eager to see you?'

'Had you really been eager, you would have come home before.'

'Well, I must say this is a fine welcome! Anyone would think you weren't glad to see me.'

Delia answered politely, 'Of course I am glad, Mamma. Did you have a nice holiday?'

Holiday! Dust and flies and disrespectful servants; contemptuous black eyes and hands forever outstretched. tedium and loneliness. God, the loneliness! Sometimes, in the stifling nights, she had tried to recall her reasons for going away, and could think of none, except that Bryant Meredith had jilted her and she hoped he was sorry and missing her.

'Very nice indeed, dear. Very interesting. I intend to write a book about it.'

'You will have plenty of rooms here to write in. Father has a nice one too, now we have moved. Did you know we had moved?'

'Yes. Your grandmother told me.' (And I am not going to discuss that with anyone but your father . . .)

Because Delia made no move toward her, Caroline was forced to go to her daughter.

'Why were you studying that portrait so intently?'

'Because he has eyes like baby Charles's.'

'What are you talking about?'

'Miss Howard's baby. He's a darling, and I'm longing to get back to him. And the funny thing is that he has eyes just like these – my great-great-great-grandfather, isn't it? A few others have them, here and there. Once I heard Kimberley call them "the Ashleigh eyes", and Mrs Parker said, "The Ashleigh inheritance, you mean," and *he* said, "It's all part of it, isn't it? Haven't you heard the legend?" so of course *I* asked what legend, and they stopped talking at once. I don't think they realised I was there.'

I am quite sure they didn't, Caroline thought grimly, resolving to exert her authority over the staff more firmly than her brother had done. He had kept them on his side with charm and generosity, when it suited him to use either, and servants always made excuses for their masters. They didn't even respect them if they failed to sow a plentiful crop of wild oats when young, nor even when older. Goodness only knew how many of Justin's escapades Kimberley had helped to cover up – and, no doubt, been suitably rewarded for. But execrable behaviour in a mistress would never be excused. She had to be a lady first, last, and foremost.

'What's this about a baby?' she asked.

'I told you, Mamma. Baby Charles. He has eyes just like these. He was born with them, and that's unusual, isn't it, because newborn babies have blue eyes, don't they? I had never seen anyone but Uncle Justin with eyes like these before. I've been taking a good look at all these pictures, and not only Uncle Justin had them, but some others before him. And all were men. Isn't that strange? Not a single lady in the whole gallery has them. But Kimberley must have been wrong when he called them Ashleigh eyes, because Charles's surname is Howard.'

So it was true. And how *dare* that ex-Gaiety Girl call her son by Papa's name! Through spite? Because Justin would not acknowledge the child? Had the creature really imagined he would? That servant girl Mama had bought off years ago had expected nothing at all, though rumour had it that her rape had led to pregnancy – a little girl, Caroline had heard, adopted by the girl's mother after the daughter, flushed with what would be, to her, unexpected wealth, went off to London and probably finished up on the Dilly. Not an offspring of one of the traditional Kingsmere estate families, of course; nothing but a local girl hired as extra help during the spring cleaning, which gave additional employment to village folk annually. Caroline could not even remember her name, let alone what she looked like, but how could one ever forget a woman like Dulcima Howard?

'Did you see any camels, Mamma?'

Caroline jerked to attention. 'Mm? Oh, yes, plenty. Filthy creatures.'

'Couldn't they be bathed?'

Caroline gave the high laugh that her daughter had forgotten, but now recalled as very much a part of her mother. A sort of dry, brittle sound that never seemed really amused.

'I should hate to try, my love.'

'Did you buy any?'

'Gracious, no! I hired the beasts for the use of servants, along with pack mules. The only animal I bought was a decent Arab horse for myself, which, I'm happy to say, I finally sold in Haifa at a goodly profit.'

The thought of her mother struggling up a ship's gangway, leading a camel, struck Delia as so funny that she went into gales of laughter.

'What's so amusing, darling?' Caroline looked at her daughter as if seeing her for the first time. Not only was she taller, but she was prettier too. Big blue eyes and a face which held great promise. Very much like myself, she thought complacently. Not a bit like Simon. Every inch an

Ashleigh. 'And that is a very pretty dress. Grand-mamma's choice, I presume. I am glad she kept an eye on your wardrobe in my absence.'

'She didn't. She said any clothes I needed could be charged to her account at Harrods, but Father never used it. Well, I mean, he wouldn't, would he? No father would like someone else paying for his daughter's clothes, as if he couldn't pay for them himself.' Delia's chin went up. 'We are not poor, you know.'

Oh, dear, she *was* like Simon, after all. That tilt of the chin, that quiet pride, that way he had of parrying slights. Difficult.

'I find it hard to believe that your father chose that dress, all the same.'

'No, Deborah did. She helps choose all my clothes. Sometimes Father comes with us, but usually we go alone, because he has the museum to run. I love shopping ex-peditions with Deborah; she makes it all such fun, even fittings, and you know how I always hated being fitted – though I expect you've forgotten by now.'

'I certainly have not. And I see no reason why some stranger should be allowed to supervise your wardrobe.'

'But she isn't a stranger! She is *Deborah*. Are you looking shocked because I call her by her Christian name – is that why? I know I should call her Miss Yorke, but I have thought of her as Deborah ever since I've known her, and it began to slip out gradually and became stuck for always. And she doesn't mind. She likes it. It's friendlier, she says. Less formal. And after our shopping we always have tea at Gunter's and some of their delicious chocolate cake –'

Caroline interrupted sharply, 'You'd better get ready for the children's party. Kimberley will be coming to tell us they are ready for the tree, before we know where we are.'

'I am ready, Mamma. That is why I am wearing this dress. It's my best, and even Grandmamma likes it. I'm glad you do, too. Deborah says blue is my colour, because . . .'

But her mother was hurrying away to her room, and Delia could have sworn she was angry, though she couldn't think why.

20

Once she was in her room, Caroline's fury increased. Her bags had not been unpacked, her maid had not been near. Dust sheets were still on the bed and holland covers on the furniture, and the place had the unlived-in atmosphere of a room which had been kept dusted and cleaned but not occupied. Then she recalled that preparations for the children's party must have started shortly before she arrived, and of course she had not been expected.

'Did you send a telegraph, madam?' Kimberley had asked in a tone which clearly implied that she should have done. 'If so, the village post-master must have forgotten to deliver.' A touch of sarcasm there? Kimberley, despite his impeccable manners, had always conveyed a secret lack of respect for her. He needed taking down a peg or two.

She was incensed, and not merely because her room was unprepared, or because her mother's attitude toward her was unchanged, or even because her brother had sired another bastard, but because some chit of a young woman in London had the impertinence to choose her daughter's clothes. It was more insulting than leaving the choice to a dressmaker or governess.

Obviously this Deborah Yorke took after that fast relative of hers – aunt or cousin, which had she been? – insinuating herself into Simon's affections, just as the scandalous Dulcima had insinuated herself into Papa's. The fact that she and Simon had fallen out of love long ago had no bearing on the situation. A married man was a married man, and a married woman was entitled to her husband. Divorce? He hadn't a hope! What's more, she would tell him so the moment they met. Also that their daughter was to remain at Kingsmere instead of returning to that infamous house.

'And if you return to it yourself,' she would warn him, 'I shall regard it as the first step in deserting me.' Oh, yes, she would be very firm this time. 'We must be a united family,' she would insist, 'and Kingsmere needs an heir now, more than ever it did. I might have a son, and a son would take precedence over an older sister, and I don't really think Delia is cut out to be mistress of Kingsmere anyway. She is too . . . too . . .'

Defiant? Was that the word? Well, whatever she was, Caroline didn't like it. She sensed in her daughter a future antagonist.

Caroline flung off her travelling clothes, scattering them about the floor; then she tipped the contents of a case on to the bed and pulled out the first dress to hand, which happened to be the graceful tussore that had won appreciative male glances in Alexandria. Heavens, there wasn't even a towel to hand! Every female member of the staff was down there at the Christmas party, so to ring was useless. She brushed her face with a leaf of *papier-poudre*, jabbed at her upswept hair with a comb, wished to heaven she could heat her curling tongs to frizz the cluster of curls on top, fished in corners of the case to find some artificial ones, and failed, rubbed her lips with salve, and resolved that however much Mamma might frown on makeup, declaring that only actresses and street women painted their faces, she would use it herself if she wanted to. Mamma was right – she was horribly sallow. A touch of colour would have restored her morale considerably.

Downstairs in the great hall Kimberley made his way across to the housekeeper, where she sat gossiping with a cluster of estate wives. He could scarcely hear himself speak above the din. '*She's back*!' he mouthed.

Mrs Parker put a hand behind her ear and mouthed in return, '*What did you say*?' Then she grasped it. 'Oh, mercy be, not Miss Caroline!'

She jumped to her feet, looking agitatedly around for Simpkins, only to see her dancing with a ring of children and making as much noise as the lot of them. Once a year the hall was taken over by the estate folk, and a real good time they had. This year it should have been quieter, out of respect to his late lordship, but you couldn't expect children to remember the dead in the middle of a party.

Mrs Parker grabbed one of the passing housemaids. 'Shush them, for goodness' sake, Mary-Ellen! Shush them, can't you?'

'Oh, Mrs Parker, they're enjoying themselves, bless 'em, and Christmas comes but once a year, as the saying goes – '

'I know, my dear, I know – but she's back!'

Mary-Ellen's jaw dropped. 'Not Miss Caroline, for goodness' sake!'

'Hurry up and send Simpkins to me. Pull her away from those mites and tell her to come at once. She's going to be needed.'

A long case clock in a far corner struck five solemn notes, and cheers went up, echoing to the rafters, for five o'clock heralded the tree, the peak of the party, after which there would be games for an hour before the clock struck six and everything came to an end. As the cheers died down, Kimberley made his stately way to the door.

He was going to fetch the dowager, and since everyone knew her son-in-law and granddaughter were here for Christmas, everyone expected them to accompany her. What they did not expect was that the procession would be headed by Caroline – 'That Bitch', as she was called downstairs. In she sailed, tall and thin – thinner than ever, some thought – and in the silence, as Mary-Ellen said to Cook later, 'You could've 'eard a pin drop, that you could!'

Behind her came the dowager, and somehow everyone knew that she had refused to enter on her son-in-law's arm. Preferred her ebony stick, that one did, so proud she was. You had to respect the old tartar, really you did. Then came that nice Mr Davidson with his daughter. Somehow everyone thought of Miss Delia as being solely his. How pretty she looked in that blue dress with its deep collar of white lace, and pearl buttons down the front, and white lace trim round its square yoke. Colour of corn-flowers, it was, and suited her a treat. Lace cuffs fastened by more pearl buttons, and pumps of patent leather with ankle straps, and white stockings flashing every now and then beneath the long skirt of her dress. She'd be kicking up her heels later on, laughing with the lot of them, having the time of her life. Kingsmere hadn't been the same without her, even though Mrs Parker did call her a cheeky brat on occasion.

But what would happen now her mother was home? Would Miss Delia be coming back too? Was it true that she had gone to live permanently with her father in London, or only while her mother had gone on that long trip abroad?

Kimberley called for silence, and with a dazzling smile the new mistress of Kingsmere made her speech of welcome. 'Though I am sure all of *you* want to welcome *me* just as much as *I* want to welcome *you*,' she added, and Simpkins thought irreverently: Like hell we do!

She had gone to serve the old lady at the dower house in Miss Caroline's absence and liked it a whole heap better than dancing attendance on her daughter – but now, alas, she would have to come back to the big house and return to the old routine, and lawks-a-mussy, how much ironing would be waiting for her upstairs after she had unpacked for her ladyship! Standing beside Mrs Parker, Simpkins knew what the housekeeper was thinking – that the moment the speech was over they would have to forgo all the fun of the tree and hurry upstairs to uncover furniture, strip and make up the bed, light a fire, fetch towels and new tablets of soap, and keep their thoughts to themselves even though their Boxing Day was ruined – and no doubt face her ladyship's sharp tongue into the bargain, even though everything was her fault for turning up without warning.

Delia accepted the presents her mother handed down from the tree, read the names aloud, and handed them one by one to eager, outstretched hands. If it had been she, she would have torn away the tissue-paper wrapping at once, but in the presence of the new mistress of Kingsmere the estate children had been warned not to do so until she gave permission; and not until the last gift was taken from the tree did permission come.

'*Now* you may open them, and when you have done so, Kimberley will give you an apple and an orange each, *not* to be eaten here in the hall, but only when you get home.'

Caroline's bland glance settled on the butler's astonished face. It was Mrs Parker's task, not his, to hand out the apples and oranges, while he looked on benignly. He supervised the party, made sure the housemaids kept the children in order, but did not demean himself by doing more than that. But when Caroline's eyes met his, he recognised the command in them.

'I am sure you don't mind relieving Mrs Parker, Kimberley. I need her. *And* Simpkins. Come, Delia.'

'But I am staying, Mamma. I always do. I've been listening to the games all afternoon, and now I can join in. Have you forgotten?'

'I have not forgotten things as they *used* to be, my love.' Their voices were low, unheard by anyone except Simon and his mother-in-law, and even she looked faintly surprised by Caroline's pronouncement. It was traditional for the children of the family to join the party for the final hour; a condescension but still a tradition.

'Things are changed now I am mistress here, Delia. You will do as I say, and remember that one day you will follow in my footsteps. Ask your grandmother. You are back at Kingsmere now.'

She sounded just as dictatorial as Grandmamma herself, and Delia promptly answered, 'Not for always, I'm not. Father and I go home the day after tomorrow. And now I am staying for the rest of the party.'

As stubborn as her father, Caroline decided, managing to check her anger. She was about to take her daughter by the hand very firmly, when Simon put in, 'Of course Delia is staying for the rest of the party. She is wrong only about one thing – we leave tomorrow, not the day after. Off you go now, my dear, and enjoy yourself.'

With a bound, Delia was in the middle of the hall, crying, 'Who's for Sir Roger de Coverley? I know you've had it already, because I heard you, but I wasn't here to join in the fun, so . . . please, does anyone mind doing it again?' And to shouts of agreement she was rushing to join them while her mother, smiling stiffly, waved a gracious hand to everyone and bade them good-bye.

'Until six o'clock, remember. Not a moment later, Kimberley.'

'That was an admirable display of dictatorship.'

These were the first words Simon had spoken to his

wife, and he had waited until they were alone. His mother-in-law had retired to her room, pleading fatigue and saying she would be content with a light meal served in bed after the exhaustion of Christmas, but managing to convey that she wished to be tactful and leave them alone. 'After such a long separation, the three of you must have a lot to say to one another.'

Like her daughter, the old lady chose to ignore his announcement about returning to London tomorrow. The two of them played a game of eternal pretence, he thought impatiently, the one as bad as the other.

Now he confronted Caroline in the drawing room, where she had promptly demanded a brandy to recover from 'that unholy din'.

'Dictatorship?' she echoed coolly. 'I don't know what you are talking about. And I hardly detect a welcome in your voice.'

'Did you expect one?'

'Not if all Mamma told me is true.'

'What did she tell you? That I have a mistress in Hanover Square?'

'So you admit it!'

'I admit nothing so untrue.'

'And I suppose you also deny that you hoped I would not come back, so you could divorce me for desertion.'

'No, I don't deny that.'

'Then I am sorry to disappoint you,' she snapped.

He was sorry, too. His disappointment went deep, but he answered practically, 'We must get around it some other way.'

'Get around what?'

'The obstacle of our marriage.'

'If you hope to do that by divorcing *me*, you will be unlucky. But desert me and continue to live with that young woman Deborah Yorke –'

'Not *with* her. In her house, which is a different thing.'

'From what I hear, the place is as scandalous as it ever was, and no suitable place for our daughter.'

'I see your mother has been feeding you with untruths, though I will politely call them false assumptions. The house in Hanover Square is anything but scandalous. With Miss Yorke as its mistress, it could never be.'

'Not even with bohemian actresses and artists living there too?'

Simon shouted with laughter. 'Chrystal Delmont – bohemian! She is highly regarded both professionally and personally. As for the artist, you should meet the boy – a fledgling from a country doctor's home, so inexperienced as to be positively naive.'

He turned away impatiently.

'Wait! We must discuss things, Simon. After all, we *are* still a family, and I am sure you would want Delia to be brought up worthy of her inheritance.'

'That depends on whether she wants it or not. She may prefer an entirely different mode of life, and from the example you set out there in the hall, patronising the estate children, I wouldn't blame her if she did.'

He was gone before she had a chance to reply.

Moodily Caroline sipped her brandy. She was beginning to wonder why she had ever been nostalgic for home. Now she was here, she felt unwanted. Her mother's only desire for her return was to stave off scandal – in what way did not matter, so long as the name of Ashleigh was not dragged through the mud.

There had also been hostility in the eyes of the staff. Kimberley resented taking orders from her, and as for Simpkins, that young woman's seemingly blank face spoke volumes. And now her husband and child were leaving at the earliest opportunity and she was powerless to stop them. Simon had the legitimate excuse of his work to take him back to London, and no doubt he could think up a convincing one about Delia's schooling not being interrupted. She had always known he had firm ideas about education for his daughter, disapproving of isolation with governesses and strongly in favour of companionship with other children. He had even talked about a college education later on. Caroline couldn't think why.

Idly she picked up a discarded newspaper, the last to be delivered before Christmas Day, but she scarcely was aware of the newsprint. Her mind was occupied with that house, bought by her father for his scandalous mistress. Was there something about the place that exercised a fascination for men, even studious men like Simon, whom she had never thought capable of falling in love with another woman? She had taken his loyalty for granted, believing he owed it to her because she had chosen him as a husband instead of someone in her own level of society, but she had quickly learned that her level of society left him unimpressed. Delia would no doubt grow up with the same attitude, or else become like that dreadful Lady Warwick, who had actually become a socialist. No wonder the king had ended his liaison with her, even though, as always, he remained on good terms with an ex-mistress. But what a fool the woman had been to sacrifice royal favour for her outlandish ideas, stubbornly remaining deaf to all his remonstrances, and how awful it would be to have a daughter with such revolutionary thoughts!

Idly she turned a page. The paper was *The Daily Chronicle*, semi-intellectual, touching on the arts as well as the news. The arts had never interested Caroline, but she did like to know what popular musicals were running, particularly those of George Edwarde, like *The Orchid* and *Our Miss Gibbs*. The straight theatre had never held much appeal, though to appear at prominent first nights during the season was obligatory, also enjoyable as a fashion parade. It also held the promise of being mentioned in social columns next day – and, of course, she had been a devotee of Bryant Meredith for a long time before she met him, so she never missed any play he appeared in, even those by that new dramatist Bernard Shaw, whose plays seemed to consist of endless dialogue and precious little action, and whom the king called 'a damned crank'.

She had suffered boredom on several occasions just for the pleasure of seeing Bryant onstage. Dramatic critics were apt to deride him as an actor, but he packed in a female audience, chiefly because his name was involved in frequent scandals, and always with women. Such things increased an actor's popularity with the public. For the same reason, people had always loved Edward even when he was Prince of Wales and forever gossiped about – three involvements in court cases concerning gambling or other men's wives, and goodness only knew how many others he had escaped. Life was very unfair, thought Caroline. Scandal in a man's life seemed to do nothing but good; in a woman's, nothing but harm.

Her glance slid to the Entertainments column and suddenly Bryant's name leapt from the page, printed beneath that of Chrystal Delmont at the Comet Theatre. Immediately Caroline forgot everything else, even her ill humour. Chrystal Delmont was the actress now living at 20 Hanover Square; well-known indeed, and, as Simon said, highly respected, but the important thing was that Bryant was playing opposite her.

Interesting. Even exciting, for it might not be too much to hope that, with skilled manipulation, she might meet him again through the medium of this woman who lived beneath the same roof as her daughter.

Caroline knew how useless it would be to call on Bryant at the theatre, for his dismissal had been final, and she would not expose herself to the risk of further snub. Imagine being presented with some trumped-up excuse via a stage doorkeeper! But to scrape acquaintance with Miss Delmont, even if it meant pocketing her pride and calling at that house, might be well worthwhile.

'I have come to see my darling daughter,' she would say, choosing a time when Simon would be at that dull museum, and an afternoon when no matinee was being performed at the Comet. Such a ruse offered no guarantee of meeting the actress, but was worth a try and could be persisted with. She could establish a pattern of weekly visits to her child, thus serving the additional purpose of suggesting to the world that there was no rift between the Davidsons, and that Caroline remained at Kingsmere only because her new position there demanded it for the present.

A pity Justin had not run a town house, or she would have inherited that too, but bachelor quarters in Albany were merely leased and had apparently suited him better. And Mamma had long ago given up Ashleigh House in Park Lane, because London's society never meant anything to her. It was the landed gentry, the country gentry, who mattered in Elizabeth's eyes. She considered them the true aristocracy, not to be compared with some of the jumped-up financiers who had bought their way into the London scene, and whom the king included amongst his friends. Poor Mamma, how hopelessly out-of-date she was!

It did not occur to Caroline that she confused some of her mother's standards with her own, to be adhered to or ignored when it suited her. Now it suited her very well to recall her mother's insistence that she should swallow her pride and visit number 20 Hanover Square, and to forget her own avowed declaration never to do so, for through the doors of that house, fate might bring her in touch with Bryant again.

There was also the amusing possibility that it might give her the opportunity to see the baby whose eyes were so like her brother's. How would dear Mamma react when she returned and told her about it? 'There is no doubt,

Mother dear – the child is an Ashleigh, and no mistake.'
But on no account must she call her 'Mother dear'. That
had been Justin's pet name exclusively, and whatever
made her think of it now, Caroline couldn't imagine.

Not for a moment did she question that the child was
her brother's. It had to be, if the eyes were the same. The
coincidence would be too great otherwise. And what malicious enjoyment could be derived from bringing the child
to Kingsmere as a nice surprise for dear Mamma, who
had always refused to acknowledge what kind of man her
adored son really was!

21

Chrystal Delmont had soon realised that Simon and
Deborah were in love and not for the first time in her life
wished the human heart could regulate its emotions, for
she could see no future for a young unmarried woman in
love with a married man. The pity of it was that she liked
them both, so could take no sides one against the other,
which would have been a great deal easier than simply
looking on and wondering how things would eventually
work out. Sympathy loaded in one direction was easier to
deal with, because then one need have no compunction
about trying to wean them apart.

She wished Simon's wife had never come back. Delia
had returned with the news, though she didn't seem very
excited about it. 'Mamma is back,' she had announced,
skipping into the house while her father paid off the cabby.

'No one knew she was coming. Before we left, she told me she intends to visit here as often as possible, and hopes very much to meet you, Miss Delmont. She says you are the best actress in London, though when I asked her what plays she had seen you in, she couldn't remember.'

How very flattering, thought Chrystal in amusement. But if she has never seen me act, why want to meet me?

Deborah had been standing in the hall and, shocked by Delia's news, vanished into the nursery, closing the door behind her. Then Peter Maynard had come bounding up the front steps in Simon's wake, catching the front door before it shut and calling, 'How's everyone? Nice Christmas, everyone? Kent was lovely and Tenterden like a Christmas card in all the snow, but I can't wait to get back to the theatre. Did I hear you say your mother is back, Cleopatra?' Peter had experienced a disturbing feeling when his arm fell across her shoulders as they headed for the stairs, and suppressed it by saying quickly, 'How would you like to visit the scenic workshops tomorrow? You'd enjoy it, I'm sure.' And over his shoulder, as Chrystal waited in the hall for the arrival of a cab to take her to the theatre, he had called, 'That will be all right, won't it, Miss Delmont? You can charm everyone backstage, from old Freebody downwards . . .'

Freebody was the stage director, and permission for visitors to come behind the scenes, except to the lead dressing rooms when invited, had to be obtained from him.

'Leave it to me,' Chrystal had said, and thought about Caroline Davidson all the way to the theatre. She had a feeling that the woman's name had once been whispered in connection with Bryant Meredith's, and while waiting in the wings with him that night, she seized the opportunity to find out.

'Didn't you once know Caroline Davidson?'

She saw his handsome face give that irresistible smile

which won the hearts of countless women – slanting, mischievous, like a guilty schoolboy in no way repentant. Except that he was no longer boyish. Stage makeup concealed the hint of advancing years, and across the footlights no one would guess that he was nearer fifty than forty. What would happen to the man when not even makeup and lights could conceal these betraying signs? An actor with talent could advance to character parts and a whole new sphere of success, but the career of one who could never be anything but himself would fade with his looks. Such would be Bryant's fate, speedily assisted by his fondness for wine and women.

To be linked with some well-known woman in society had become almost part and parcel of his career. He thrived on the publicity. But his rumoured *affaire* with Lord Ashleigh's sister had been carefully covered up – not by his own wish, Chrystal suspected, but because Caroline chose that it should be. The woman had had everything to lose by exposure; he, everything to gain. So why had he not persisted with the affair, extracting out of it the maximum notoriety? Even being cited as co-respondent never worried him. It lent glamour to him as an actor, and since his career had been steady and profitable and money was something to be squandered in the pursuit of it, paying damages to wronged husbands had been made with grandiose gestures, applauded by the public.

How much of Irving's career had been bolstered by gossip, and how much less would he have been loved if whispers about his famous mistress had been suppressed? Bryant Meredith secretly likened himself to Irving and other actors whose private lives titillated public fancy, but he always took very good care to remain a bachelor.

'Well, *didn't* you know her?' Chrystal persisted. In a few minutes her cue would come, and she might not have another opportunity to corner him.

'Darling, there's hardly a man in London – the London that counts – who hasn't enjoyed the predatory Caroline.'

'But the affair didn't last long, did it?'

'Now, what is that to you, dear?'

'I'm curious, that's all.'

'Why? Do you know her?'

'No. We have never met.'

'In that case, I'll admit that I did tire very quickly. Not only was she physically exhausting, but her determination that everything should be so damned hush-hush made it very boring. Would you believe that I once spent weeks with her holed up in my flat? Can you imagine any woman not wanting to have her name linked publicly with mine? But my long-lean-lovely merely wanted to entwine her body with mine – I tell you, darling, she was insatiable! Matinees and twice-nightly performances were not enough for the lusty Caroline. Even that I wouldn't have minded had I been allowed to emerge for air sometimes.'

'Bryant, you are incorrigible!'

'Maybe, darling, but I don't exaggerate. I used to sally forth alone when she slept, to gather strength for the next bout and to fortify myself with a few drinks in the Ritz bar – also to lay in fresh stocks of wine while she was around to foot the bills. Well, darling, I earned it, didn't I? Besides, I was out of a "shop" at the time, and you know the financial embarrassment "resting" can cause an actor. I am up to my eyes in debt even now and could do with a wealthy patroness or a good scandal involving one. I can always make money by selling the story to the less salubrious press. But with Caroline there was never a meal in public, never a dinner at the Savoy despite the fact that women are dining alone in restaurants more and more nowadays. "We mustn't be seen together, whatever we do!" she always insisted, until in the end I decided we'd better make for Paris. But it was not different there. It had always been the Meurice or the Crillon for her, but this time she avoided both in order to dodge recognition. Wouldn't even dine at Maxim's, for the same reason. So there we were, holed up again in a discreet hotel, totally unobserved. We might just as well have stayed in London, because we didn't make the Paris headlines as I hoped, and you know how the French enjoy illicit love affairs, even vicariously. On the strength of the publicity, I might have landed a part in a Paris production, think of that! Now, *I* enjoy sex as much as the next man, and possibly more than some, but an animal like the lusty Caroline wore even me out. I was getting nothing out of the affair except exhaustion. No juicy scandal to bring me back into the limelight; no irate husband chasing us; no member of her titled family racing to Paris to bring her home and plunging us into the headlines. Well, darling, no actor can afford to continue with anything so unremunerative, can he? In no time at all he can be forgotten, but a good society scandal can put him right back on top. So I decided she wasn't worth the hotel bill she was paying. Had she but realised it, I had more to lose than she – my career, my reputation with women, not to mention the auditions which other actors were grabbing while I did nothing but serve her in bed – but she was so damned selfish, worrying all the time about preserving her good name and not caring a fig about preserving my bad one!'

Chrystal was laughing. Bryant was a rake, but an honest one.

'So you ended the affair?'

'Naturally.'

'And she?'

He shrugged. 'Last I heard, she was off to the mysterious East. I remember seeing her picture in the press and reading some garbled interview that sounded just like Caroline at her most self-centred, dramatising herself ridiculously.'

'She is back. She has inherited the Ashleigh estates, and

all that goes with them, following the death of her brother.'

Bryant gave a low whistle. 'Kingsmere! One of the most famous in England. Needless to say, *I* was never invited there, though perhaps I missed a chance to be, ditching her the way I did. A pity I didn't have a crystal ball, but I thought that brother of hers would live forever, and after all, the family fortune was his. He was likely to remarry and produce heirs, and she wouldn't get much more than she already had – which was considerable, of course, but not enough to entice me forever. And now she has the lot, you say?'

'I gather so.'

Chrystal paused to listen to the dialogue onstage; soon her cue would come.

'You could drop a line of condolence about her brother's death,' she suggested. 'Why don't you, if you want to pick up the threads again?'

'A little too obvious, don't you think? Besides, she won't have forgotten how I walked out on her, and she certainly will not have forgiven. There's your cue, darling. You're on.'

Chrystal made her entrance, stepping onstage and losing herself in the character immediately. As always, she had the true professional ability to reject anything extraneous to it, such as her present and wholly unaccustomed desire to meddle in the affairs of others. Throughout her career she had kept her own counsel on all things, but since moving to 20 Hanover Square the lives of its occupants had become of increasing interest, particularly Deborah's and Simon's, and, inevitably, that likeable young daughter of his. So she felt no pangs of conscience for wanting to interfere on their behalf. It seemed to her that Caroline Davidson was a totally selfish woman who thought she could take from life whatever she wanted, and give nothing in return. She and the unscrupulous Bryant were two of a kind, and well deserved each other.

Besides, Justin Ashleigh had been her brother, and in helping to outwit his sister there would be a tinge of retaliatory satisfaction.

Peter Maynard could not help being pleased about Caroline Davidson's return, because it would surely put an end to the situation between Deborah and Simon. A wife was always in a strong position, so there could be no chance for Deborah now, but there might well be a chance for someone like himself to step in and comfort her. He must be careful not to thrust himself forward, but she must become aware that he was there, waiting in the background, and that the difference between their ages was negligible.

Earning regular money gave him confidence. He had repaid all Bruce Whitney's loans, a pound a week regularly since he began working at the museum, and a final payment of three pounds just before Christmas. This last payment had been accompanied by a note. 'I am indebted to you for your help, old chap, but now I'm in the clear and doing fine. Remember your suggestion that I should go in for theatrical design? Well, I haven't advanced that far yet, but I have a permanent job at the Comet Theatre, in the scenic workshops, and a good studio here at 20 Hanover Square into the bargain. Again, many thanks for your help.'

He might have guessed that Bruce would immediately come back into his life, curious about the change in his circumstances. The studio met with his approval. 'A damn sight better than that Pimlico cellar, I must say, and you're a lucky bounder to get behind the scenes at the Comet. Any chance of introductions to a few pretty actresses, eh?' A characteristic nudge in the ribs accompanied that, but what jarred even more was his comment about young Delia, whom he chanced to encounter on the stairs. 'A couple of years or so, and she'll be ready for it. She's a natural, I can tell. Lucky devil, you'll be on the spot, but what's the betting I beat you to it?'

No amount of discouragement seemed to deter Whitney in his calls, either at Hanover Square or at the theatre. Peter regretted revealing his address, but had been unable to resist it because this was where it had all begun. If Bruce had not brought him along that night, and landed him in trouble, he would never have met Deborah, never have fallen in love, never have arrived on her doorstep the next day with the picture she had accepted in lieu of his gambling debt, which, he suspected, had led to the closing of the card salon. He had never been certain on that point, but guessed Dillon must have been angry with Deborah for waiving the debt, the man having been part of the setup. Or so Bruce Whitney had implied. So if his folly had led indirectly to the final breakup, he was no longer sorry that his old school friend had landed him in what could have been an unholy mess. Out of that had come not only his meeting with Deborah but also his employment at the museum, his job at the Comet, and even accommodation beneath her roof. Deborah had been his angel of mercy, which made him love her even more.

Since Christmas he had seen little of her, no more than a glimpse every now and then as he came into or went out of the house. She seemed to avoid everyone except Delia, and, heaven knew, that young lady couldn't be avoided no matter how hard one tried. She had kept him to his promise to take her to the theatre workshops, waylaying him every day to remind him, and this morning the great day had arrived. She was banging impatiently on his door at this very moment. 'You said ten o'clock, Peter, and I'm ready and waiting. Do hurry!'

Deborah was coming out of the baby's nursery as they descended. She had just given him his ten-o'clock feed. Peter knew her routine, and it seemed to centre round the child exclusively. The picture of her with the baby in her arms touched him profoundly. She should have babies of her own, but that was unlikely to come about so long as she wasted her heart on a married man whose wife had come back into his life. The woman had called a few times already, each time when Simon was at the museum, but making herself very much at home in the Davidsons' apartment. Delia had introduced them.

'This is Mr Maynard, the artist I told you about, Mamma. He is terribly clever. That is why Miss Delmont got him into the scenic department at the theatre.'

Peter had seen cool eyes appraising him, and sensed surprise. What had she expected? Someone with a flowing beard and paint-smeared smock, emulating Augustus John? He knew he looked exactly what he was, a young man from a good middle-class home, and no doubt that stamp would remain with him to a large extent, no matter how long he stayed in the unconventional world of the theatre.

He had returned her appraising glance, admiring the sleek elegance of her — black astrakhan trimmed with a huge shaggy collar of black monkey fur, and a wide-brimmed hat adorned with shining cock feathers, set straight upon her head and speared with hat pins crowned with knobs of polished jet. She had pushed back her coat with its enormous raglan sleeves, revealing a lot of shiny jet jewellery, the whole effect of mourning unrelieved except by her skin, which had been lightened with a heavy application of light face powder. Beneath it, he suspected, her complexion was sallow — the result of her travels abroad? — which she doubtless found unbecoming back home in England. Apart from that, she was very striking. A little terrifying, though, to a young man unaccustomed to making small talk with society hostesses.

He had the impression that she intended to pay these visits regularly, even that she planned to stay sometimes, because she had told Delia that as soon as she had got things running the way she wanted them at Kingsmere, she would be free to spend more time here in London. 'I am so glad your dear papa has found this roomy apart-ment . . .' Then she had added that she would like to go downstairs to see the baby. 'From what you tell me, Delia my pet, he sounds quite adorable.'

Delia had been despatched to find out if it were con-venient for her to call on Miss Yorke, only to return with the message that Garfield had just taken the baby out for a walk. That, Peter knew, was untrue, because from the dormer window of his studio he had seen Deborah putting the child in his perambulator at the bottom of the small garden, settling him for his afternoon nap.

Somehow he knew there would never be a meeting between Deborah Yorke and Caroline Davidson, if Deborah could help it.

Delia found the world backstage completely different from her imagining.

'It's so bare and bleak – all these long stone passages, and no roof at all to the stage, just space going up and up to a lot of tangled metal and ropes! I never imagined anything like this. I thought you just opened a door and walked on to the stage from another room.'

'Disappointed, Cleopatra?'

'N-no – not exactly. Just surprised. What's up there?' She pointed to the dark and distant heights, and he identi-fied the galleries and grids and their uses. 'Do you mean that stagehands actually walk about up there on those narrow platforms?'

'Some do.'

'They must have a good head for heights! Oh, Peter, how exciting it all is, and how nice of Miss Delmont to arrange for you to bring me. Show me *every*thing!'

So he showed her the prop room, and the scenery dock,

and the prompt corner, and the place beside it from where Lights sent signals to the men operating spotlights above-stage, and to Number 1 Limes in his nest behind the grand circle and higher still to Number 2 Limes above the gallery. But she couldn't see the dressing rooms; no one could visit those unless personally invited by leading members of the cast, but the men's were on the opposite side of the stage from the women's or, in smaller theatres, on separate floors. He had anticipated an unending spate of questions from Miss Curiosity, and they certainly came, but he found he was enjoying himself as much as she. Finally he led her belowstage past the master carpenter's shop to a vast basement area from which large sliding doors opened on to a side street.

'Those are to admit new flats and take out old ones,' he told her. 'Down the side street are the Comet storerooms, where stock sets are kept until needed again, but down here we paint all the smaller stuff that can be hoisted up to the stage.'

Delia watched him at work for a while, then wandered away to explore. He was so absorbed that he did not hear her go, so she crept unobserved into an area immediately beneath the stage and saw a small door ahead, so low that a person would have to stoop to go through. Nearby were musical instruments in their covers – the orchestra's, she guessed, but what a place to store them! She had always imagined that the orchestra emerged from a splendid, roomy place, a sort of vast green room where they took their ease in armchairs covered in red plush like the seats in the stalls, but here there were only packing cases and a few broken chairs and all sorts of discarded junk. There were also funny things like levers overhead, to release trapdoors in the stage; the low-hanging ceiling, which formed the floor of the stage, was crisscrossed with them. And someone was walking about up there. And talking. It sounded like a man and a woman, speaking lines. If she opened the low door and crept into the orchestra pit, she would be able to sit there, quiet as a mouse, and watch.

She almost knocked over a music stand in doing so, and beside it, a fragile chair. In a corner of the orchestra pit stood kettle drums beneath covers – too big to cart into that untidy place beneath the stage – and in the centre was the conductor's rostrum, nothing but a wooden stand, without even a bit of carpet on it. Beyond the polished brass rail with its concealing curtain, the auditorium spread away into shadow, and above her the tabs were drawn back.

'Would I might but ever see that man!'

Delia recognised not only Miss Delmont's voice, but the words as well. Also those that came in reply:

'*"Now I arise – Sit still and hear the last of our sea-sorrow. Here in this island we arrived, and here have I, thy schoolmaster –"* Oh, hell, Chrystal, I shall never master Shakespeare!'

'You must, if you hope to remain with the company, Bryant.'

'I'd rather do Shaw, Sheridan, anyone but Shakespeare!'

'What actor can afford to pick and choose? Certainly *I* can't.'

'Darling, you know the Comet would be lost without you.'

'I doubt it. No one is indispensable.'

The man grimaced. 'Which means me, I suppose.'

'Both of us. Now, let's take it again. We have two weeks before the Shakespearean season opens, and – '

' – and I *don't* like being cast in parts such as Prospero. Your father! Why couldn't I play Ferdinand, your lover?'

Because you are too old, thought Delia, staring wide-eyed from the orchestra pit. Of course, Miss Delmont was too old also, too old for Miranda really, but Peter had said she looked very young from out front. But this man – who else could he but but Bryant Meredith, whose name was on the billboards? – looked so cross that there was nothing youthful about him.

Miss Delmont said patiently, 'Let's take it again. That's why we came, remember? If you are not going to try, I might just as well have stayed at home.'

'Darling, forgive me! How much easier life must be for an actor with a rich woman to support him – he can pick and choose his parts then.'

'Bryant, I warn you. If you don't concentrate, I am not going to waste any further time on you. Now, take it from "thy schoolmaster . . ."'

'Oh, very well.' He glanced down at his script and continued, ' " . . . *made thee more profit than other princes can –* "'

'Without the script, Bryant.'

He hurled it aside petulantly, almost shouting, ' " . . . *that have more time for vainer hours, and tutors not so careful."* There, dammit, I hope you are pleased?'

'When you throw away the script, I will be.'

'Doesn't Ariel come on now?'

'Not yet – I have four more lines and you have ten before I fall asleep and you summon Ariel.'

Delia listened, absorbed. So this was what rehearsing was like – two people speaking lyrically, then snapping at each other. So different from school, where the English teacher had them out in front of the class to recite their lines, and corrected them quietly if they stumbled. She was astonished that a professional actor should not be word perfect, since it was his job to be. It seemed that this was the reason for their being here alone, with no other members of the company. How like Miss Delmont to want to help the man, though he didn't seem to deserve it, or he would surely not be so cross. However, he now proceeded with better grace, though not entirely without the script, until he reached the final lines:

' *"Come away, servant; come, I am ready now. Approach, my*

Ariel; come!"'

Delia piped loudly, ' *"All hail, great master! Grave sir, hail! I come to answer thy best pleasure; be it to fly, to swim, to dive into the fire, to ride on the curled clouds –"'*

'Good grief, who's that?'

The actor spun round, and Chrystal Delmont stared at a pair of round eyes peeping up from the orchestra pit.

'It's me. I. Delia. I couldn't help joining in, because we're doing *The Tempest* at school next term. The day before prize-giving. And I'm to be Ariel and I know everybody's lines – well, almost everybody's – besides my own. You said a word wrong just now, Mr Meredith. You said, *"If now I count not."* It should be "court not". Would you come to see us when we do *The Tempest*, Miss Delmont? Could you spare the time? Everyone at school would be so excited if you did, and besides, it would prove that I do know you. I have a feeling some of the girls don't believe me.'

'Well, I'll be damned,' said Bryant Meredith. 'This is the first time I've ever been put right by a chit of a child! Who let her in?'

'I did.' Chrystal was laughing. 'I arranged for her to come with Peter Maynard, though I must confess I didn't expect to see you in the orchestra pit, Delia dear. I thought you were in the scenic shop.'

'I was, but I got bored. Peter seemed to forget I was there.'

'I can't imagine anyone forgetting you were there, or *you* letting them.' Bryant Meredith's voice was half amused, half rueful. 'What did you say your name was?'

'Delia, sir.'

'Delia Davidson,' Chrystal added pointedly. 'Now, I suggest you join us, darling, and we can all three rehearse together. It will be useful to have someone who knows Ariel's lines, won't it, Bryant?'

Delia bounded beneath the stage, across the cluttered

space, and up into the wings, unaware of the actor's sudden interest.

'Davidson, did you say?'

'I did.'

'Not the same Davidson, of course.'

'The very same. She and her father occupy rooms above mine, and her elegant mother has begun to visit there. I can more or less estimate the day and time of her arrival, because I see her from my windows. She chooses an afternoon when I have no matinee and an hour when her husband is at his museum, her hope being to meet me, but not to meet him. Why she wants to meet me, I can only guess, because she has never seen me perform. But *you* are acting with me now, and she is probably aware of that. Since you abandoned her in Paris, she would hardly come crawling back to you. I imagine the most thick-skinned woman would fear a rebuff in such circumstances, but to meet you through someone else . . . with all her newly acquired wealth . . . *would* she be snubbed?'

'Not if I met her away from the vicinity of her husband. I don't mind confrontations with enraged spouses if the timing is right, but never at the beginning of an *affaire*, or the renewing of one. But how like you to think of my interests, darling Chrystal. I always knew you had the kindest heart in the world.'

Chrystal smiled, saying nothing. They certainly did deserve each other, these two.

It was through Garfield that Caroline first saw her brother's child.

Beside the front door of number twenty, bells communicated with the separate occupants. A few days later, Garfield was on her way to the nursery when the Davidsons' rang upstairs. Knowing they were out, she answered, and came face to face with Caroline Davidson for the first time since that weekend at Kingsmere.

Of course, the woman didn't remember her. How could she be expected to recall a mere lady's maid whom she had only seen flitting along a corridor to serve her mistress? But Garfield recognised that striking face, and stiffened defensively. 'They're out,' she said abruptly. 'Miss Delia's at school and her father with her. That's why I answered the door.'

Caroline answered frigidly, 'Then perhaps Miss Delmont —'

'I doubt if Miss Delmont receives folk she isn't acquainted with, but she happens to be out too. A dress rehearsal for a play at Miss Delia's school. They've gone together.'

The woman was not only insolent but also dismissive. Another moment, and the door would be shut in her face. Caroline checked her rising indignation and asked for Miss Yorke instead. 'Or has she also accompanied my husband and daughter?'

Garfield echoed the woman's tone. 'Step inside, and I'll find out if she cares to receive you.'

Turning her back, she left Caroline to enter and even to close the door behind her. She then walked away down the hall, saying over her shoulder, 'Wait here, if you please. I've something to attend to first,' and opening a far door, she entered without even knocking. What a household! Plainly Deborah Yorke had no idea how to train a servant.

Caroline sat down automatically, then stood up again. Never would she sit waiting in a hall, like someone applying for a situation. For two pins she would walk out of this house! She paced up and down indecisively. Being left in the hall was insulting, but to walk out would indicate that she had accepted the slight and did not know how to retaliate. When that insolent woman returns, she vowed, I will put her in her place and *then* she will see how someone accustomed to authority deals with ill manners.

But the next moment the woman came back with an

infant in her arms. Halting in front of Caroline, she said abruptly, 'He's getting on for six months now. Premature, he was, but he's thrived well, thanks to my care—and Miss Yorke's. Take a look at him. Take a *good* look.'

This was the moment Garfield had longed for. To have confronted Justin Ashleigh with his child would have been more satisfying, but this stuck-up sister of his was the next best thing.

'See the eyes?' she demanded. 'They're proof, aren't they? Those are the Ashleigh eyes, and no mistake. Not that there could *be* any mistake, for my dear mistress was faithful to that brother of yours, which was more than the bastard deserved, and if you think that's insulting, it is meant to be.'

The drawing-room door opened. Deborah stood there, and behind her, Dulcima looked down from her portrait.

Deborah glanced from one woman to the other, from Garfield's truculent face to Caroline Davidson's outraged one, and immediately sized up the situation. 'I see you have wrapped up Charles very thoroughly, Garfield. Are you putting him out in the garden or taking him for a walk? The day is dry and sunny and the fresh air will do him good.' Then she stood aside, silently inviting Caroline to enter. 'I think I heard you ask for me?'

Against her will, Caroline found herself in the drawing room dominated by the portrait of Dulcima Howard. It was a beautiful room. A beautiful room for a beautiful woman, paid for by her father, as this whole house had been. And now all these people were occupying it. How would Papa feel about that?

Remembering her father's generous nature, she grudgingly admitted that he might be glad for it to be put to good use, but she kept her face averted from that commanding portrait. Despite this, she was aware of the lush beauty of the sitter, the sensual curve of her mouth, the smiling blue eyes, the full breasts subtly shadowed so that one was wholly conscious of them. Sargent had excelled himself in conveying not only the uninhibited generosity of the woman's nature but also the warmth of her personality and the invitation of her body. He had captured Dulcima Howard for all time.

Caroline surmised correctly that her father had commissioned the portrait. Her mother's had also been painted by Sargent at a much earlier date, and now adorned the gallery at Kingsmere – handsome, austere, unyielding. These were the two women in her father's life, and she hated both.

'So you have seen my aunt's child at last,' Deborah said.

'Your aunt? I thought she was supposed to be your cousin, or was that pretence on her part?'

'She was young enough to be my cousin. Does it matter?'

There was nothing meek and mild about this young woman. Caroline remembered her as a quiet, self-effacing girl, so unsophisticated that her notorious relative had whisked her away from feminine after-dinner gossip, to everyone's amusement, and particularly to that of the old Duchess of Dorking, whose ribald laughter had echoed the moment the pair of them disappeared. Then she had deflated everyone by rasping, 'Well, I do believe she's a damned sight more ladylike than the lot of us!' A detestable woman, Dorking, *and* that sharp-faced Leonora Crossley, *and* that two-faced Moira Balcombe; the whole lot of them, in fact. She had seen none of them since that house party, though black-edged letters of condolence had been sent by all. '*Dear* Justin – so noble of spirit, such a loss to society!' Who had written that? Old Dorking, her sarcastic tongue in her cheek, no doubt.

Caroline had never given another thought to Deborah Yorke, until her mother's recent news. Now she studied her as if seeing a different person. She had a poise and self-confidence which had certainly not been there before. Is that what being my husband's mistress has done for you? she wanted to ask, only to find she could not, because the serene face before her took the wind out of her sails.

'Charles is five months old now,' Deborah said, to make conversation.

'So that woman told me.'

'You must excuse Garfield's manner. She is very abrupt, and was possibly more so because you were related to the baby's father. Charles is the apple of her eye, and any slight on her late mistress is a slight on her child. It so happens that I agree with her.'

'Being very much like Dulcima Howard yourself.'

'I wish that were true, but I lack her beauty and possibly her courage.'

'You apparently have enough allure to entice my husband, and sufficient effrontery to steal him.'

'I didn't have to try. You had lost him already. And surely you don't imagine that Simon would be so unwise as to risk losing custody of his daughter by indulging in some hole-and-corner love affair, as a result of which he might be condemned as an unsuitable father? If you can imagine that, you don't know your husband.'

'But you do, I take it.'

'As a friend. A good friend –'

'– to whom you would like to be a great deal more.'

'I would indeed, but I can never be so long as he is tied to you. Since your return I have been more aware of that than ever, and so, I think, has he. I see little of him, and never alone.' She burst out, 'You have so much, what more are you seeking, coming here so regularly?'

'I come to see my daughter. My husband too, perhaps.'

'In that case, you should call when he is at home. But you never do. So you must forgive me if I doubt your motives. What they are exactly, I don't know, but your indifference toward Delia in the past hardly convinces me that you now find separation from her so hard.'

'I want to make up for lost time. I want to make up to her for many things. Why else do you imagine I can swallow my pride sufficiently to visit this house? I have every reason to hate this place. It was bought for your scandalous relative by my father – that shows what sort of a woman she was, mistress of a man old enough to be her father too, and then, after his death, accepting his son in his place.'

'Dulcima is gone. I loved her and will always love her. That is one reason why I care for her child, the other being that I love him also. Now you have seen him, please go.'

'Not until . . .' Caroline checked an involuntary gesture of pleading. She had never pleaded with anyone in her life, except Bryant when he began to tire of her. She didn't know exactly why she was pleading now, but some picture lingered in her mind which was becoming irresistible – the picture of herself arriving at the dower house with Justin's child and saying, 'Look, Mamma, doesn't he remind you of his father? And what do you think his name is? Charles – after Papa. Now, isn't that a nice thought?'

Deborah was studying her curiously. 'What is it?' she asked. 'What is it you want?'

'To take my brother's child to Kingsmere. I'm sure you would wish me to do the right thing by him. I could arrange for him to take the family name by deed poll.'

'His name is Howard, and will remain so.' Deborah moved to the door. 'He is my cousin, my only relative, and I refuse to be parted from him. Much less will I agree to your taking him to Kingsmere, where his mother was so cruelly treated.' The drawing-room door was open. 'I will see you out myself, and I will let Delia know that you called. And, of course, her father.'

Caroline answered curtly, 'Don't trouble,' and swept from the room. All she wanted to do was get away from the disconcertingly cool Deborah Yorke. What am I doing wasting my life like this? she mused angrily. I'll find another lover to restore my confidence. A fig for Mamma's sanctimonious preaching, and a fig for the good name of Ashleigh! Many a male ancestor had dragged it through the mud: such as the early Ashleigh who had been beheaded for ravishing the seven-year-old daughter of a king; another imprisoned in the Tower for abducting the wife of a notable earl and forcing her to yield up her body to him while holding her as hostage for a thousand crowns; another sentenced for bigamy; and yet another guilty of something quite unmentionable.

'So why should you preach to *me* about preserving the family's good name?' she would demand of her mother when next they met. 'There is a child in that house in Hanover Square who bears the unmistakable brand of the Ashleighs, and if all that legend claims is true, he will follow in their worst footsteps.'

22

It seemed to Delia that life was changing in a strangely frightening way, as if happiness were slipping away from it, leaving empty patches in which she felt lost and alone. The worst of these was the widening gulf between Deborah and her father. Neither had offered any explanation, nor even referred to it, but it was there. The Sunday walk in Regent's Park had come to an end as far as the three of them were concerned; it was a twosome now, herself and Deborah, and even this was spoilt by a feeling of restraint, as if, despite her friendliness and affection, Deborah now hid behind a screen.

Delia's first intimation that something was wrong came when her father made an excuse not to accompany them as usual. 'He is going to the museum – on a *Sunday*!' she protested to Deborah, who glanced away as she answered, 'Why not? Many London museums open on Sundays. For most people it is the only day of the week they are free.'

'Then he should have it free, too. Can't you persuade him?'

'No, darling. Your father must do whatever he wants to do.'

'But he always comes! Why should he change now?'

To that, Deborah made no answer. She avoided a lot of questions these days, pretending all the time that every-thing was as usual. And in some ways it was. Delia met with the same welcome in the kitchen, and in Deborah's sitting room, and in baby Charles's nursery, also in Miss Delmont's apartment and in Peter's studio. He had started doing portrait sketches of her, pigtails over her shoulders or with her hair loose beneath an Alice band, and never would he allow her to dress up in her Sunday best. 'I want pictures of a schoolgirl, and you are right for the part.' The pictures went into the portfolio he carried wherever he went; it was crammed with studies of people seen in the parks and in the streets. 'I would have thought you had enough work in the theatre without continuing outside,' she said, but he answered, 'This isn't work. It is what I love doing.'

'You say that about the theatre, too.'

'*And* mean it. Find out what you want to do most in life, Cleopatra, and stick to it. Fight for it, if you have to, but *do* it. That way, you'll be a fulfilled person.'

'Meaning happy?'

'Of course. A contented person is always happy.'

He had given her one of the sketches, framed, for her

birthday, and another to Deborah, who had begged for it and gave it pride of place in her bedroom alongside the painting of the Thames at dawn. 'That is because I treasure it,' she had told Delia. 'I want it near me.' At moments like that, the fear that life was changing ebbed a little, but Delia could not understand why her father looked sad when she told him what Deborah had said.

One of the things which promised to brighten life these days was Pru's enrolment at Delia's school. Her father, elevated from being a counter assistant at Harrods to the lofty position of floorwalker, had elected to send his daughter to the progressive school Simon Davidson had chosen, and Pru, feeling superior to those schoolfellows who went by foot, travelled by horse-drawn omnibus from Kensington daily. Since her father's promotion Pru seemed to have become somewhat uppish. '*We* don't have to share a house with lots of other people,' she had remarked after coming to tea one day, 'and Mamma says she cannot think why your papa chose to.'

'Because we have bigger accommodation than we had in the flat above yours, and because we like it, and anyway, we don't share with other people. And we are right in the West End. My mother says Hanover Square is as good as anywhere in Mayfair or Belgravia, and when she can be spared from Kingsmere, she intends to join us.'

'Will you like that?'

'Of course,' Delia lied. Not for the world would she admit that she was by no means certain. Pru came from an united home, and if her father was what Peter would call a bit of a stuffed shirt, her mother was a darling. Never chilling, like her own mother, whose visits Delia had begun to dread, because she always seemed bent on criticism. '*Must* you wear that hideous skirt and blouse and that awful straw boater, like any middle-class schoolgirl?' she would say, frowning upon the school uniform which gave Delia the satisfactory feeling of being on a par with other girls, not segregated from them, as at Kingsmere. 'If you have to wear those garments at all, my child, do *not* do so when with me.'

Even worse was her mother's condemnation of the clothes Deborah had chosen. 'The creature has no taste,' she declared. 'We must put the matter right,' and promptly carried Delia off to Knightsbridge, where she chose a whole new wardrobe in complete contrast. Delia, forced to try on endless garments, all elaborately befrilled and beribboned and overdecorated, disliked each one but had no say in the matter. Deborah had never gone about things in this way, silencing protests and declaring that no girl of her age could possibly have any taste, but with Deborah no protests had been necessary, for she could tell at a glance whether Delia was happy or unhappy in a dress, and certainly whether it suited her or not. In some of the garments her mother chose, Delia felt bedecked like a Christmas tree or some elaborate confection.

Even the saleslady's reactions to Madam's choice were plain to Delia, though not to her mother. The woman's comprehensive glance scanned the girl's straight dark hair, parted in the middle like a young Mona Lisa, and the features which, though Delia did not realise this, were of classic simplicity, and the glance said eloquently enough that the young lady was not the type to wear fussy, over-elaborate clothes.

Delia was intelligent enough to realise that her mother's selection was influenced solely by a desire to choose a wardrobe which Deborah Yorke would never have chosen. 'Why, she hates her!' Delia thought in astonishment. 'She hates the thought of another woman choosing her daughter's clothes,' and wanted to point out that Deborah had done so only because her mother had been away, but refrained. She was learning that it was never wise to oppose her mother or to argue with her.

Worst of all was the scene on returning home. The dress boxes and band-boxes almost filled the cab and necessitated two journeys to carry them upstairs. For this Caroline summoned Cook and Garfield, as if she were mistress of the establishment. Delia's embarrassment was so acute that she snatched as many boxes as she could, dropping most of them as she hurried for the stairs. It was humiliating to hear her mother ordering servants about who were not in her employ, and Delia did not blame Garfield for refusing. 'I work only for Miss Yorke,' the woman pointed out, and went back to the kitchen, her back rigid with indignation. Cook had obliged, but in a familiar manner which was plainly unacceptable to Caroline.

'My, but you've been on some shopping spree, haven't you, love?' the woman said to Delia. 'Wot'll your dad say, I wonder? Are we going to 'ave a fashion parade later on? Bring 'em all down into the kitchen, ducks, and I'll do the buttoning-up.'

'Dreadful creature!' Caroline said when at last the door of their sitting room was closed. 'Is your father aware of the woman's familiar manner? If so, it is time I stepped in.'

'No!' cried Delia. 'No, Mamma. Cook is a darling, and I won't have her hurt. Besides, you don't live here, so you have no right to order her about.'

'Then it is high time I did live here. I will see your father when he returns, and arrange things. I am not needed at Kingsmere so much these days.'

'Where will you sleep?'

'That, my child, is not a question for you to ask.'

'But we have only a spare single bedroom, and I don't think you would like that.'

'I have no intention of sleeping in the spare room. Now, let us unpack these clothes, and those uninteresting garments you possess can be sent to an orphanage.' She was in Delia's room in a trice, flinging the contents of her wardrobe on to the floor and not even caring when she stepped on them. Close to tears, Delia picked them up and laid them aside whilst Caroline flung box lids and tissue paper all over the place, shaking out the new dresses and looking very pleased with her selection. Delia could not understand why her mother, who had an excellent dress sense for herself, should fail to show the same good taste today, and without thought she burst out, 'You did it on purpose, didn't you? You chose everything that Deborah would never have chosen, just to show her up or to hit back or something.' Her voice rose on an angry note. 'You hate her because Father and I love her, but it's your own fault, Mamma, truly it is!'

Caroline's hand flashed out, stinging the girl's cheek. 'How *dare* you speak to me like that!'

Instead of bringing forth a stream of sobs, the blow silenced Delia. Her face froze into an immobility which conveyed more emotion than her outburst. It was like a mask suddenly donned to hide her deepest feelings, and for the first time in her daughter's life Caroline realised that there was more to her than she suspected. That still, shocked face made her feel uncomfortable, so she turned away abruptly and pulled the last item from the wardrobe. It was the cornflower-blue dress chosen to match Delia's eyes.

'*That* can be thrown on to the rest of the pile,' she declared, suiting the words to the action.

'*No!*' Delia snatched it up and clutched it against her thin body. 'I won't part with this – never, never!' Without warning she burst into tears, weeping more bitterly than her mother's stinging slap across the face could have been responsible for.

'Be *quiet!*' Caroline rapped, but now that Delia's unhappiness had burst its bonds, nothing could dam it. Sinking on to the side of her bed, she rocked back and forth, cradling her blue dress against her cheek, soaking it with her tears. *Please God, help me to stop*, she prayed, but not even God could stem her weeping, and the more her mother scolded and protested, the wilder became her grief and the greater her defiance.

'You are doing this to hurt Deborah, I know you are! How do you think she will feel when I stop wearing the clothes she chose for me? And you want to hurt me, too, because you know I hate all these things. I won't wear them, I swear. Nothing will make me. Send *them* to an orphanage if you like, but not this dress – my favourite.'

Renewed sobs choked her, more agonising than before. *Do help me to stop, dear God, please help me to stop!* But perhaps God knew that the tide had to exhaust itself, for it flowed on until Caroline, after trying threat and cajolery, finally yielded to impatience, calling her an ungrateful child, an impossible child, a thoroughly stupid and hysterical child.

'I will wash my hands of you, Delia, if you don't pull yourself together!'

'G-good. I want that, I want it!'

'My God,' her mother burst out, 'what am I to do with you? Don't you realise that everyone in this building must be able to hear? Miss Delmont, for instance – what will she think of you? Do you imagine she will ever invite you to tea again?'

Caroline was chagrined because she had never yet managed to meet Chrystal Delmont, who represented the only avenue back to Bryant Meredith. Sometimes she suspected that the chance encounter she had hoped for was being deliberately thwarted, so she enjoyed this opportunity to vent her chagrin on someone else. Besides, her recalcitrant daughter deserved it, so let her cry her heart out for reasons it was impossible to understand. Why so much fuss about that blue dress? Of course, those she had bought today were not in the best possible taste, but did it matter if an eleven-year-old looked a freak occasionally? Most girls were gauche at that age, anyway.

These reflections lulled vague stirrings of guilt, and the added thought that the new clothes could all be replaced when they had served the purpose of stressing a mother's rights quietened Caroline's conscience finally.

But nothing seemed to quieten Delia, who now lay face down on her bed, the blue dress crumpled beneath her, stifling her sobs in her pillow. Caroline picked up the new dresses one by one, thrust them on to hangers, and slammed the wardrobe door before stalking from the room. If scenes like this were commonplace in this house, she was glad she lived elsewhere, though convincing herself on that point was difficult when she recalled the dullness of Kingsmere. Country pursuits had always bored her and, now that she was owner, her mother's vigilance was irksome. Elizabeth was constantly on the watch, criticising everything she did. Mother and daughter were long-established antagonists, but the situation between them was now worse than ever. It was about time this dreary pattern of life was broken, and there was no better place in which to do it than London.

But an establishment of her own was not desirable. Women who lived alone could have a lean time socially and that held little appeal for Caroline. It was here, in this house, that she should gain a foothold, thus forestalling any action Simon might try to take against her and, at the same time, thwarting any plans he might have for replacing her with that chit of a young woman from below. The fact that her attitude was dog-in-the-manger did not occur to a woman so self-centred as Caroline. It was self-protection she was after, and on this she grudgingly admitted that her mother had advised her well, but beneath this aim was a restless longing to win back a man who had jilted her. Pride would be appeased only when she achieved this, and then punished Bryant by turning the tables. To do that she had to cultivate Chrystal

Delmont. Occasional visits here were useless. A more permanent arrangement had to be achieved, and while her daughter was left to weep in private, Caroline settled down in the sitting room to await her husband's return.

Bruce Whitney's arrival was, as always, unexpected. His habit was to drop in on his old school friend when fancy took him or when time hung heavily. He had not yet succeeded in meeting any pretty actresses through Maynard, who seemed to spend his time exclusively in the theatre workshops, but one never knew . . . Pete would rise in the theatre, without a doubt, and a chap could do worse than know someone who hobnobbed with the acting fraternity. To be acknowledged by some famous actor in Monico's or to bow to some popular actress when supping at the Savoy did not seem an unattainable ambition. So he cultivated his old school friend even though Peter was still on the lowest rung of the ladder.

Going downstairs to answer Bruce's summons, Peter heard stifled sobs from behind Delia's door and, shocked, paused to listen. There was no mistake. She was in there, weeping her heart out.

Without thinking, he opened the door and looked inside. All he could see was the back of her head, her face buried in a blue dress and the room littered with empty boxes and tissue paper, plus a pile of discarded clothes on the floor. Why had she been chucking her clothes away like that? And why in the world was she crying?

He had seen Delia in many a tantrum, he had teased her until she rounded on him, but only once before had he seen her close to tears. Now her unhappiness made greater impact, and he went over to her, taking her by the shoulders and saying, 'Hey, what's all this about? Tell me, Cleo – tell me.'

Her face was blotched and swollen. She looked a sorry sight, but far from finding her repellent, he was so touched that he gathered her up and rocked her like a child. But she wasn't a child. Close contact with her body brought the fact home. Already immature breasts were forming, soft little mounds which were beautiful in their innocence. Never before had he realised that the halfway stage between childhood and young womanhood was something to be protected and delicately nurtured. Perhaps more at this stage than in any other of a young girl's growth should she be handled with understanding and care.

He said no more. He just sat there, holding her but not pressing too close; holding her as a brother would, comforting a little sister. He must not think of her in any other way, or his feelings would communicate and frighten her.

His doorbell jangled again. Whoever was ringing it could go away. Then the sound cut off, replaced by distant voices, but still he paid no heed.

Delia's sobs were diminishing, followed by only spasmodic shudders, the aftermath of desperate weeping. Then she drew away, pushing back her hair and hiding her swollen eyes with her hands. 'Sorry, Peter. Take no notice. Mamma was right – I shouldn't have behaved like that.'

'Your mother – is she here?'

Delia nodded.

Then why the hell isn't she with you? Peter wanted to ask. Why isn't she comforting you, as a mother should? But somehow he could not imagine the intimidating Caroline offering a motherly shoulder for anyone to cry on.

'Want to tell me about it, Cleopatra?' He forced a light note into his voice, though all he felt was anger. Something, or someone, had hurt the child desperately.

Delia shook her head, so ashamed that she could not look at him. She also hated the thought of anyone seeing her in such a state, so she hung her head and let the curtain of her hair conceal her face. She was still clutching the blue dress, and a crumpled mess it was.

'Anything to do with that?' Peter asked, nodding toward it.

'Sort of. But it doesn't matter.'

'And you don't want to talk about it?'

Again she shook her head. He knew that he could now leave her alone, for her weeping was exhausted, but he still wanted to know the cause. Such a bout could have been prompted only by deep unhappiness. He suspected that she had been bottling things up for a long time before the dam burst. He was aware that things had changed in this house since Delia's mother had returned from her travels, and after her visits Delia always seemed particularly prickly, either putting on one of her shows of bravado or cheeking him thoroughly, either of which he knew to be defensive, but today her armour had been pierced and if that brittle mother of hers had been responsible, he would very much like to give the woman a piece of his mind.

That something was wrong with Simon Davidson's marriage had been evident for a long time. A wife who loved her husband did not go journeying off alone, and a husband who cared about his wife showed some signs of missing her when she did, but throughout his wife's travels Simon had appeared to be a happier man than now. The only good thing about Caroline's return, in Peter's eyes, was that Simon no longer spent any time with Deborah, for to love a married man was just about the worst complication she could land herself in. Eventually she would get over it, and that would give another fellow a chance.

At the door he looked back at Delia and said, 'It's Saturday tomorrow. Would you like to come to the theatre with me? I've some new sets you might like to see.'

She nodded in mute gratitude, taking a frilly pink dress from a hanger and replacing it with the crumpled blue.

'Heavens,' he said, 'that isn't yours, is it? I can't imagine you in pink frills.'

'Nor can I,' she answered with a rueful smile. 'And no, I am not going to wear it.'

'Thank God for that.'

Her attempted smile became a real one, linking him as a conspirator. He didn't know why, but he liked it. Bless the kid, she needed a friend, and he was glad to fill the role. He waved his hand in farewell, and she said, 'Thank you, Peter. Thanks for being so kind. I know I made an exhibition of myself, crying like that.'

'You don't imagine you're the only person in the world to weep occasionally, do you?' He gave her a big brotherly grin. 'It does no harm to turn on the tap occasionally. Helps to wash things away. Next time you want to, borrow my shoulder.'

Outside, he came face to face with Bruce, who raised expressive eyebrows and asked what he was doing, coming out of there. 'Isn't that young Delia's room?'

Peter wanted to ask how he knew, but was too annoyed by Bruce's implication to answer. Instead, he asked how his friend managed to get in.

'That straitlaced woman who looks after Dulcima's child opened the door in passing.' Bruce gave a mock shudder. 'Gruesome, isn't she?'

'Not really. Garfield's a good soul underneath.'

Peter began to climb the stairs to his studio, and Bruce followed, saying he had just dropped by to say cheerio and that he had seen Delia with a stunning woman getting into a cab in Knightsbridge, which had reminded him that he hadn't seen his old school pal for ages. Peter didn't believe a word of it, since Bruce had called only a few days ago, asking how he was going to celebrate the coming coronation. 'They'll be having a party backstage at the Comet, won't they?' Bruce only ever dropped by for a purpose, his object, that time, being to scrounge an invitation in the hope of meeting some pretty and obliging actress, but what was his object now?

That became plain when Bruce saw sketches of Delia on the studio walls. 'Using her as a model, are you? Anything in the nude to show me?'

'Not of a child that age. Do you think I would ask her to pose that way? What's more, do you think she would agree? She would turn tail and run. She may be only eleven but she's not gullible.'

'I thought she was older. Tall for her age. Struck me as quite a good-looker when I saw her this afternoon. Tremendous potential there, old chap.'

'If you came just to say cheerio,' said Peter, 'say it and get out. And don't drop by again in the hope of pestering young Delia.'

'Keeping a watching brief, are you?' Bruce sneered.

'You can call it that. One wrong step, and I'll make sure you are never admitted into this house again.' Peter opened the door and held it open. 'Cheerio, old chap. Now I've said it, you can echo it and be on your way.'

Simon was surprised to find his wife lolling at ease in the sitting room. She was smoking a cigarette in a long silver holder.

'So you've come at last,' she said. 'I've been waiting.'

'Where is Delia?'

'Sulking in her room.'

'Sulking? That doesn't sound like her.'

The elegant shoulders shrugged. 'She's at an awkward age. The best thing to do is to ignore adolescent tantrums. Don't play up to them by asking what is wrong.'

'But I want to know what is wrong.' He made for the door.

'Simon . . . wait. I will tell you what the trouble is. She needs a mother. She needs *me*. She needs parents who are not divided. What she does not need is a stranger deputising as a mother.'

Meaning Deborah Yorke. He could read Caroline like the proverbial book. She was up to something, and he would find out what it was soon enough. He ignored her and went to his daughter's room. Opening the door, he found it empty and guessed she had gone downstairs to the kitchen in search of comfort. Or perhaps to Deborah? If so, he could not call to see if she were there. Deborah's door had been shut on him, not angrily, but quietly, erecting a barrier he was not in a position to break down. He was well aware that his wife had been calling here in his absence, laying claim to her daughter and thereby reminding everyone that she was Simon Davidson's wife. He was wise to Caroline's subtleties and determined to be a match for them, though, so far, all the moves she had made were safe moves, forcing him to play a defensive game. To deny her admission to his home would be to hand her a trump card which she would surely make the most of, for he had no legal cause for rejecting her, only suspicions which he had never been able to prove.

The sight of littered boxes and tissue paper led his eye to a neat pile of clothes upon the bed, carefully folded as if ready for packing. They were Delia's, and his heart lurched in alarm. Was Caroline planning to take their daughter back to Kingsmere? Was that her game? Had she commanded Delia to get ready, and was that why she now claimed that Delia was sulking? But, as he had said, Delia wasn't a sulker. Her habit was to protest volubly, but never to sulk. Possibly she had then fled down to the kitchen to hide until he came home, safe in the knowledge that her mother would never descend to the servants' quarters. Short of dragging their daughter from the house, Caroline could do nothing but cajole or threaten, and wait until she yielded. But it was too late now. He had come back in time.

He wheeled round, determined to face Caroline once

and for all.

Then the dress boxes and tissue paper attracted his attention again. Freshly unpacked, they told their own story. He flung open the wardrobe and saw a whole new array of clothes, with the exception of a crumpled blue, which he recognised as one chosen by Deborah.

He guessed at once that Caroline had bought all the rest, including a pink affair tossed over the back of a chair. That told its own story, too. His daughter had ripped it from the hanger and replaced it with the crumpled blue, and she had done it in a defiant mood, for the pink dress was ripped on one shoulder. He picked it up, examined it, dropped it, and went back to his wife. 'Did you tell her to discard the clothes Deborah Yorke chose?'

'Naturally. *I* am her mother and my daughter's wardrobe is my concern, not another woman's.'

'You weren't here at the time, remember?'

'I am here now.' She flicked ash into the hearth. 'And here I mean to remain. I shall be perfectly content to visit Kingsmere only at weekends, as my brother did, and this place will pass muster until we find a house of our own. Chester Place or Eaton Square, perhaps . . .?'

'No,' he said firmly.

'Darling, are you refusing to live with me? Are you refusing me a home? Is that wise, do you think? Mamma tells me that a husband's refusal to house his wife constitutes the first step toward divorcing him – one of the very few open to a wife, alas. And you would need good reason for refusing me admission. Infidelity, for instance, which you certainly cannot level against me.'

'Because, like your brother, you are skilled at covering the truth, but don't try to be too clever, Caroline. If I can ever lay my hands on evidence of past infidelity, I won't hesitate to use it, and to move in with your husband now would not place him in a position of condoning behaviour which came to light only later on. In any case, I have no intention of sleeping with you again, even if you do choose to move in – and I cannot prevent that without appearing to be in the wrong. Is that your game, so you can take Delia away from me? By God, Caroline, will you stop at nothing?'

'Why should I?' she answered stonily. 'Delia is as much my child as she is yours.'

'I won't allow her to be used as a pawn between us!' he stormed. 'I have already told you that.'

A sound distracted him. It was the closing of Delia's door, and at once he was striding from the room, wondering how much she had overheard. On his way to her, he flung over his shoulder, 'Those new clothes you bought for her will be sent back at once. I will see to that myself.'

Delia's face looked taut and wretched. So she *had* heard, and, avoiding quarrelling parents, retreated to her room. He held out his arms and she went into them, saying nothing and shedding no tears, but he knew that in her heart was the deepest misery she had ever known. Their happy life in this house had been destroyed, and the sound of wrangling voices stressed the fact. She closed her eyes and rested her head against her father, and he could say nothing to comfort her. False assurances would not ring true, and she was too intelligent to be fobbed off with them.

From the door Caroline's voice said, 'Delia mentioned a spare room, but you wouldn't want me to occupy that, would you, Simon?'

'You mean that you want to stay the night?'

'Why not? I don't fancy travelling down to Kingsmere so late in the day.'

'You can have my room. I will take the spare one.'

'And tomorrow,' she said, 'I will tell Mamma that we are all going to be together again. I must go back to Kingsmere to see that everything is under control, but I will return as soon as possible, and we will be a family once more.' She looked from one to the other and smiled. 'Won't that be nice, darlings?'

23

It was Peter who told Deborah that Simon's wife was back with him. 'She arrived yesterday, and I know she spent the night, because I saw her drive away in a cab this morning. If they are together again, I suppose they will move into a place of their own.'

He wasn't sure why he had spoken, but mixed with personal relief because Caroline had come back into the scene was a desire that Deborah should not be taken by surprise when the Davidsons were reunited as a family. It would be awful for her to come face to face with the woman, unaware that she was in the house. But afterwards he cursed his lack of tact, because it was a long time before Deborah was able to speak. Then she said quietly, 'Thank you for telling me, Peter.'

That was all, but he knew that he had shocked her. Waiting to take Delia to the theatre, he felt wretched because he had caused Deborah distress, and even more wretched because it indicated that she still cared about the man.

After that, the news that Caroline Davidson had rejoined her husband spread rapidly, coming to Chrystal Delmont via her daily servant, who had it from Cook, who had it

412

from Garfield, who had it from no less a person than Miss Yorke, who had intimated that the Davidsons' quarters would no doubt be available for reletting before long. 'I cannot imagine Delia's mother being content with anything less than a house of her own,' she had said, which told Garfield how badly Miss Deborah needed someone to talk to, for confidences did not come easily to her.

This was followed by the news of Elizabeth Ashleigh's sudden indisposition, keeping her daughter at Kingsmere. That was a merciful reprieve for everyone at 20 Hanover Square, said Garfield when Deborah showed her the brief paragraph in the morning paper. Anything to do with the Ashleighs made news, even the dowager's sudden chill. But what difference did Caroline's absence make? Deborah thought unhappily. Husband and wife had spent the night together, and that was enough to end her own hopes. The dreams she had dreamed seemed ridiculous now, but how important they had become, how dominant in her life! The kind of dreams from which it was difficult to shake free.

The news accelerated Chrystal Delmont's plans to bring Bryant Meredith and his former mistress face to face again, but to succeed in the way she hoped, the meeting had to take place in the presence of witnesses, and the forthcoming coronation gave her an admirable excuse to stage a private celebration party. Public excitement was gathering, coupled with relief because the unpopular Boer War seemed to be dragging to an end at last. The public wish for an early crowning had been dashed when the king chose 26 June of 1902 in the hope that it could be celebrated in time of peace, but not until 31 May of that year was the treaty signed. Immediately, excitement rose, only to be dashed again when rumours of the king's illness at Windsor began to circulate, then contradicted by the announcement that he had merely caught a chill, from which he would have recovered long before Coronation Day.

Being an expert on ceremonial etiquette, the king was also determined that the coronation should be thoroughly rehearsed to prevent the slightest mishap from marring the most colourful state ceremony of all, and one which had not been seen since his mother's, sixty-four years earlier, when innumerable things had gone wrong. Then he startled everyone by planning to give a fillip to the rising motor industry by driving to the abbey in a 'motor coach' instead of the state coach, provided the vehicle could be made noiseless and odourless. To the relief of the populace, this could not be guaranteed, so the golden coach would be seen in all its splendour as the culmination of a magnificent procession.

'We will see it, won't we, Father?' Delia demanded excitedly. 'All of us – you and me and Peter and Deborah, and Miss Delmont too, perhaps, because she is such a good friend now. Do you know she is reading my plays, though she does say I shouldn't write in such a hurry and that acting experience would help me. Peter once said I would make a better actress than a dramatist, and I think perhaps Miss Delmont feels the same, because ever since I did Ariel that day at the Comet, she has encouraged me.'

'I know. She told me all about it. She has distinct views on the way your future could go.'

'She *has*? Then she must really mean it, mustn't she? Oh, Father, would you let me become an actress, even though Grandmamma would disapprove?'

'I would never prevent you from doing anything on which you had set your heart, though you do realise, don't you, that the training Miss Delmont recommends would have to replace Girton?'

Delia nodded. 'I know. I have thought about that too, and though I think it would be very interesting to become a female undergraduate, even though everyone calls them blue stockings, I think it would be a great deal more interesting to belong to the theatre. I go there sometimes with Peter. I know everyone at the Comet, even the stage-hands. I know all the theatrical terms, too, so I am not a bit confused when hearing them talk. I wish I were old enough to act professionally now. I am getting tired of amateur productions at school.'

But that, she knew, was hoping for too much. 'When you are older, perhaps,' Miss Delmont said.

'But Ellen Terry acted when she was much younger than I.'

'That is true, but your father's wishes must be considered. I am sure he would not allow your education to be interrupted too soon, but if he would agree to your leaving school at sixteen, I know of a new drama academy you could attend for three years and finish your scholastic education there in conjunction with training for the stage. This is a new innovation, and I know your father is never averse to new innovations for women.'

And now she had actually spoken to him about it, and he was not refusing! Dear Father. Dear Miss Delmont. Dear Deborah, too, to whom she still poured out all her hopes and dreams. No gulf existed between them, as, alas, it continued to exist between her father and Deborah. Delia feared that the breach would never be healed between them, but for the moment her father's news drove all that out of her head.

'Have you heard, Charles?' she demanded of him one day in the small back garden, where he was enjoying the sun in the wicker bassinet which replaced his solid winter perambulator. 'You are going to know a real live actress when you grow up. *Me*, no less!' And he gurgled his pleasure, as he always did whenever she appeared.

She adored Charles. 'Couldn't we take him to see the coronation procession, Father? Stands are being built all along the route, and he could sit on my knee and see everything over the heads of people in front. There would be problems about nappies and feeds, of course . . . No? Well, I suppose he is a bit young. I will just have to tell him all about it when we come home. He understands every word I say, and everything Deborah says too. That makes Garfield jealous, so Deborah and I have agreed not to let her know, but it is true — Charles recognises Deborah's voice even from the other side of a door, or through an open window, and bounces up and down for joy. Have you noticed what a happy baby he is? He never seems to cry at all.'

'Except when hungry, like all healthy little animals.'

'So you *have* noticed? I thought you saw less of him now, and of Deborah too, until she explained how a man in your position has the demands of work to occupy him.'

Her father turned away. Delia could not see his face, but had the oddest feeling that he did not want her to.

The impasse in Simon's personal life was becoming more unbearable every day, as was his desire to overcome the ever-lengthening shadow between himself and Deborah. Peter Maynard, rapidly developing from a gauche young man to one of increasing confidence, was taking the fullest advantage of the situation, and Simon was well aware of the ripening friendship between the two. Though he had previously dismissed the young man as adolescent, he could do so no longer. Jealousy of Peter's freedom to woo Deborah was keen, and so was his own frustration. He felt that unless something happened to break the deadlock in his life, he would have to break it down himself before Caroline walked back into it finally. But what could he do? How could he fight? Caroline had been only too right when reminding him that a husband could not refuse to house his wife, without reaping the consequences, and while he didn't give a damn for himself, he cared deeply on his daughter's behalf. Delia would be hurt were her father to be condemned for being in the wrong, and even more hurt when her mother obtained custody of her. That was something he had fought against all along, and he had to continue the fight even at the cost of losing Deborah.

His case seemed hopeless, and life was rapidly becoming a thing of despair. He could take no interest in the coming coronation, nor share Delia's excitement about it. He had to force himself to listen to her chatter about the lavish preparations, about the brightly painted stands, about the flags of visiting nations flying from public buildings, about the gaily coloured coats-of-arms and enormous crystal constellations for illumination above the Mall and along the processional route from the palace to the abbey.

Never in living memory had any royal preparations been so lavish or costly. Food ordered by Buckingham Palace for the entertainment of royal guests amounted to 2,500 quails, hundreds of chickens, partridges, and sturgeons; fruit, sweets, desserts; colossal wine bills. St George's Hospital made no secret of the fact that it had spent £2,000 on the erection of stands and contracted for £500 worth of refreshments. Gunter's was catering for 6,000 guests for the Royal Garden Party and for 1,000 luncheons at the House of Lords. Florists and fruit-growers throughout the country were flooded with their biggest orders for years.

In the second week of June, the distinguished guests began to arrive; from Russia and the United States; Japan, Siam, and China; Spain, Zanzibar, Egypt, and Abyssinia, each guest with at least a dozen attendants. Trains poured into London carrying illustrious crowned heads and their attendants; separate trains followed with their mountains of luggage. From the provinces came an endless flood of vehicles with thousands of devoted subjects; private carriages, omnibuses, charabancs; country carts fitted with planks for seats; spring carts, traders' vans, and costermongers' carts, all pitching their spots in Hyde Park and surrounding areas, where their occupants lived, slept, cooked, and ate, awaiting the great day.

Londoners gathered in the streets to watch the arrival of heirs-apparent, foreign heads of state, and high-ranking guests of all nationalities, for whom a state banquet was to be held on the evening of 23 June, but when the king arrived at Paddington Station from Windsor that day, his appearance shocked everyone. His face was grey, his eyes closed, he could scarcely raise his hat to acknowledge the cheers, and rumour had it (later confirmed) that Queen Alexandra received the guests alone at the state banquet that night, and at the reception that followed.

Next day, while the coronation rehearsal was in progress at Westminster Abbey, the thunderbolt fell. The ceremony was postponed indefinitely and an emergency operation was performed on His Majesty. From rejoicing, the people were plunged into anxiety. The flocks of distinguished guests departed, and the lavish food ordered by the palace was sent to the Little Sisters of the Poor and other charities, so reaching many poor families living in London's East End. Stands were dismantled, catering orders and celebrations cancelled, and again Chrystal's desire to bring Bryant Meredith and Simon's wife together was frustrated, for the intimate party she planned, and which Bryant would certainly have attended because never had he been known to decline a meal at someone else's expense, had to be postponed.

But this waiting only increased Chrystal's determination. She was resolved that when the coronation finally did take place, nothing would stop her from using her celebration party as a means to the required end, and nothing would stop her from plying Bryant with plenty of champagne beforehand. He could be wildly indiscreet when he had had enough to loosen his tongue.

*

On 5 July, when news of the king's recovery was announced, her invitations were sent out. First, a personal letter to Caroline, at Kingsmere.

> Your daughter has often mentioned your desire to meet me, and I, equally, would like to meet you, but alas, your visits have so often coincided with my performances, and I understand that your mother's recent indisposition has kept you away from London. I trust she is now fully recovered and hope you will give me the pleasure of your company at a small supper party I am giving to celebrate the delayed coronation. No doubt you will be attending the ceremony, but my party will be later on that night, after the theatre, since my guests will be mainly the leading players from the Comet . . .

No names. No specific mention of Bryant. Just a hint, as bait.

Caroline accepted promptly. So did Bryant and other members of the cast. The remaining guests were Simon, Deborah, and Peter, for Chrystal was also aware of Peter's attentions to Deborah. All too often he would be lingering in the hall on some pretext or other, and all too often Chrystal had seen them out walking together, or leaving and entering the house together. Their friendship was warm, but Chrystal suspected that on Deborah's side it mainly acted as compensation for the loss of Simon.

About Peter's infatuation, Chrystal was not unduly worried, because he was young enough to recover, but if things could come to a head at her supper party, it would be better for all three.

Chrystal was enjoying her self-elected role of manipulator. She had never had a daughter of her own to plan for, no family to fight for, and no thwarted love affair to watch over and scheme for, and once the scene was set, hope increased with her determination. On the night of the party she whisked Bryant back with her from the theatre, where, behind the scenes, the cast had been toasting the newly crowned king and queen. It was 9 August, seven weeks after the original coronation date, and although almost all the distinguished visitors had left, the event proved to be anything but an anticlimax, and far surpassed Queen Victoria's in pomp and splendour. From all parts of the empire came units of armed forces – Sikhs from the Viceroy of India's Bodyguard, Maoris from New Zealand, soldiers from Africa, Jamaica, and the Barbadoes; even Dyaks from Borneo. King Edward's Russian Regiment of Guards vied with the Danish Regiment of Hussars, and the Austrian Regiment of Hussars with the German Regiment of Dragoon Guards, but perhaps most splendid of all was the magnificent array of Indian princes in their state uniforms and turbans. Back had come all the street decorations and, at night, the illuminations. Most stirring of all was the patriotic excitement of the multitude.

Inevitably the Comet's audience was particularly light-hearted. Applause was prolonged, and the reception Bryant received, particularly from the female section, went to his head as intoxicatingly as the backstage festivity. He was mellow, amenable, and totally uncaring as the hansom drove them to Hanover Square where a buffet had been provided by Fortnum & Mason, together with a waiter to assist Chrystal's daily maid.

Bryant swooped on the champagne and toasted Chrystal with lavish endearments, but despite smooth running so far, Chrystal knew that everything hinged on correct timing. Their fellow actors had followed and were already imbibing when Simon and Peter arrived, followed by Deborah a few minutes later. Chrystal had taken the precaution of naming a time to Caroline Davidson which would bring her on the scene last of all.

The stage management seemed faultless, and the only

difficulty was in avoiding an introduction between the now slightly intoxicated Bryant and Caroline's husband. To realise the identity of the blunt-featured man with the scarred face and the slight limp might put Bryant's guard up, light-headed though he was, so Chrystal promptly swept Simon away to meet other guests, leaving Deborah with Bryant.

With an elaborate bow, the actor swooped over her hand and kissed it. 'A pretty woman, begad! As for you, knave, out of my way!' With an histrionic gesture he swept Peter aside. 'You, I have already met, sir, amongst your paint pots and your brushes, and though I grant thou art a fairsome youth, methinks at this moment I wouldst have thee gone. Shakespeare, though God knows from which of his plays . . .'

From none of them, Peter wanted to point out, well aware, as were all at the theatre, that Meredith would never master Shakespeare, but this was a night of celebration and he joined in the laughter, though he considered the man singularly unamusing. Nor did he like the familiar way his arm slipped round Deborah's waist. He was pleased when she eluded it with ease and charm, and the champagne quickly sent his own spirits soaring. The food was good, the company was good; he liked everyone, admired his hostess, adored Deborah, felt sorry for poor old Simon, because now that his wife had returned from her sojourn abroad he hadn't a hope of winning Deborah, and thought how wide-eyed Delia would be were she old enough to be allowed downstairs to meet all these famous people away from the stage.

Two of the actresses were paying marked attention to her father. They seemed to find his rugged face very attractive. Well, good luck to him, thought Peter charitably.

Bryant Meredith, at the end of the room near the door, was well away. Chrystal seemed to have cornered him there, which surprised Peter, because more often than not she was impatient with him at the theatre, and not without reason, for he was a lazy actor, fluffing his lines so that she had to cover up for him all too often. Peter was surprised that she had invited him tonight. He always felt she had enough of him at the Comet, but now she was laughing at every quip he made and encouraging him to let himself go.

Peter looked around for Deborah, who had eluded Bryant and was now caught up with two other actors from the cast. He tried to catch her eye, and failed, and at that precise moment the doorbell communicating with Miss Delmont's apartment rang clearly. More guests. At this rate the place would become overcrowded. He hoped it would be someone he could talk to. He disliked being on the fringe.

The new guest, ushered in by Chrystal's maid, paused on the threshold, a striking woman in a gown of gold lamé which bore the hallmark of Paris. Only Maggy Rouff used such striking materials, skilfully swathing it round the hips beneath an Empire sash of bronze silk which trailed in long swathes down the fishtail train, but perhaps the most striking effect was the extreme décolleté of the neckline, the nakedness of shoulder made doubly provoking by the use of an ostrich-feather fan dyed to the bronze shade of her sash. For a moment the woman held the pose, gently fluttering the ostrich feathers above her breasts, then letting the fan glide away slowly. No unveiling could have been more effective.

There was an immediate hush.

Directly opposite the door stood Bryant Meredith, regaling his hostess with some unending and apparently hilarious tale, but his voice cut off abruptly. The next moment, with outstretched arms, he swayed in the newcomer's direction and embraced her fondly. 'Caroline, my lovely! How wonderful you look! Life has been desolate without you, and I hope it has been the same for you, or I shall think you didn't care as much as I believed . . . and no, don't tell me you have replaced me, or my heart will break. I left you when you were still hungry for me, and it serves me right that I have been hungry for you ever since. Remember Paris, those nights we had? Those endless nights – *and* days. And before Paris, alone for weeks in my flat with the world shut out . . .'

He raised his glass to the startled company. 'Ladies'n gen'lmen, meet the most passionate woman I ever bedded! It isn't women like the king's giantesses who satisfy a man – the buxom Lillie Langtry and stout Mrs Keppel would make substantial figureheads on the prow of any vessel, but my darling Caroline is the longest, leanest thing I ever saw naked and has a sexual appetite equal to all those lumbering women put together! Like a tigress she was in bed – are you still the same, my lovely? I am sorry I deserted you in Paris, but never mind – I am ready for more, anytime. I never had a mistress to equal such a savage as you.'

24

Delia knew that the unpleasantness of her parents' divorce would remain in her memory permanently, even though she had been aware, in childhood, that they no longer loved each other. Years later she would still recall the squalid details of her mother's affair with a notorious actor, and the distaste she felt for both of them. And she would never forget the way in which everyone tried to keep the newspapers from her – unsuccessfully.

Newsboys carried placards announcing 'ASHLEIGH HEIRESS SUED FOR DIVORCE', 'FAMOUS ACTOR TELLS ALL', and 'THE SECRET LOVE LIFE OF SOCIETY HOSTESS'. It was the scandal of the year, lapped up by readers of the more sensational Sunday press, to whom Bryant Meredith sold his story for an enormous sum, concealing nothing.

It made no difference when Cook tried to console her with, 'Never mind, love, these things happen, and some-day the world will think nothing of it – not the way it's going, which is to the dogs, I always say.'

As for her mother, Caroline did not get in touch with her daughter throughout the prolonged and unsavoury proceedings, during which Elizabeth Ashleigh swallowed her pride and came to London to call on Simon. From her room Delia had heard her grandmother's voice queru-lously demanding that he should drop the proceedings for the sake of their good name.

'Whose good name, Mother-in-law? The Ashleighs'?'

That was all Delia heard him say, for she turned on her side, burying her head in the pillow, and there her father found her later and gathered her up, holding her close for a long time.

She didn't want to talk about it. What was the use? Apparently it was something one had to go through, like measles, but anyone who believed that when the marks disappeared the memory of them would also disappear was wrong. And there were some particularly bad moments which she would never forget. When visiting Pru's home one day her friend had blurted, 'Your mother is an adulteress. The papers say so, and my papa says so, too,' and although Pru's mother punished her and held out kindly arms to comfort Delia, her friend's accusation left behind a sort of stigma which could be applied to none of their schoolfellows, all of whom came from homes untouched by scandal.

Of course, Pru said she was sorry, but Delia guessed that her mother had ordered her to, so nothing was mended. Behind Pru's owlish spectacles her face displayed nothing but shocked curiosity, which made Delia realise that they could no longer communicate in their old, easy way. She left as soon as possible, hiding her tears.

Later, in Charles's nursery, she confided to the baby, 'I am never going to marry, and I'd advise you not to, either. It seems to make everyone unhappy. Your own mother was never married, and she seemed the happiest person I'd ever known. I remember her well, laughing and smiling that weekend at Kingsmere, until she suddenly left next day and I never saw her again,' and Charles looked back at her through his pale Ashleigh eyes, as if he understood.

Perhaps it was then that Delia guessed the identity of his father, though later she decided she must have realised it at Kingsmere before the estate children's party, when studying the portraits in the long gallery and remarking to her mother on the strange coincidence of the Ashleigh eyes. And she remembered how Dulcima Howard had once walked amongst the guests with Uncle Justin's possessive arm about her. They had been lovers, of course, but they had been lovers openly, not furtively, as her mother and that actor had been.

One thing sustained Delia during this unhappy stage of her adolescence. Throughout the whole squalid exposure – for details of his mistress's sexual proclivities added spice to the story Meredith sold to the press long before the case reached the courts – the understanding and affection of her father and Deborah provided a bulwark during this unhappy stage of her life. Divorce cases waited a long time after suits were filed, and after they had at last been heard, a further six months had to elapse before a decree nisi could be granted, during which time the innocent party dare not commit any misdemeanour or the court decision could be reversed and the final decree withheld. But was it really necessary for Deborah to take Charles away with her to Brighton, Garfield accompanying them?

'Why should *she* have to go away?' Delia asked Peter, who said that he supposed it was better so.

'Tricky lawyers might try to turn the tables by pointing out in court that your father and Deborah share a house.'

'They don't share it alone. Other people live here. You and Miss Delmont, for a start.'

'Yes, but as far as the rest of us are concerned, there is no emotional involvement.'

'You are emotionally involved with Deborah.'

'Not with her, *for* her, if you know what I mean.'

'Meaning you're in love with her? Poor Peter.'

'Don't worry, Cleo. I'll get over it.'

'Good. I don't like to think of you being unhappy as well.'

'Besides yourself, you mean?' He patted her cheek affectionately. 'You won't believe this now, but someday you will be able to look back without wanting to cry. In fact, you'll even be glad it happened. Marriages aren't made in heaven, they are made here on earth, and some badly need rearranging. Your father's is one. Know something? I think he's a lucky devil, and I wouldn't be surprised if he knows it too, so you can't blame him, or Deborah, for not wanting to chance their luck by continuing to live beneath the same roof.'

'If lawyers are that cunning, they can accuse them of living together all the time my mother was away.'

'Living beneath the same roof and living together are two different things, and open to misinterpretation only when someone needs to make them so. Such as now.'

'But *we* can tell them it has never been true. You and I and Miss Delmont, and Garfield and Cook — '

'And so we all would, if necessary, but I imagine that is the last thing your father would want, especially for you. Not that I think any such defence will be necessary, in view of all that's come out. Sorry, Cleo, but you're a big girl now, and it's no use pretending that your mother's story isn't pretty indefensible. It's better that it should remain so, and the divorce go through without any risk of complication or trumped-up falsehoods. You must believe that whatever your father and Deborah do is for the best.'

'I hope you have brought your play for me to read, Delia, my dear?'

'I'm afraid not, Miss Delmont. I'm stuck. Somehow I can't concentrate these days.'

'Never mind. I'll give you something to read instead. That will help you. It is to be the next Comet production. *Twelfth Night.*'

'Are you playing Viola?'

Chrystal shook her head. 'I'm rather too old. I play Olivia.'

'She's the beautiful lady the Duke of Orsino loves.'

'That's right. But she falls in love with Sebastian, who is really Viola in disguise. Would you like to read their scenes with me?'

Delia's eyes lit up. It was the first time they had brightened for a long time. Did I really do right in bringing matters to a head? Chrystal wondered. She had considered Simon and Deborah, but not Delia. Why did adults so often imagine that children could be untouched by the affairs of their parents? She had not given this sensitive girl a thought, and while she had no regrets as far as Simon and Deborah were concerned, she wanted to beg Delia's forgiveness. Not until she had begun to notice a change in her recently had she realised that the child was unhappy. And why had she regarded her as a child? During the months of waiting, Delia had grown up not only physically, but also emotionally. There was an air of maturity about her which had never been there before. Yet another birthday had come and gone, and beneath the school blouse her immature breasts were now noticeable. Delia seemed to have left childhood behind overnight. By the time she was sixteen she would be a young woman, and through these difficult growing-up years she needed all the understanding she could get.

Chrystal remembered her own adolescence, the bewilderment attendant on physical change, and the deep sensitivity accompanying it. Whilst waiting for her father's life to be rearranged and for Deborah to come back into it, there was only one person who could tide Delia through this difficult phase – another woman.

'Let's take it from Act I, Scene 2 – *"What country, friends, is this?"* '

Thus began Delia's initial training in drama. Though Chrystal gave her no formal lessons, these readings developed her theatrical sense. Reading lines aloud with an experienced actress was wholly different from performing in school plays. Instead of uttering drilled responses, she was encouraged to react spontaneously, and it mattered not in the least if the rendering was bad. It was *fun*.

She began to look forward to the sessions, racing home from school to catch Miss Delmont for an hour before she left for the theatre, and never was she unwelcome. It became as natural to visit the apartment below as it had been to visit the one on the ground floor. She wrote lengthy letters to Deborah, telling her about the visits. 'Today we did *Romeo and Juliet*, all the scenes between Juliet and her nurse, and Miss Delmont praised me.' . . . 'We are reading parts of Oscar Wilde's *Chamides*. Miss Delmont says I can read the rest when I grow up. I have to memorise several stanzas because Miss Delmont says that Wilde is appreciated only as a dramatist, but his poetry deserves study.' It was always 'Miss Delmont', emphasising the woman's professional standing, which placed her just that little bit out of reach. And it was satisfying to bask in the actress's aura, to be able to boast that she was being coached by one of London's leading actresses. Boasting was not one of Delia's faults, but she needed some defence at this particular time, and the awe and envy of her schoolfellows went a long way to bolstering her. They soon ceased to look askance because of the scandal of her mother; instead, they looked impressed, and there could be no better satisfaction than that.

By the end of 1904 the creaking wheels of the law ground to an end and the whole traumatic period was over. Her parents' marriage was ended, and with the granting of the decree nisi, public interest ended too. Meredith could extract no further publicity and retired from the scene well content with what he had netted.

When Deborah returned to 20 Hanover Square, she brought home a chubby toddler who looked more like his mother than ever, but such perfection of feature could not hide the fact that young Charles was essentially mascu-line. He promised to be devastatingly handsome when older, Delia reflected as she stooped to hug him, but Charles disliked being cuddled and pushed her aside. Even Deborah's fond gestures were sometimes dodged, though it was plain that he loved her more than anyone else. Garfield's effusive attention irked him, and affec-tionate overtures from her were tolerated with obvious distaste. 'He's such a manly little man,' the woman said in excuse. 'Can't bear to be fussed over. Nothing namby-pamby about *him*! Very independent, is his lordship.'

Later, sounds from the bathroom confirmed this. Thrusting her head round the door, Delia saw Charles struggling to grab the sponge for himself and soaking Garfield in the process, but even then the woman did not scold him. 'Well, it's certain you're the master here, and no mistake, my little lordship.'

Delia slipped away and went downstairs to seek out Deborah and her father. She was not surprised to find them in Deborah's ground-floor sitting room, nor to find them embracing. The action dispelled once and for all the rift which had entered this house many months ago.

They drew apart when she entered, and both held out a hand to her.

'We are together again,' Simon said. 'The three of us.'

'For always, Father?'

'You can count on that, my dear.'

'Will you be married?'

'Yes.'

'I hope you will be happy about it,' Deborah added, and Delia flung her arms round her neck, unable to find words to tell them how she felt. It was all coming right, after all. Everything was coming right, just as Peter had said it would. She hoped they would do it quickly; then life could really return to normal. She was anxious to get on with the business of living and, in particular, the exciting prospect of the dramatic academy.

When Simon and Deborah married, Chrystal bought a terraced house in Chelsea. 'I have always wanted a small house and garden,' she insisted, but the Davidsons guessed she was leaving because the time had come for 20 Hanover Square to change into a family home. Peter began to pack reluctantly, but was urged by Deborah and Simon to retain his studio, whereupon he unpacked again with alacrity. 'After all,' he said to Bruce Whitney later, 'good studios are hard to come by,' at which Bruce smiled knowledgeably and remarked on how rapidly young Delia had grown up and what a pretty filly she was.

At moments like this Peter realised that Bruce's secret observation of Delia had never ceased and that, at the rate she was developing, she could well become the focus for his fuller attention. Peter didn't like that at all, but Bruce was not the kind of chap to heed any 'Hands off!' warning. He had been pampered and indulged by his doting mamma and considered that whatever he wanted in life, he had only to take. Peter became even more concerned when Delia finally left school, discarded the regulation blouse and skirt, and put up her hair.

The Regent Academy of Drama was situated, not surprisingly, in the vicinity of Regent Street, tucked away in a less impressive thoroughfare known as Carnaby Street. It was an area rapidly becoming the centre for the millinery trade, but the academy occupied number sixteen exclusively. Stepping across its threshold was like entering another world. Off endless stairs opened endless studios, and from behind endless doors came the sound of voices intoning singly or in groups, vying with background street noises or rival classes on the other side of adjoining walls. Here were taught singing, elocution, mime, dancing, deportment, the mastery of dialects, character acting, the art of makeup, and skills such as fencing to develop dexterity of movement and grace. Branches of stage management and design were encompassed within a separate department of training.

Classes were segregated between male and female, which, to Delia's mind, was a mistake. Surely, she argued with the staid secretary who showed her to the female locker room and pinned a notice, bearing rules and regulations, on her locker door, if actors and actresses were to act together, they should study together?

'That comes later, Miss Davidson. You will undergo a preliminary term as a beginner before you advance to the classes for ladies and gentlemen, and if you fail the seeding at the end of the first term, you will qualify for no further training.'

'Seeding?'

'Sorting the wheat from the chaff, as one might say. The academy must concentrate on students with real potential.'

Delia threw herself wholeheartedly into the course, fully expecting it to be exciting from the start. Instead, much of it was tedious, and all of it hard work. Not surprisingly, many students fell by the wayside at the end of the trial term, and even those who got through complained of the grind. As for acting, chanting vocal exercises and practising breath control was not their idea of it. Nor was there anything glamorous about walking up and down a room balancing books on one's head until the neck ached; and the first lapse brought a sharp reprimand, sometimes accompanied by a rap between the shoulder blades. 'Straighten up, young lady, straighten up! You are walking an unseen stage, remember, and an audience is watching. What sort of an impression will you give, slouching like that?'

And then came lessons in sitting correctly, in rising from a chair or couch, opening a door, entering and exiting, kneeling and rising, bowing and curtseying, turning the wrist, inclining the head . . . over and over again these things had to be practised until the body tired and you wondered why you ever thought acting would be easy. And before advancing to the study of plays, poetry had to be mastered, memorising difficult lines and reciting them in class, enduring the titters of fellow students and the teacher's scathing comments, until the only thing you wanted to do was run from the room and never come back.

Then suddenly the preliminary grind was over and the scene changed. You were studying roles and rehearsing with male students, and if you worked hard enough, you would be auditioned for the annual drama production in the academy's small theatre. Only a limited number of parts would be available, so not everyone could be cast; therefore it was up to you to do your best. In this, Delia felt she had an advantage; her preliminary sessions at home with Miss Delmont would surely help her through.

The notice posted in the main hall announced that students had to perform a compulsory piece set by the judges, plus one of their own choosing. The compulsory piece would be announced individually when one walked onstage, and the only certainty was that it would be from work already studied in class. For the optional piece, Delia decided to choose something she had already studied with Chrystal. Blandly assured, she sailed out into the street after reading the notice, and walked straight into Bruce Whitney.

'Are you waiting for me?' she asked, surprised.

'For who else? I've hung around this place several times, never sure when you would appear. Luck is in today.' He offered her an immaculate arm, and she enjoyed taking it. She felt very grown-up as they walked toward Regent Street, and conscious of the envious glances of other female students. Bruce's admiring eyes made her conscious of her femininity. She hesitated only briefly as he hailed a cab, and deliberately thrust aside her father's warning never to ride in hansoms alone with gentlemen with whom she was unacquainted. Since Bruce was Peter's friend, he scarcely came within that category, so she stepped into the cab with all the grace learned in class. The only disconcerting thing was the proximity of Bruce's shoulder as they drove away. Was it really necessary to sit so close?

Edging away slightly, she tried to hide the fact that this was a new experience for her, but Bruce's sidelong glance was amused, indulgent, and to cover her discomfiture she said, 'The driver is going the wrong way. Surely he knows that Hanover Square is north of Regent Street, not south?'

'I daresay he does, but I haven't directed him there.

Did you think I only came to take you home?'

'Yes, I did think that.' At least her voice was steady, even if her heart was not. 'I am expected to go straight home, so will you please tell the man to turn round?'

'What's the hurry? The afternoon isn't over, and the sun is shining. A walk in St James's Park would be pleasant, don't you think?'

A walk in the park – was that all? How ridiculous of her to be alarmed! She agreed that it would be most pleasant. 'And after that, you could come home for tea. I am sure Deborah would be pleased to see you.'

Bruce wasn't so sure. Deborah was always polite, always pleasant, but she made him feel that she didn't wholly like him. The feeling had increased since Delia grew up, and he resented it. Deborah Davidson seemed to be self-appointed watchdog to her stepdaughter, which only made him more determined to see as much of the girl as he wanted to.

'I thought tea at Gunter's would be enjoyable,' he said. 'I remember you once telling me you liked Gunter's.'

'How nice of you to remember that!'

'I remember many things about you, right from your childhood. I have always been enchanted by you.' That wasn't strictly true; once upon a time he had found her rather precocious, though he had recognised her potential even then. But those days were gone, and the present was with him. He intended, as always, to make the most of it.

After that, Bruce met her regularly, sometimes walking her home to prove that his intentions were entirely honourable, but gradually extending their meetings to take in visits to art galleries or other respectable places to which her father could raise no objection. Bruce knew he had to step carefully where Delia was concerned, for though she was inexperienced, she was not naive; one wrong step, and she would shy away. And he wasn't averse to breaking in a filly; it could be enjoyable, especially with one like this. So he bided his time, only occasionally putting his hand beneath her elbow and feeling encouraged when she did not draw aside. She was enjoying his company as much as he enjoyed hers, and he lent a willing ear to her chatter about life at the academy and all she was going to achieve when she graduated. Meanwhile, the coming auditions dominated her horizon.

'I wish you could come to the annual production,' she said one day. 'Friends and relatives of students taking part are invited.'

'Will you be taking part?'

'I won't know until I am auditioned, but I am determined to succeed.'

He said lightly, 'I would prefer to come as a relative than as a friend, but for the time being I'll be content with things as they are.'

She found, to her surprise, that she was too shy to answer. She was confused by her reactions to this man, and by the unfamiliar physical awareness he stirred in her. Could this be love? And was this how Bryant Meredith had affected her mother? For the first time, she felt a certain pity for Caroline. If a man stirred a woman so deeply that she was unable to resist him, perhaps she was to be pitied more than condemned. All the same, the things the actor had revealed about her mother's sexual behaviour could hardly he interpreted as love. People believed she had not read about them, but she had. He had stated that his mistress had behaved like a wild animal in bed. Surely lovemaking wasn't like that?

Only two weeks to go, and Delia had not yet decided on her voluntary piece. Juliet's balcony speech, or Portia's immortal one on mercy? She knew both well, and others besides. She could take her pick of several. While fellow students worried and studied, she put classes behind her the moment she left the building, for Bruce was always waiting, and always some new treat was planned.

'You know you'll get through,' he assured her, 'so forget it; let's enjoy ourselves.' He was now the proud owner of a motorcar, which, he told her, had cost as much as the king's. His habit of quoting the prices he paid for things jarred on her, as did the flamboyant way in which he tipped cabdrivers or tearoom waitresses, but the novelty of being escorted about London by a sophisticated man helped her to shut her eyes to such things. She felt very adult these days, and a grown woman accepted a man uncritically. So off she would drive with him to Kew Gardens, or to the river at Richmond, such things as auditions and examinations forgotten.

'You're flattered by his attentions,' Peter told her angrily. 'I thought you had more sense. Can't you see what he's after?'

'You are mistaken. You don't know him as I do.'

'I know him very well, but go ahead and make a fool of yourself if you want to. And if you fail your audition through wasting your time with him, don't come to *me*.'

She was very much at loggerheads with Peter these days, and somehow their sparring lacked its former spice. No longer could it be forgotten in five minutes; their disagreements rankled, and his warnings about Bruce only goaded her into seeing the man more. Peter was aware of this, cursed himself for not keeping his mouth shut, and found it increasingly difficult to do so. Avoiding her didn't help much either. Nor did obliging artists' models, or flirtations with understudies or small-part players at the Comet. He had imagined himself in love a dozen times since Deborah married, and even that had not hurt as he had expected, nor affected him the way Delia's friendship with Bruce affected him. He became moody, touchy, and decided that the only worthwhile thing in life was work.

Even so, he could never resist challenging Delia when

they met. 'Has he seduced you yet? Has he taken you to Solferino's or the Café Royal? Private rooms there are well-equipped, even with beds which a maid lets down from a wall before helping the lady to undress.'

'Indeed? And how do you know? From personal experience?' Her anger had been as stinging as her voice, and as she flung away from him, he knew he deserved it.

On the eve of the auditions, Bruce announced that they must have a celebration dinner. 'Let's not do the conventional thing and celebrate afterwards.'

It sounded a lovely idea, but impossible. Her father would disapprove of a girl of seventeen dining alone with a man; afternoon outings to art galleries or Kew Gardens were one thing, but suppers in fashionable restaurants were quite another. What married women could do, unmarried girls could not. Besides, auditions started at ten tomorrow, and she had still not settled on the piece of her choice. But she remained unworried, for there was no chance of her forgetting lines she had read so many times with Miss Delmont.

Even so, she declined Bruce's invitation. 'I really must study. It's terribly important.'

'It hasn't been important up to now. You've never made work an excuse before. Are you afraid of parental disapproval? Is that it? I thought you were more independent.'

'I am, but . . .'

'But you're afraid of being found out? Don't be silly. All you have to do is say you have extra classes. You do have them sometimes, I know. Evening sessions for one thing or another. So you have one lined up tonight. What more natural, with auditions coming up? You can smuggle a valise out of the house when you leave at the normal time, and change at the academy. I'll pick you up there at seven. I have reserved a table at Kettner's for seven-thirty, a ridiculously early hour; you see how thoughtful I'm being. We'll have time for a leisurely dinner, and I'll still get you home by ten – well, maybe ten-thirty. You've been that late before, haven't you, when study sessions have kept you and you've gone home with a friend to run through lines afterwards?'

'Yes, but I don't like deceiving them.'

'Them? You mean Deborah as well as your father? Since she isn't your mother, I can't see that you owe her any allegiance. Your father's a different matter, and I wouldn't want you to upset him. That's why I've planned everything so carefully. Come, Delia! Even your father was young once, and he loves you so much he'd forgive you anything. And I'm not asking you to do anything disgraceful.' When she still hesitated, he added, 'Of course, if you lack the courage, we'd best forget the whole thing . . .'

And put an end to our friendship, his tone implied, whereupon she reacted as he expected.

'All right – I'll do it.'

Mingled with her guilt was a feeling of adventure, of challenge. The whole thing promised to be a delightful escapade, with no real danger, because she knew Bruce could be trusted. She chose her gown with care before she went to bed that night; it had to be something which could be folded into her commodious satchel. That would attract no attention when she departed in the morning.

So into the satchel went a simple white chiffon, with matching court shoes in satin. Thank goodness, skirts were long and straight these days. The only other necessary item was a small beaded evening purse, tucked into a corner.

She went to bed in a state of excitement, which was still with her when she awakened. She could not face her father across the breakfast table. She had never lied to him in her life, and he would surely see through any attempt, so she waited until he had left for the museum before she descended, and yawned elaborately when she entered the breakfast room.

'You slept late this morning,' said Deborah, looking up with a smile. 'I hope you are not overworking because of tomorrow's audition?'

'I admit I'll be glad when it's over,' Delia answered truthfully.

'You must have an early night tonight,' Deborah advised.

'I wish I could, but there's to be an extra study session for anyone wishing to take advantage of it.'

'And you are.'

Delia nodded, tackling a boiled egg with such concentration that Deborah watched her thoughtfully, then turned away.

'Try not to be too late,' she said. 'I will tell Simon for you. He will fetch you home.'

Delia took a gulp of coffee, then shook her head. 'No need. I'll walk home with other students coming this way.'

By the time she left the house, her excitement had diminished. It had been horrible, lying like that.

Excitement returned when she saw Bruce, immaculate in evening wear.

'You look beautiful,' he said. 'Virgin white becomes you.' His tone implied that purity was something not to be despised and certainly not to be defiled. His manners were impeccable, his care of her everything that it should be.

'I took the precaution of reserving a table where no one can see us, just in case any acquaintance of your father's should chance to be there.' The words were accompanied by a smile which was open and trustworthy. 'I want nothing to mar our evening, and any possibility of your being taken to task later would distress me.'

His reassuring tone relaxed her. He didn't even touch

her hand or sit close to her during the drive to Soho, so when they reached the restaurant, she felt no qualms when they entered by a side door and were ushered along a passage beside the main restaurant to a room at the back. He was being wholly considerate in ensuring that they should not be seen. It would have been fun to dine in the elegant restaurant she glimpsed in passing, but she appreciated his thoughtfulness, also the room, which was brilliantly lit and beautifully decorated, dominated by the dining table set mid-centre beneath a glittering chandelier. This was no setting for seduction, for the only other furniture was a serving table in one corner, with a chair beside it, and a chaise longue by the opposite wall, champagne in an ice bucket close by.

She relaxed on the chaise longue with all her recently acquired grace, and he sat apart from her, being his most charming and entertaining self. He wanted her to forget the coming strain of auditioning, he said, and what better way than this? 'Champagne and a good supper, and then home to Hanover Square.' As he said that, his eyes slid to the satchel he had taken from her when they met. 'There will be a room here where you can change into your day clothes before we leave; then, if ever-watchful Deborah sees you on your return, she won't suspect a thing.'

'Why do you speak of her like that? You make her sound like a jailer, and she is nothing of the kind.' She still felt guilty for lying to Deborah this morning, and even a hint of criticism of her put Delia on the defensive.

Sensing this, Bruce said easily. 'Of course not. She's a little overprotective, that's all.'

He dismissed Deborah, and refilled Delia's glass. It was the first time she had ever drunk champagne, and it was all she could do not to crinkle up her nose. He laughed and told her not to gulp it, and after a sip or two she enjoyed it very much.

She enjoyed the whole evening very much. The food,

the wine, the flower-perfumed room, Bruce's sparkling companionship. What on earth was wrong with dining with a man in a private room? The warnings she had heard were ridiculous, and as for Peter's views on such a situation, he must have gleaned them from some sensational novel, and she very much wished she could tell him so.

Time sped far too quickly. The meal over, the waiters withdrew, and Bruce smiled at her across the table and suggested they should finish their wine more comfortably. She found herself back on the chaise longue, with Bruce seated nearer to her this time, but not touching her. He took his watch from his waistcoat pocket, glanced at it, and put it away again. 'Just making sure I am not keeping you out too late,' he said. 'I haven't forgotten my promise to get you home at an uncompromising hour.'

She stretched luxuriously. What an adventure, and how she wished she could boast about it to her friends! Pru, for instance. How shocked the dear girl would be! Delia was still fond of Pru, though she seemed more prissy than ever these days. 'I wonder your father allows you to become an actress, knowing what actors are like,' she had said, reminding Delia of that horrible man Bryant Meredith. Not that she had meant to. Pru had merely been tactless, but a tiny cloud now stirred in Delia's memory, a cloud she thought she had forgotten. She drank some more wine to chase it away, and felt deliciously light headed after it. That warned her to lay her glass aside. Soon she would go home, and evening sessions at the academy didn't send her home light-headed . . .

Bruce promptly topped up her glass. 'There's no hurry,' he said. 'I'm keeping my eye on the time, and we have plenty in which to enjoy ourselves.'

That was when he reached for the bell on the wall and pressed the knob with three decisive touches. Two long and one short. Like Morse code, she thought. Was he ringing for a cab to be fetched already, even though he had just remarked that there was plenty of time? Was he tired of her, wanting to curtail the evening because she had not proved to be the scintillating companion he expected? Enjoyment gave way to a sense of failure, though the smile he was levelling at her belied it.

Then the feeling gave way to surprise, for a maid entered and, crossing the room, opened a door skilfully designed as a wall panel. From behind it she took out a screen and spread it across the corner containing the side table and chair. Then on the table she placed a mirror and hairbrush, silver-topped perfume bottles, crystal powder bowl, and a selection of face creams. All appeared like magic from the concealed cupboard. Delia watched in astonishment, and was even more astonished when Bruce strolled to the end of the room, turning his back, and the woman bobbed a curtsey before her, asking if Madam was ready.

'Ready for what?' Delia asked, light-headedness rapidly departing.

'For my help, ma'am.' The maid was holding the screen for her to step behind. She was even scanning Delia's figure with an experienced eye. 'Not much unlacing, I can see,' she commented in a low and approving voice. 'That always pleases the gentlemen. They don't like to be kept waiting.'

'Get out,' Delia said in a voice which quelled the woman and brought Bruce's head spinning round in astonishment.

'But, ma'am, I have my orders–'

'*My* order is for you to get out.'

She was on her feet, trembling with anger. The woman beat a hasty retreat. The minute the door closed, Bruce demanded, 'What the devil are you playing at? Why do you think I brought you here?'

'For a "celebration dinner", you said. Celebrating

what? Another seduction?' She snatched up her satchel. It looked incongruous against her white chiffon dress. 'I don't like being tricked.'

'Nor do I,' he rapped. 'Do you think a man spends all his money for nothing?'

'Damn your money. Spend it on someone else.'

'You stupid little bitch! You must have known what to expect, without being told. You must have learned a thing or two from that mother of yours.'

She reached out blindly and struck him. He caught her wrist and held it, enraged and yet excited by her. 'Stop playacting, Delia. Keep that for your precious audition. The minute you entered this room, you must have guessed what was expected of you, but you went along with me just the same. And you're ripe for it, ready for it. Virgin white may become you, but virginity does not. It's high time you quit that state.'

'In return for a good meal?' The way in which she wrenched free expressed her contempt. 'I can enjoy one of Cook's good meals anytime I like, without having to earn it, and if and when I do allow myself to be seduced, it won't be in some private supper room, no matter how fashionable or expensive the place, nor by a man I don't love. The last point happens to be the most important.' She crossed to the bell and pressed it. 'I don't know the signal for a cab, but this should bring *some*one.'

It did. The waiter who answered had difficulty in hiding his astonishment, and the look on the man's face did nothing to ease Bruce Whitney's humiliation or diminish his rage.

She made no attempt to slip into the house unobserved. She went straight to the drawing room to face her father and Deborah. Both looked in surprise at her white chiffon dress and the bulging satchel containing her day wear.

'A rehearsal of some kind?' Simon asked tactfully.

'No, Father.' She took a deep breath. 'I want to say I'm sorry. I lied to Deborah this morning, and I'm ashamed. And there's something else.' She looked at each in turn, half afraid and yet compelled to own up. 'I did something this evening of which I know you won't approve . . .'

'You have been out with a man, not at the academy, as you said?'

There was no reproach in her father's voice. It even seemed as if he were trying to help her over the moment, so she said in a rush, 'I dined in Soho. In a private room.' Seeing the expression in his eyes change from indulgence to concern, she hurried on. 'I didn't enjoy it. I mean, I didn't enjoy finding out why I'd been taken there, though I was stupid not to guess. I did enjoy the meal, though, and the champagne. It made me feel sophisticated, and that was enjoyable too, but it shows how unsophisticated I really am, not to guess what was expected afterwards.'

'By whom?' Simon demanded.

'It doesn't matter. I shan't be seeing him again. And nothing happened – nothing of the kind you fear. But I do want to apologise for being deceitful. I feel worse about that than about anything.'

His eyes softened. 'I gather you took care of yourself.'

'That was easy. I was livid, and told him so, and I had to order a cab to get myself home and I hadn't enough money to pay for it, so I'm afraid the cabby is waiting outside.'

Simon laughed, and kissed her as he went to pay the man. 'Do the same again when in a tight corner, though it's wiser not to get into them,' he said.

'But not always easy, is it?' Deborah added sympathetically when she and Delia were alone.

They really were the most understanding people in the world, Delia decided as she went upstairs, but though her feeling of guilt was lessened, her self-reproach was not. Nor was it helped by the reflection that Peter had been right. Throughout a restless night this thought troubled her continuously.

Downstairs, Deborah said, 'I'm glad she told us. I've had her on my mind all day.'

'You guessed she was up to something? Why didn't you tell me?'

'And worry you unnecessarily?'

'If she was on your mind all day, that means *you* were worried. Don't ever do that again, my love. Don't keep things from me.'

She curled up against him on a sofa before the fire. 'I might have been imagining things.'

'But you weren't. I can guess who the man was, can't you?'

She nodded. 'She's been seeing a lot of Bruce Whitney, and I never did like that young man. Nor does Peter, I'm sure.'

'And not without cause. Peter has certainly changed since those days. Delia too. That's what security does for the young. That she wanted to own up and wasn't afraid to is a good sign.'

Deborah nodded. 'We're lucky, Simon. Delia's course is set fair, and Charles is positively angelic.'

Too angelic, Simon thought secretly. The boy would be more natural if he were less well-behaved. Never could he be accused of real naughtiness, and his moments of defiance were no more than flashes of growing independence, mostly against Garfield's doting attentions. The woman's adoration could be dangerous, particularly if, as Simon suspected, she cherished the belief that the child had been defrauded of his rightful heritage. Legal aspects would not enter into things, as far as Garfield was concerned. 'His lordship', to her, was not a pet name, but a title which should rightfully be his, particularly since there was no male left in the Ashleigh line. It was useless to try to instil into her that there was no way in which Charles Howard could ever be legally acknowledged by that family. Simon had tried to make her understand this, without success. The woman had closed her mind to both truth and reasoning on that point.

But enough of Garfield and the boy. Enough even of Delia, who, thank heaven, had found her feet after that unhappy period in her life. Simon had known what his daughter had endured through the attitude of her school-fellows, and never had he felt less capable of protecting her than at that time. Only by keeping her constantly aware of his love had he been able to tide her through. He rarely let his mind dwell on that unpleasant yet – as far as he was concerned – merciful chapter in their lives. It was over, Delia had emerged a somewhat quieter girl, but one who had lost none of her individuality, and he and Deborah were together at last. Many had been the times when he had despaired of such a miracle.

Now she stirred in his arms and said, 'There is only one thing I want to make life perfect – a child of our own. More than one, Simon.'

As always, the closeness of her body quickened his blood, and when her arms curled round his neck and the sweet curve of her mouth touched his, desire leapt between them with its unfailing urgency. Deborah was a passionate woman, ever responsive, seeking him as eagerly as he sought her and finding in their union total fulfilment. Forgotten were the years of her restricted upbringing and the months of despair when a life with this man seemed beyond her reach. Her cup of happiness was full, and when he led her upstairs to bed, she knew that this night she would conceive.

After fitful slumber, Delia wakened in the early hours of the morning, shocked by the realisation that the day for auditioning was here and still she had not selected her voluntary piece. Appalled, she scrambled out of bed and reached for her volume of Shakespeare. She would not choose Juliet – she was out of love with love, so definitely it would not be Juliet.

Portia, then. She was in the mood for spirited defiance and the need to put the opposite sex in its place, and Portia had done that admirably. *'The quality of mercy is not strain'd, it droppeth as the gentle rain from heaven upon the place beneath. . .'* Not that *she*, Delia Davidson, felt inclined to dispense mercy, incensed as she was by Bruce's assumption that she could be his for the taking, and by Peter's equally infuriating assumption that she might have already surrendered. But why think of Peter now? Why think of him at all? Why remember his jibes and his warnings, why imagine how gleefully he would say, 'I told you so!' were he to learn about last night? She would take good care that he never did – so forget him, and concentrate on Portia instead.

It was now five A.M. By ten she would be in the wings awaiting her call. She had no fear of the piece set by the judges, because it was sure to be something studied during the term, but when it came to her own selection, she faltered. How *did* Portia's speech continue? *'It is twice bless'd . . . .'* She had to glance at the book to recall even that line, and she had been so confident that she knew it by heart. Juliet, then? Should it be Juliet after all? The balcony scene? No! She would not acquit herself well in that, feeling as she did this morning, anything but responsive to masculine advances. Rosalind? How about Rosalind? *'Come, woo me, woo me; for now I am in a holiday humour, and like enough to consent . . .'* That would not do, either. Besides, she had not studied Rosalind enough.

Despairing, she wondered if she had studied anything enough.

She crept down to the kitchen, made some tea, and carried it back to bed. Wrapped in her eiderdown, book propped on knees, she sipped the hot liquid, and her apprehension dwindled. Portia – yes, she would definitely do Portia, and what better speech than the one on mercy? '*It is twice bless'd, it blesseth him that gives and him that takes; 'tis mightiest in the mightiest . . .* ' There! She did know it. Why was she worrying? She laid the up aside, and the book slid to the floor, but scarcely had she dozed off again than the household was astir and it w s time to get up.

She scarcely touched her breakfast and she scarcely heard the good-luck wishes everyone showered on her when she left. Even Garfield dragged herself away from Charles at the breakfast table to wish her well, and Cook was waiting in the hall with a rabbit's foot in her hand. 'They do say it brings luck, Miss Delia. I've heard tell that theatrical folk set great store by them. I've cleaned it well – no need to worry on that score.'

Delia flung her arms round the woman's neck and kissed her soundly. 'Bless you, Cookie, bless you! When I'm an actress, I'll use it for my makeup. Always. I promise!'

The rabbit's foot comforted her. She clutched it in her pocket when waiting in the wings. Her turn was a long time coming, and she grew colder and colder in the chilly area between the stage and the high brick walls beyond the flats. And oh, how tired she was! An emotional evening, an experience that had shocked her more than she realised, followed by little sleep, had left her feeling drained. She yawned frequently, and her head ached. Perhaps she had been unwise to eat so little breakfast? On the other hand, perhaps not. Feeling as she now did, she would have been sick. *Was* she going to be sick? Oh, God, I wish I were home in bed! I wish I hadn't been a fool last night, imagining myself a woman of the world dining clandestinely in Soho . . . I should have known what to expect. I've ruined my chances, I know I have.

I haven't, I haven't, every word will come to me once I step onstage . . .

Her eyelids drooped. Her head felt dizzy with fatigue. Only vaguely was she aware of voices onstage and of others in the auditorium saying, 'Thank you. Next student, please.' Then someone was calling her name from a long way off, and from behind she was given a push. 'You're *on*, Delia! Hurry, or it will go against you!'

'Delia Davidson! *Where is Delia Davidson?*'

It was the stage manager, audition sheet in his hand. 'What's the matter, Miss Davidson? Are you dreaming or something?' His tone was impatient. She stammered an apology and stumbled onstage. A single spotlight from above shone down centre, and three naked footlights focused on the same place. The pitch of the stage seemed steeper than it really was and the auditorium as dark as a cave, even though some of the houselights were on. The flickering gas jets at her feet and around the dim recesses of the auditorium floated hazily before her. She could dimly discern the judges in the stalls, and amongst them a woman's face. Miss Delmont, thank goodness! She couldn't go wrong with Miss Delmont there, looking up at her with that friendly, confident smile which always gave her courage.

One of the tutors was onstage to give her cues. He was holding out a script and saying 'Act II of *An Ideal Husband*, Miss Davidson. The scene between Lady Chiltern and Mrs Cheveley.' *That* was all right; as expected, it was a study piece from last term. She heard the character of Mason announcing Lady Markby and Mrs Cheveley, and then a voice greeting them, and was astonished to realise it was her own, because it sounded totally unfamiliar. The tutor glanced at her in surprise, then in encouragement, and she realised he was trying to help her through. That should not be necessary; the judges would notice and mark it against her. She rallied and found her natural voice, and throwing her lines across the footlights at the right moment, but with a turn of the head which was jerky and mechanical, she saw Miss Delmont's face down in the stalls, clear as in a mirror. It was no longer smiling. It was surprised, puzzled . . . Then somehow the scene was over and she was alone.

'Your chosen piece, Miss Davidson?'

'The trial scene, *Merchant of Venice*. I'm sorry, I mean Portia's speech of course.'

'Commence, please.'

The opening words came; then she realised that she was too far downstage. She should have been up centre, but did it matter? Of course it mattered; everything mattered. Movement, gesture, timing. On "Tis mightiest in the mightiest' she stumbled backward, trying to find the right position, then panicked and forgot the words. She should not have moved at all. Portia delivered her speech to the court without moving, except for gestures to emphasise her words. Wrong movements distracted from the importance of a passage. An inner voice commanded, '*Stay where you are, you idiot — pull yourself together!*' Her aching head groped for the words, found them, and by force of will she delivered them, but the continuity was destroyed.

'Thank you, Miss Davidson, that will do.'

Dismissal was abrupt, and she did not have to wait for the list of successful candidates to be posted next morning. She knew she had failed.

'What went wrong, Delia? You were not suffering from nerves. Signs of nerves are allowed for, lack of study is not.'

'I'm sorry, Miss Delmont. I was tired.'

'Tired and ill-prepared. Why?'

'Because I've been a fool. Because I was flattered by a man's attentions. Because I was overconfident and thought I could dredge it all up from memory with ease.

Because when I should have been studying I was out enjoying myself with Bruce Whitney. Because I haven't studied hard enough,' she said honestly. 'I have only myself to blame.'

Chrystal Delmont had been angry when she came backstage. Now her anger retreated. The girl had learned a lesson she would never forget, which meant that she had taken the first step in becoming a pro. She had not been wrong in her judgment of Delia, as, during those anxious moments out front, she had begun to fear.

She touched the girl's cheek compassionately. 'Go straight home and get the sleep you plainly need – and next time, don't disappoint me.'

Delia choked, 'Yes, Miss Delmont,' and turned away blindly. Outside, someone took her arm and a voice said, 'Here, use this. Those scraps women call handkerchiefs are no use – and if you need a shoulder to cry on, mine's still available.'

Peter squandered one-and-sixpence on a cab so she could take advantage of his offer. It was worth every penny, plus the tip. He had been waiting outside the building for over two hours, but he said nothing, asked no questions, and to say 'I told you so' never entered his head.

25

Delia never disappointed Chrystal Delmont again, and by 1910 she was established as a lesser actress with the Comet Theatre company.

That was the year, 1910, when King Edward died. His golden reign had lasted only nine years, and was memorable not merely for its glitter and opulence, but for its achievements, its progress in aviation, wireless communication, the cinema, motoring, and much more which was brought to fruition through his enthusiasm and determination. Behind his role of gay boulevardier he had worked as a diplomatic agent on his visits to Berlin, Paris, and St Petersburg. Mistrusting his nephew the kaiser, and more deeply aware than many of his ministers of the impending threat of war, he had finally turned to France in an endeavour to avert such a catastrophe, and achieved the *entente cordiale*, but society in the Edwardian era was concerned only with enjoying itself, with staging elaborate parties such as Krupp's, when the majolica fountain in the old courtyard of the Savoy Hotel gushed with champagne, and the Pilgrims' Club gave a dinner there to celebrate the discovery of the North Pole by Commander Peary, for which the Winter Garden was turned into a realistic illusion of snow and ice and the waiters were dressed in Eskimo furs; but the Savoy's elaborate staging was excelled when the courtyard at the back was made water-tight, flooded, and transformed into a miniature Venice, with dinner tables placed inside gondolas and covered with canopies of silken gauze. In these the diners floated, served by waiters garbed as Venetian gondoliers and serenaded by mandolinists brought over from Venice for the occasion. How could anyone be expected to heed the king's pessimism about impending war, when life could be so enjoyable?

And so this age of gaiety and frivolity went on, the extravagant parties, the eccentric dinners, the daring of women who considered feminine advancement to be achieved solely by dining with men in fashionable restaurants, wearing naked-backed evening gowns, smoking, taking lovers, and being a great deal more skilful than Caroline had ever been in adhering to the eleventh commandment. It was bad enough to be debarred, as a divorcée, from the Royal Enclosure at Ascot, but society's attitude toward her was even more marked at the famous Monte Carlo dinner at the Savoy, given by the man who broke the bank, and to which she had been surprisingly invited. Erstwhile friends cold-shouldered her, whispering behind their ostrich-feather fans that she was present only because she was having an affair with their host.

The whole evening was unfortunate for Caroline, for red was not her colour, and because the man had won on *rouge*, that was the only colour used in the decorations — the ceiling painted red for the night, red carpet on the floor, tablecloths to match, flowers also, and even the food: prawns, *queues de langouste, mousse au jambon, choux-rouges braisés*, with strawberries as the dessert. All the waiters were dressed in red, with shirts, ties, and gloves to match, and the long dining table was laid out to represent a huge roulette board, with thirty-five guests, each seated at one of the roulette numbers and the host at the number that had brought him success. 'Dante's Inferno', someone called it, and it marked Caroline's last venture into any London social affair. Women who were unwise enough to be caught breaking the most important commandment of all could do nothing but retire from the public eye and hope that time would not drag on too endlessly before the scandal of it was forgotten.

But to Delia, life was bounded by the excitement of growing up, and to the young such things as wars and rumours of wars skated over the surface of life. Progress was marked by the wooden-cased telephone in the hall – all one had to do was turn a handle to call the operator – and the electrification of underground trains which rid them of sulphurous smoke choking the lungs of passengers. Most impressive of all was the transformation of London's streets by night. No longer was it necessary for her to walk to the theatre through the half-light of gas jets and fishtail burners; shop windows were lit up, and remained so even at weekends. Brilliance replaced gloom and reduced the molestation of women on main thoroughfares, though Simon insisted on her returning by cab after an evening performance.

Sometimes Peter called to bring her home. His own work at the theatre excluded evenings, but when he was not painting in his studio, the theatre always beckoned. Their sparring continued, but without animosity, and their friendship remained alive and important to her. It was part of her background at 20 Hanover Square.

The house had indeed become a family home, Garfield now busy with the twin sons Deborah had given birth to, but still harbouring the softest spot in her heart for Miss Dulcima's boy, who was turning out to be all that Deborah expected – bright, alert, and kind. If school reports made no comment on his ability to get on with his schoolfellows, they did stress that he was above average in intelligence.

He also displayed an unusual interest in religion, and when Deborah's third child was born in October 1911, a little girl named Sarah-Dulcima, Charles even argued that he saw no reason why he should not be godfather.

'Is there anything in the prayerbook which forbids a boy of ten to be one? I have swotted up everything about a godparent's duties.'

Deborah pointed out that such responsibilities were really for adults, and the promises made by godparents had to be maintained until a child came of age. 'And as yet, you are not even confirmed.'

The next thing Charles announced was that he had talked to the vicar of St George's. 'I'm younger than average for confirmation in the Protestant church, but not in the Roman Catholic, but he sees no reason why I shouldn't be prepared for it.'

Charles's enjoyment of church services from a very early age had surprised everyone. From the time he was a toddler sitting on Deborah's knee, he had tried to join in the hymns and listened entranced when the choir sang. When other children grew restless, he remained quiet and absorbed. Being taken to church was no penance, and when Delia had yawned during the sermons, he had been fascinated by the imposing white-surpliced figure in the pulpit, even though the sermon was beyond him. The ritual, the robes, the altar, the organ music, the whole atmosphere of reverence seemed to cast a spell on him. He was never, ever bored.

So even though, at the age of ten, he was unable to stand as a youthful godfather to Sarah-Dulcima, for Peter acted in that capacity, with Delia and Chrystal as the little girl's two godmothers, he was incapable of resentment. 'Perhaps I will be godfather next time,' he said amicably, and led everyone in the hymn-singing with his clear, piping voice, was first on his knees in prayer and the last to rise, and admitted to Delia later that he thought the christening service the most beautiful of all. And he said it sitting on the grass beside some bushes in the Square gardens, slowly and deliberately pulling the wings off a sparrow.

When he saw her face blanch and her hands fly to her mouth to stifle a cry, he said with that sweet smile of his. 'Don't worry, Delia. He can't feel anything. I killed him first.'

'On no account must we tell Deborah, but what am I to *do*, Peter? He didn't pay the slightest heed when I told him it was a diabolical thing to do. All he said was, "What does 'diabolical' mean?" and when I said "Cruel, most horribly cruel," he simply argued that the sparrow couldn't have felt a thing because he killed it quickly, so that wasn't cruel! He even described how he did it. "I clutched it ever so tightly round the throat, and the beak jerked open with a squawk and the head lolled over and he was dead, so he couldn't have felt anything, could he?" Oh, Peter, he *choked* the poor little thing.'

She had raced upstairs to his studio. Ever since she had wept on his shoulder following that tragic audition, the studio had become her refuge as well as the place where she could be sure of finding a ready ear for her dreams and ambitions and disappointments and fears, her excitements and achievements, her good news as well as bad.

'It was horrible, Peter, seeing Charles with his angelic smile and the poor little strangled bird in his hands. I felt sick. And then what do you think he did? Threw it away quite casually, and began to pick clusters of veronica from a nearby bush to bring home for Deborah. He never visits the Square gardens without coming back with a small bouquet of something for her, even if it is only sprays of leaves. I can't make him out. To be honest, I'm frightened.'

Peter didn't like it either, but hid his reaction, telling her that he had read somewhere that boys had to go through a cruel phase. 'Like tying cans to the tails of puppies.'

'Did you? Go through a cruel phase, I mean?'

He couldn't honestly remember doing so, but admitted to chasing the cat round the kitchen at home.

'That's not the same thing. That's just fooling about, and I daresay the cat knew it was only a game. You are trying to reassure me, and you're not succeeding. Did you ever strangle a bird?'

'No, but I used to have a good time with a catapult, shooting into the trees to scare them off Dad's vegetables.'

'Oh, Peter, what am I to *do*?'

'Nothing, old dear. There's nothing you can do, other than tell him to stop it. *I'll* talk to him.'

He did, and Charles listened with polite interest. He really was the most courteous little devil Peter had ever met, quite unlike Peter's young brothers at his age, and when the lecture was over, Charles even thanked him. 'It is nice of you to take time away from your work,' he said, 'just to talk to me about birds.'

'I am not "just talking to you about birds"! I am talking to you about cruelty, and how wrong it is.'

'Yes, I know, and I agree. That's why I did it quickly, so the bird wouldn't suffer.'

'Why do it at all, for heaven's sake?'

'Because I enjoy it,' Charles answered simply.

'Good grief – you mean you have done it before?'

'Of course. That's why I can do it so quickly now.'

Like Delia, Peter felt sick. I can't talk to this little blighter any more, he thought, but knew he had to.

'I hope you have never let Deborah see you at it?'

Charles reflected for a moment. 'I don't think so. You mean she wouldn't like it either? Then she would tell me, wouldn't she, the way you are telling me now? Well, she never has, so that means she hasn't.'

The boy's logic left Peter bereft of words; then he burst

out, 'Listen, you little monster, if you ever frighten Deborah with this nasty trick of yours, or if you ever upset Delia again the way you upset her today, I'll tan the hide off you so you won't be able to sit down for a week. Do you hear?'

Charles looked hurt. 'You know I would never frighten Cousin Deborah, and I didn't mean to upset Delia. I can't think why she ran away like that. I *told* her –'

'I know what you told her. Now, listen to what *I* am telling *you*. Do you know what keeping a promise means?'

'Of course. It means keeping your word.'

'Exactly. So now *I* am asking *you* to promise that never again will you ill-treat a tiny harmless bird, or do anything to hurt another human being. You have a Bible of your own, I believe?'

Charles nodded proudly. 'Deborah gave me one for my last birthday.'

'Bring it to me.'

Charles rushed to fetch it. 'Look,' he said proudly, 'Deborah wrote inside –'

Peter took the Bible. 'There is something you have to learn, young Charles – that apart from promises made in church, any promise you make with your hand on the Bible is sacred and must never be broken. Understand?'

Charles nodded. 'Of course I understand.'

'Right. Then place your hand on this and make that promise I said just now. Repeat it after me, word by word.'

Charles did so. He said every word with quiet solemnity, not liking to point out that to make him promise on the Bible was not necessary. Long ago he had learned that promises were important, and never to be broken. He could remember the day quite clearly. Deborah had held his hand and stood with him beneath his mother's portrait. The picture of the lovely lady had always fascinated him, and he loved to hear about her.

From babyhood he had known she was his mother, and whenever he asked questions about her, Deborah always answered truthfully. What was my mamma like? Was she fun? Did she love me? Was she as old as you? 'Older than I,' Deborah had said, 'and the greatest fun in the world, and yes, she loved you more than anyone.'

When he was five he had asked about his father. 'Did she love me more than she loved him?' To be told that she had loved his father in a different way was very satisfactory; it was nice to feel loved in a way not shared by anyone else, and since there was no picture of his father in the house, he never existed as a person in the boy's mind.

'She was loyal, too,' Deborah had added, and explained what loyalty meant. 'When she made a promise, she never broke it.' So really, he thought now, Peter ought to know that he doesn't have to make me promise on the Bible, because if my mother kept her promises, I shall always keep mine.

26

Delia had little time in which to think about Charles's frightening behaviour, for Wilde's play *An Ideal Husband* was going into rehearsal and she was cast in her first responsible role as Mabel Chiltern, with Chrystal as the lovely Lady Chiltern. To speak Wilde's lines was sheer joy, and Delia's enthusiasm infected everyone. Even the stagehands, blasé as only stagehands can be, would emerge from their posts backstage to listen from the wings when she and Chrystal Delmont were on stage together.

Acting with Chrystal was inspiring. The woman drew the best out of her, and made no attempt to hide her pleasure over the fact that Delia showed promise of being on a par with her one day. 'She will take my place when I retire, if not before,' she commented to Peter. 'That is, if some demanding husband doesn't lure her away and put an end to her career.'

Now scenic director at the Comet, Peter never missed a rehearsal of Delia's. He would appear in the wings shortly before her cues and then return to the workshops following her exits. His sets were designed on his drawing board at home, then put into execution with his team of three — master carpenter, master joiner, and assistant scenic artist. Life was so satisfactory for both of them that such things as unrest in Europe meant no more than the newsprint which reported them. The kaiser was being tiresome. But the kaiser was always tiresome! He was over there in Germany, a long way from the Comet Theatre, and the government knew how to handle him. So did his cousin, King George V. So leave the man to them.

Time passed, and the world moved from 1912 to 1914. The season of Wilde's plays exceeded the success everyone expected, with alternating runs of *An Ideal Husband, The Importance of Being Earnest, A Woman of No Importance*, and *Lady Windermere's Fan*, but when launched into the final double bill of *Salomé* and *The Duchess of Padua*, box-office receipts fell sharply following the assassination of the Archduke Franz Ferdinand and his consort at Sarajevo on June 28, plunging the nation headlong into war the following August.

No one believed it. In the world of the theatre, reality rarely penetrated beyond the stage door. Delia was aware that her father had been following the newspapers closely and silently, but politics had never interested her, and the scaremongers who had been crying war for so long had, she believed, only been crying wolf. But now the wolf howled in earnest and darkness fell.

It won't last, everyone said. A few months, a year perhaps, but no more. But when tramping feet marched into railway termini en route for Dover and Boulogne, and lines of khaki-clad boys departed for training camps on Salisbury Plain and elsewhere, and London's streets were suddenly depleted of their young men, optimism was silenced.

The theatre management called the company onstage to listen to their leading lady.

'The theatre must *not* close,' Chrystal announced. 'Our boys will need entertaining when home on leave, but we must stage plays with a minimum of male parts. All our young actors will be called up when their age groups demand, unless medically unfit, but we must remember that a soldier home on leave wants nothing so much as the sight of actresses onstage who look as if the very thought of war has not touched them.'

Chrystal, of course, remembered the Boer War. So did Simon. But that war had been a great deal farther away than France and Belgium, and even than Germany itself.

'I have something to tell you,' said Peter. 'I have enlisted.'

'No! Oh, *no*!'

Delia's reaction took him by surprise. Women were urging their men to go to war. Kitchener's finger pointed accusingly from hoardings. '*Your Country Needs You!*' A man in civilian dress could scarcely look him in the eye. Even worse, women in the streets walked up to them, handing out white feathers. It had happened to him, and it had even happened to Simon, whose limp was scarcely noticeable now, but whose hair was grey. But what did grey hair matter? Many a soldier had grey hair.

'My husband has gone, and he's as old as you,' the woman who presented him with a white feather had taunted.

Simon had merely flicked it away and walked on, but Delia, with him at the time, had rounded on the woman furiously. 'My father fought the Boers. He was wounded by the Boers. He was in hospital for a long, long time. Do stupid women like you ever pause to think that a man may have done his bit already, and not be passed as fit for any more?' Anger had blazed in her voice and in her eyes, anger in every line of her indignant young body. 'I should think your husband enlisted just to get away from you! Go home, you cruel woman, and do something practical to help the war effort instead of roaming the streets looking for men to insult!'

Quietly Simon had turned, taken his daughter's arm, and headed for home. Later, in the studio, Delia had poured out the story to Peter, tears hot on her cheeks. He had kissed them away, but even after they had dried on his lips the taste of them remained.

It was the first time he had ever kissed her in anything but a brotherly way, and neither spoke for a long time afterwards. Her large eyes had stared at him, then fallen. She had busied herself in the cubbyhole which served him as a kitchen, making tea. She had looked everywhere but at him.

Now she looked at him directly, shock in her voice and her face.

'Why, Peter! *Why*? Your age group won't be called up yet. Please, oh please, don't go!'

The intensity of her distress surprised her. The reason for it, even more so.

He said, 'I have to. I know dozens of men of my age who

have gone already.'

'Let them – but not *you*!'

'You don't understand. The war has been going on for several months.'

'Four. That's all. Four. That's not "several".'

'It is to me. More than that. I have to go, Delia. This may be something you won't understand, but I have to go to be able to live with myself.'

'But I want you to live with *me*!'

She flung herself on him, clinging, pleading, raging. 'It's that damned Lord Kitchener poster that's done it! They are everywhere! I'll go all over London myself, ripping them down, I swear it. *Damn* Kitchener!'

He held her close. 'What was that you said? Not just now – before.'

A stifled sob was his only answer.

'Say it again,' he commanded. 'I want to hear you say it again.'

She lifted her face and repeated, 'I want you to live with me. I'm not asking you to marry me, but I do want to be with you, to mean more to you than that model of yours. You lock the door when she comes, and I know why. Well, I want that too, but for a different reason. I love you, Peter. I didn't know it until this moment, but I must have been in love with you for a very long time.'

She scarcely heard him say her name. All she heard was his incredulity and joy, and all she felt was his mouth on hers, encompassing, demanding, and the strength of his body against her own, matching her urgent desire.

Much later, cradling her, he said, 'I shouldn't have done that. I shouldn't have touched you.'

'Why not? I wanted you to.' She nestled against him. 'I could purr with contentment. What a wonderful feeling! It was all so beautiful. And now I feel glowing all over as well as deep inside me, my mind all alight with happiness.' Her fingers touched his face, tracing his features with mute gratitude. 'Such a wonderful, wonderful way to be loved . . . '

Her face lay on the pillow beside him. He saw her sparkling eyes and radiant smile. She was like a newly awakened flower, he thought, and tried to fight a feeling of guilt. It was the first time he had ever seduced a virgin, a thing he had always regarded as dishonourable. On the rebound from Deborah, he had sought forgetfulness with several women, all experienced and none meaning anything beyond physical satisfaction. Now, unbelievably, this had happened, and it mean everything in the world to him. That was why rapture had been followed by a feeling of shame. With anyone but Delia, it would not have mattered so much. With her, it mattered immeasurably.

'You were virgin,' he said. 'That is why I should not have touched you.'

'But I wanted you! Darling Peter, I had to lose my virginity sometime, and I couldn't have lost it with anyone nicer than you. I do love you, but please don't think I expect you to love me in return.'

'Good God, of course I love you! Couldn't you tell? Do you think it has ever been like that for me with anyone else? Dear, sweet Cleopatra, for a man there is a world of difference between lying with a woman and making *love* to a woman, as I have been loving you this past hour.'

'More than an hour,' she gurgled. 'Look at the clock.'

'I don't want to and I don't mean to. I want to keep you here in my bed forever, the world shut out.'

'Shall we sleep then, and make love again? I did so enjoy it, even at the beginning.'

He said anxiously, 'Did I hurt you? I tried not to.'

She pressed her soft cheek against his. 'Not so much as I expected. I've always understood that losing one's virginity was painful, but you were so gentle, so kind, and it was drowned in love so quickly.'

He kissed the tip of her nose and then the dimple beside her mouth. 'You don't know how often I have wanted to do that. The tip of your nose, and that dimple, are entrancing.'

'You haven't always found *me* entrancing.'

'Nor you, me, my dear sparring partner. But no more sparring from now on.'

'Never, never, never!'

She nestled against him, and for a time they lay without speaking, quiet and at peace; then her young blood began to stir again, and her leg slid over him, drawing him to her, the softness between her thighs close against him until passion flared again and their bodies merged once more. Dear God, how I love her! Dear God, bring me back to her! Dear God, don't let any other man touch her while I am away!'

The lovely abandonment of her body moved with his instinctively, rising and falling to his rhythm until their senses mounted on a rising crescendo which was at once urgent and yet unhurried, prolonged and yet surging. Her little moans of ecstasy seemed to come from a long way off, and yet were part of him as they soared together into a blinding burst of delight.

It was dusk when he wakened. She lay half on her side, exactly as she had fallen when he slid from her, one leg still across him, her bare breasts drooping sideways in soft domes. One was cupped in his hand, smooth and round and sensual. He hated to release it, but did so, feeling the lovely movement of it as he withdrew. He raised himself on one elbow and watched her as she slept. Very gently he stroked her, moving from the narrow waist over the curve of hip and down the firm thigh to knee and calf, then slowly up her back, marvelling at the loveliness of her. Every part of her seemed moulded in perfection. And, dear God, she was his, discovered on the eve of separation.

Surely no God could be so cruel as to end something so newly found and precious to both?

Her eyes opened. Her lips smiled. He said, 'Someday I am going to paint you, lying here as you are now. And we must be married, my darling, before I do. It is terribly important to me that we marry.'

For a moment he thought his words had not penetrated the mists of her sleep, for she lay looking up at him, not speaking. Then she whispered, 'Before you go? But it won't be yet, will it? It won't be for ages yet? They don't whisk you away the moment you have enlisted, surely?'

'Sweetheart, I enlisted some time ago. I didn't tell you or anyone until my papers came this morning. I leave for a training camp on Salisbury Plain tomorrow afternoon.'

Getting a special licence proved impossible. When the shops opened next morning, they were already at a jeweller's, waiting for the doors to open, and then, armed with a narrow gold band, and a broader one which Delia insisted on buying for him, they found the nearest regi-strar's office, where they were faced with queues of young men and women, all pressured by imminent separation into a desperate need to belong together, to make a bid for permanency in a threatening world.

'Come back tomorrow,' the clerk said. 'There aren't enough application forms to go round. We may have a fresh supply by then. But don't forget,' he added to their crestfallen faces, 'marry in haste and repent at leisure. Too many young people are rushing into it, if you ask me.'

I'm not asking you, Peter wanted to say, and this isn't a hasty thing. We have known each other for years, and couldn't know each other better. But he said nothing, taking Delia's arm and turning away, sick with dis-appointment.

'And it won't be much use trying elsewhere,' the clerk

called after them. 'Wherever you apply, one of you at least has to be resident in the area, and special licences are expensive.' He sounded as if he enjoyed frustrating young love.

Outside, Delia said, 'Darling, it doesn't matter. I said you didn't have to marry me.'

'I *want* to. It is important. I want to go away knowing you are my wife.'

'I feel I am already. Won't that do?'

'No. I want you to belong to me both legally and in the eyes of God.'

Delia halted. They were walking up Hanover Street toward the square, and ahead of them stood St George's Church. At this hour of the morning it would be quiet, perhaps even deserted except for a cleaner or two, and it wouldn't matter in the least if they looked on. Perhaps they would even smile and give them their blessing. . . .

'Peter . . . let's marry ourselves. Let's go to church this very minute, and make our vows, and surely God will hear us and bless us, and that will be as real and sacred as anything could be.'

The church was empty. They knelt before the altar, holding a prayerbook between them, and quietly read the important parts of the marriage service, and exchanged their vows, and placed their bright new rings on each other's fingers, then said the Lord's Prayer together. The light from the high window above the altar shone down on them, and a ray of sunshine touched their upturned faces. It was like a benediction, sanctifying their union.

The Comet Theatre was one of the few to remain open throughout the war, playing to spasmodic houses and barely paying its way. Everyone in the company took cuts in salary, for it was better to be in work than out of it. By the end of the first year all stagehands had been replaced by older and less active men, and the cast kept scenery painted and repaired, with the aid of an aged carpenter, long since pensioned off. Even the wardrobe mistress had left to work in munitions, and the company had to care for their own costumes.

The first rush of patriotic enthusiasm for the war had diminished; optimism and a display of confidence had become forced. Wars in living memory had been conveniently far away, but this one raged only on the other side of the English Channel, where gunfire roared and shells blasted men to bits in the trenches. Pessimists began to predict that it could even last another year, and when that passed and reversal followed reversal, voices that had scoffed at Kitchener's prediction of a three-year war were silenced for good. And white feathers had ceased to be handed out on the streets.

Delia's first confrontation with the horror of it all came within the first twelve months, when she saw, across the footlights, a group of wounded soldiers who were sufficiently convalescent to be brought by ambulances to the theatre. Some were in wheelchairs, some had crutches propped between their seats, all seemed to make up a pattern of white bandages and the bright blue of 'disability' uniforms. Many faces were almost unseen behind their dressings, and empty sleeves were pinned neatly out of the way. Later, when the group was brought backstage and served with refreshments supplied by the cast, the spectacle was even worse.

They were nothing but boys, some below the call-up age of eighteen. Some admitted to faking their ages in order to fight for King and Country. Some would never walk again, see again, use hands or arms again. Delia knelt beside the wheelchair of a boy whose face was so heavily bandaged that he had seen nothing of the play. Only his mouth was exposed, and to this she held a glass, thankful he could not see the tears that blinded her. Then someone began to play the piano down in the orchestra pit: 'Pack Up Your Troubles', 'Tipperary', 'Keep the Home Fires Burning'. It was almost more than she could bear. And any one of these men could be Peter, who had been posted overseas very quickly.

His letters came regularly, always cheerful, always hopeful of leave. He had had a brief twenty-four hours before embarkation; no time in which to get married, but time enough to be together. Now he wrote, 'I should think that within a few weeks we'll get a spell, then we'll see about those marriage lines for you,' to which she had answered, 'Darling, marriage lines couldn't possibly make me belong to you more than I already do. I don't care a fig about marriage lines!'

'That's all very well, dear heart,' he had replied, 'but if anything should happen to me, marriage lines will be essential in claiming your war widow's pension. It is important to me to provide for you in *some* way.'

That had sent her heart lurching. She had drowned her fear in work, and now she was face to face with these butchered men, valiantly singing their war songs to drown the memory of recent horrors and the fear of going back to the stench of death, to bodies blown to pieces in trenches knee-deep in mud, to the screech of shells, and the explosion of bombs obliterating men who, moments before, had been cracking jokes to keep up their spirits. Beneath bandages, she saw eyes that had looked on death and were haunted by the memory of it.

'Chrystal, I can't go on like this, comfortably acting at the Comet.'

'Comfortably? I thought we were all finding it extremely *un*comfortable.'

'You know what I mean. Those boys out front last night – trying to make them forget was not enough. Nor did we really succeed.'

'I know what you mean.' Chrystal's hand touched hers. 'I have been expecting something like this, knowing you as I do. You want to do something more active. You don't feel you are doing your bit just by entertaining men on leave, so I suppose it is useless for me to try to persuade you that what we are doing here at the Comet is valuable in its way.'

'I know it is – in its way. But it can't be my way any more. I can be replaced with another actress easily. Many are available, with so many theatres closed. But hospitals are crying out for help. I am volunteering as a VAD. Did you know those boys had been prematurely discharged from hospitals to convalescent homes because their beds were needed? Every day, the wounded are arriving from the front in shiploads. And it is getting worse. Any day, one of them might be Peter, and I would be eternally grateful to any nurse who cared for him, and think how much more worthwhile her job was than mine. So back me up, Chrystal, when I tell the management I am leaving. If I stay, I shall be repeating my lines parrot fashion, uttering words which have no meaning for me, standing on the sidelines while other people do the real work, the useful work.'

It was drudgery at first. The menial tasks, the degrading tasks, the filthy tasks. She did them all, returning home, after long spells of duty, so white and tired that Deborah became worried. Delia drove herself relentlessly, refusing to go off duty if another batch of wounded arrived and nursing staff was inadequate. But nursing staff was always inadequate, and male nurses unobtainable, except for older men like Simon, who worked part-time at their jobs by day and did voluntary hospital work afterwards. Bruce Whitney had headed for home on the outbreak of war, receiving a letter from his father saying, 'There'll be plenty of damaged ships being towed into these docks for repair, and an administrative job in the office will keep you out of the forces. . . .'

He wrote to Delia once or twice, but gave up when she failed to reply.

Even Deborah spared time from caring for three children and running a home to give two afternoons a week to tasks for the wounded -- writing letters for them, reading to them, holding the hands of those who were past hearing or talking, so they would know they were not alone, wiping foreheads beaded with sweat, lifting the injured to sip from the spout of an invalid cup, or sitting silently beside them until they found merciful oblivion at last. Then she would walk home feeling drained, and Garfield would take one look at her and put the kettle on at once, shooing away the twins and the bubbling Sarah-Dulcima. ('A minx if ever there was one, that one is!')

Peter's letters ceased, and Delia was plunged into weeks of anguish, dreading the knock of the telegraph boy, which had become all too familiar in hundreds of homes. None came, but neither did his letters. Her life seemed to exist in a vast emptiness, haunted by dread, least of which was the fear that he had met someone else – a French girl, or an English nurse, perhaps. That would be better than his death, however painful it might be to herself. Then back would come that certainty that he was as loyal to her as she was to him, that he loved her and would die loving her – but not yet, dear God, not yet! Not until they had lived out their lives together.

She volunteered for overseas duty, asking particularly to be sent to France, cherishing some remote hope that if she were there she might find him. Her application was rejected on the grounds of insufficient experience and the fact that no more nurses could be spared from her present hospital. So back she went to the loneliness of waiting, the empty silence, the haunting dread, the fruitless waiting for the postman, who never brought what she prayed for. Torture and despair, hope and prayer . . . and the aching void that seemed never-ending.

Then came the unexpected sight of her father walking into the ward one day. 'Matron gave me permission to see you . . . ' A paper in his hand. A white paper. Too big for a telegraph. A letter perhaps – an official letter? She swayed, and her father's arm steadied her.

'Hold on, my love – it's from the Red Cross. A list of prisoners of war. It takes time to trace them . . . but Peter is safe. He's wounded and in a prison hospital just now. When he is fit enough, he will join the rest of his fellow prisoners. The camp number and address are here. At least you will be able to write.'

Peter – a prisoner of war. For the duration. Safe, but not writing to her. Why not? Mixed with relief because he was safe was a new alarm.

By 1916 the need for convalescent homes was acute, and Delia went down to Kingsmere to visit her mother. After her parents' divorce she had paid duty visits, from which she had always returned with a feeling of relief mixed with bewilderment, for her mother's attitude baffled her. Caroline seemed to regard Deborah and Simon as the sinners, and herself as the tragically misjudged scapegoat. Even Grandmamma commented on this. 'Not that I hold any brief for your father and that woman of his, but I daresay they are better suited to each other, and now you are grown up, I can tell you quite frankly, Delia, that I have never been able to understand my own daughter.'

After Grandmamma's death in 1912, Delia's career had put an end to these duty visits, and no pressing invitation to renew them came from Caroline, but now Delia arrived unannounced and came straight to the point.

'The country desperately needs more convalescent hospitals, Mamma, and Kingsmere would make an excellent one. Just look at it – all these bedrooms unoccupied! All these reception rooms which could be put to better use, and all these grounds for wounded soldiers to recover in! What do you *do* with your time here? I see you even manage to have servants.'

'Precious few, I'd have you know. The mere remnants of former staff, all too old to be much use. Servants are impossible nowadays. So independent. Within a week or two of war being declared, all the young men had volunteered, and all the maids were off to work in munition factories. The ingratitude! They needn't think I shall take them back when it is over, and so I told them in no mean terms.' (Good gracious, she sounded just like Grandmamma!) 'As for what I *do*, I would have you know that I contribute nobly to the war effort. Three times a week I have the women of the village here to sew and knit for the soldiers – socks and scarves and mittens, also gloves and Balaclava helmets, for which I buy endless supplies of khaki wool, plus yards and yards of foul-smelling muslin for antivermin underwear, so you can imagine how much I spend out of my own pocket. On top of this, I organise parcels for the Red Cross, *and* supply produce from the kitchen gardens to those religious fanatics who have taken over the old manor house at Fenfield for precisely the purpose you expect me to hand over Kingsmere. Isn't that enough?'

'No. Playing the role of Lady Bountiful doesn't seem much of an effort to me. And what religious fanatics are you talking about?'

'Some weird sect or other, led by a man who was once a doctor and still practises as such. I suspect they are conscientious objectors who have managed to escape arrest by serving the war effort in this way. They are deeply religious, I understand, and dedicated to serving humanity, which is fine, of course, though I do think there is something peculiar about men who choose to be monks. Not that this lot are real monks. I understand they are of mixed faiths, belong to no traditional order, and they don't shave their heads or wear those silly little skullcaps, but they do go around in robes and sandals. This doctor – his name is Sanderson – started the whole thing and won quite a lot of followers. Now I hear there are goups in other parts of the country. They must get money from some- where, because they built their own chapel in the manor grounds, and replaced the wrought-iron gates with big, solid, studded ones which make me think, "Abandon life, all ye who enter here!" whenever I deliver vegetables and fruit – for which, I might add, I make no charge. You see how much I do and how I demean myself, loading up Mamma's old dogcart with the stuff and driving with it to their gates and ringing the heavy iron bell just like any servant. Never did I think that a mistress of Kingsmere would stoop to do anything so menial. Lady Bountiful, indeed! You should show more respect, my dear, for someone who is doing more than her bit for this horrid war.'

'Fenfield Manor isn't very large. It can't accommodate many wounded. Kingsmere would be much better. I think you should approach this Dr Sanderson and offer to co-operate. If you don't want to, I will.'

'Don't be ridiculous, Delia. One doesn't call on men like that.'

'Why not? Have they put up a notice saying 'Women, Keep Out'? If you are taking vegetables while I'm on leave from the hospital, I'll come with you, but I have only forty-eight hours.'

'What hospital? Don't tell me you are one of these VADs, carrying bedpans and doing unmentionable tasks?'

'That, and more besides. And like every other hospital, we are over-crowded, desperately in need of beds, and being forced to discharge patients before they are fit to go. We try to get them into convalescent homes, and mercifully, more and more country-house owners are offering them. I hope you will do the same. If you don't, the place may be requisitioned, and you won't have any say in the matter.'

Her mother said sulkily that she might think about it. 'Only *might*, mark you, for I'm not sure that you are telling the truth about this requisitioning.' She shrugged the matter aside and asked what in heaven's name Delia had done to her hair. 'It looks frightful.'

'It is called a bob. I cut it myself, but one of the nurses trimmed the uneven edges for me. There is scarcely a working woman today who hasn't cut her hair. It is practical, easy to cope with, and fits snugly under a nurse's cap or factory headgear. Nurses don't have time to spend coiling and pinning up their hair at five in the morning. Even plaiting takes up too much time before charging down to the wards to wash the men and attend to their needs before racing on to the ward kitchens to collect their breakfast trays. And I'm willing to bet that the bob remains fashionable after the war.'

'I pray not. It is most unfeminine. Nothing becomes a woman so well as a good head of hair, and nothing displays it so well as a splendid hat. You'll be telling me next that women are dispensing with those!'

'Some are. Busy women are even appearing on the streets without hats and coats *and* gloves occasionally.'

'I don't know what the world is coming to,' Caroline complained, sounding more like her mother than ever. She continued to grumble throughout dinner, served by aging Mrs Parker, now forced to accept the lowly position of cook-housekeeper. She grumbled about rationing, despite the plentiful stock of fruit and vegetables from Kingsmere's gardens and orchards, and eggs and dairy produce from the few remaining home farms. She grumbled about shortages, about the incivility of shop-keepers, about the mess the village women left behind after their knitting and sewing sessions. ('Fluff and threads all over the place, and they don't even notice, let alone care – nor do they appreciate the privilege it is to spend their time in such a place as this. One even had the impertinence to ask what on earth I did with so many spare rooms!') And finally she grumbled because Delia had left the stage to become a nurse.

'I would have expected you to frown on my becoming an actress, just as Grandmamma did.'

'Why? It is becoming quite respectable nowadays. Look at Sybil Thorndike – I understand she is a clergy-man's daughter. Of course, had you become a flashy chorus girl, I would never have approved, but the Comet company has a good reputation, thanks to Miss Delmont's influence. Not that I have cause to like that woman, but I am charitable enough to believe that the part she played in my past unhappiness was entirely inadvertent. So how you could turn your back on a promising career, I cannot imagine, but I don't suppose your father tried to dissuade you.'

'You are right, he didn't. He knew exactly how I felt. He has been very understanding about everything, and so has Deborah. Sorry, Mamma. I don't suppose you like my mentioning her, but she is part of my life as well as Father's. They even understood about Peter and me, and said we can have the whole of the first floor, the one Miss Delmont occupied, when he returns from the war. It has a small kitchen, plus bathroom and everything we need, and will make a lovely home.'

'And who is Peter? It sounds as if you plan to marry him.'

Delia held out her left hand.

'Good gracious, you *are* married! Why didn't you write and tell me? As always, of course, I am ignored. Well, girl, well? Who is this Peter, and what is his full name?'

'Peter Maynard. He is – was – scenic director at the Comet, but when he is demobbed, which won't be until the end of the war, because he is a prisoner of the Germans, he plans to start his own scenic studios with his service gratuity.'

'Peter Maynard? The name sounds familiar. Wasn't he the artist inhabiting an attic in that house?'

Delia nodded, checking a smile.

'Well, I must say I am glad your grandmother isn't alive to hear this. She had such plans, such hopes for you. A title, at the very least. And now you are plain Mrs Maynard.'

'Not yet, Mother.'

'What do you mean? That is surely a wedding ring you are wearing?'

'Yes. And Peter put it on my finger, and I put one on his, in church. We also exchanged marriage vows, except that there was no priest to hear them. We married our-selves, you see. There wasn't time to do it any other way.'

'I never heard anything so ridiculous! You are not married at all!'

'In our eyes, we are. Particularly in mine. Peter was determined that it should all be done legally after the war.'

And why did I say *was* determined? she wondered with a now familiar lurch of apprehension, for Peter's silence had been maintained, her letters unanswered. There seemed only one possible explanation for this – that he had ceased to love her, or had met someone else. This dread thought haunted her life, an ever-present under-current of pain.

Caroline declared, 'I am shocked that a daughter of mine should live with a man to whom she is not married. I suppose you *have* lived together?'

'If by that you mean have we been to bed together, the answer is yes. And after we had gone to St George's, we went straight home and told Father and Deborah. I think they were touched by our going to church like that, alone, making our vows. They gave us their blessing, and Peter's father has done the same. I visit him whenever I can – he is a darling. I hoped you would give us your blessing too. And forgive me, Mamma, but I don't really think you, of all people, can condemn me for sleeping with a man I am not married to. And now I am off to bed, and I hope you will think over my suggestion about Kingsmere and put the place to good use before it is requisitioned, as I am quite sure it will be. It is happening already to other places.'

In the morning her mother agreed, stipulating that she should retain her own wing and declaring that when the war ended she would claim good financial compensation and the restoration of any damage, and she made sure that the news of her latest patriotic act circulated through the district. People had never been quite the same toward her since that horrible divorce. Local society had cold-shouldered her. Invitations to the best houses had ceased. Her mother had become a recluse at the dower house and she herself had been forced into a solitary existence here at Kingsmere.

In time, the whispering had ceased, though no doubt the scandal was remembered throughout the country and beyond – but she could afford to ignore everyone because she was mistress of Kingsmere and, as Delia put it, Lady Bountiful of the neighbourhood. She enjoyed patronising the women doing the khaki knitting; she enjoyed being seen driving to Fenfield Manor with a generous supply of produce for the soldiers those eccentric men were looking after, and she now enjoyed making the grand gesture of offering Kingsmere as a convalescent hospital for the wounded.

Delia wrote to Dr Sanderson:

You may have heard that my mother has offered
Kingsmere to the government for use as a convalescent
hospital. I understand you have put Fenfield Manor to
similar use, but knowing the manor from childhood, I
feel you must have limited accommodation. All but one
wing of Kingsmere will be in use, and I have obtained
provisional release to serve there as sister-in-charge
until I can be spared to return to my base hospital in
London.

If you feel that co-operation between us would be
beneficial, perhaps by transferring patients when you
are in need of beds, I am sure the medical authorities
would agree. I am preparing a report on accommodation and facilities at Kingsmere and could include any
suggestions you care to make.

Dr Sanderson replied:

Dear Miss Davidson,

We accommodate here a maximum of thirty
specialised patients who cannot be treated in a general
hospital, but my fellow servers and I gladly offer co-
operation in any other way we can. Some of our
members, like myself, have medical qualifications, and
we have trained others of our community on the nursing side. You may find yourselves in need of male
nurses, since they are in short supply, and in that we
can give part-time help.

Meanwhile, I must mention that we are a group of
practical men, dedicated to serving God through
humanity, thereby remaining part of the world and
segregating ourselves only by our vows. I mention this
to clear any misconceptions.

By which, thought Delia, you mean you are not a bunch of religious fanatics hiding from reality. That pleased her.

Kingsmere was well established as a hospital for the war-wounded by the time Charles reached his sixteenth birthday in 1917. On the morning of that day Garfield said to him tentatively, 'Master Charles, have you ever wondered who your father was?'

'Sometimes, but I have never asked because I felt that if Cousin Deborah wanted to tell me, she would, and since she has always refrained, I concluded that telling me would cause her pain, and this is something I could not bear to inflict on a woman like Deborah.'

To Garfield, there was nothing pompous or pedantic about the way in which her young master spoke, and she would have been astonished to learn that his schoolfellows regarded him as a prig and a bore. She was impressed by his grown-up manner of speech and said admiringly, 'You're an unusual young man, and no mistake. Many born in your circumstances would have been demanding the truth years ago.'

'But I guessed it years ago. I am a bastard. How else would my surname be that of my mother? She was Deborah's aunt, which makes me Deborah's cousin, and Howard was the maiden name of Deborah's mother, Sarah. Sarah and Dulcima were sisters, which is why Sarah-Dulcima is called after them. Many sons of kings have been bastards, and they couldn't help it any more than I could. You don't have to explain anything to me, Garfield, though I appreciate your interest. As for my father, I have never wanted to know about him because he was a sinner, and God disapproves of sinners, so *I* disapprove of my father. You know your Bible as well as I, so I am sure you should understand my not wishing to bear a sinner's name.'

There goes Preacher Howard, his schoolfellows would have said, shunning him as they always did, but Garfield said admiringly, 'Master Charles, you take the wind out of my sails, that you do, though I've always known you to be an intelligent young man. I don't say that what your mother and his lordship did wasn't wrong, but it was quite common in society and still is, though secretly, of course. So if you condemn your father, you condemn your mother too.'

'Indeed not. She was used for an unscrupulous man's pleasure and no doubt cast aside. But why do you refer to him as "his lordship"?'

'Because that is what he was. Lord Ashleigh. Lord Justin Ashleigh, and high time it is that you knew, because by rights, in my opinion, you should be his heir.'

For the first time, the cool young man's composure was shattered. His face paled, then flushed, then paled again. 'You mean Delia's uncle, the one who was drowned? *The one who committed suicide?*' The thought of having a father who had taken his own life, and therefore did not qualify for burial in hallowed ground, was a greater shock to him than the confirmation of his own illegitimacy. He could bear the latter stigma as a misfortune shared with many others, and the private picture he cherished of his unfortunate mother's abused innocence even lent a touch of romantic drama to it, but to be the son of a man like Justin Ashleigh, of whose reputation he had heard whispers from Cook, and whose death, the woman had hinted, had always been open to doubt, made him feel sullied and unclean.

'He came here the night Bella was murdered,' the woman had once told him, 'and within a couple of days he was gone too. You won't remember Bella; she was housemaid here, and no better than she should've been, and I only know Lord Ashleigh was here because she came downstairs and told me. That was the night Miss Deborah closed the card salon, and Bella was all aflutter with the news. She'd seen Lord Ashleigh on his way out, and mighty angry he looked, she said. Then she went off in search of Dillon, the butler, and little did I dream that was the last time I was ever to see the poor creature. And a few days later Lord Ashleigh's body was found floating in the lake at Kingsmere. Slipped on the bank, they said, but I should've thought the owner of such a place would have known what spots to avoid. . . . '

Now Garfield said briskly, 'He didn't commit suicide, Master Charles, and don't you even think it. The verdict was accidental death, and rightly.'

But what the boy said about his mother being cast aside by the man was true enough. His young lordship had uncanny perception in some ways, and sometimes Garfield found it very strange, coming from a boy of sixteen. It's all that religion, she reflected. Had too much of it, he has, though it's never been drummed into him overmuch.

Church attendance had been no more than average in this household, even though Miss Deborah was a clergyman's daughter (an ordinary clergyman, never a bishop, as Garfield had found out long ago), so for a child to be attracted by the psalm-singing and ceremony, the robes and the chanting, seemed to indicate that it was really in his blood; not a bit like the average child, and not a bit like the average sixteen-year-old either, but Charles had always been way above average, in Garfield's opinion. In the circumstances, she had not been in the least surprised by his announcement about entering the Church, and though Miss Deborah and her husband had declared that he would no doubt change his mind later on, Garfield knew that this young man wasn't given to changing his mind. When he said a thing, he meant it. When he made a promise, he kept it. And when he wanted something, he went right after it and got it in the end.

Cook used to say she'd never understand him, but Cook had been a fool. '*I* think he's all mixed up,' the woman had said, to Garfield's indignation. She had given Cook the sharp edge of her tongue at that, but the woman had shrugged and said, 'You know what I mean. He's . . . wotya call it? All contrarilike. One minute you feel he's one thing, and the next he's another. Contradictory. That's the word for Master Charles.'

Well, if he was, perhaps he took after his mother in that respect, for Miss Dulcima had often been contradictory. Look at that trip to Brighton, years ago, when she had sent Garfield to Whiteley's to buy a good holland dust coat for travelling in, not stinting on the cost, yet made her travel back third-class. Lavish with one hand, cheese-paring with the other. Often it had hurt. Garfield found she could now look back at her beloved mistress without the intensity of grief she had once felt, because all her love had been lavished on her son instead. And here he was, being cheated out of his heritage. In looks, in bearing, and in manner he was every inch the gentleman, and if anyone should be lording it at Kingsmere, it was he.

Now he said thoughtfully, 'Isn't Kingsmere the Ashleigh home, the place where Delia's mother lives?'

'That's right, and if Lord Ashleigh had had the decency to marry your mother, you would have been his heir. A right shame it is, that you should be done out of things just because he wouldn't give you his name, especially since there's no one left in the male line. When Miss Delia inherits, as she will after her mother, there'll never be another Ashleigh to keep the family name going, and it has been associated with Kingsmere since the sixteenth century. One of the great houses of Sussex, it is. I admit I never cared much for his lordship, but it's sad to see a famous name die out. Of course, there's nothing to stop you from changing yours by deed poll, or whatever they call it. Anyone can do that, I believe. But I understand it wouldn't give you Kingsmere.'

Charles said vehemently, 'I wouldn't want it. What would I do with a place like that? If it is one of the great houses of Sussex, it must be enormous.'

'It is. A kingdom on its own, as you might say.'

'Then apart from not wanting it, I couldn't possibly afford it, nor do I want to change my name from Howard.' His reactions were under control now; he was his cool self again. 'I am sorry you told me, though I know you meant well.'

He left her then and went across to the Square gardens, his secret refuge all his life. When a child, they had seemed large; now they seemed small. He also remembered how he used to watch the birds, stalking them and sometimes catching them, and feeling the softness of their feathery bodies in his hands and the sharp crunch of their necks as ne broke them. He could remember how they used to squawk, and how the sound wasn't very pleasant because it made him sad. He would tell them how sorry he was. 'Next time, I'll do it quicker, and then you'll hardly feel it.'

But that pleasure had to stop, because Delia and Peter told him not to do it. Peter had even made him promise on the Bible, which, looking back, he now considered insulting, a slight on his honour, but he had never injured another bird. Actually, he had found small kittens even lovelier to touch and much easier to catch. The mews had been the place for that. Cats were kept in stables to catch mice, and they were always having kittens. He had seen the first cluster of sleepy-eyed furry creatures when he was about six, and been enchanted by them. The jobmaster who had taken over the coach house and stables of 20 Hanover Square had had a big fat, friendly wife who always welcomed him when he went down there through the garden at the back of the house. There was a door leading into the stables, and he would knock on it, and her head would appear at the window high above.

'Lift up the latch and walk in, as the wolf said to Red Riding Hood!' she would call merrily. 'And come up the loft ladder to my kitchen – I've some hot scones straight out of the oven.'

Now the jobmaster had been called up, and so had his stable lad, and his wife had gone to join her sister in Essex for the duration, and they had given their cat away long ago, so no more kittens were born in the straw down there. But that day, when he was six, he had gazed at a bunch of beautiful little creatures, mewing helplessly, and loved them so much that he wanted to stroke them forever. The jobmaster's wife had let him pick them up, and he had loved helpless little kittens ever since, but never harmed them until after he made that promise to Peter, which had said 'never again to ill-treat a tiny harmless bird or do anything to hurt another human being'. There had been no mention of any other creature, so when his fingers sank into the soft fur of a kitten's neck and he felt its purring go right though his fingertips, he had experienced an excitement which made him giddy and breathless – until one writhed and scratched him so savagely that he had dropped it with a cry of pain and, for the first time he could remember, felt so wild with anger that he wanted to hurt the creature, really *hurt* it, because to be jolted out of such a moment of ecstasy was a terrible shock.

But with the coming of the war, and his school evacuating to the country when the zeppelin raids began, his visits to the stables had ended. Most of them stood empty now, the horses gone and carriages abandoned to collect dust, and mice no doubt running all over the place because there were no cats on the premises any more. But at school in the country there were several cats, and once – but only once, because he had nearly been expelled for it – he had played with a small kitten for nearly an hour, hiding in the woods while the other boys were playing cricket (sports of any kind never appealed to him) caressing the little creature's neck until its purring stirred that almost forgotten excitement and he closed his eyes and surrendered to it. Such a tiny neck, such a soft, beautiful little neck! Both hands had closed about it, tighter and tighter, and the sensation was so delicious that he could not hear the kitten's helpless, choking cry. Only the sports master had heard that, running into the woods to retrieve a cricket ball which Clarke Major had sent crashing beyond the boundary.

The next thing Charles had felt was a stinging box on the ears and the sports master dragging him out of the woods by the scruff of his neck, shaking him and calling him a sadistic little swine. Charles had cried unashamedly, and mercifully his tears had been mistaken for shame and contrition, so he didn't let on that he was crying because he had been jolted violently out of the most delicious excitement.

He didn't like boarding school. He made few friends. He always longed to get back home, because everyone there loved him, so it was easy to love them in return. He was always sure of a welcome in the kitchen, where Garfield sat beside the enormous kitchen range, her feet out-thrust to the warm glow, and Delia, before his school had evacuated and he became a boarder, would help him with his homework and spend any amount of time with him (though not so much after the incident of the bird).

And Cousin Deborah was always pleased to see him. She had taken the place of his mother, but never let him forget that his own mother was the beautiful Dulcima Howard, of whom he had every right to be proud. Even after her own children were born, she still paid as much attention to him, making him feel that she loved him as much as her own children. Simon, of course, had always been kind, even if he did look a bit anxious when hearing that he wanted to enter the Church. 'A man must be absolutely sure that a religious vocation is the right one for him. I should wait until you are older before you really decide.' Unnecessary advice, though Charles would never be so impolite as to tell him so. He had always known what he wanted to do in life, and still did.

The old man who swept the gardens was still employed there. He had been old when Charles was small, and now he was bent and gnarled like an ancient tree. Impulsively Charles dipped into his pocket and pulled out half a crown. 'You look cold, Billings. Buy yourself something hot to drink.'

The old man took the coin with a trembling hand. 'Gawd bless yer, young sir, Gawd bless yer.'

'And God bless you,' said Charles benevolently, then asked how long Billings had worked in the gardens. 'I have seen you here all my life, or so it seems.'

Billings peered closer. 'Blimey, I'd never've recognised yer, sir, so growed-up y'are! 'Course I remembers yer, now I see them eyes, though I must say I useter steer clear o' yer. The way y' useter catch them birds fair gave me the creeps, if y'll fergive me sayin' so, sir. A real little varmint fer the birds, y' were. 'Course I niver told on yer, though I useter feel p'raps I oughta, next time I saw yer mum or that big sister, but I were afraid o' losin' me job, an' I'd kept me mouth shut about many a thing I'd seen in this 'ere garden – like the married gent from number fourteen who useter meet the daughter o' the 'ouse from thirty-nine and take 'er into the bushes. Shockin' things went on in the dark afore the war, sir. Now all the blokes are in the army and I don't 'ave the worries I useter. I'd search the plice every mornin', 'case somethin' were lyin' around as no little 'un oughta see. Worst of all, o' course, was that no-good 'ousemaid as were done to death in them there bushes. Strangled, she were, but some said she arsked fer it, but a'norrible sight she were, all the sime. Fair turned me stummick, it did. So a little 'un catchin' birds an' torturin' 'em weren't nithin' compared wi' that. "Gotta get it outta 'is systim," I'd tell meself. "Boys will be boys," as the sayin' goes, an' I dessay you did get it outta your systim, didn'tya, sir?"

His voice echoed after Charles's retreating figure. He wished he had not gone into the gardens now, and if that old man were around, he would take good care not to, in future, because reminding him about the birds, in the same breath as talking about a woman being strangled, was strangely frightening. He wanted to put as much space as possible between the old man, the Square gardens, and himself—and that was when he decided to go down to Sussex and find this place called Kingsmere. Just out of curiosity, of course. The place wouldn't mean anything to him, and whatever Garfield's views, he wanted nothing belonging to his sinner of a father. His mother had left him the house in Hanover Square, and Simon and Deborah had told him long ago that when he came of age they would either move out or buy the property from him, whichever he wished, but meanwhile they would continue to run it and maintain it and meet all the costs. Naturally, he would never hear of their leaving. In his eyes, it belonged to them as much as to himself, since they had spent so much on it all these years.

But to take a look at Kingsmere, perhaps even explore the grounds if he could — why not? And of course it would be nice to see Delia, who was now sister-in-charge there. That made an excellent excuse for calling.

27

Delia had been retained permanently at the Kingsmere Recuperation Hospital, as it was now called, where every bed was filled the moment patients were discharged. She and the minimal nursing staff were thankful for help from the religious servers of Fenfield Manor, plus a few young women from the village who worked as ward maids. Two or three of the Fenfield monks came daily, shedding their robes for white gowns and doing the more harrowing tasks that many a man was sensitive about a woman doing for him, also to lift those who were helplessly crippled into their wheelchairs or carry them outside for fresh air. To call the place a home for convalescents, or even a re-cuperative base, was a misnomer, for many patients would not be at the really convalescent stage for a long time to come. But the beauty of Kingsmere, with its undulating acres and quiet peace, was something every man marvelled over. It was like reaching heaven after journeying through hell.

Casting her mind back, Delia found it difficult to recall Kingsmere as it had once been. Her childhood here seemed remote and unreal, her uncle's crowded house parties impossible to conjure up. Had these rooms, now filled with hospital beds, ever echoed with the shrill, arti-ficial voices of overdressed women, self-indulgent dilet-tanti, and social parasites? Had the endless bedrooms, which now housed three or four beds to a room, really been the settings for casual love affairs, and had the long reception rooms on the ground floor, now turned into wards for the severely handicapped, once been the setting for lavish dinner parties and receptions?

And had lines of black-and-white housemaids, streamers flying from their frilly caps, really hurried along the lengthy corridors bearing jugs of hot water, and then back again with breakfast trays, and had beels really rung impatiently, bringing ladies' maids on the trot because milady was incapable of dressing herself? And was she, in this year of 1917, in her starched uniform with a large red cross on the front, really that long-ago child who had watched Deborah Yorke approaching along the gallery, pretending to be interested in the family portraits to cover her reluctance to go downstairs? Now a hundred years seemed to have passed, and Kingsmere's past with them. And what of the future? Would the place have a future? Would *she* have a future?

She could picture none without Peter, whose silence had been maintained, a silence which could now be interpreted in only one way — he did not want to write, which meant he did not want the letters she continued to send, but nothing in the world could stop her from doing so, because reaching out to Peter kept her going in the back-breaking, heartbreaking routine of her present existence. 'If you have stopped loving me, I shan't complain,' she wrote, 'but until you tell me so, I shall go on writing and hoping.' She prayed too, very often, but did not tell him that. 'Whatever has happened to make your feelings change, don't tell me yet if you don't want to, but I must know someday, sometime. . . .' After that, she kept strictly to everyday things, news of her family, news of the theatre, which she gleaned every now and then from Chrystal, news of how civilians were enduring wartime life in Britain, news of anything and everything to foster her illusion that he was still interested enough to read her letters.

She knew he had been discharged from the prison hospital, because his father had let her know. Relatives of wounded prisoners received formal reports of progress or change, and Peter's father had written to her the moment he heard that his son had been transferred to ordinary prison quarters. 'These official notifications are so damned impersonal,' he wrote. 'All I've had is the address to which I can now write – a different camp, as you'll see, since he is now with ordinary fellow prisoners. He drops a line occasionally, but only briefly, telling me nothing, and his handwriting has deteriorated so much that I scarcely recognise it.'

No mention of whether Peter had enquired after her, which confirmed that he had not. And why had his hand-writing deteriorated? Because his experiences at the front had left him exhausted? That she could understand, but even a brief line, badly scrawled, would have been solace. More and more she sought refuge in work, and since sleep mainly eluded her, she welcomed longer and later hours on the wards. Month followed month relentlessly, each day a repetition of the last, until it seemed that the present was merely an extension of the past, leading to no positive future.

She had ceased crossing the days off the calendar because they were nothing but meaningless numbers following each other in an endless and uneventful chain. Sunday, Monday, Tuesday, Wednesday . . . and back came Sunday again, differing only from weekdays because prayers were said on the wards, and matins and evensong conducted in the hall for those mobile enough to attend, and a Roman Catholic priest came to hold mass and take confession for members of his faith, and for others who declared themselves to be agnostic, Dr Sanderson's apostles came to chat but never to preach. All this was poured into her unanswered letters.

Because she now felt that no future could be planned for herself and because in wartime the only thing to get one through was to think of a future of some sort, she tried to focus her mind on Kingsmere. A place so lovely should have a better future than its past, something as worthwhile as now, but when the war ended, Caroline would take over again and all this would disappear.

The thought was depressing. Eventually, Grandmamma had frequently reminded her, she would come into this inheritance herself. The old lady had wanted to incarcerate her here, drilling her into the role of future chatelaine, and from that her father had mercifully rescued her. Peter would have hated to marry an heiress. He would never adapt to the role of consort to the lady of the manor. Was it possible that since their separation this thought had crossed his mind and triggered his rejection? In the whirlwind days before his departure, there had been no time in which to think of such things, but in the monotony of a prison camp a man had little else with which to fill his days. One patient, repatriated with a batch of incurables who were nothing but a burden to their German captors, had told her so. 'You've so much time on your hands, you see everything either completely in focus or completely distorted. Whichever way, you know you can't return to things as they used to be, or even as you thought they would be. You've changed. You're not the same man any more.'

It also seemed useless to dream of a future when one doubted whether the country had a future in store for it at all; useless to imagine that she and Peter would simply pick up the threads where they had been dropped and step back into the theatre world together, she on to the stage as if she had made only a brief exit and he launching the scenic studios he had planned. And the fact that logic dismissed the idea of another woman in his life was cold comfort. German prison hospitals had only male orderlies, no pretty nurses, and before his capture he had surely had no time for more than a brief acquaintanceship or mild flirtation. There was a deeper and stronger reason for his silence, and the repatriated patient had given it to her. Peter had either changed his mind about their future together or no longer wanted it.

Chrystal wrote, 'You know there will always be an opening for you at the Comet. The management hasn't found a young actress of your calibre since you left: good and competent performers, yes, but none with what is now occasionally referred to as "star quality". When I was a young actress, that term was unknown, though I remember old Bernadette Boswell sticking a star up on her dressing-room door and announcing to everyone in the company, 'That's what *I* am, darlings – star of the Boswell Theatre!' Of course, she was slightly tipsy at the time, a Christmas party, I remember, and I suspected she only did it because she was jealous of her husband's fame as the theatre's actor-manager. Dear Sir Nevill – the audiences loved him. As you know, I stayed on at the Boswell for many years after his death, until the Comet management approached me to play permanent leads at their newly built theatre, and Lucinda Grainger (Sir Nevill's daughter) knew I couldn't afford to turn down such an offer. The Boswell, which she now owns, couldn't match the Comet's financial offer, though her theatre pays its way very well indeed. She could have held me to my contract, but never would Lucinda stand in anyone's way – particularly someone who had loyally played supporting leads in her father's company for so many years. Which brings me to this "star quality" I was talking about – I read the phrase only the other day, coined by some new theatre critic, saying that Lucinda Grainger had always had "star quality", and I must say I thought it very apt.

And I believe it applies to you, Delia, so hurry back to the
Comet just as soon as this beastly war is over. . . . '

It was like dreaming dreams, and Delia had never been
averse to doing that. She had indulged them as a child,
with her fanciful plays, but start reality now dominated
her life, recorded in a diary during nights when she was
too fatigued to sleep, and as she wrote, an idea was forming that at some distant time, when she could look back
and see it all in perspective, she would bring all this
material to life in dramatic form, particularly from the
viewpoint of a woman suffering the anguish of waiting and
serving and hoping and loving.

The drama could not be written until the final curtain
came down, but she scribbled feverishly, her notebooks
forming a pile of recorded history for which an audience
would be ready one day. Not immediately after the war,
with memories too raw to want anything but forgetfulness, but after a passage of time, when a new generation
would be ready for it, a generation very different from her
mother's.

And that thought brought her right back to Kingsmere
and its future. She sighed, wondering why she wasted time
speculating about it when the place was her mother's
responsibility and would be for many years yet. Caroline
spent no time worrying about the fate of her ancestral
home; all she thought about was the inconvenience of life in
wartime, deploring the fact that she was reduced to living
alone with Mrs Parker and only daily help from the
village, the mother of that 'no-good girl' Justin had
seduced years ago. The girl had borne a daughter, and the
daughter, now grown up, had entered a convent. Molly,
one of the ward maids, was her cousin and had told Delia
about it.

'Imagine, Sister, living with all them nuns! Wot a life!
I'd hate it, but I think Ruby was afraid she'd go the way of
her mother, who cleared off to London with the money

your grandmother bought her off with, and was never heard of again.'

Delia couldn't help liking Molly, brazen young miss though she was. Rosy-faced, like a russet apple, she worked like a Trojan and flirted like mad with the soldiers. 'Poor dears, how they must miss a good time in bed – eh, Sister?' A grin and a wink, and Delia would be laughing with her. One forgave Molly anything because she was a willing and inexhaustible worker, and that infectious and meaningful smile of hers cheered the patients as she crawled on her knees about the ward floors, cleaning and polishing and wiggling her bottom to make them laugh.

And there she was now, coming down the long hall toward her, polishing materials in hand for the bare wooden tables from which mobile patients had just eaten their midday meal – a transformation of the ancient banqueting hall, where balls and receptions had been held in the old days. Now its guests were soldiers in their bright blue disability uniforms, or dressing gowns if heavy bandaging made dressing impossible, and the voices it echoed were the cheerful cockney, or the West Country burr, or the broad, flat syllables of the Midlands or North, or the rolling r's of the Scots. A whole new world, a whole new life.

Molly's piping voice announced, 'Please, Sister, there's a young gentleman to see you. Says his name is Charles Howard, but I didn't believe it at first, he's so like your uncle . . .'

Delia didn't hear the last words because she was racing to the front steps, where Charles was waiting.

'Good gracious, you are taller than ever! It's good to see you, Charles, but shouldn't you be back at school? Surely the summer holiday is over? It's nearly the end of September.'

'Back next week. Four more masters have been called up, and replacements don't arrive until then. One form without a master could be coped with, but not four. Not that I want to go back, now I see what is going on here. I'd like to help.'

'Next holidays, perhaps. We can do with every available hand. There are lots of things one do for the wounded, besides nursing.'

'May I really come then? I saw some of the chaps as I walked up the drive. Poor devils, they look as if they've gone through hell.'

'They have.'

'And, my word, Delia, what a magnificent place! Will all this really be yours one day?'

'Who told you that? Not Deborah, I'm sure. She has never mentioned Kingsmere for as long as I can remember.'

'No. Garfield. She told me other things, too. Who my father was, for instance.'

Delia took his arm and led him away from Molly's eager ears. The girl was standing at the far end of the banqueting hall, straining to listen and gazing at the tall blond young man with that particular look Molly had for tall blond young men.

'Let's talk in the summerhouse.'

They walked past soldiers on crutches and in wheelchairs, and spinal cases prone in long, flat, wicker-railed carriages, their faces upturned to the late-September sun, and Delia saw Charles react to them with a compassion he was quick to hide. She was grateful to him for that, because pity, shock, and repugnance were reactions the men found hard to take and not all visitors were adept at concealing them.

'About your father . . .'

'I know who he was. An uncle of yours. I don't want to talk about him and I'm glad I never knew him.' He changed the subject at once. 'Who are those monks in sandals and robes?'

'They are not monks. They are members of a self-formed religious group from nearby. Men from all denominations. Conscientious objectors and therefore despised by many, but they don't ape those objectors who seized the chance of comfortable seclusion in camps on the Isle of Man and elsewhere, working on the land and at other "essential occupations" but refusing to succour the wounded because they claim that to heal someone trained to kill is aiding the war by making them fit to go back and kill again. The men from Fenfield Manor are different. They care for severe cases of shell shock, and men suffering from brain damage who will never be mentally normal again, and others who have temporarily lost their reason. I have seen some of their patients – helpless as babies when they arrive, and some, poor souls, remain so. But Dr Sanderson and his men have nursed many back to sanity and helped them to face life again. Before the war, that was his field of medicine. They handle cases we are not equipped to handle here. No wonder the government didn't clamp down on them and pack them all off to prisons for conscientious objectors!'

Charles was silent; then he said thoughtfully, 'Why have I always believed that religion was confined to the Church?'

Charles returned to Kingsmere at Christmas, and again at Easter the following year, working unstintingly. No job was too menial for him, none too horrendous. He helped Dr Sanderson's men with tasks which Delia expected a boy of his age to shrink from. She was proud of him, and told him so. He looked at her as if he failed to understand why. His compassion was so great that she could not believe he had ever sat beneath those bushes in the Square gardens pulling the wings off a bird.

Perhaps it was true that boys went through a cruel

phase, and outgrew it. Certainly there was no trace of cruelty in Charles now.

Sometimes he visited Fenfield Manor and came back full of the conversations he had with Sanderson. 'Did you know that he replaced the original wrought-iron gates with those solid doors because they give a feeling of security to his patients? Village people used to stare through the wrought iron, as if looking at freaks. Now they can't. I think that was a fine idea, and they certainly make you feel wonderfully safe when they shut behind you. You've been there. Didn't you feel it, too?'

Delia couldn't honestly say she had, but she saw the sense of it and decided to tell her mother next time she saw her. Perhaps it would make Caroline a little less contemptuous of the men she still regarded as cranks. But Delia rarely saw Caroline, who kept strictly to her own wing and her own part of the grounds. 'Lend a hand?' she had echoed when Delia suggested it. 'Aren't I doing enough by sacrificing my home and putting up with so much inconvenience?'

Molly, the ward maid, quickly realised she was in love with Charles. He seemed older than his age, which was two years younger than herself. She was delighted whenever he came to stay, and wished his room could be near to her own so she could slip along the corridor and into his bed. She wondered what he would be like in bed – wonderful, she was sure, with that tall fine body. Just to think of this awakened a very familiar sensation that going to bed with a man always satisfied. She was a totally amoral young woman with a generous heart, and she was ready to give Charles whatever he wanted without expecting anything in return except the gorgeous thrill of being made love to. There was something potent about him, even though he was so reserved. But she would very much like to know how he came by those Ashleigh eyes.

She remembered Lord Ashleigh well. As a little girl she had been brought to Kingsmere by her mother when extra help was needed for the spring cleaning. She had played in the stable yard with other children who were too young to be left at home, and often seen him mount his horse and dismount when he returned. Sometimes the animal would be in such a lather that the head groom would utter a stream of abuse behind his back, keeping it under his breath until his lordship was out of hearing, but letting it rip then. 'Doesn't give a tuppenny damn for any horse he rides, the bastard! He fair flogs them to death. I'd like to see him thrown so hard he'd break his bloody neck.'

He didn't give a tuppenny damn for women, either, according to the gossip of her mother and her auntie and the neighbours. And that proved true when auntie's girl Edith had a baby by him and Lady Elizabeth bought her off. 'It's the eyes,' Molly had heard her mother say to auntie. 'The Ashleigh eyes. A pity you didn't warn that Edie of yours to watch out for 'em.'

One day Molly managed to corner Charles after supper. The ward maids ate in the kitchen and the nursing and medical staff in what had once been the long dining room. When at Kingsmere, Charles had his meals there with the others. Molly was very glad that he didn't pay particular attention to any of the nurses, though she knew that some of them were as much aware of him as she was herself. He was a very quiet young man who worked hard, even taking on additional night shifts so the nursing staff could get more rest. She wished that maids could enter the wards after their chores were done, for she would certainly have made some excuse to do so when Mr Howard was on night duty. Most of the domestics went back to their homes in the village, but she offered to 'sleep in' after

Charles Howard appeared on the scene. 'I'm used to getting up early,' she had said to Sister Davidson, 'and I'd be on the spot to get the breakfast trays ready.'

So here she was, on the spot and ready and willing. Didn't he see how the poor devils of soldiers eyed her? Why didn't he eye her himself? He seemed aware of nothing but the needs of those men, but surely he'd like a break from them sometimes? Perhaps he would take more notice of her out of domestic uniform. She had a nice floral dress with a low neck, which Ma said should be filled in with a fichu. Not likely! She wasn't going to hide her bosom beneath a fall of lace, like some old maid. There wasn't a man of her acquaintance who hadn't wanted to get his hands on her breasts at some time or another, especially when she wore her floral.

She timed the meeting well. When the service door from the kitchen was left open, she could hear the staff leaving the dining room, and she knew Mr Howard's step very well by now. He had come off the wards later than usual, so he started his meal after the others. That made him the last to leave. She hurried from the kitchen just in time to bump into him as he left the table, and of course it was natural that she should stagger from the impact. She hoped he felt the softness of her body, and when he grasped her arms to steady her, she moved so that she faced him, standing close. He couldn't fail to see the low neck of her dress then; scooped right down, it was, showing more than Ma considered decent.

'Oh, Mr Howard, I'm sorry, sir! I wasn't looking where I were going. I was in a hurry to clear the table because I'm going off duty.' She put a hand to her breast in embarrassment, drawing attention to that area of her body of which, she knew, she had every reason to be proud. *Look*, the gesture said. *Look at me*.

It worked. His eyes went to her hand. She removed it so that he could see the mounds of her breasts, and she took a deep and fluttering breath to display them better. A tide of colour flooded his face, and he looked away swiftly. Well, well, who'd have thought he was so shy? If that was the reason why he kept to himself so much, she could soon cure him.

'Don't you ever take a turn outside when you've finished for the day, Mr Howard? It'd do you good. Fresh air makes you sleep better – if it's sleep you want when you go to bed.' She ended on a note of invitation.

To her astonishment, he turned and fled. Good gracious, he *was* shy, and certainly not so experienced as she'd imagined. But that didn't matter. It would be fun teaching him.

The more Charles saw of Dr Sanderson, the more interested he became in the man's work, and particularly in his views. He had heard of Freud and such people, but never paid much heed. He had even thought that mankind had no right to meddle with the minds of God's people, a viewpoint he now realised was adolescent. God, Sanderson pointed out, needed some practical aid from man in helping people both mentally and emotionally.

'We are God's servants, so let us serve him in whatever way we are best equipped. *This* is my way, and the way of my companions. Every human being has problems, some greater than others, and it is this awareness that drew us together. Some of my servers are medical men, some have been patients of mine in the past, and in doing this work I have overcome many problems of my own. You could do the same.'

The keen, kind eyes had met Charles's briefly and looked away.

But I haven't any problems, Charles reflected. Life has been good to me. I belong to a loving family. I can forget about my father because I have a good home and many advantages, and I'm healthy and normal.

But even normal people had emotional problems, according to Dr Sanderson.

'Of course,' the man had added, 'one needs to learn self-discipline, and that is never easy. That is why we at Fenfield take religious vows. Chastity and obedience are the first steps, more difficult for some than for others. Then there is greed – that has to be overcome too. So we bring to the movement all our worldly goods. We keep nothing individually, and that removes the temptation to covet anything belonging to others, for nothing does belong to others. "If thou wouldst enter the Kingdom of Heaven," said Christ to the rich young man, "sell all thou hast and give to the poor." Each of us here sold whatever he possessed and put the money into the cause. First we needed a place in which to practise our work, so we bought this house and restored it with our own hands. It was in a bad state of repair and had stood empty for a long time. Then we built the small chapel, essential for our spiritual needs and for those of the patients. We became self-supporting by investing what money was left over, and the money brought by others who have joined us, to yield an income for the upkeep of the place, also by cultivating our own food, though we have cause to be grateful for the overflow from Kingsmere since the war broke out.'

'It sounds a hard life.'

'A difficult life, perhaps, but not hard in the general sense. Striving to achieve better things is always difficult. There is no easy way to salvation, and all of us here happen to feel that the best way for *us* is our way. That doesn't mean it is the only way. We must each choose our own.'

I suppose, Charles thought as he walked back to Kingsmere, Delia chose hers when she gave up a promising career to become a nurse. He knew how hard she had worked to climb in the ranks of VADs, and although known as sister-in-charge, she really did the work of a matron now. She was much thinner than in the old days, but so was everyone, since the country was existing on the barest rations. The war was still dragging on, and the civilian population was losing hope. Some had already lost it. Nineteen-seventeen had seen Haig's campaign in Flanders, the collapse of the Nivelle offensive, destruction by air at Cambrai, and the triumph of the Austro-German offensive against Italy. But gradually the Central Powers were being strained economically due to the blockade, and shortages of foodstuffs and raw materials must surely help to wear them down. Exhaustion due to continuous fighting could be the last nail in their coffin.

But the Allies were becoming exhausted for the same reason.

Entering the house in the evening quiet, Charles met Delia. Despite her thinness, he was struck by her rare kind of beauty. He had never noticed it before. To him she had always been like an older sister, though of course they were not related — or so he had thought until his sixteenth birthday. Since then he had begun to think of her as a cousin, which she was on his father's side. Knowledge of their shared Ashleigh blood had begun to have another effect too — he was beginning to identify himself with Kingsmere.

'You look very thoughtful,' she said. 'A penny for them.'

'Do you ever feel like a blood relation to me? I suppose not, since the relationship isn't a legal one.'

'Oh, that.' She brushed it aside. 'What makes legal relationships different from the other kind? Nothing, as far as I can see, except domestic considerations. I suppose Garfield told you? I suspect she feels you have been cheated of your rightful inheritance, but is that so very different from my being cheated of my rightful marital status? Don't look so puzzled. Haven't you noticed my wearing this before? I don't all the time, of course. Not when working. But I always wear it when out of uniform.'

She was holding out her left hand, and he was startled to see the gold band on the left finger.

'I didn't know . . . '

'That I was married? Well, I'm not.' There was a catch in her voice. 'Nor do I know that I ever will be, but apart from a bit of paper, I became Peter's wife before he went away. You look shocked. Why? Because I'm no longer a virgin? Does that offend your religious conscience? If it does, I'm sorry, but I have never regretted it, nor ever will, and furthermore,' she added almost angrily, 'if you knew the agony of waiting, the *awfulness* of wanting someone physically and being denied them, you wouldn't sit in judgment. Simon and Deborah don't, but of course they love each other too, and had to wait a long time to be together. And I'll tell you something more – I wish I had had a child by Peter, despite this bloody war and despite the fact that it would have been illegitimate in the eyes of the law. I am quite sure it would not have been in God's, any more than you yourself are. It wasn't God who wrote the marriage service, as far as I am aware.'

She whirled away from him then. It was the first time she had shown signs of cracking. Many other people had, but not Delia. He wanted to go after her, but could think of nothing to say. He *was* shocked that she had committed sexual acts out of wedlock. That was sinful. Hadn't he branded that father, whom he had never known, as a sinner? But not his mother, smiling down at him from her portrait on the wall. There had been warmth and kindness and generosity there. A woman with a smile like that couldn't possibly be bad.

But Delia had been part of his life too, a big sister always. She had represented fun and gaiety and affection, and this had been unchanging until that incident in the

Square gardens. Even now he could recall the horror in her face and his own failure to understand it, though now, having witnessed the suffering of others at close quarters, a depth of compassion had been aroused in him that he had never known was there, and remembering the torture he had inflicted on those helpless little creatures, in what he now chose to call ignorance, filled him with shame. So why couldn't he feel compassion for Delia, or make excuses for her? Because she had Ashleigh blood in her veins?

As Charles approached his room, a figure moved out of the shadows. It was Molly, her hair streaming over her shoulders. She wore a robe in gaudy colours. He was unaware that she had bought it at a jumble sale and prized it highly. He only knew it was wide open at the neck, revealing a lot of bare flesh. He stood still, unable to take his eyes off her body. It was very beautiful. White and soft. Lovely to touch, if he had the courage to.

She stood very close.

'I couldn't sleep,' she whispered. 'I've been on the go all day, and thought I would go to bed early, but when I got there I was too tired. I need someone to snuggle up to. I don't like being alone in bed – do you?'

'I have always slept alone.'

'*Always*? A fine young man like you? I don't believe it. I'll bet you've taken many a girl to bed.'

'Of course, not. I've lived at home or at school. In neither place would I be taking a girl to bed.'

'You don't always need a *bed* . . . ' She was pressing her young body against him. He thought she was shivering, until the same kind of trembling started in himself. 'I know what schoolboys are like,' she said. 'I've worked at that big public school over beyond Ashdown Forest. Ma got me a place there when I was fourteen, but I only lasted a couple of terms because the senior young gentlemen wouldn't leave me alone, and they didn't need the dormitories for it, neither.'

She opened his bedroom door and drew him inside. It closed behind them.

'Haven't you made love to a girl *ever*?'

He shook his head.

'Then it's about time you learned, isn't it, love?'

She taught him all sorts of things he had never dreamed women did to men. He had indulged in sexual fantasies from time to time, boyish dreams of lying with a naked girl and mating in the conventional way. One learned about the functioning of male and female in Biology, but always being the odd one out at school had debarred him from the sniggering conversations of his schoolfellows, which always broke off when he appeared.

Sometimes they taunted him: 'Haven't you ever done it, Howard? Are you a virgin? You poor miserable devil, you don't know a thing, do you?' When he coloured, they laughed, and when he turned away in embarrassment, their laughter followed. He remembered one calling after him, 'Try that girl from the laundry, old chap! Knows a thing or two, that one does. And there's a nice warm spot off the drying room where she'll do it for half a crown. Ten minutes for a tanner, if that's all you can spare.'

He had put as much distance as possible between them, hiding in the stables and nestling his face in the warm fur of the stable cat, but the softness had been strangely exciting, and his hands had tightened. He had meant only to caress, not to hurt, so he had been shocked when it fought and scratched and escaped with a screech.

Now he felt the softness of Molly's flesh beneath his hands. She had dropped her robe and was naked beneath. His jacket was off, and she had even unbuttoned his trousers and dragged them down; then her hands were stroking him. They were work-roughened, the fingernails broken, but their touch made his senses reel. On the bed they were both naked and her legs were open for him. He went into her on a tide of delirium, rising and falling with the movements of her hungry body, devouring her breasts with his mouth and hands, stroking and then clutching her, spinning in a sensuous whirl toward a climax which was coming . . . *coming* . . . He sought it violently, because all his senses screamed that only with violence could he reach that blinding peak. He raised the upper part of his body, still riding her but striking with his fists as he would whip a horse to go faster. *Damn you*, his brain shouted, *help me, help me*! He saw her face threshing this way and that to avoid his blows, and that enraged him, because it was her fault, not his, that something was going terribly wrong.

He couldn't stop, though his heart and lungs and every vein and muscle were threatening to burst in this agonising struggle to reach a climax that eluded him. Blood was pounding in his ears, noises resounding in his head, rage driving him in a frenzy of frustration pierced by her screams. He clamped a hand over her mouth, and the sound cut off, but her body was threshing, squirming, fighting. There was no rhythm left, but he would not let her go; he had to reach that fantastic summit, no matter how.

Instead, he felt a searing pain on both sides of his face. Her jagged nails were clawing him so savagely that shock sent him crashing away from that unattainable peak. His body sagged and his hands fell away.

With one desperate heave she rolled from beneath him. She was off the bed and kneeling on the floor, drawing deep, rasping breaths. Then she dragged herself to her feet, hands covering her face. He lay limp, too exhausted to move, wild with anger because ecstasy had been denied him.

He hated her.

His eyes slid sideways to her work-worn hands with their horrible, jagged nails, and he could not think why she was sobbing so wildly. He had been making love to her, hadn't he? She had wanted it, begged for it, and now she was calling him all sorts of foul names. They came streaming from her throat: '*Swine . . . bastard . . . a wild animal couldn't be worse than you . . . you filthy beast, you savage!*'

He closed his eyes. He couldn't bear to look at her. She was a slut whose ugly hands had left blood on his face, but at the same time she was a horrifying reproach in a way he could not understand.

'*. . . you nearly killed me, you swine . . . my God, is that the only way you can enjoy yourself?*'

A creeping horror began to stir. He remembered his violence, and recoiled. He felt as if he had been dragged back from the edge of a precipice beyond which madness yawned. He began to shake with terror. That man possessed had surely not been he? He was conscious of fear and a deep, dark hatred of himself, a terrible loathing. Dear God in heaven, don't let that ever happen to me again! Dear God, help me – I don't know myself! Dear God, help me fight whatever monstrous thing is in me.

She was scrambling into her tawdry robe, sobbing hoarsely. He wanted to shut out the sound, and could not. 'I should've listened to my ma – she always said them Ashleigh eyes were a sign of cruelty, and you've got 'em, all right!'

'What do you mean?' he managed to ask. 'What Ashleigh eyes?'

'Take a look for yourself,' she rasped from the door, one rough hand clutching her cheap robe about her, the other still at her face. 'They're all on the stairs in the family wing. The mistress had them moved there when the place became a hospital – lots of pale-eyed Ashleighs like yourself who have done terrible things in their lifetime!'

<h1 style="text-align:center">28</h1>

It was easy to get into the family wing. There was a communicating door which Delia used when she went to see her mother, who never used it because she never visited the hospital side. He had heard that she couldn't bear the sight of sick people, and had despised her for it, but in the aftermath of his experience with Molly he had felt the same revulsion for a girl's work-roughened hands. These did not strike him as pathetic until he had recovered himself, when the memory of them came to him with a sense of pity and shame.

He wanted to forget every moment of that encounter, but he could not forget her final words. The girl had been hysterical, but her reference to his eyes had startled him. The only other person to comment on them had been the old gardener in Hanover Square, who had not recognised him until he saw 'them eyes'. And the gardener had told him of some poor creature who had been strangled there, and the story had revived memories of his own treatment of birds in his childhood – scruffy little London sparrows whose feathers had been as soft as any exotic birds', beautiful to touch. The memory alarmed him now, because it seemed to be linked with Molly's final taunt.

Of course, he didn't believe her. Not even Garfield had told him that he had inherited any specific Ashleigh feature. Even so, he was curious to see the portraits. Curious, and yet, in a way, fearful. But he had to prove to himself that Molly had made it all up.

He had lain for a long time after the girl had gone, too spent to move and too disturbed to think coherently. He had even dropped into unconsciousness for a while, only to waken shivering. He dressed, anxious to get out of this room where emotions beyond his understanding had torn him apart. He walked in stocking feet along the corridors, past the wards where dim lights burned, pausing, if the doors were open, to make sure he would not be seen. It would not be easy to explain why he was prowling around without shoes, because that was what it would look like – puzzling and suspicious. He could easily say he was restless and wondered if he could lend a hand, but even so, the absence of shoes would be difficult to explain. But no one heard or saw him, and an oil lamp was burning on a table by the communicating door. He picked it up and slipped through.

The whole wing was silent. He found the stairs, and descended slowly, holding the lamp aloft, pausing on every tread to examine the age-old paintings, studying the thin Ashleigh features and the high foreheads and, in some, the generosity and kindness of mouth and eyes. But in those cases the eyes were never pale. In others, the cold and unfathomable ones, his own looked back at him, and in all cases they belonged to men.

'Bruce Carruthers Ashleigh, 1528.' 'Humphrey Prendergast Ashleigh, 1556.' 'Charles Patrick Ashleigh, 1594.' 'Joseph Steven Ashleigh, 1662.' A lull up to 1731, when they appeared again in Justin Malven Philip Ashleigh. A shorter span to the birth of Frederick Charles Wentworth Ashleigh in 1761. A father-to-son inheritance? Then no more until 1802 – Alfred Charles Ashleigh, followed by Bruce Joseph Ashleigh in 1832. In all these, the eyes were repeated.

Then finally Justin Malven Ashleigh in 1864 – his own father, surely, since the birthdate would be about right.

Charles held the lamp higher. Between Bruce Joseph, of 1832, and Justin Malven in 1864, there was a Charles Carruthers Ashleigh with the warm brown eyes and the gentle mouth he observed in several. He liked the look of this Charles Ashleigh and wished he resembled him. He was unaware that in some respects he did – he had the same compassionate mouth, but not the eyes, which were those of Justin unmistakably. Did they really signify cruelty, as Molly said? If she really believed that, she would surely not have pursued him so blatantly. Every time he had come to stay to Kingsmere, he had been aware of the invitation in her glance, and no girl would be so brazen were there any reason to fear him.

But he had given her plenty of reason, once in bed with her. Then he had become a different person, possessed by instincts of which he was now not only bitterly ashamed but also fearful. Had they been there all his life, warring with his belief in God and the Church – or perhaps, even as a small boy, he had been drawn to God and the Church through an unconscious awareness of this other thing, this cursed thing which had made him enjoy pulling the wings off helpless small birds after killing them.

He was trembling so violently that the lamp shook in his hand. He turned away, stumbling on a step and banging the base of the brass oil lamp on the wrought-iron banister rail. It made a resounding noise in the silence, and within seconds a door on the landing above was flung open and a voice cried, '*Who's there?*'

A woman was silhouetted against the light of the room. Electricity had been installed at Kingsmere some years ago, and oil lamps were used in the hospital corridors at night only because they were economical and shed a softer light. Now Charles was unaware that the even ring of flame shone directly on his upturned face, spotlighting it.

The woman's hand flew to her throat. '*Good God . . . Justin!*'

He stammered, 'I'm sorry . . . I'm Charles Howard and I help in the hospital wing. I come to stay every now and then during school holidays. I . . . I apologise for intruding . . .'

She was tall and incredibly thin. He knew she could only be Delia's mother, for no housekeeper could afford such nightwear. Beneath costly satin, elaborately trimmed with lace, the lines of her body were long and angular.

'Come up here at once!' She went back into her room, and returned a moment later, pulling on a wrap. 'What did you say your name was?'

'Howard. Charles Howard.'

She was a good-looking woman, with high cheekbones and a firm jaw, but there was a hardness about her which was lacking in her daughter. At close quarters the angular face looked almost haggard.

'You gave me the fright of my life,' she scolded. 'Whatever made such a noise? Luckily I wasn't asleep. I thought perhaps it was my daughter, though she never comes at such an hour, and when I saw you . . . dear God, I thought you were my brother.' She peered at him. '*What* did you say your name was?'

He repeated it. Her eyes widened, and remained so for what seemed a long time; then she rapped, 'What are you doing here?'

The tone was not encouraging, but there was nothing he could say except the truth. 'I wanted to see the Ashleigh portraits.'

'Then why not ask to, instead of creeping in at dead of night?'

'I . . . I'm sorry . . .'

She peered closer. 'What have you done to your face? It looks as if a wildcat attacked you.'

He had forgotten Molly's claw marks after he staunched the bleeding. Everyone would see them and comment, of course, and he would have to explain them away satisfactorily, but what of poor Molly? How could she explain her bruised face? For his part, he could say he had been torn by brambles, taking a shortcut from the village across the common and into the woods. He tried the excuse now, and it was accepted.

'You certainly *were* torn, from the look of you.' Again the long level glance, the piercing concentration. 'So you are Charles Howard, my brother's illegitimate son – or perhaps I should say one of them, though I have met none of the others.'

'Others?'

'Oh, I am sure he sired plenty, quite apart from the one my mother handled so well. She bought the girl off. Not *your* mother – she was well provided for, and in any case, Justin disclaimed being your father. I hated your mother, Charles Howard, and with good cause. I suppose that daughter of mine has been inviting you to Kingsmere without my knowledge? Trust Delia not to confide in me. I have always been the one to be ignored.'

Her voice held the plaintive note of a thoroughly spoiled woman. He didn't want to talk to her, and he didn't like the tone in which she spoke of his mother.

He said again, this time very coldly. 'I apologise for intruding,' and turned to go.

'Wait!'

He obeyed unwillingly. To walk straight up the stairs and on to the communicating door, slamming it behind him – as he wanted to – would be ill-mannered, and Charles had never been that. Even as a child he had known that people commented on his courtesy.

'Why did you want to see the family portraits?'

He was silent for a moment, then shrugged. 'Curiosity, I suppose.'

'About what?' When he made no answer, she pressed on relentlessly. 'Was it the eyes? Are you curious about the eyes? You have them, you know, and so did Justin. They are a legacy in the male line of this family. Would you like to know what kind of legacy?'

He remained silent, torn by a desire to know and a fear of doing so. Then he said, 'Obviously you are wanting to tell me.'

'For one so young, you are quite astute. A characteristic of your father, I would say, though I believe your mother had her fair share of shrewdness and did very well for herself as a result.'

'You were talking about some kind of physical legacy, not my mother, and I won't have her belittled.'

'What makes you think I am belittling her? You never knew her. She died when you were born.'

'I know that. I also know she was warm and generous and kind.'

'A picture nurtured by Deborah Yorke, I fancy. I mean your cousin. You can hardly expect me to call her by her present surname, and I don't suppose she has ever told you about my generous offer to bring you here, which she flatly refused. A pity . . . I would have enjoyed showing Justin's offspring to my late and unlamented mamma, who always swore Justin could do no wrong. But let us get back to the Ashleigh eyes. Since your curiosity about them was strong enough to make you break in at this hour, I think it should be satisfied. Come. It is all in the library. You can read it for yourself.'

She touched a light switch at the head of the stairs, and swept down. He put aside the lamp and followed. In the library she unlocked a glazed door and gestured toward morocco-bound volumes.

'The family archives – take your pick. These bound ones are official histories, written by biographers over the years. Others are boxes designed to match; they contain letters and diaries and personal recollections of the family. The only missing ones are those which I may take the trouble to record myself one day – my father's story, and my mother's, and my brother's – perhaps even my own, but all from my point of view, since that has never been heeded. No one has ever been interested in me, though I did think my father . . . long ago . . . ' The note of self-pity hovered again, then changed to a briskness which held a touch of malicious enjoyment. 'The legend is repeated again and again, starting with an early Ashleigh who was beheaded for ravishing the seven-year-old daughter of a king, and another imprisoned in the Tower for abducting the wife of a notable earl and raping her frequently whilst holding her to ransom. That was Bruce Carruthers Ashleigh, I believe. Then there was Joseph Steven Ashleigh, sentenced for bigamy with no less than four women, and another for something so unmentionable that it isn't even whispered about. That was Frederick Charles Wentworth Ashleigh. Another was a member of the Hellfire Club, though I am not sure which one – you could work it out from the date, I suppose. In my own girlhood, a village wench was raped and strangled in the Kingsmere woods, but it was never laid at my brother's door, though some people thought . . . Anyway, the rest of it is here, everything about the pale-eyed Ashleighs, the ones who fulfilled the legend and passed on their toublesome seed. Thank heaven it has never been passed on by their womenfolk, as you will see from all this evidence. A biological quirk, my ex-husband called it, and though I may have become a bitch in some ways – and not without cause, mind you – I wasn't actually born one, and I do know that any child my daughter bears won't be tainted either. By the way, there's brandy in that cupboard over there. Young as you are, I rather think you'll need it.'

She gave a throaty laugh and departed.

He read until dawn, then returned to his room feeling ill.

Next day he went back to Hanover Square, but before leaving he paid a visit to Dr Sanderson and asked how old a man had to be for entry into the brotherhood. Promises could safeguard his future, and except for that one deviation in the woods at school, for which he bitterly reproached himself, he had always striven to remain constant to any he made. Religious discipline would help. For this reason he determined to take vows which would bind him for life, particularly the vow of celibacy, so that his seed would never be passed on.

Deborah had kept Peter's studio cleaned and aired throughout the war, leaving everything exactly as it was so that when he came back he could walk right in and know he was home. She refused to contemplate the possibility of his not wanting to return, though in her way she was as anxious was Delia. She knew he had been discharged from hospital and that his father sometimes heard from him, albeit briefly, but it was impossible not to realise that his silence must be deliberate as far as everyone else was concerned.

'He doesn't write to you and me, Simon, because he knows he can't do so and continue to ignore Delia. I can't forgive him for hurting her, I really can't.'

Simon made reassuring answers, contrived though some of them were. 'It takes a man a long time to recover from war wounds' was the best he could think of, to which his wife replied, 'Yes, but what kind of wounds? They can't be serious, or the prison hospital wouldn't have discharged him. And if he is disabled, why not write and tell us? Delia wouldn't love him any the less, no matter what had happend to him,' to which Simon could only murmur that they must be patient and have faith, but it was not easy to utter such assurances when in doubt.

'War changes people,' he said, then wished he had not,

for Deborah immediately replied that if so, the least the boy could do was say so. 'Delia isn't a coward. She would accept the truth. The bewilderment in her eyes distresses me, and I suspect she is forgoing much of her leave because she can't face coming home even for forty-eight hours. Last time, she couldn't bring herself to go up to his studio, which speaks for itself. She used to head straight for it in the early days, making it her first duty, her first pleasure. She feels close to him up there, but now . . . well, it is almost as if she can't bear to be reminded.'

Simon, too, found the situation disturbing. 'If you would just let us know how you are,' he wrote, 'for Delia's sake. She isn't the type to reproach you if you now feel differently about her . . . .' This too brought no reply. After prolonged waiting, Simon's fatherly concern developed into anger, which was useless, since he could vent it on no one but an absent soldier. By the end of 1917 resignation seemed to have replaced the despair in his daughter's eyes, and that was almost worse, because Delia had never been the kind to resign herself to situations. If she could not readjust them, she would at least put up a fight, but now the heart seemed to have gone out of her. She was on his mind more and more, and automatically, when he came home each day, he would ask whether there were news. Deborah knew what he meant. Not war news, but of things nearer home.

She did not tell him that she, too, had written to Peter. 'We know you must have gone through a great deal,' she said, 'but, in her way, so has Delia. Your silence makes it worse.' Nor was she prepared to accept Garfield's hopeful suggestion that perhaps he was no dab-hand at letter-writing. As for Charles, the boy declared that it was disgraceful 'in view of the situation between them', whereupon Deborah rounded on him, angry with the boy for the first time he could recall.

'Don't sit in judgment,' she said sharply. 'Their union

was sanctified in church, which should ease your pious conscience.' She was as startled as he, but she meant it.

Simon had hinted once or twice that he found Charles almost too good to live up to. 'There has never been any real naughtiness in him, at least not that we have ever seen, and that's unnatural in any lad.' She had sprung to the boy's defence at once, insisting that he had his mother's sweetness of nature and if that meant lack of aggression, perhaps it was all to the good.

Now, standing beneath the studio skylight, he looked exactly what he was – a clean and wholesome youth hurt by her words.

'A pious conscience,' Charles answered, 'is a mainstay in life. You should be glad I possess one,' and though the answer might sound smug if taken literally, she felt it was somehow defensive and that he was wishing he could have the strength to live up to it. She looked at him for a long and questioning moment, wondering if he had come up here for reasons other than to say hello to her and her small daughter, who staggered around on chubby legs in her mother's wake all day. Sarah-Dulcima was fond of Garfield, but happy that her brothers took up much of her time. From birth, Deborah had been the most important woman in the little girl's life. Already she had a passion for dressing up in Deborah's clothes, were she able to sneak into her parents' bedroom and lay her hands on them. For this reason Garfield had opened up Dulcima Howard's old theatrical skip, unearthing moth-proofed relics of her beloved former mistress, to the child's delight.

Now she startled her mother by appearing in the open doorway clad in a trailing black velvet cloak many sizes too large and an enormous hat with sweeping black ostrich feathers. She had had to allow Garfield to carry her upstairs in such unwieldy garments, but now she stumbled into the room, chortling with glee and clutching the enormous cartwheel hat with plump little hands.

'Look, Mamma, look!' And behind her Garfield sniffed audibly and wiped her eyes with the back of her hand, for beneath the sweeping brim the little girl's face dimpled wickedly.

'She's come back, hasn't she, Miss Deborah?' Garfield said with a catch in her voice, and for the life of him Charles could not understand why both women should have difficulty in checking their tears.

'You kept them, Garfield, all these years!'

'I had to, Miss Deborah. I know you told me to get rid of the rest of her clothes, but these I couldn't part with. . . .'

Charles guessed at once that they were talking about his mother. 'Did she really wear things like that?' he asked in surprise. 'I imagined she was more ladylike.'

'She wore them magnificently,' Deborah told him, and Garfield declared indignantly, 'And a lady she was, Master Charles!' This was the second time he had been spoken to in a way he had not expected. 'How *could* you?' the woman went on. 'Your mother was a lady through and through.'

So he had become 'Master Charles' to her at last. He was glad of that, having no desire to be reminded of his father or to bear either his name or his title, but he sensed a subtle change in Garfield's attitude. His nose had been put out of joint by this toddler. Garfield was gazing adoringly at the child as she danced around the room, stumbling over the trailing cloak, picking herself up with a joyous squeal and dancing on, an entrancing little creature with a smile to melt anyone's heart. He smiled back at her and clapped his hands in applause, whereupon she dimpled even more, loving it. Then he turned to the door.

'If Simon isn't home yet, I'll wait for him in his study. I have something to tell him. You, too, Deborah.'

Germany's assault of St Mihiel in the spring of 1918

meant a desperate renewal of the Allied struggle, but Marshal Foch dealt with further German blows whilst Ludendorff's massive effort was checked by the French counter-attack at Château-Thierry. Hope began to stir at last, gathering momentum with the victory at Amiens in late summer, but British Tommies incarcerated in German prison camps had no inkling of what was happening. For them, life had halted on the day of their capture and had marked time ever since. For Peter, in Hut Seventeen, Stalag Nine, Gottesberg, the longer this situation continued, the better it was, but the more he chafed against it. Sometimes he thought this was a coward's attitude, and sometimes he thought it was the only possible one until he had learned all he had to learn, mastered all he wanted to master. Until then, he would be unable to come to grips with any sort of future.

Surprisingly, the camp's visiting MO had been helpful, smuggling a package of watercolours and sable brushes and a supply of cartridge paper to him amongst the monthly Red Cross parcels, and risking a lot in the process. He was a newly qualified doctor and therefore of low rank, so Peter had never run the risk of thanking the man or indicating in any way that he guessed who had sent them. He limped across the exercise yard for his weekly medical inspection with other disabled prisoners who had been prematurely discharged from the hospital five miles away; the injured hip didn't matter, but the amputated arm did. His right arm, too. His working arm. He had gone through months of torture because of it, the worst of which was continuing. This was the knowledge that his career was finished. He would never paint again.

'Try with your left hand,' the young German doctor had said. He was the first to take any interest in his plight. In the hospital, butchered bodies had been things to patch and despatch, not human beings with emotions and problems. Doctors and surgeons weren't bloody mindmenders, and injured soldiers should be thankful to be alive. That was the attitude he had to face, but even more difficult to face was his own – the conviction that it would have been better for himself and Delia and everyone else if he had gone the way of Corporal Stevens, who had fought beside him in the trenches amidst the stench of mud and decomposing bodies, so many bodies that orderlies hadn't time to gather them in. The dead were dead; even those with only a flicker of life had to yield to the living. At first the horror of walking on half-buried human corpses, some of which moved and twitched when your mud-caked army boots skidded on them, had been a paralysing nightmare. You stumbled to a halt, trying to stifle screams which mercifully turned into vomit, and behind you Stevens shouted above the shriek of shellfire, 'That's right, mate – bring it up an' you'll feel better. It'll be my turn next!' And it was. He had been laughing, cracking jokes, and then he was silent, his laughter cut off when the blast came, and when Peter turned to help him, taking hold of his arms and dragging them round his neck to get him back to base, no head lolled between them.

The nightmares began then, and still came back to him.

'You have to *try*,' the young German doctor had said. 'Just *try*.' He was a decent chap, unwise enough to have compassion, which did not recommend him to the camp commandant. He spent too much time talking to his patients, questioning them about their symptoms and the extent of their pain, and how well or how badly they slept, when five minutes should have been sufficient to cast a clinical eye over their injuries and pass on to the next. No wonder he was replaced by one who kept his eye on the clock, ready to take off for the next prison camp the minute it was time to go. The indulgence of a resident medical officer was not justified here. The place was only a huddle of huts, twenty prisoners to each, and two more which served as separate messes for officers and men.

It wasn't until the young doctor had been delegated to other duties that Peter began to stir from his stupor. He felt he owed the chap something, and was ashamed because he had not thanked him or heeded his advice. As belated atonement he turned to the painting materials, knowing it was hopeless, that he would never master painting with his left hand, but, as the doctor had said, he had to give it a try. So he did, tearing up every effort until his supply of cartridge paper ran out. And that, he thought, was that, until Perkins, in bed number ten, brought him some wrapping paper from the cookhouse. 'I saw the horsemeat going in, and nabbed it when the stuff was unwrapped. The red will merge with the water-colours, won't it? There's a blob there which looks like the start of a sunset. . . .'

So he was under another obligation, because Perkins and others scrounged paper of all kinds, wrappers from Red Cross parcels and the boxes they were packed in, slit and opened flat, and he couldn't let them go to all that trouble without showing some appreciation. They decorated the hut walls with his daubs, but he kept none for himself. The only things he kept were Delia's letters, in a kitbag beneath his bed read and reread and never answered because what use would he be to her now?

'You ought to answer them,' Perkins said. 'It isn't kind, not to.' But it would be even more unkind to make her feel that he was binding her to him, keeping her to promises which would condemn her to no sort of a life. What could he offer her now? What of the dream of his own scenic studio? It would never be. He couldn't paint anything of a decent size, let alone quality, and at his present rate of progress, God only knew how long it would be before he could.

An injured hip could recover or remain as a manageable handicap, but a lost arm could not be replaced. His had gone clean from the shoulder, and no artificial limb had yet been invented that could be attached to a place where there was no stump. He would be a liability, a burden. The very idea was an insult to his independence. Even worse was the insistent fear that when Delia saw him undressed, she would be repelled. He would no longer be the splendid young man who had initiated her into the joy of love, strong-armed and strong-limbed, without a blemish on his body. Her hands had explored him in delight. How would they touch him now? At the most, he thought, with pity. At the worst, they would shrink from him. He could face neither.

'I could write for you,' said Perkins, 'as I do to your father.' It was a stroke of luck that Perkins's handwriting faintly resembled his own. 'You are a chump, Maynard. They've got to know sometime. You've hidden the truth for too long.'

But 'sometime' was a long way off, a vague horizon which never drew near, so he didn't have to face it yet. Their German jailers enjoyed relating British adverses, which came thick and fast, and it was plain that nothing would change for a long time yet. Years, some said in pessimistic moments, when the depression caused by captivity and stultifying boredom was as its worst.

It was then that he surprised the lot of them by hitting on the idea of getting up a Christmas snow. 'We could rig up a stage of sorts in the mess, and I could paint scenery of some kind if the rest of you chaps will knock up the flats. The bloody Boche can't object to that. They'll sneer at our stupid British humour, but at least they'll know we're not up to any mischief, like trying to escape.'

Escape attempts had brought such heavy penalties that few even thought of attempting them now. Solitary confinement in underground dugouts in which some poor devils had cracked and gone off their rockers, and starvation diets which led to innumerable physical ailments, were the finest deterrents, and their captors used them well. So there he was, saddled with the job of staging a show, and cursing himself for thinking of it. *He* must be off his rocker to say, so unthinkingly, that he would paint the scenery, but now he had to do it. Large frames were made, covered with whatever paper could be collected, even small pieces stuck together to make large sheets, and he was faced with the task of turning them into backdrops, painting the damn things with his left hand. He thought the results hopeless, but no one agreed, and Perkins said, 'We'll tell your father about this in the next letter, and he'll know you're going to be A-one.'

But his father would pass on the news of his disfigurement to Delia. Peter knew they kept in touch, for in her letters she referred to him frequently. So he told Perkins he would write himself now he was mastering the use of his left hand, and, satisfied, Perkins let it go. But at least one fear was being eliminated. With constant practice, he could still have a career of sorts, but it would be a long and painful rehabilitation, perhaps never reaching his previous standard. How could he ask Delia to share that with him? So her letters continued to be stored away, unanswered, and when still they came, he read and reread them, though he was convinced that she now wrote only from a sense of loyalty.

After the temporary stimulation of the Christmas show, life returned to the deadly stagnation of prison routine, and the under-officers' taunts in the parade ground each morning became worse. 'You are a defeated race,' they jeered, and laughed at the prisoners' straightened shoulders and stiffened backs. Such taunts increased in proportion with the prisoners' stubbornness, goading their jailers to either rage or laughter.

Then, suddenly, the insults and the taunts diminished. 'Something's happening,' said Perkins when bread – real bread, not the coarse, stale black stuff they were accustomed to – appeared at breakfast one morning. And the coffee wasn't that bean-tasting muck, and the under-officers weren't patrolling the tables, thumbs stuck arrogantly in their belts, watching with derision. They were quiet, almost civil. 'Anyone would think they wanted us to like them,' Peter said, as puzzled as the rest.

That was at the end of September 1918. None of the prisoners at Gottesberg knew that the German initiative had been brought to a halt by the Allies' assault on the Hindenburg Line; they could only sense, by the change of attitude toward them, that something was indeed happening.

On 3 November an armistice was signed, and on 11 November came the cease-fire. A weary world at last rested on its arms, and the prisoners heard that they would be repatriated as soon as possible. The announcement was made with much heel-clicking and correct military salutes, for they had ceased to be regarded as subhuman cattle. The were soldiers of the conquering armies, but to Peter they were simply men bound for home at last. That nebulous horizon had taken a giant leap toward him, and had to be met.

Dear God, he thought for the hundredth time, I can't face her. I won't be able to endure her shock, her flinching away, or even her pity.

His prayer now was that she might no longer feel the same about him, for that would be more bearable than losing her because of his maimed body, as some men had lost the women they loved, or to have her stay with him from some galling sense of duty. If his silence had driven her to someone else, it would be better that way.

He would know, as soon as he saw her, exactly how she felt.

29

Charles had said, 'I want to talk to you both. I wanted to tell you when I first made up my mind, but one gets so little chance of privacy in this house; I mean, with the children and everything.'

'Family life is like that,' Deborah answered, wondering what this self-sufficient son of Dulcima's wanted to discuss. Charles was not in the habit of seeking private *tête-à-tête*, and though open and friendly and considerate, she had become aware as he grew up that he was not one to need a confidant or to seek one, so she asked, in some surprise, what he wanted to talk about.

'My future. I have taken the first steps already.'

'The first steps toward what?' Simon asked.

Charles told them. They shouldn't be surprised, he said, They must know how interested he had been in religion since early childhood. 'Don't you remember my saying that I wanted to go into the Church? Well, this is a practical extension of it. Dr Sanderson says that if I complete my education first and have your consent at the end of it, I can enter for a trial period, then leave if I want to. None of the men is forced to remain if they wish to return to their former way of life, and all are reimbursed should they go. Very few do. Only two in the last five years. But I will never want to.'

It was impossible to argue in the face of his quiet determination, and if Simon felt there was a deeper reason for his choosing such a life, he did not probe. Charles was something of an enigma; self-contained people so often were. That was their way of hiding their innermost feelings, and despite the boy's frank and considerate nature, Simon suspected that Dulcima Howard's son was a law unto himself. Always he was the calm, well-mannered, dutiful young man, but what went on beneath the surface of his mind, only he would ever know.

'Is a lifetime of religious devotion and self-sacrifice really something a boy of your age should decide upon?' Simon said. 'Don't you agree that it would be wiser to wait for a few years and think again?'

'Not for me. This is right for *me*. You know I never change my mind once it is made up.'

That was true enough, thought Simon. Stubborn as a mule, was Charles, once he had reached a decision. He was the only person in this house who made good resolutions on New Year's Day and really tried to stick to them.

Deborah said a trifle bleakly, 'It sounds as if you have everything cut and dried.'

'I have. You should be glad I've found my true vocation.' He still spoke in that somewhat pedantic way, but no doubt he would grow out of it. Adolescence was an ideal time in which to discover what one wanted to do, and in that they were luckier than most parents or guardians, who bemoaned the fate of offspring lacking in such decision. To Deborah, Dulcima's son had always seemed more like her own child than a cousin.

But something beneath Simon's manner troubled her. She sensed an underlying curiosity, almost an anxiety, about him. He was studying Charles in that penetrating way of his, and it didn't disturb the boy at all. He simply met Simon's glance and said, 'Is there anything else you want to know, sir?'

Simon shook his head. How could he ask: What are you running away from, and what makes it necessary for you to seek such security? Instead he asked, 'What about university?'

'I'd like to skip that, if I may. What I want most is an occupation with a worthwhile future, and I have found it.'

'I would like to meet Sanderson, have a talk with him.'

'He would be delighted, I know. So would I. You would then see what a splendid cause I shall be working for.'

Or what a splendid refuge you have found? wondered Simon, looking at the pale Ashleigh eyes and moved by pity for the boy, but saying only that he would write to Dr Sanderson without delay. Perhaps, during this final school year, his ideas might alter, but in a way, he hoped they would not.

'You needn't think I shall change my mind,' Charles reiterated. 'Nor my plans concerning this house. I want to take you up on the idea you mentioned years ago, to buy the place. I would value the capital more than the property. I don't want to own material things, but the money would be useful. I intend to invest it, and it would make me happy to know that 20 Hanover Square belonged to you both, your home forever. Well,' he finished, 'that covers everything, I think.'

It was impossible to argue in the face of his quiet determination, and Simon's suggestion that they should review the situation at the end of the school year met with only a faint smile, as did Simon's stipulation that if and when Charles withdrew from Sanderson's commune he should take up his postponed university course. The smile was positively benign, suggesting that he accepted the stipulation only to indulge them, which happened to be true. Charles knew full well that he would never withdraw. There was a niche for him at Fenfield that he would find nowhere else. There was also safety behind its doors and in the sanctity of its vows.

The last person for whom Delia felt in the mood was her

mother. It was the first time Caroline had crossed the dividing line between house and hospital, and she walked into Delia's room without knocking. 'I came to find out when my home is to be evacuated. Now the war is over, I see no reason for it being occupied any longer. And why are you crying?'

Delia lifted her head, hiding neither her tearstained face nor the letter in her hand.

Caroline's sharp eyes noticed it at once. 'What is that? Who is it from? Is that what's upset you?'

'No . . . yes . . . it's from Peter's father.'

'Not bad news, I hope?'

Delia was surprised and touched. 'No, Mamma. Good, really. Peter is on his way home. Time schedules are uncertain, but he should be crossing from Dieppe to Newhaven sometime tonight.'

'Well, that's nothing to cry about, surely? I thought you were in love with the man. And now the war is over, you will be released from all this drudgery for which, frankly, I have had no sympathy, because there was no necessity for you to do it. Many a young actress must have been stealing a march on you, and you have only yourself to blame for that. Well, Delia, when *can* I expect these men to go? And what a mess the place is in! This is the first time I have ever set foot – '

'I know it is. And I can't admire you for it.' Delia was more composed now, but unable to hide her feelings. 'You have kept to your comfortable quarters while everyone around you was either working or suffering, and now at last you "set foot" in here and all you can see are signs of wear and tear. "Mess", you call it! What did you expect? Spotless walls and paintwork? Everything immaculate and unmarked? Men have been carried on stretchers, and no doubt nurses have accidentally marked the walls as they carried them. Crutches have knocked against things, chairs and doorframes have been damaged by men learning to propel wheelchairs, hurting themselves in the process far more than they hurt the woodwork. They've been sick in the wards, bled in bathrooms, stumbled blindly with their white sticks in an effort to be independent and a trouble to no one, yet you complain and demand that they shall go as soon as possible!'

'Don't speak to me like that.'

'I'm sorry, but nothing can stop me. Are you already thinking of compensation, calculating how much you can demand for the damage these tragic men have done?'

'Of course, I must be compensated. That was understood from the start. And why are you crying again? What you have to cry about, I cannot imagine.'

'Of course you can't. You cannot imagine any woman weeping for love of a man, waiting and longing for him to come home, praying night after night for the end of a bloody war that killed off thousands of brave men and mutilated thousands more. How do I know what state Peter will be in after incarceration in a prison camp? I don't even know how he was wounded, or how badly, but at least he is coming back, and he has to return to 20 Hanover Square, because it is still his base. So he can't avoid seeing me.'

'Why should he? I thought you both took your mock marriage seriously.'

Delia took a deep breath. After that brief touch of concern, her mother's self-centredness had returned, making it impossible to communicate, impossible to say that even if Peter were scarred and maimed, she couldn't wait to take his body in her arms and lie close to him in bed and make love to him – real love, as, she remembered unhappily from Bryant Meredith's frank revelations, poor Caroline had never been able to offer. *Poor* Caroline? Was she actually pitying her mother, and beneath her choking anger, was that really compassion she was feeling? She fought against it, because Caroline had come here feeling none herself.

'What's the use?' Delia cried. 'You can never understand how I feel about Peter. How can you? All you ever did was give your body to a man and conceive a child, which, unfortunately, happened to be me, but you didn't conceive in love, because had you really loved my father, you would never have turned away from him following the Boer War. Do you think I can't remember how you complained because he fought in it, and how you made his disability an excuse to remain at Kingsmere, living in a state of luxury he could never provide? Go back to your comfortable wing where you have hidden yourself away from the sights and sounds and smells of this part of the house, and grumbled because you had only a housekeeper and a daily servant to look after you!'

Rigid with shock, Caroline said, 'I shall never forgive you for this. You don't deserve to become mistress here after I die.'

'I don't want to be. When Kingsmere becomes mine, I will offer the use of it to some worthy cause — Dr Sanderson, perhaps, to turn into a larger hospital for his tragic cases.'

'You wouldn't dare!'

'If you think that, you don't know me.' Delia ran a hand through her short hair, and continued tiredly, 'Don't you realise that life is never going to be the same again? The glitter and the gold of Edwardian society is over, and nothing like it will ever be seen again. You think that, overnight, Kingsmere will go back to being what it was before the war, but it won't. Look at the old men who have remained here, coping with the place inadequately — do you think that the sons and grandsons who are lucky enough to be returning will be willing to follow in their footsteps, their ideas unchanged? There is going to be a tragic shortage of men, and women who have been earning money in munitions aren't going to settle for less as domestics. They will be off to the towns, seeking jobs in industry, in shops, in all sorts of things, and if there is ever another war – '

'*Another?* Don't talk such nonsense.'

'I am facing facts, as a lot of other people are. Listen, I beg you – don't turn these men out. Not all of them have families to go to, and many are incurably crippled. Why don't you do what the actress May Whitty and a group of other leading actresses have done for that home called the Star and Garter on Richmond Hill?'

'The Star and Garter? My dear, that was a fashionable hotel in King Edward's day. I remember it well. One used to drive out there to dine on its terrace overlooking the Thames.'

'Like everything else belonging to those days, it is gone now. Chrystal told me how they raised money worldwide to launch it as a permanent home for the disabled. Now it is known as "The Memorial to the Great War by the Women of the World". Think of the renown Kingsmere would achieve, the renown *you* would achieve, if you did something so noble.' Delia warmed to her theme, aware that she was planning Kingsmere's future because she wanted it to be a worthy one. The place did mean something to her. She was proud of it. '*Think,*' she urged. 'Your name would be honoured. You could be its patroness and continue to live as you are living now, and everyone in the county and beyond would admire you for it.'

A glimmer of interest shone in Caroline's eyes. To be accepted again, respected, looked up to, no longer ostracised by those with long memories, which seemed to include just about everyone of her acquaintance; to win the renown she had once sought unsuccessfully . . . how much more comfortable to achieve it this way than as an intrepid woman traveller! And there would be money-raising projects to bring her into the public eye. The prospect was pleasing. 'It sounds a feasible idea,' she said carefully. 'I will consider it.'

Delia kissed her mother soundly. 'Thank you, Mamma, *thank* you!'

The spontaneous gesture took Caroline by surprise. She was also surprised by her reaction. 'Please,' said she who never said 'please' to anyone, 'come and see me now and then. . . .'

'Of course, Mamma. Of course I will.'

'Not that I make any promises, mind you. About Kingsmere, I mean.'

'I understand,' said Delia, well satisfied because she knew she had won, but equally satisfied because her scheme would make her mother think of something other than herself.

Delia delegated her work among the senior staff nurses and caught the first train to London. At Victoria a row of blackboards detailed the arrival of troop trains and those of repatriated prisoners. No mention of Gottesberg. Hurrying to packed 'Enquiries', she queued with suppressed impatience, eventually learning that no contingents from that area were scheduled for Victoria. 'Try Charing Cross, miss – some routes have been diverted to Folkestone or Dover.'

She boarded one of the new steam omnibuses, which seemed to go slower than the old horse-drawn affairs, stuttering its way up Victoria Street and Whitehall to Trafalgar Square and the Strand. Much of the evening had gone, and dusk had given way to winter darkness, but fishtail flares lit up the station blackboards with their notices in white chalk, and there she saw it – due at seven-thirty A.M., 29 November. Tomorrow morning, and one of the early contingents, thank heaven. She wanted to stay here all night, just in case the notice was wrong and his train arrived early, but apparently it was more likely to arrive late.

'Bin waiting 'ere all arternoon, me and me ol' man,' a woman told her. 'Our Mike was due in midday, and we're still 'ere. Channel's rough, they say, and crossings delayed over there.' She nodded toward the railway lines as if France lay at the end of them. 'But we ain't budgin', are we, Joe? We 'aven't seen the lad since Gawd knows when.' Her motherly face creased with tears and excitement. It was turning chilly, and both she and her husband looked cold. Delia bought two mugs of piping hot tea from a Red Cross trolley, with a couple of Chelsea buns apiece, and took them over to the couple before going home to Hanover Square, where Deborah, after hearing the news, insisted on bringing her supper in bed.

'And then a good night's sleep,' she ordered, though she doubted whether she would get much sleep herself. Curled up against Simon later, she whispered, 'Perhaps I should have given her some of those sleeping drops Dr Anderson prescribed when Garfield went down with influenza,' to which Simon answered that he doubted whether Delia would have swallowed them. 'She would be afraid of oversleeping. She'll be off to Charing Cross long before his train is due, if I know my daughter.'

'How long have they been apart? Three years?'

'Slightly more, I think. Amazing how one loses a sense of time during a war. Now, go to sleep, my love, though I doubt if any of us will get much of it tonight.'

The whole house was tense with expectancy. Cook, discharged from her hospital kitchen, 'and not 'arf glad to be 'ome', had promptly set to and prepared some of Mr Maynard's favourite foods the moment Miss Delia walked in with the news of his impending return. 'He's sure to need fattening up,' Cook said practically, and Garfield had hastened to the studio to make up his bed and to air clothes long stored away. 'A bit out-of-date,' she commented, 'but I daresay he'll be glad to get back into civvies, no matter what they're like.' No one made any reference to the long silence, or revealed their private thoughts or fears, for Delia's sake. Everything would come right. It had to. Cook even said she saw it in the tea leaves, and for once, Garfield didn't scoff.

Even after the house was silent, tension was in the air. Delia could feel it pulsating through her. She was alternately terrified and excited, her thoughts swinging like a pendulum between hope and despair. Would he search the platform for her the moment he stepped from the train, or would he pray she was not there? His father's note had contained only the news of his return. 'That's all I know myself, dear girl. I would travel to London to meet him, but I can't leave sick patients at short notice. Besides, it is you he will want to see first.'

But would he? After not writing for so long, and not revealing the reason for it? There had to be a reason, and all sorts of possibilities chased through her mind, amongst them the possibility that he had been blinded, or too maimed to hold a pen, but both were contradicted by the fact that his father had received letters at fairly frequent intervals. She was tormented by fear and longing, seized by hope and then by apprehension. When they met, all would be explained . . . but what if he did not recognise her, or she him? What if his experiences had changed his looks as well as his feelings for her? What if he passed right by her and she failed to know him?

That thought sent her padding barefoot to her dressing table, and in the flickering light of a candle she studied her face. White. Strained. Blue shadows beneath her eyes. Surely she looked ten years older? Her collarbones showed more prominently; she had lost weight. But hadn't everyone, on sparse war rations? She snuffed the candle and went back to bed, tossing and turning until she knew that sleep was finally out of the question. She rose then, plunged her face into cold water, and sponged her body to chase away fatigue. It was hard to control her trembling hands as she brushed her hair. Tying her shoelaces, her fingers felt all thumbs. Then she belted a warm coat over her ankle-length dress and crept, hatless, from the house.

Simon heard the creak of stairs, the careful drawing of bolts, the quiet shutting of the front door. God go with you, my dear, and bring you back to this house in happiness.

It was half-past five, and a dark winter's morning. With the end of the war and zeppelin raids over, gas jets flared again in streetlamps, their pale glow appearing brilliant after four years of total darkness. Soon the shop windows that had shone with electricity shortly before the war would be permitted to display it again, lighting up a whole new world. But what sort of a world would it be? A better one, surely. Wasn't that what the war had been fought for?

She walked from Hanover Square to Piccadilly, then across the Circus and down Haymarket, left into Trafalgar Square, and then alongside St Martin's-in-the-Fields, crossing the Strand to Charing Cross station. The Eleanor Cross in the forecourt looked as gracious as ever, miraculously unscathed.

The cockney woman and her husband had gone, reunited at last with their Mike. The station was packed, and more helpers were dispensing Red Cross tea. She bought a mugful and drank it in a forlorn attempt to steady her inner trembling. The walk from Hanover Square had warmed her, but not calmed her.

The time was six-thirty. If the train arrived promptly, he would be here in an hour. If not, she would wait and go on waiting, and when at last she saw him she would know exactly how he felt.

Also in Hamlyn Paperbacks

Drusilla Campbell

BROKEN PROMISES

A terrible secret lies buried in the Hopewell past – a mystery that haunts the dreams and hopes of beautiful 18-year-old Suzannah Hopewell.

Born the daughter of a rigid New England mill-owning family, Suzannah longs for a love that will take her away from the cruelty and injustice that surround her.

Though she finds tenderness in Travis Paine, a brilliant young architect, a new passion sweeps her into the arms of Roberto Monteleone, a sculptor from far-distant Sicily.

But as she struggles with her deepest feelings, a ruthless tyrant stands in her way, covering up an unspeakable crime. He is the man she must call "Father".

Here is a brilliant saga of shattering love, and a young woman's conflict with destiny.

Judith Saxton

THE GLORY

The continuing saga of Ted and Tina Neyler's family.

After his years in America, Mark returns to New Zealand. There he finds a son he cannot understand . . . and the beginning of a new romance.

In England, Tina's family is growing up. When the Great War starts, Frank joins up, but one terrible day in the trenches will change him forever . . .

Louis, the eternal optimist, returns unscathed from the War to find that his wife and mistress have met, and that fate is catching up with him at last.

Spanning two continents, the family's zest for living carries them through joy and suffering alike,